Spirits Entwined

The Legend of Ghaleon Series

By Theresa Biehle

BOOK 1: SPIRITS ENTWINED

BOOK 2: STARS CALLING

Spirits Entwined

Book 1 of the Legend of Ghaleon

Theresa Biehle

This is a work of fiction. All of the characters, organizations, and events portrayed in this novel are either products of the author's imagination or are used fictitiously.

First Edition

ISBN: 9781521532713

Edited by Patricia Gentil and Justin Fox

Artwork by Theresa Biehle

www.theresabiehle.com

Dedication

For anyone who has lived in a moment that felt like an eternity;
Who has believed in something enough that it became reality;
Who has ever thought they couldn't do something but did it anyway;
Who has ever contemplated the meanings of their dreams;
And especially for those who find the strength to smile when the world wants you to do anything except that.

Cherish the moments you have while they are here, and believe that more will come to you through the choices that you make.

Acknowledgements

A special thanks to my Mum, Alex Williams, Justin Fox, and Coleby Wilt for providing all the input and support that they did during the creation of this book.

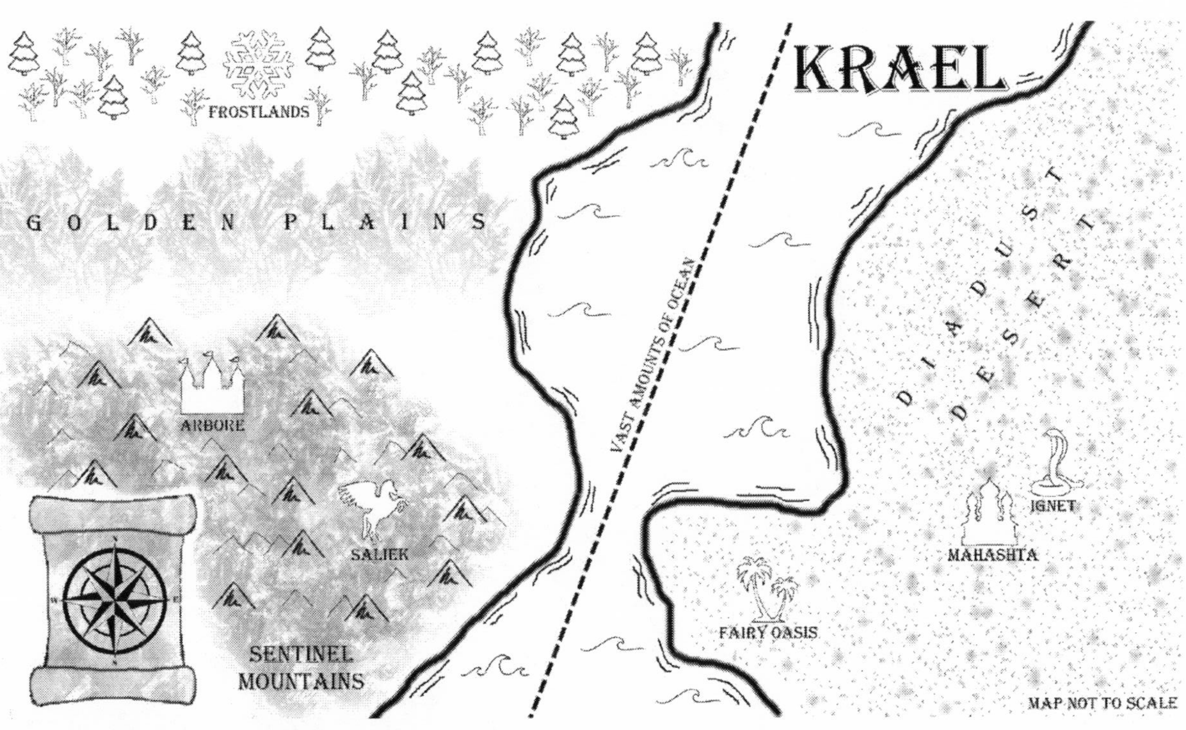
KRAEL
FROSTLANDS
GOLDEN PLAINS
ARBORE
SALIEK
SENTINEL MOUNTAINS
VAST AMOUNTS OF OCEAN
DIADUST DESERT
IGNET
MAHASHTA
FAIRY OASIS
MAP NOT TO SCALE

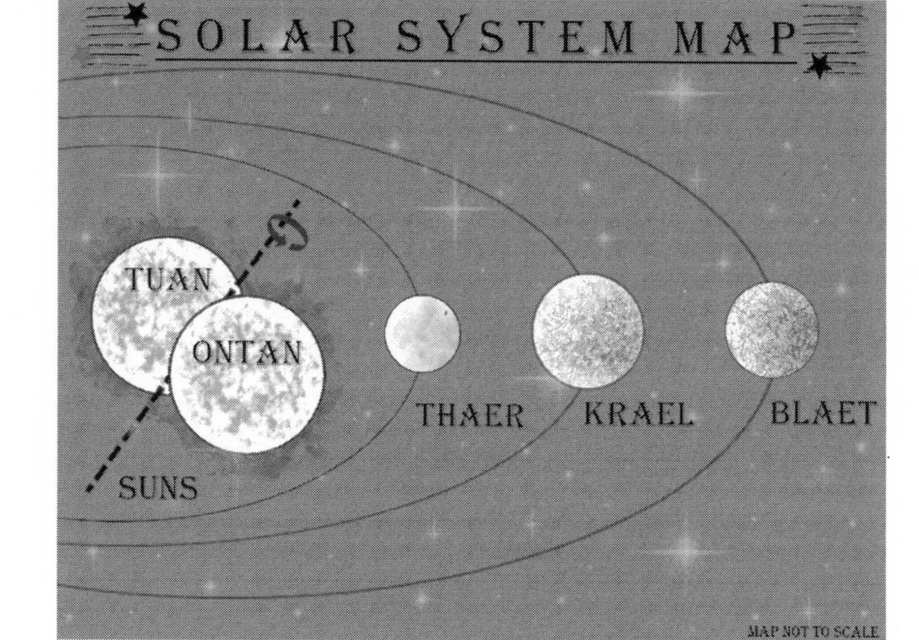
SOLAR SYSTEM MAP
TUAN
ONTAN
SUNS
THAER
KRAEL
BLAET
MAP NOT TO SCALE

Chapter 1

The darkest hours of the day had come once the second sun had set. Massive thunderheads denied the light of thousands of stars entrance to the world below and promised an imminent storm with their booming clashes. Three dark figures took to the sky on their powerful steeds over a city in chaos. The only light to be seen was the red glow of the flaming fireballs being launched and the sporadic sparks that hurtled between the clouds. Any noise that was made by the beasts' thundering hooves or buffeting wings had been covered by the roar of the ever-growing fire raging below and the wailing screams of where the fireballs fell. The riders all but ignored the destruction as they dutifully flew towards the mountains that encircled the city, the mountains that had been the city's sentinels for ages. A lone woman watched sorrowfully out of a castle spire until she could no longer distinguish the riders' flapping black cloaks from the darkness. She prayed that the treasure they carried would make it to safety and that someday she could arrange for its return.

Years later…

Mount Liriken gazed down from the dust-hazed clouds onto the rooftops of a small, dry village. Grey vapor spewed every so often from its top, blurring the intensity of the suns and sky from the village occupants. Red dust swirled up from the crossing of the two streets that lay at the village's center as the occasional passerby hurried back into one of the wooden houses lining the roads before both suns would set for the day. Grass sprouted in greenish brown shoots above the clay-ridden soil in a field to the west of town before ending at the largest house in the area. The most color lay to the east of town, where the molten center of Mount Liriken's belly warmed and nourished the ground, coaxing more flowers to sprout along a river silently weaving its way across the land, painting a sparkling blue streak in an otherwise colorless world.

Where the roads crossed, an impressive building dwarfed the rest of the town in size and magnificence. The walls were made of a rock that shined black in the sunlight, and a shimmering blue rooftop peaked high above the ground, swooping in an elegant curve away from the building. At the four corners of the roof, the head of a horse, dragon, serpent, and fish were carved and kept watch below. The obsidian walls of the building were etched with immaculate images that provided endless rumors and stories for those who lived in the town and made time to visit the library.

"Kylie! Where are you? I need your help with these new books," boomed a woman's authoritative voice down one of the many rows of dusty bookshelves. Kylie, sitting in one of her preferred alcoves that featured a purple, feather-cushioned bench encircling a gigantic geode rock sliced open to create an amethyst tabletop, quickly shoved the wooden figurine that she was whittling into her satchel and flipped a discarded book beside her open to a random page. Kylie loved the library and the librarian that she had been apprenticed to for five years now, but sometimes she just needed a break from all the reading. After all, she was assigned to read every book in this extensive library and attempt to memorize their contents. Who would begrudge her a little down time? Unfortunately, she knew that Scilla would indeed. Sometimes that woman acted as though the survival of the worlds depended on Kylie memorizing as much written material as possible. "I'm back here Scilla, studying like always," Kylie replied exasperated as her finger absentmindedly followed a crystalline pattern in the table while she firmly held a book with her opposite hand.

A chuckle sounded from a nearby corner, and Kylie whirled around to give the lanky young man leaning against the stone wall, book in hand, a frown. He was wearing a white linen button-down shirt, top few buttons undone, and casual brown working pants today. "What are you laughing at, Mory?" Kylie asked pointedly. He shrugged as he tossed his shaggy blonde hair out of his eyes. Kylie held a stare with his mischievous blue eyes long enough to give him a good angry look, then flipped her long, wavy, sandy blond hair out of her face as she turned back around to make it look as though she were intently reading the book in front of her. Mory, two years Kylie's senior, had always seemed a nuisance while growing up with all his teasing and pulling pranks on her. Although, since she'd turned 14 five years ago and had been assigned the same apprenticeship as him, he'd become one of her closest friends. She could almost find the humor in the teasing and the pranks now. Mory was much better at his assignments than Kylie. Not that Kylie wasn't talented, he just seemed to have a longer attention span than she did when it came to reading and memorizing book material of sciences and ages gone by. It also may have come easier to him since he had been living with Scilla since he was found by her as a child, abandoned by the river on the east side of town.

Just as Kylie had situated herself, Scilla's slight figure

came into view from the corridor of bookcases. Her short, dark hair flicked past her dark eyes and pointed face as she made her way to the study area that Mory and Kylie currently occupied. Click, click, click, went the heels of the impossibly high, jet-black, leather boots that she was wearing as she approached. Scilla had always seemed to have a fascination with darkness. Her floor length dress was nearly as dark as her hair. It contained small, dark stones embroidered into an inverted triangle beginning at her neckline that shimmered blue when they caught the light. She wore the deepest of reds for lip color and had heavily shaded her eyelids. Both had the effect of severely accenting her ghostly white skin. Kylie always wondered if Scilla's darkness fascination was why the library seemed to lack an appropriate number of windows to adequately light some parts of it during the day. The windows it did have were of a stained glass, which although beautiful, hardly let in enough light to properly read without an additional source of illumination.

"Kylie," Scilla asked, "could you please help me organize this new batch of books that just arrived from Syrvio? They are of a unique nature, and I would like you to make them next on your reading list. I think you will find them most interesting." Scilla was an ever-vigilant book collector and was always looking for new volumes to expand her vast library. As such, Kylie was not surprised that she was able to get books from such a faraway nation, but the fact that she wanted Kylie to bump them up in her reading order was intriguing. In the entire time that she had been working here, Scilla had never made that request before.

As Kylie stood to follow Scilla to the entrance of the library, Scilla looked her up and down and scowled at Kylie's attire before scolding her, "Kylie, dear, you turned 19 today. Do you believe that you will soon begin adorning appropriate attire for your age?" Like usual, Kylie was wearing tan trousers, plain green blouse, and riding boots instead of the customary dress or skirt that other women her age wore. Kylie simply ignored the comment and began to walk with Scilla. She found dresses and skirts highly impractical. How could anyone run or maneuver in such a monstrosity? Kylie's mother agreed with this sentiment and had been the one to teach Kylie everything she knew about survival. Not that she'd ever need to use it, but it was always good to know.

It took a while to weave through the maze of bookcases within the Ancient Archives, as Scilla endearingly called this place, not because the library was in disarray, but for the exact opposite reason. Every place was extraordinarily neat and all the lines of bookcases were identical. It was hard to tell exactly where you may have been, if you didn't know the place as well as the occupants. The quaint little alcoves tucked away in various locations throughout the corridors of books were the only way to help an outsider distinguish where they were. Each had its own unique twist to it, such as the wondrous geode table that Kylie favored.

The clicking of Scilla's boots began echoing with each step on the smooth stone floor as they entered the maw of the entrance hall. There were four magnificent stone columns near the main entrance with ornate twists and curves engraved into them that towered to at least three times her height. The inside of the roof was made of a shiny black material that seemed impervious to everything. It came to a point in the center and swooped outwards beyond the edge of the building to produce an overhang of weather protection for those walking along the outside walls. The floors were a smoothed rock of some sort with worn images of animals and people painted upon it. They seemed to be telling a story that no one could ever decipher. The walls of the library were made of stones so large that nothing currently living on Thaer could have lifted them. It was truly amazing, and no one could explain how something of this grandeur could have been made with the tools and expertise that were currently available. To be honest, the entirety of the Ancient Archives was quite a marvelous mystery.

The Ancient Archives had originally been found in a desolate area of Thaer, and the town of Liri had grown around it as the years carried on, taking advantage of the warm waters of the Zula River. The plains near the river would flood during the rainy season, and when the waters retracted, the fertile soil in between was ideal for growing various crops. Mount Liriken, in the distance, had never shown any signs of eruption as it burped steam into the atmosphere and only seemed to bless the waters and grounds surrounding it with a soothing warmth.

Scilla stopped walking and gestured towards a travel worn crate near the front door. Engraved into the door was an intricately carved warrior who was shrouded in an ornate cloak and carried an impressive looking sword and shield pair. Obviously, Scilla would expect Mory or herself to unload the books from here and move the crate as needed. Kylie refocused her attention to the task at hand and examined the new book shipment. The crate was labeled in a red ink: “Legends, Myths, and Tales of the Universe.” She thought that had an interesting sound to it. Noticing the sun’s angle through a nearby window, Kylie took a weathered book off the top of the stack, tucked it into her satchel, and turned to Scilla with hope, “My mother is going to be making me a delicious birthday dinner today, so I was wondering if I could take this book home to read and organize the shipment tomorrow morning?” Scilla showed her consent with a slight nod of her head, as most of her attention seemed to be focused on reading another one of the books from the recent shipment. Kylie pushed hard to swing open the heavy front door opposite the warrior, which also contained an intricate carving. This carving was of a muscular, demonic looking creature, and she barely cast it a glance before beginning her short walk on Liri's well-packed dirt streets home.

As she was walking home, thoughts of her father who had mysteriously disappeared when she was 10 years old crossed Kylie's mind. She wished that he could be there for dinner; it'd been years since she'd seen him. She remembered him lovingly and thought of all the great times they had together while she was growing up, as well as the valuable skills and lessons that he had taught her. Those memories were often one and the same. He always seemed to know what she was thinking and would protect her from any fears conceived by her overly vibrant imagination. Even now, she thought that she could almost feel his presence in the back of her mind, which made her believe that he was still alive. That gave her hope that one day she would see him again. She never believed the rumors around town that he had decided to abandon his family or had been killed during a hunt. Her father was too kind of a man who loved Kylie and her mother dearly and was a master of knives and swordplay. She was quite sure nothing alive could match his agility and accuracy with a knife or a sword. Kylie should know, he had helped train her.

As her mind wandered, she fingered the concealed knife that she always carried up her sleeve. Her father had given it to her years ago, and it seemed to be made of such a high-quality steel that it had never needed sharpening in the many years that she had owned it. It also shined as brightly as it did the day that he had given it to her. Since he had disappeared, she had taken to carrying it everywhere, if just to keep his memory nearby. Her mother had seemed to approve of this acquired habit and had skillfully altered the sleeves of all her shirts so that she could carry it about unnoticed and with easy access.

As Kylie was about to turn down the road that passed a large, open grass field before arriving home, she was roughly awakened from her reverie by a loud resounding thump. A person had dropped from the last of the of the red, clay rooftops in the town, creating a small whirlwind of dust about them. Kylie instinctively pulled her knife on a very startled Mory. "Spirits girl! What are you thinking?!" he exclaimed as he threw his hands up in the air to surrender to her.

"Sorry... I was deep in thought, and... and... you startled me," she stuttered ashamedly. "How'd you get out of the library anyway?" It was a rhetorical question, as she was aware that Mory knew of a multitude of secret passages hidden throughout the Archives. Kylie hastily put her knife away, kicked the dirt, and continued walking towards her home. She should have heard Mory coming long before he dropped from the roof, she berated herself. Her mother wouldn't be happy if she knew that Kylie had let her guard down enough to be startled like that, and by Mory nonetheless! Mory gave her a brief concerned look but didn't question her further. He knew her talents in knives went far beyond whittling and began walking beside her.

"Never mind that, I got you a gift for your birthday!" Mory exclaimed excitedly. Kylie hesitated. She wasn't quite sure if she wanted this 'gift'. In past years, gifts had consisted of frogs, mud, sparking objects, or other things of that sort. Before she could object, he thrust out his upturned, clenched palms towards her with an enormous grin on his face. With a sigh, Kylie stopped walking, turned towards him, and reached out to slowly pull his fingers up from his palms. After all, she had to admit that she was a bit curious. She gasped at what she saw. It was a beautiful rock attached to a durable cord. It was the most interesting rock she had ever seen. It had swirling color patterns that she had never seen before in a rock, and it shone vibrantly when the light hit it in certain ways.

"Mory... you got this for me?" Kylie was speechless as she looked up at him, mouth gaping open, and green eyes showing nothing but pure surprise. She then began inspecting the rock and cord as it begged her to do.

Mory replied proudly, "Well, more of I found it, shined it up a bit, and then gave it to the tanner to make a durable neck rope out of hides for it. You're into strange things, so I thought that you may like it." He was looking rather proud of himself and had a crooked smile on his freckled face as he cocked his head to one side. Before any more could be said, Kylie's mother called out and beckoned them both to come eat the dinner that she had prepared. Kylie quickly put the necklace on and made her way alongside Mory to her home. As they neared the cozy cabin, she felt Mory's arm brush up against her shoulder, and their eyes met for a moment. The smile he gave her seemed in some way different from others, and it made her cheeks flush slightly before entering her house. Maybe those freckles under his eyes, that she had often teased him about, weren't so bad after all

Chapter 2

Darkness seeped through the cracks of Thaer, coalescing into multiple shapeless shadows. A ghostly warrior with a great sword, impenetrable shield, and a magnificent cloak stood guard alone to protect his old home from the evil forces gathering within it.

"Well now, I suppose I won't have to ask how your day has gone young lady!" Kylie's mother, Zhannah, said with a smile as her gaze shifted from Kylie's new necklace to Mory's arm around her waist as the two walked into the house. At that comment, Kylie's cheeks turned an even brighter color red than before, and she hastily shook off Mory's arm. When had that mongrel done that! He was getting far too sneaky for his own good Kylie concluded. Twice in one day he had snuck something by her! This was absurd.

The house smelled too wonderful for her to remain concerned about Mory for very long. Kylie followed her nose to the dining room table and sat down, closely followed by her mother and Mory. Her home wasn't nearly as grand as the library. It was just a simple wooden cabin that was large enough for her mother, father, and herself to live comfortably, yet it was the largest house this close to town. As she sat down, she took a moment to scope out the wonderful dinner that was laid out before her. It was her favorite: chicken and dumplings, mashed potatoes smothered with savory gravy, mixed vegetables from the garden, and sweet cornbread muffins. Scilla always warned her about how eating meals like this would ruin her perfect figure one day, but Kylie had been eating like this for as long as she could remember. Besides that, her mother had always told her that muscle burned more energy than fat. Using that logic, she figured that if she ever stopped eating this way that she would become too scrawny and began gobbling away her portion of the delicious dinner.

As her mother was bringing out a juicy looking fruit cobbler for dessert, a low roar suddenly began rumbling from the direction of town followed by shrill screams of terror. Kylie, Mory, and Zhannah all paused briefly, dropped what they were doing, and rushed to the yard to see what was happening. The sight that met their eyes was one of chaotic confusion so extraordinary that it was difficult for their startled minds to grasp. Fire had been set to the Spirit's Church, which was centrally located in Liri, across the street from the library. The fire itself could be disastrous to most of the town since the buildings were mainly constructed of wood and hides with the exception of a few stone ones, but what looked more frightening than the growing crackling flames were the short black creatures with glistening fangs dancing around the fire. Though they couldn't have been more than three feet tall, they were each wielding a torch and felt no remorse for flailing it towards anyone who looked as though they would try to put out the fire. Mory stood behind Kylie, gripping her shoulders protectively as they watched. Both were frozen in horror and disbelief.

Reality seemed to have suspended itself as Kylie stood in the yard. She didn't feel as though a disaster of this magnitude could touch her small town, so it played before her like she was watching through eyes that were not her own. She could feel the heat of the flames billowing towards her, smell the tinge of smoke in the air, and hear its growing roar as it consumed more of the church as well as the shrill shrieks of the creatures wielding the fire. Even with her other senses corroborating, her eyes refused to accept that the imagery she saw was happening in front of her. She drew back into Mory's arms, like she never had before, as she felt tendrils of fear begin to wrap themselves around her stomach. The gentle warmth of his body was comforting in contrast to the searing heat of the fire advancing slowly in their direction. Mory's arms grasped her more firmly, whether in an attempt to protect her or in response to his own growing fear, Kylie was unaware.

***

Zhannah whispered, "Firelings," under her breath. She had known this day would come, but any day would have seemed too soon for her. Kylie had been more of a daughter to Zhannah than she had been a refugee to be protected, and Zhannah was crestfallen to know that Kylie's peaceful life would now be uprooted. But as the caterpillar was sure to emerge from its cocoon as a butterfly, Kylie had always been destined for something more. At least Zhannah had the peace of mind of knowing that Kylie had been as best prepared to face the future as she could have possibly been with her own and Regithal's training combined with Scilla's education. What troubled her the most right now was not being able to help the village as it rapidly burned to the ground. She had the ability and knowledge to help destroy the firelings, but she could not risk blowing her cover, not yet. There was too much at stake.

Zhannah decided to grab Mory and Kylie and herd them inside away from the mayhem. Their cabin was far enough away from the town that the fire shouldn't bother it, for now. Until it reached that open grass field, she still had time. Just as she was shutting the front door behind them, the cellar door flung open and slammed against the floor with an imposing man quickly emerging from it. He was near seven feet tall with broad shoulders, black hair that fell to them, and ice blue eyes. He wore all black clothing with occasional glimpses of steel where a knife had been made purposefully visible. The only splash of color amidst his figure was the hilt of his broadsword, which had been decorated with a pattern of sapphire, emerald, and diamond and tucked into his jet-black scabbard. Even that was only visible when he began his purposeful stride and his shadowy cloak swept back. Anyone in their right mind would be intimidated by him.

Zhannah couldn't help but smile as Kylie ran into Regithal's open arms proclaiming him father, and he picked her up like a rag doll and twirled her around as though she were a small child again. Her laugh sounded like the first songbird of spring, and he smiled back at her with the proud twinkle of a father's love in his eyes. After briefly watching the gleeful reunion, Zhannah hastened to Regithal's side to give him a kiss. It had been years since she had seen him, although not as many as it had been for Kylie, and her heart was racing in excitement to see him again. Simultaneously, it was drenched in sorrow at what she knew she must do. Curse her strategical mind and allegiances! They always seemed to turn her away from the trails she would prefer to follow. A tear trickled off her face and into her blonde hair. Regithal delicately dried the stream it left on her face with his thumb and asked, “Why the long face, my Z? I've come to take you and Kylie back home! A home that is in a time of war and troubles, but we will be together.” He held her at arm's length and looked straight into her eyes with a jovial glint despite the terrors that were unfolding outside the house.

Zhannah swallowed her sorrow deep within to deal with another time and found her courageous self again. She drew him in closer so that she could speak into his ear conspiratorially, “The boy is talented in stealth and trickery. He even bests our Kylie when her guard is not up. With the right training, he could be of use to us in the future, if the need arises to return to this world. In addition, his affections for Kylie, will make him all the more eager a student if I tell him that he could see her again," she paused to let her words sink in, and then continued, "Scilla would agree. She’d have never let him out today otherwise.”

Zhannah leaned back and saw the agreement shaded with a hint of disappointment in Regithal’s eyes. She had almost wished that he would have a logical argument against it. Instead, his gaze became more intense, and he promised to her, “I will not be away as long as last time. Krael may need me, but I also need you.”

When she let go of his strong embrace, Zhannah made her way to Kylie. She was next to Mory cautiously peering out the window in dismay at the flames that were slowly, but deliberately, destroying their childhood haunts. She wished her ‘daughter’ the courage to survive her life's journey, as she knew today would just be the beginning. If only she could take on some of the burdens for her instead, she would, but she had not what Kylie possessed, and as such, she could only support her as she had. She hoped it was enough. Zhannah gently pulled Kylie away from the window and hugged her tightly, speaking softly into her ear, “There are so many things left unsaid and many secrets that have been veiled from you. For that, I am truly and deeply regretful. In time, I promise you, these mysteries will be revealed, for better or for worse, and I can only hope that you will find it in the kindness of your heart to forgive us. There is no time to explain right now." A fireling let out a piercing demonic screech as if to emphasize her point, before she continued, "So I ask you to trust in me and your father, until the immediate danger has passed. I love you dearly, Kylie. I'll miss you! Be good, and remember your training. I promise we will see each other again." Releasing her embrace of the now trembling girl, she suggested, "You may want to say your goodbyes to Mory. Quickly now!"

Zhannah watched as a confused and glowingly angry Kylie received a hug from an even more confused and very cautious Mory. It would have been quite comical to watch in a different situation. It was a shame that those two couldn't be together. At least not without certain complications. Kylie could expect to live a full 1000 years while Mory would probably live 1/10th of that, if he were lucky.

Regithal beckoned Kylie to come with him back into the cellar with an outreached hand. They hadn't much time left now. The firelings' chattering and clambering was increasing in intensity towards their little house. Luckily, the fire had died out before reaching the field. It seemed the church was the primary target. Kylie took Regithal's hand, and they disappeared down the stairs into the cellar. Once the cellar doors had firmly shut, Zhannah, determined in her new mission, turned to Mory, "We have work to do. First, let me explain what must happen now."

Chapter 3

Smoke and debris sting the eyes of a black dove as it circles a dragon's lair ablaze in the fire of its own belly. Bursts of the grey smoke blot out the light from the sky. Gently grasped within the dove's talons is a sleeping baby dragon. Barring fear from its mind, the dove swoops into the heart of the fire, into a burning building. Fruit is smashed everywhere in a colorful mess along the charred wooden beams that remain of the house. Sitting untouched under a fallen beam thwarted by a table is a bunch of purple grapes. The dove places the sleeping dragon under the table and retrieves the bunch of grapes, then flies until it can no longer be seen through the smoke cloud.

Kylie was beginning to be entirely irritated at the day as she clomped down the stairs to the cellar. She did not like being held in the dark, and she did not like being forced to say good byes like that. Honestly, how far could she be going if her father was taking her to the cellar? It was not a very big area. And what was with all those dancing demons around the fire? "Father," Kylie demanded, "it's really great to see you and all after all these years, but could you *please* tell me what in the name of the Spirits is going on here?" Kylie was not usually an insistent person, but she thought that under the current circumstances, she was entitled a little more information despite her mother's plea earlier.

"All in due time, my Ky, but for now you must take shelter beneath my cloak. And you shouldn't swear like that, it's unbecoming of a lady," Regithal said with a playful smirk as he uplifted a muscled arm like a wing for a young bird to take shelter under. Kylie crept in close, and thankful for her father's guiding hand in the darkness of the cellar, she took a few steps with him towards where she knew the back wall would be. Suddenly, an icy flash of cold engulfed her, like needles to her skin, and she felt her stomach drop as though she were falling down an endless pit. Then as fast as it came over her, the sensation was gone, and she was in a new dark place. This place reeked of fungi and dampness. The pungent odor paired with whatever she had just experienced, made her retch behind a nearby rock.

"I'm afraid you'll have to get used to that eventually," soothed her father.

"What do you mean!? What just happened!?" Kylie was on the verge of infuriation at this point.

"We just entered and exited a gateway that helps one to travel through the universe between various worlds. Your other questions will have to wait for now, as I am afraid that we might be followed from here. It would do you well to control that temper of yours just now." Regithal strode lithely towards a boulder embedded in the wall that was larger than he was and placed both his hands on the boulder. He gently laid his forehead between his hands to touch the rock.

Kylie unceremoniously pulled herself onto the rock that she had retched behind, dismissing her father's strange actions for the time being, and began to take in her surroundings. They had 'landed', for lack of a better term, in a cave just as dark as the cellar they had left. She listened as her eyesight slowly improved in the dark cavern. There was the dull thrumming of insects and the soft plinking of drips that were falling from the ceiling into a body of water slowly manifesting itself in front of her rock. The water was so still that faint ringlets from the drops could be seen merging with one another across its surface creating an intricate web. This fascinated Kylie.

Moss and fluorescent glowing mushrooms covered the many rocks and boulders surrounding the pool making them slick to the touch. She noticed that she had smashed a few of these mushrooms as she had hastily climbed her rock earlier and identified them as the source of the rancid smell of this place. As she was lifting her gaze to peer across the stagnant pool again, she caught a glimpse of her reflection. Did her hair seem lighter, and what was with her irises? She tried to examine herself more closely, but she didn't want to lean much further forward, or else she might fall into the pool. She dismissed it as her eyes playing tricks on her in this dark cave.

Before she had time to contemplate more, her father called her over. She carefully descended her rock throne without crushing anymore of the rancid mushrooms and approached the boulder that her father had been touching before. There was an opening at the boulder's base, just large enough to fit her father's brawn through. She didn't think there had been a hole there before, but she hadn't paid much attention to her father after her eyes had fully adjusted to the darkness. In a short explanation he said, "This boulder is made from much smaller building blocks that are interconnected in such a way as to make an impenetrable rock. If you understand how these connections are made, the much smaller building blocks are easier to convince to sever their connections than dealing with the entire boulder itself. Surely this must sound similar to the information that you have read in Scilla's books?" As if that explained everything she would have needed to know, he turned away, lowered himself to his stomach, and shouldered himself through the opening. Once through, he turned back and signaled her to hold tight for a moment. Then he stood up on the other side of the tunnel and disappeared for what seemed to be an eternity for Kylie.

Lying on her stomach on the moss-covered floor in this smelly cave, peering into a hole in a boulder that she was pretty sure her father had just willed into existence was not how Kylie had expected to spend her birthday. She thought about what her father had said about Scilla's books, and figured he must have been talking about the molecular structure of the boulder. Severing molecular bonds required energy though... Her elbow slipped on the moss-covered stone, and she jarred her teeth as her chin smacked the floor. The drips that she had heard falling into the pond earlier were also trickling down her whole body resulting in a slight chill. The air seemed colder here than back home, but that may have had to do with the fact she was in a cave. As she was starting to envy that nice black cloak her father had, she saw his face appear on the other side of the short tunnel. He proclaimed, "It's safe, you may come through now."

Kylie shimmied herself through the tunnel, thankful that she was not claustrophobic and nowhere near the size of her father. Once she reached the other side, her father helped her to her feet and must have noticed that she was shivering slightly. He reached into the vast blackness of his cloak and produced another cloak for her to wear. It looked nice and warm and smelled like her father, even if it looked slightly worn and not as magnificent as the cloak that he wore. She gladly took it and wrapped it over her shoulders, tying the front shut. It seemed to fit her perfectly now, even though it had originally looked oversized for her petite body. The warmth it provided was intoxicating.

The cavern they now occupied was larger than the

last. That must have been why it took so long to investigate. It was largely an open cavern, but off to one side there was a cluster of rocks, which her father led her towards. As they approached, it appeared to be a small hidden camp of sorts with the essentials provided for a night's stay. There was firewood shoved into a tight cranny in the rocks as well as two bedrolls tucked into another corner. Thankfully, an overhang protected an area large enough for two people to sleep around a fire and be safe from the abhorrent dripping.

As her father began coaxing the kindling to ignite from a source that Kylie did not see, he began to explain, "I prepared this about a week ago," his hand sweeping open across the camp, "when I had heard of Scilla's predictions. She is not often wrong about happenings of this magnitude. She knew I'd be coming back for you when the firelings came but not exactly when." He started wafting air to increase the intensity of the flames and sighed, "She used to be quite the seer back here on Krael before she was stationed on Thaer by her own choice. Her abilities are considerably dampened there, although the Ancient Archives help. Only one of her strength of skill would be able to have any ability at all on that world. It's such a tragedy that a talent so strong would have to be crippled in the name of duty. I expect that she will return here soon now that her players are in motion." The last bit of what her father said seemed to be more to himself than Kylie.

Kylie set the satchel that she had carried with her from the library under a protective-looking rock. The book she had promised Scilla that she would read was in there, her half completed carving and knife, as well as other various items that she carried with her day to day. Kylie realized just how tired she was when she unrolled and snuggled into her bedroll near the welcome heat of the crackling fire, but she was not about to let her father escape more explanation with her sleepiness. As she was about to say as much, he looked down at her with a warming smile, "How about I tell you a bedtime story like I did years ago, but instead of a story, this will all be history leading up to this point. Don't worry if you fall asleep midway through. Your rest is more important than your knowledge at this point, as we both need to be strong and alert for our travels tomorrow. As your mother promised, all will be made clear to you in time." Kylie agreed to this as she sleepily laid her head down on the small feather-stuffed pillow that had come with her bedroll.

***

Regithal felt the heat billow off the growing fire as he watched the dancing flames. He now faced the moment in his life that he had been dreading for the past many years. Of all the horrors and truths, he knew that this bedtime story would reveal, the one he feared the most was the revelation to Kylie that he and Zhannah were not truly her parents. Although, he felt that she was a daughter to him nonetheless. He only could hope, as Zhannah had told her earlier, that Kylie could find it in the kindness of her heart to forgive them for what their duty had called for them to do. Being not only a member, but the commander of the Saliek was a venerated position that he was honored to hold, but the necessities of duty often weighed heavily on his heart. Wasn't he getting too old for this? He ran one hand through his jet-black hair that did not betray any silver streaks as he stoked the fire with the other and began his story.

"Seventeen years past, upon this world of Krael, a great city known as Arbore was under siege. Arbore, surrounded by the Sentinel Mountains, had been thriving in relative peace for hundreds of years prior to that day, as it had been the home of the great peacemaker, Spirit Master Andolin. Andolin was no ordinary Kraelian. He was the thousand-year mage of that age. As such, he was the most powerful being in the known universe. Not only was he powerful, but his intentions were well-placed. He never used his Spirit to harm anything, only to heal and protect. Andolin passed away two years before the siege on his 1000th birthday, as is how the lifespan of those particular beings' work, causing the 1000-year cycle of war to begin…again."

"It is well known that on the day of the Spirit Master's death, another will be born with his Spirit. The means through which this transfer is determined and completed is unknown. Around Krael, every child born on that day is carefully watched and protected by those who care for them as the caretakers hopefully, and often selfishly, await some sign indicating a manifestation of the Spirit Master's powers. The Spirit does not discriminate between the noble and the common. Andolin himself had been the son of a woman who diligently pushed a fruit cart around the bazaar."

"This uncertainty combined with evil locked within the hearts of many people generated an incredible number of false claims, which has unerringly culminated in war between various cities in Krael every thousand years. Wars in which many children that had the misfortune of being born on that day are slaughtered. This was exactly what the cause of the siege on Arbore was seventeen years ago."

Regithal glanced down at Kylie to find her still holding her heavily drooping eyelids up and continued.

"The royal family of Mahashta, a city on the opposite side of Krael that is an oasis surrounded by miles of desert, had given birth to a daughter on that momentous day. She had shown signs of powerful Spirit, even as an infant. Mahashta royalty was not fond of their city's location, as it was difficult to access for many types of trade unless the traders contained Spirit and understood portal magic. This increased the cost of trade significantly. So, they were usually limited to whatever goods they could grow and manufacture inside the oasis, unless they paid exorbitantly high prices. They saw their daughter's possible status as a way to expand their boundaries and had openly spread the word that Elasche was the thousand-year mage reborn."

"As news has a way of travelling fast, especially in worlds riddled with various magics, Elasche's family soon heard about another talented child in Krael. This child was born in Arbore. It was not just a normal child of Arbore though; it was of the royal family of Arbore themselves. This gave the child a similar status to that of their own daughter and could not be tolerated by Elasche's parents if they were to maintain their claim on her status, which they had decided they would not revoke, no matter how pressing the evidence was. And so, they marched to war against Arbore in 'honor' of their two-year-old daughter."

"The Starbow family had attempted to keep all knowledge of their child's talents secret as long as they could. They knew too well the heavy price someone may claim on their family if the secret was betrayed too soon. Andolin, the peacemaker, and his stories of years gone past had informed them as such. Unfortunately, this secret was indeed betrayed by someone close enough to the Starbow's that they felt them trustworthy with this information.

"So, for the first time in centuries, the Starbow family called upon Krael's most trusted and talented guards: The Saliek. Many had dispersed to various locations on Krael in those centuries of peace, but all returned to duty once the call was given. The Saliek are those who are strong in Spirit and willingly devote their services to the protection of the world of Krael. The initiation ceremony includes a ritual that results in nearly immortal lives to those who serve. Through their longevity, they have seen the histories of the worlds, and even when the last of an era is deceased, there exists no better documentation of history than those of the Saliek."

"The Starbow's made their case to the Saliek to help to protect their child that they believed to have inherited Andolin's Spirit. Upon meeting the child, it was obvious to any member of the Saliek that it must be protected at all costs. The future of the universe could be tainted if they let this child fall victim. And so, myself, Zhannah, and one other member of the Saliek carried this child away from Krael, amidst the siege on Arbore, to a world where magic was known to be suppressed. A world often used as a threat of exile to those who wield their Spirit wrongly in Krael. Thaer."

To her credit, Kylie was still just barely awake. Even in her tired state, she had made the connection, "That child is me isn't it, Father?" Regithal nodded and combed her now golden hair back with his fingers as she finally let the blanket of sleep overcome her. There was so much more to tell, but it could wait for now. His heart was swelling, and a great burden lifted as he watched her drift off into a peaceful rest. She had still called him father.

Chapter 4

A child places her worn favorite book on the ground opened to the very first page of the story. She takes a few steps away and turns back to look at her book with a mischievous grin and giggles. Images and colors begin streaming up from the open book painting the world around her, the pages steadily turning until it reaches the end. The book slams shut with force enough to bounce it from the ground. The child stares in wonder at the masterpiece she has created, then begins to walk through it, leaving the shell of the book behind in a cloud of dust.

The wind had a cool bite to it as it swept past Mory's perch on the cabin's rooftop. A hint of smoke from the recent fires marred its usual fresh scent. The sky was beginning to don the pastels of the first sunset, but its usual beauty was fragmented by smoke tendrils snaking up from the town. The second sun would set in a few more hours this time of year and night would come.

Mory had always been entranced by the sky and its inhabitants. He had read countless books on them in Scilla's library, and yet his hunger was still not sated. How had the universe come to be? How large was it really? Was there an outer limit? Had anyone seen it? How many different life forms existed? The number of questions he could ask were as vast as the number of answers that could exist for each question. The two suns that were in the process of setting were the center of Thaer's solar system. Ontan and Tuan twirled in an endless waltz that brought evening and night upon their planets at varying intervals throughout the year. Once every month, they would come together in an alluring eclipse rumored to be the cause of mysterious occurrences.

The legend of Ontan and Tuan was one of Mory's favorite stories that he had uncovered in his studies. Tuan was a beautiful maiden whose parents had promised her to a boy of a wealthy family in return for a trade alliance once she had come of age. Her family kept her locked away in their estates to 'protect' her from any that might try to woo her until then. Ontan, a soldier, was a dreamer and bard at heart who, upon striking up a playful conversation with Tuan morosely peering from her bedroom window one evening, fell madly in love. He would often call upon her from the shadows of the forest behind her home to sing her stories of wondrous places and heroes when her family was unaware.

Eventually, it would seem that she loved him back, as she would anxiously await his signal from the trees to not only hear his stories but to be near a friend. The fateful day came when she was shipped off to the household of her groom to be, and Ontan was severely distressed. He concocted a hasty plan to steal her away from the carriage so they could run away and live happily ever after, as his stories to her would often end. And so, Ontan endlessly chases Tuan, and once every month he catches up to her carriage, and he sweeps her away for one enchanting night before she is taken from him again. Hence the eclipse. The part about this legend that was Mory's favorite is that he knew the true ending. Ontan did not chase Tuan, but they held each other in an eternal circular dance that orbited about a shared center of mass. So, he must have rescued her after all! It was all about having the right perspective.

A bone chilling screech brought his eyes off the sky as Zhannah had slain another fireling. He felt quite amazed and a little worthless as he watched Zhannah's own deadly dance with the firelings in the grassy field. What seemed like moments ago, she was inside the cabin below relaying her plan to him as she located her short swords and braided back her long blonde hair. She would go take on the ten or so firelings, while he would scramble onto the rooftop and lay hidden. He had tried to tell her that no such thing was going to happen, but she had talked too much sense pointing out, among other things, that she was a sword master, and he had not a weapon to use. Now he found himself entranced in the fight below, as though it were some sort of theater, as he peered over the edge of the roof.

Zhannah's dual-wielded swords were flashing as the light reflected off their sharp edges, slicing through air and fireling alike. She had baited the firelings into following her to Kylie's knife practice area where targets dotted the field and provided her a small amount of protection against the onslaught. More than once, Mory had gasped as a fireling's glistening fangs would nearly find a way to penetrate Zhannah's pale skin before she would agilely twist away from or slice through the opposing fireling. She would dart behind a practice target and emerge swords flying and braid twirling to behead a fireling then slice one's stomach open in the same wide sweep.

The firelings' weaponry consisted of fangs, claws, small backwards curved horns on their heads, and their sheer ugliness. By the time there was only two of them left, they decided to attempt a coordinated attack. If those creatures had been smarter and tried that at the beginning when it was twelve on one, then they may have had a chance. As it happened though, they both squatted on their little legs and sprung up aiming for Zhannah's head. He thought he may have seen her smile as she realized what they were doing. She back-stepped quickly and let the last two firelings launch, fangs flying, at each other. They smacked together with a loud crack of their skulls, and then both fell to the ground. Zhannah was apparently not a woman who took any chances, as she took the opportunity to stab each of the firelings through their hearts as they lay either unconscious or already dead on the ground.

Zhannah had taken on twelve of these mythical creatures who had obviously wanted her dead, killed them all, and had made it look easy. Mory was impressed. She made eye contact with him and motioned for him to come down. He jumped first onto a barrel near the cabin and from there to the ground. He had been scaling the roofs of Liri for years, so this was no special feat for him. As a matter of fact, he had been on this particular roof more than most as he had often found it fascinating to watch Kylie practice her knife throwing skills. He wasn't sure whose skill he was more impressed by.

Mory decided that it must be Zhannah with whom he was more impressed, seeing as her targets had been alive and attacking whereas Kylie's targets were just waiting for her knife to be thrown at them. He would never tell her that though... especially since she didn't even know that he enjoyed watching her practice. He knew that sounded creepy, but he had never found a polite way to tell her that wouldn't end in her forbidding him to watch and a possible knife thrown his way if he neglected her orders. He could already imagine the thwack of the knife in the roof underneath his chin with splinters flying into his face.

Not that her knife threatening him would have been a new occurrence. Since Mory had known her, he had been on the wrong end of Kylie's knife several times. Never once had she actually harmed him with it though, so he counted himself lucky. He was becoming far too accustomed to having the pointy edge of a knife aimed at him than any person should ever be. For some reason, this just made her more appealing to him. He had always known that he was a bit crazy anyway.

He made his way across the field of bloodied corpses towards Zhannah, carefully picking his way to avoid stepping in anything too disgusting. Zhannah's hair was plastered to her head with sweat, and she was still breathing hard as she was poking around the dead bodies as if looking for something. Strangeness must run in this family. Zhannah looked up as he approached, "Did you happen to see anything out of place as you walked out here?"

Mory paused for a moment, looked around, and with maybe a little too much sarcasm responded, "You mean other than the bodies of mythical creatures that I never knew existed? No, other than that I haven't seen anything out of place around here."

"Get your head out of the clouds and start looking!" Zhannah scolded him with her hands on her hips and swords sticking out like two silver plumes with crimson tips, "There has to be some clue as to who summoned them here or why. Look for brand marks, or jewelry, it could be anything really. Firelings are often either bribed or frightened into action, as they have no specific agenda of their own." Then she carefully wiped one of her swords clean on her bloodstained pants, sheathed it, and began to use the other to maneuver the carcasses in all directions to ensure a thorough search.

And with that detailed description of what to look for, Mory began helping her. He was thankful that she had the foresight to keep her blood bath behind the cabin in the target practice area so that no one could see them poking and prodding at the dead bodies. Come to think of it, no one had seen her act of valor besides Mory himself. Zhannah was definitely a woman of secrets. She was lucky that the town had just been relieved to see the firelings leave and was currently occupied in cleaning up the carnage they had left in their wake, or else someone would have surely seen her in action.

***

They continued searching until the second sun was an hour from setting. Zhannah dejectedly declared their search over since they had to dispose of the bodies while there was still some light to work by. Her muscles were aching as she helped Mory pile the firelings' now reeking bodies onto a pyre behind the cabin. She had not fought that hard in decades. To some extent, it felt good. She would have to increase the intensity of her workouts now that trouble was rising. She did not want to be caught exhausted if the time was ever needed for her defenses again.

Zhannah's thoughts were troubled as she watched the pyre burn. Why had they not been able to find any clues? Firelings weren't particularly intelligent, and the bands that were bribed usually carried their treasures with them. The bands that were threatened or tortured would bear some signs of their previous torment. Neither of these seemed the case for the band that burned Liri. The only other possibility that she could fathom was some powerful dark magic. If that was indeed the case, Kylie and Regithal were in more trouble than they originally assumed. Zhannah would check in with Scilla tomorrow to get her take on this situation.

It had helped having a Saliek friend here these last years while she had scarcely been able to see Regithal. It would have been difficult to be in a situation where she was the only person that knew what was going on. At least having Scilla to converse with privately, she was able to talk through some of her more troubling worries as well as possible courses of action. Not that she didn't trust in her own ability to make the correct decisions, Zhannah just found that it was often helpful to talk through a problem or get a new perspective on an issue. Two great minds were better than one!

As the remaining pyre was smoldering in ashes, she turned her attention to Mory who had found a seat on a nearby log. She walked over and sat next to him. She spoke as she patted him firmly on the back, "Mory, I want to thank you for your help today."

He shook his head, probably thinking that he hadn't been much of a help overall and responded, "Where did they go? When will they be back?"

Zhannah knew these questions were inevitable, but she still sighed in resignation before answering, "They went to Krael in an attempt to restore peace to that world. A peace that will in theory manifest itself on Thaer as well. You see, Kylie was born on Krael, not Thaer, and many believe that she will play a vital role in its restoration. As to when they will return, I truly don't know, Mory. Believe me when I say that I wish I knew." She waited for his reaction, knowing that he was aware that Krael was a neighboring planet to Thaer.

Mory bent over and with his elbows on his knees, planted his face into his hands and groaned, "So let me guess, you and Regithal are some all-important king and queen on Krael, and Kylie is a warrior princess. You guys were exiled from your home on Krael due to some revolution or something and took refuge on Thaer until she was old enough to return, and you will all take your places back on your rightful thrones, leaving Thaer forever."

For not knowing what was going on he had done a

decent job at piecing together a rough story, and he hadn't freaked out about their travel to another planet. Zhannah was happy with his overall reaction.

"More or less, you are correct. Let me clarify for you. Kylie is indeed a princess on Krael, though she has no knowledge of this. Regithal and I are no king or queen though. We are her protectors who rescued her from certain death as a young child on Krael. She is thought to possess the Greatest Spirit within her, which on Krael means that she has access to powers beyond her wildest dreams. Regithal's goal in the near term on Krael is to educate her in the use and control of her Spirit, which she will hopefully be able to use to purge the evil from Krael."

She paused before continuing, "My goal in the near term, however, is to teach you how to wield a weapon skillfully, if you choose to accept my education. This will be done in the hopes that one day you and I will follow Regithal and Kylie to Krael and lend our assistance. You must know by now that you have a specific talent in stealth, I believe that we can use that to your advantage in your training."

Mory nodded, agreeing to her proposition, "I accept your offer of education and desire to become even half as skilled as you, but I still have many questions. Such as, if Kylie had 'magical powers' of a sort, why hadn't she used them here on Thaer? Also, how did they travel in between Thaer and Krael safely?"

Zhannah held up her hand to quiet the boy before he could go on and interjected, "I will talk to Scilla tomorrow and see that she gives you access to the rest of the Ancient Archives. I am sure you will find the answers to those questions and many more that you hadn't even thought of yet in your future research."

Mory's eyes lit up as he exclaimed, "There is more of the library!"

Zhannah couldn't help but laugh, "Yes, there is more to the library, and I am sure you will find it to suit your needs. It's getting late now though, and I think you should head back home. It's been a long day for both of us. We will talk again soon. I look forward to working with you." Zhannah took his hand and gave it a hearty shake as if they had just brokered a deal, which in her mind they had. Mory stood up then and started the dark walk-through town back to the Ancient Archives.

Chapter 5

The hero watched the young dragon from a distance through his metal helm as it raged inside its cavern. For years the dragon had kept to itself and lived in a semi-harmonious state with the nearby village. Now it hissed and roared even when no villagers were nearby to agitate it. The villagers had nominated their local hero to slay the dragon. Now, he sat atop his black war steed fully adorned in armor assessing the situation. If only he could communicate with the dragon from afar, maybe then the village and the dragon could resolve their concerns. Maybe even become allies.

Kylie awoke the next morning to the sizzle of cooking meat. The smell wafted in her direction and sent her stomach growling. Not even the warmth of the bedroll could keep her away from the scrumptious aroma. She scooted out, disregarding the chill of the cavern's air, grabbed her satchel, and took a seat on a rock across the fire from her father. His story last night had been a flood of information on her sleepy mind, but she was still sure of at least one thing, Zhannah and Regithal had been the only parents she had known, there was no way she would forsake them for some king and queen of a world unknown to her. Besides, who else but a father would get up early and make her breakfast

"Good morning, Ky, did you sleep well?" her father's deep jovial voice echoed slightly in the cave.

"Yea, really well. I was exhausted!" she replied, watching the grease of the cooking meat hiss as it dripped onto the hot coals of the fire.

"Good to hear! We have a long day of travel ahead of us and wouldn't want your sleepy head slowing us down," her father said with a wink.

Kylie had found a brush squirreled away in her satchel and began brushing the tangles out of her hair while she waited for the meal to be completed. "So, I've travelled through space to the planet next door and have some sort of magical powers, huh?" Kylie asked rhetorically. "I sure hope you know more about them than I do because I think I'll be darn near worthless in this campaign of yours without some proper instruction." As if to prove her point, she pointed towards her bedroll with her brush in hand and commanded it, "Pack yourself!" Nothing happened and she shrugged in a show of helplessness.

Her father chuckled at her, and then tried to explain, "Well now, you are not in charge of the world! If simple commanding was all it took, there would be no need for the extensive education that most of us who can wield our Spirit actively pursue. Remember the boulder tunnel from yesterday?" Kylie's eyes followed his gesture and with slight surprise noticed that the hole was gone. It was only slight surprise because how could much surprise her after what she had learned last night. Her father continued, "I have an understanding of the molecules that make up rocks in general. Using that knowledge and focusing in on what I knew and what I desired, I convinced the molecular bonds to separate for a small amount of time to create the tunnel we used to gain entrance here."

"Using Spirit costs your body energy, so always think of the most efficient way to accomplish a task and your energy reserves should last you a good long time.

Packing a bedroll is a benign thing that I would not generally suggest wasting your energy on, but it is a simple task that I believe you know well. I think it would make a good teaching moment. Imagine what you would do to pack away the bedroll, the more detailed the better."

Kylie closed her eyes, and she could see herself rolling the blankets into a tight cylinder around her squished feather pillow then stuffing it into a pack. Her father said, "Nice job! Now *will* it to happen. No words necessary." She did just as he said and felt a strange sensation almost akin to tingling. When she opened her eyes, the bedroll was packed! Her father was beaming at her, still sitting on his rock. Had she done that? She felt so happy that she couldn't help giggling a little.

"Well enough of that for now. Eat some of this breakfast that I agonized all morning over," her father said smiling and handed her a piece of the meat and sweet roll from his pack. Her morning hunger sated, Kylie helped her father pack up the rest of the small camp manually before they began moving.

He walked to the opposite wall of the cave and she followed. As they came to what Kylie thought was a solid rock wall, her father took a sharp right and vanished. She paused for a moment to take it in, then realized he had not truly vanished but had only stepped into an optical illusion formed by the rocks. As she approached the wall, she could see that an area of the rock jutted out to the left, and her father had just turned behind it. He obviously expected this to confuse her because he had stopped and waited for her just behind the curve with a smile upon his face. Just as she was going to say something, he turned about another rock formation jutting towards the right. After they had completed the approximation of an "S" shape, they found their way into another room of the cavern where stalagmites and stalactites disappeared into the distance. They were so long that they nearly met in the center of the room. It almost looked as though they had stepped into the maw of a giant predator.

Kylie turned around to look at the path from which they had come. The rocks they had walked through looked exactly like the wall of the cavern. She only knew that there was a passageway since she had just walked through it. "This is amazing!" she uttered to herself slowly looking from the wall to the room around her.

Her father nodded agreeing with her, "Nature is a brilliant artist." He let her have a moment to ingest the beauty around her. Too soon they started meandering through the towering spires. Veins of crystal spiraled through the dark rock formations creating intricate patterns that goaded Kylie to examine them. It was far more striking than her favorite geode table in the library Kylie thought as she bent close to, but did not touch, the fragile formations. The crystal embedded within them and crawling across the walls gave off a faint glow that prevented the cavern from being enshrouded in blackness.

As they began their walk, her father started to talk more about information that he undoubtedly thought Kylie should know. He was profoundly proud of the Saliek that he commanded and talked about various members' prowess at length. It would seem that she would be meeting one of them upon their exit from this cave. He talked of Krael, the magical beauty it possessed, as well as the creatures that strode upon it. She thought that if it was anything like the cave they were currently trekking through, she would not be disappointed. He also talked about her royal family. She took after her actual father in looks and had a brother that was ten years her elder. That seemed a little strange to her, but nothing she couldn't handle.

He paused for a second and cocked his head slightly, remembering something of particular importance to tell her, "When Zhannah and I secreted you away from Arbore seventeen years ago, I cast a strong spell upon you and myself. This spell is not easily cast upon two people, as it takes such a large amount of knowledge of not only oneself but of the other person it is being cast upon. It also requires extensive knowledge of the human brain, which I had fortunately studied. You were practically a baby and had not really become your full self yet, making the process easier."

Kylie listened intently, hoping he would get to the point soon.

"It seemed necessary at the time," he explained, "in case we became separated and has actually come in handy frequently throughout the years, such as the impeccable timing of my arrival in Liri yesterday. I imparted a connection between your thoughts and my own. I can hear what you are thinking, and with some practice, I can teach you to read my thoughts as well."

Kylie wasn't sure how to react to this. It made sense in a way that he always seemed to know what she was thinking, but she had always assumed that was just because a father knew his daughter very well. A shadow of doubt and fear suddenly crept over her as she thought of the additional implications of a bond like this. Could she ever have thoughts that were only her own? What else had he been privy too of which she was unaware? Her eyes got larger, and she began rubbing one of her arms with the opposite hand as her cheeks reddened slightly.

He must have sensed her troubled thoughts, as he continued hastily, "There are ways to build blockades in one's mind, and I have only reached out to you when needed. You have some sort of sense of how to reach out to me already. Throughout the past couple of days, I have answered those questions that you have directed towards me."

She supposed this seemed to explain a lot of situations recently and lamely responded to him, "Oh, okay... Thanks." After a few moments, she recovered her words again, and her curiosity took over, "Do others have the power to reach into my mind as well?"

"No," he answered, "At least not through this link. It is plausible however that someone with a strong Spirit could have researched and mastered the art, though I do not know of one. The human mind is an incredibly complex system, as I mentioned earlier, and unless they have found a way around knowing the object of their mind reading very well, I do not know of another way for it to be possible."

"Will you teach me how to block my mind soon then?" Kylie asked eagerly.

Her father agreed that the sooner she knew, the better, and he began teaching her as they made their way through the rest of the cave. Kylie was a quick learner and an eager student in their endeavors. She was soon able to block out her father when she didn't want him there, as well as sense his presence, and consciously send him messages of her own. It was almost fun to communicate this way.

"Will it ever go away?" she wondered aloud to him after a time.

"Not the way I designed it. It is possible that the connection could be removed but only with much study on my part. You have become a human being with much more complexity than a baby. I would have to know you much better than I do now to be able to remove it without fear of damaging the rest of your mind in the process. I... I am sorry for leaving you for a decade," her father hung his head in dismay. "Maybe if I hadn't, I may have known you well enough to offer this option. But even if I did, knowing that this is an advantageous tool that we can use in freeing Krael from the clutches of Elasche, I would not recommend its removal."

Kylie understood and had already forgiven him for leaving her. After all, he had come back for her in the end, and that had to mean something. He had also told her earlier of the troubles on Krael that demanded the Saliek's, and therefore his, attention. Being their commander meant a certain amount of sacrifice on his end was inevitable. He needed to be their example, to help bring the best out of every member he interacted with, and ultimately help each Saliek to succeed in their own specific talents and interests that were pertinent to the cause of restoring peace to Krael. Only in this way could the Saliek be maintained as successful and skilled as they were. From his stories of their heroics that he had been telling earlier, it sounded like he was a very accomplished leader.

Elasche, her parents, and her minions, according to her father's stories, had taken over the majority of the cities on Krael, leaving only the ones she felt undesirable alone. Elasche seemed like a real snake to Kylie. She had decided to study seduction and deceit and used her Spirit to brainwash her unsuspecting prey who would then follow her every order, desire, and whim just to gain her approval. Kylie thought that these people she brainwashed must have been extremely weak minded to fall for something as petty as seduction, but her father had warned her to not let her guard down so easily. Where seduction didn't work, she could trick someone with pretty words to do nearly anything that she wanted. Rumor had it that Elasche had a talent for finding chinks in one's mental armor. Kylie almost couldn't wait to meet this gem, despite her father's warnings about her. It sounded like all they needed to do was be rid of her and all would be well again on Krael. She had heard that the best way to deal with a poisonous snake was to chop off their head. Well, she didn't think she could manage to do that, but sending one of her knives between the snake's eyes would probably work just as well.

She had said as much to her father, but he had found it hilarious. After laughing so hard his face turned red, he had said, "Dear Ky, if it had been that simple, I'd have done away with her myself years ago. She is but a spoiled child who has learned what she has at the encouragement of her family. Though she is the one with the power to control others' minds, the actual masterminds behind this chaos are her parents, whom have always been protected extremely well."

They walked for hours through the majestic cave, slowing only once to eat a packed lunch. All the while, they bantered about the inconsequential and mused upon important affairs until she could see a faint light that brightened with every step forward that they took. The light made the cave come alive in a spectacular sparkle. The light would reflect off one vein of crystal into the full spectrum of color and then, as if a rainbow come to life, bounce between the veins until the light vanished into the darkness of the cave. A point came where there was too much light for the dancing rainbow effect to be seen, much to Kylie's disappointment, but she could see a blindingly bright circle growing up ahead. Her heart fluttered with excitement. It must be the exit.

Chapter 6

The elements of fire, earth, water, and air swirled about each other in an ethereal sphere abandoned by its previous owner. A locally hailed hero found the sphere nestled away in his camp one evening and decided to take it as his own. After many years of training, he was able to fully tap the powers of the sphere, and the sphere morphed into a man of great potential. A man who had the ability to be compassionate and lead, as well as smile. The finder of the sphere knew that one day this man would overtake him, but it was not fear or anger that stood forefront in his feelings, it was pride and happiness.

Kylie blinked wildly as she stepped through the exit and into the sun. Her father had just signaled to her that all was clear. As it had taken her eyes a while to grow accustomed to the darkness of the cave, she stood in blindness for a few moments as they became readjusted to the light. She was awestruck at the beauty of the Krael wilderness. Her father had warned her of its extravagant colors and sheer beauty, but her actual experience of it had a larger impact than the description that words could provide.

There were trees that were bright green with the leaves around the edges fading to a sunny yellow color before giving way to the soft blue sky. Deep emerald bushes nestled in the brush were spotted with five-petaled flowers in a variety of colors painting the greens with splashes of crimsons, teals, pinks, yellows, and purples. The tall wispy stems that dotted the landscape exceeded her height and were encircled with tiny halos of blue, bell-shaped flowers near their tips. Green plants of various shapes and sizes blanketed the ground and covered her feet as she stood outside the cave. Her senses were completely saturated as the sweet smell of strange flowers also caressed her nose, and the suns began to warm her still chilled body. Compared to the dusty red-brown colors of Thaer, where the grass held a tint of green but was dominated by a brown hue and where dull trees sparsely dotted the landscape, this was paradise. She had never known what she had been missing.

A sharp whinny directed her attention away from the scenery. Her father stood caressing an enormous, pitch-black Clydesdale looking horse's head, scratching it between its ears and cooing words of praise and adoration to it. It stamped its white feathered forefeet in satisfaction. As the horse butted its white blaze against her father's forehead, she noticed a change had befallen her father. His hair had become a deeper black color and obtained a blue sheen to it when the sunlight hit it the right way. In a similar way, his eyes shone a brighter sky blue, almost emitting light from them.

Not taking his eyes off the horse, her father tried to explain, "It is the Spirit inside shining outwardly. You can generally tell people with Spirit here in Krael, due to their 'glow'. The brighter the glow, the stronger the Spirit. You should see yourself," he briefly glanced towards her. "The next chance we get to stop near a reflecting pool of sorts, you will see what I mean."

At her father's words, Kylie was anxiously trying to look at herself without the help of a mirror. The main difference that she could see was her long sandy blonde hair had turned a golden yellow color. When she examined it more closely, she noticed that as her father's hair had a blue sheen to it when light glanced off it a certain way, her hair had an emerald green sheen in the sunlight. She was very curious to see her eyes. The cloak that her father had given her to wear was a magnificent shade of deep green. She clutched the rock that Mory had given her before she left, and when she opened her hand, she saw that the colors that swirled into the rock had intensified. She tucked it back under her shirt for now.

Her father's horse then unfolded its wings... its *wings*! They were strong feathered black wings that powerfully beat a breeze into the surrounding air. When the pegasus had finished its stretch, her father beckoned her over.

"Kylie, I'd like you to meet Valor," her father introduced them, and Valor bowed his head slightly. "Pegasi are intelligent and prideful creatures. They often bond with their Saliek riders for life, if they deem them worthy. Since the day I was honored to join the Saliek, Valor here has been by my side. I'd have to say that it's been almost 300 years now. He was only a rambunctious colt back then, but then again, so was I." Valor once again bobbed his head in agreement and playfully butt his head against her father's shoulder while he chuckled.

"Can I touch him?" Kylie ventured as she stuck her hand warily out towards the creature whose shoulders were as tall as her head. Valor gently pushed his muzzle into her hand and nickered softly. His nose was silky soft to the touch and his breath tickled her hand each time he exhaled. Her eyes met his and she could see his intelligence. Was he also judging her? She moved her hand up to his white blaze and scratched it lovingly telling him what a pretty boy he was, and Valor closed his eyes and pushed into her hand grunting his agreement.

"I think he likes you, Ky," her father chuckled slightly. "Then again, anyone who gives him compliments is on the fast track to his favorites list, along with anyone who gives him one of these." Her father reached into his pack and produced a juicy looking blue fruit the size of his fist. "Blapples," he declared as he tossed it to her, “are a fruit grown here on Krael. It's basically a blue colored apple but slightly sweeter. Valor loves these things!"

Valor eyed the blapple as Kylie reached out to hand it to him. She held her hand flat with the fruit on top and her fingers out of the way of the beast’s chomping teeth just as her mother had taught her with the horses that she had met on Thaer. She felt a rough swipe of his tongue on her hand, and then he triumphantly gobbled down the tasty treat. After Valor swallowed it, he rubbed his head on her shoulder affectionately. Kylie wiped the slobber off her hand onto Valor's coat.

"Well, now I think that he will let you ride him," her father said with approval. "Rather, he’ll let you ride double with me until we can get back to the Saliek camp near here and get you properly outfitted.” Her father started scanning the horizon with his eyes and wondered aloud, “Now where is Anik? He was supposed to meet me here."

As if on cue, Kylie saw another one of the beautiful beasts descend from the sky. It looked nearly the twin of the one whose neck her father scrubbed with his hands, except only three of its four feet were white and instead of a blaze on its forehead, there was a white mask that covered its eyes. Kylie’s hair blew back in the breeze that was created by the pegasus' landing as she got a glance of the magnificent beast's rider. His black cape that signaled he was one of the Saliek flew out behind him, and his thick auburn hair with an orange sheen swirled in the wind. His eyes glowed orange... That was a little disturbing but probably only because she had never seen a person with orange eyes before. He locked eyes with her after he completed his graceful landing and gave her a dashing smile. She could then see that his eyes were actually brown in color, they only had an orange glow to them. He was a strong lad that looked about her age, but soon she realized that she was staring and after giving a quick smile and nod in return, hastily turned her attention back to Valor.

"Anik, where were you?" her father asked calmly. "You were assigned to stay here to keep Valor company and guard the entrance to the cave."

"I was doing just that, Saliek-an Regithal," Anik replied with confidence. "A group of firelings came by, whether by accident or not, I am unsure. Valor, Bandit, and myself fought most of them off here, but a couple got away. I went to chase them down in case they were planning on relaying any information. None survived." Anik motioned in the direction of the forest. "You'll find what is left of them there. I was planning on burning their corpses on my return, but if you are in a hurry," he glanced towards Kylie, "I can leave the task until later."

"A job well done!" her father complimented Anik, who kept a straight face, but Kylie could see the smile in his eyes. “We did not run into a single one in the cave, so none got by you. I think it is best if we take care of the bodies now to decrease any attention drawn to this area, but it should be done quickly."

Anik seemed to have gotten the gist of what her father was intending with that last comment and proceeded to close his eyes. Moments later, the field near the forest dotted itself with small bright fires. As quickly as the fires started, they ended. Miraculously, there were no burn marks in the grass where the bodies had lain. Anik must have studied fire and the flammability of various substances at length to accomplish that. In her experience, grass burned more easily than dead bodies. Maybe she would ask him about it later.

"Kylie, I'd like you to meet the Saliek's newest recruit, Anik," her father introduced the lad.

Anik bowed as well as he could from Bandit's back, "Pleasure to meet you, Miss Kylie." His tousled hair fell in front of his eyes in the process.

"Hello, Sir Anik," Kylie replied for lack of a better way to address someone who had just prefixed her name with "Miss."

Her father quickly corrected her, "You can just call him Anik. There are no knights amongst the Saliek, only scholars. Anik was initiated about five years ago now. It is not so often that we have new recruits into the Saliek. He is studying the physics of fire, water, wind, and earth. Quite an ambitious one we have here."

She noticed Anik flush slightly at the compliment as he tried to brush it off, "Oh it's not all that impressive in comparison to those who have been in the Saliek for years. Just somewhere to start, you know." He was rubbing the back of his head and looking down at Bandit's back as he spoke.

"Now that we are all comfortable with one another, let's take to the sky and return to camp. I am sure a warm welcome awaits us there!" her father said to get them moving.

"Kylie, I will give you a leg up onto Valor, and you will ride behind me. Hold on tight! I advise you not to look down at first if it makes you queasy. If you feel fine, just enjoy the view."

Kylie and her father mounted up, and with a nudge from her father's black boot, Valor took to the sky with big swoops of his wings. Bandit and Anik were right behind them. Kylie's golden hair swept back in the wind as they ascended towards a sky spotted with fluffy white, welcoming clouds. Kylie gasped in awe, sucking a cool blast of air into her lungs as she dared to look down over the side of Valor's flank. She saw a world from a perspective that she never had before. Beneath her extended gaze, Kylie could see miles of the Krael wilderness, that she had already fallen in love with, shrink into a colorful palette of green and golden patches with spires of grey rock breaking through the colors' barriers. The largest trees that had towered many times her height near the cave were reduced to undefined green blotches on the ground, and the cave's entrance was soon unable to be seen as it meshed in with the grey mountain sides. Kylie's head began to swirl slightly as she looked from side to side at the views surrounding her. She didn't know if it was from the heights that they were reaching or from the sheer amount of awe her mind was experiencing at the moment.

They were currently rising from a valley amidst the mountains. In one direction, she saw what looked to be a castle with a town sprawled out around it that must have been Arbore. In the other direction, there was a vast, deep blue ocean with waves twinkling in the sunlight extending endlessly to the limits of her vision. She could definitely get used to this. All too soon, her father called back for her to hold on tight as Valor began his descent into the Saliek camp nestled, unseen from the skies, in another valley between the mountains.

They landed near a herd of pegasi grazing in a large field. Their coats were not only black like Valor and Bandit, but also chestnut, bay, palomino, grey, dappled, white, and every other shade that horses generally were colored. All of the full-grown ones were built similarly to Valor and Bandit with their strong muscles, tall backs, and feathered feet. There were also a few youngsters running amuck, charging at each other playfully, romping around, and generally having a good time. They were the most adorable creatures that Kylie had ever seen.

Before her father could stop her, she jumped off, or

more like fell off, Valor's back and briskly walked over to a group of the young pegasi. They were still in their awkward phase with long gangly legs ending in tufts of fluff that would one day grow into the gorgeous feathered feet of the full-grown pegasi. The group she walked towards at first eyed her suspiciously, but they soon decided that she was an acceptable acquaintance as she began scratching behind their ears. Suddenly, Kylie felt a thump in her side and was knocked off balance to fall onto her knees. She looked up to see a golden coated filly with a cream-colored mane and tail. She held a somewhat devious look upon her face as she held her proud head up high.

"You little devil!" Kylie said jokingly, and stood up to give the foal a good scrubbing. After that, the foal would not let any of the other young pegasi get close to Kylie without a good nipping.

"It looks as though someone has found a new friend!" her father exclaimed from behind her.

"She does have a certain amount of spunk, doesn't she?" Kylie replied. She turned around to look at her father and was caught off guard by the group of black-coated individuals that had gathered to watch her. The golden filly must have sensed her unease and made a show of putting itself in between Kylie and the group of Saliek with a grunt and glared out at the crowd from its spindly legs. This just seemed to amuse them more.

"A new friend indeed," a female voice said, and a chestnut-haired woman extracted herself from the crowd. She closed her eyes for a moment and then approached Kylie, "This little filly seems to have bonded itself to you. Congratulations on your lifelong companion." The woman reached out to pat the golden filly, who tried to take a chomp out of her hand. "Slightly ill-tempered lifelong companion," she muttered as she pulled her hand back quickly. "The pegasi do not usually bond that quickly, but she must have sensed something about you... I am Phyllis," Phyllis said while beginning a bow. "It is an honor to meet you Spirit Master, Princess Kylie, as I don't believe you could be anyone else from what I have seen thus far."

Kylie was at a loss for words. She knew that this title corresponded with the tale that her father had told her, but somehow it must not have completely sunk in at the time. "Please, just call me Kylie, and no need for bowing… it doesn't feel right," Kylie said, turning down her head to look at the ground. Assuredly, her face was as red as a hot coal by now. Without further ado, the crowd started applauding and cheering at her performance, which made her even more embarrassed. She just wanted to hide.

Her father immediately stepped in and began shooing the crowd away, "Yes, this is Kylie, she is a little overwhelmed right now, so let us welcome her tomorrow. Go on now, there is a multitude of work to be done now that she has returned." Then he turned to direct specific individuals to ready a tent for her and prepare some food for an evening meal. After the crowd had dispersed, he returned to Kylie's side and poked a little fun at her, "Well you sure know how to make an entrance now don't you?"

"I just wanted to pet the pegasi foals. They looked so adorable!" Kylie defended herself while stroking her fingers through the golden filly's cream mane.

Her father laughed, "That they are! So now that this one seems to have bonded itself so recklessly to you, what will you name her?"

"Starshine," she replied decisively. Kylie had been calling her by that name silently before the crowd had encircled her.

"A fitting name," her father agreed as he ran his hand along her golden coat, nodding his head. "You know, her coat matches your hair," he said with a smile. Kylie placed a lock of her hair against Starshine's coat in response and found that he was right.

They both took a seat in the well-cropped grass, watching the pegasi roam the field with Valor and Starshine at their sides grazing. Kylie wondered aloud, "How do the Saliek keep all these pegasi nearby with no visible fences? Some sort of magic?"

"Not magic," her father replied, "unless you consider love a magic. You see, the pegasi herd follows the Saliek camp of its own accord. Whenever we move, they follow. It's been like this as long as I can remember. The Saliek take care of their needs, and they take care of the Saliek. Phyllis oversees the pegasi, making sure the herd is comfortable. Her Spirit seems to be specifically in tune with the beasts and can tell with whom they've bonded, as you saw earlier. The dark-coated ones carry a gene that makes them more likely to bond with one of us. You will notice that the Saliek mounts are black, dark chestnut, bay, or deep grey. This has helped us to travel with relative ease in the dark of night many times. Usually, a lighter colored pegasus will only bind with a person if they sense that they are the Spirit Master. Although there have been noted occasions when this was not the case, especially with particularly strong Spirited people. These instances are few and far between. Andolin's bonded pegasus was completely white. His name was Ghost. Ghost passed away within a day of Andolin, supposedly from a broken heart. What happened with you and Starshine earlier, just confirmed what everyone here at this camp has hoped for the last 17 years, which is why they couldn't help but cheer."

Kylie stared up at the sky watching the swirling colors of the first sunset. She truly hoped that she could be as great of a person as the Saliek assumed she was. The only thing that she had accomplished with her Spirit was the packing of a bedroll. All of those around her were adept at using their Spirit and had studied various topics extensively. There was no way her mind could fathom that she was greater than these extremely skilled and accomplished people surrounding her. Look at what Anik had done earlier today, and he was the newest recruit! She felt very inadequate at the moment.

"You will learn in time," her father promised quietly. “It was us who chose to sequester you on Thaer, knowing very well that this may dampen your skill initially, but your mother and I made sure you had access to most of the Ancient Archives to learn what may be useful to you here. Although you may not have had practice with your Spirit, you still have a plethora of knowledge within you that you can apply later."

Oh great, Kylie thought to herself making sure her mental boundaries were up, good thing she had spent half of that time whittling wood and goofing off with Mory.

Her father must have known that she had put up her mental shields because he shifted uncomfortably, eyeing her sidelong, awaiting a response.

"Thanks Father,” Kylie said to break the awkward silence. “I hope I learned enough from my studies or at least read the correct books. There were so many books stashed away on the shelves that I don't think I even opened the cover on half of them!"

Her father replied reassuringly, "No one can know everything, Kylie. There is a library here at camp that you can use at your leisure. My suggestion to you is to find something that interests you the most and pursue the study of that. Once you master that, move on to another topic. With any luck, you will have many years to study and increase your prowess. In the short term, I think your main purpose will be acting as a rally point for the Saliek to bring down Elasche and her family. The morale has significantly increased just by you being here. Your return has given them something tangible for all of their hard work up until now."

Kylie sighed, "So I really am going to be worthless for a while."

Her father scooted over to hug her on the grass, "No Ky, you will never be worthless. Remember your training from Thaer. No one here has ever had to survive without the help of their Spirit. You can. You have that. And I promise you that is a significant advantage now and in the long run. To the best of our knowledge, Krael is the only planet where the people who have Spirit manifest it to its fullest extent. Krael is not the only planet that is visited by evil. And Krael is not the only planet that needs protection. On those other planets, only relics imbued with an ancient magic seem to keep their attributes while the Spirit within a person is dampened." He started brushing his hand down her hair, "I suggest reading that book Scilla made sure you had in your satchel tonight. She wouldn't have gone to the trouble if she hadn't thought it worth it. Let's go eat a meal and get some rest. I'm sure tomorrow will be just as exhausting as today."

Chapter 7

Wind whipped sand across the searing heat of the desert causing a traveler to pull his headgear tighter around his face. His camel's feet sunk slightly into the sand with each step adding to the slow pace of his travels. He was accompanied by a large group of traders hoping to sell their goods in a difficult to reach city where prices would be largely set in their favor. Their maps indicated that they would be about two to three days' travel away from their anticipated destination at their plodding pace. They only had supplies enough for one more day of travel, maybe two if they rationed very strictly.

Slightly off their course, the traveler saw a beautiful oasis, bright green palm leaves contrasting the pale-yellow sand of the surrounding dunes. Between himself and the oasis lay a gargantuan snake ringed in black, red, and yellow. Tales told of the horrors that this snake had committed in guarding its precious oasis. Tales so horrible that the rest of the group of travelers decided to risk carrying on as opposed to restocking at the oasis. This specific traveler had studied animals rather thoroughly, and upon closer inspection of the snake, the traveler noted that the red rings were surrounded by the black rings before the yellow. In his studies, snakes with this specific pattern were harmless, and it was only when the red rings were surrounded by the yellow rings that the snake was dangerous. He left the group to restock himself at the oasis, safely passing the snake.

Kylie was tucked away in her very own tent for the night. The hard-packed dirt on the ground was covered by throw rugs of various colors so she wouldn't have to get her bare feet dirty. An oversized cot had been placed in a corner and outfitted with a surprisingly comfortable mattress, fluffy down pillow, and soft warm blankets. The days and nights here on Krael seemed significantly cooler than on Thaer. She wondered if that was because Krael was further out from the suns than Thaer, or if maybe it had to do with the atmosphere, or if it was as simple as her specific location on Krael was in a different part of the seasonal cycle than where her cabin was on Thaer. Anyway, she was happy for the warm blankets as she snuggled into her bed with a full stomach.

The food they had provided her at dinner had warmed as well as filled her stomach. The Saliek must not move their camp very often since the kitchen tent that the food had emerged from looked very well established, and the food that came out of it looked as if it could have been made for royalty. Oh wait... She was royalty here. Eh, she didn't feel any different. Kylie, her father, and Anik had eaten in her newly-erected tent, which had enough room for a small table and some chairs. Kylie was thankful that her father had declared it a private dinner, as she had had her fill of excitement for today. Anik had seemed to have gained a certain amount of respect from the other Saliek when she had said it would be nice if he could join them as well.

They had talked about what Elasche and her family had been up to recently and complained about how they were slowly destroying Arbore. It was said that Elasche had decided that Arbore was her favorite of the cities of which they had seized control and had set up her very own realm in a mountain paradise. The majority of the city had been brainwashed into her slaves to the detriment of the city. It is often the merchants working for their own best interests that keep cities alive, her father had explained. If they always sell for less than it costs to create a good, just because it is to someone who mentions Elasche's name, then they will never be able to make a profit to stay in business. As the businesses closed one by one in Arbore and the un-brainwashed occupants moved elsewhere, the once prosperous city was slowly edging towards its demise.

The king and queen of Arbore, who had been held hostage for seven years by Elasche and her family, were rescued ten years past with the intervention of the Saliek and were currently hidden in a clandestine location. Unfortunately, it seemed that Elasche had previously gotten to Prince Sonu, as he could not be persuaded to leave the city with his parents during the rescue. He had fallen victim to Elasche's charm when the city was taken over and attended to her every waking need. The rumors were that they had been engaged for two years now, ever since her parents left her alone in Arbore.

Sonu saw the Saliek and his parents as his enemies, and any attempt to rescue him had been met with his own resistance and attempts to kill his rescuers. Sonu believed that he and Elasche were the rightful rulers of Arbore now since his parents had ‘defected’. They were also involved in some other mission that they had hidden quite well. Sonu often was gone from the city, from what the Saliek intelligence believed, searching for something.

Anik and her father had talked at length about their plans for tomorrow. The Saliek were planning an ambush on one of Sonu's search parties that had been away from Arbore for weeks. Their theory was that when a person was away from Elasche they could realign their thoughts properly, and a few weeks seemed an ample enough amount of time. Kylie hadn't much to contribute to the conversation after both her father and Anik had simultaneously said, "No!" when she had asked to come along. Once again, that worthless feeling had engulfed her.

After the food was all eaten and the conversation had died down, Anik and her father had excused themselves, and Kylie had taken a warm bath within her tent, rinsing off the grit and grime that had accumulated over the day. She had found a trunk of clothes someone had thought to give her, and then had found her way into the bed she was in now. Her father had suggested that she read Scilla's book, but she felt so tired, and the soft pillow was lulling her to sleep. Then she remembered that terrible sinking feeling of worthlessness that kept overwhelming her and reached her hand beneath the cot to grab her satchel. She found it quickly and pulled out the book. She ran her hand across the rough, dark brown leather cover and her fingers swiped away dust that had covered the title written with gold leaf: Legends, Myths, and Tales of the Universe. The cover had been etched with a warrior holding a great sword standing in opposition to a demonic looking creature. It was eerily similar to the carvings on the front doors of the Ancient Archives.

Legends, Myths, and Tales of the Universe. Isn't that what the crate had been labeled that she pulled the book from? Unsure of any significance there, Kylie propped herself up to a more comfortable reading position and opened the book. The pages seemed brittle and were acquiring a slight brown tint around the edges. It smelled like the books in the Ancient Archives that hadn't been opened in years. She would have to treat this book carefully. The first page held a faded table of contents. The book was, as advertised by the title, a collection of short legends, myths, and tales. She supposed that she could read at least one tonight, and where best to start other than at the beginning? She turned the page.

Legend of Ghaleon

A renowned warrior of ages past lost his beloved wife and beautiful daughter to a man who came to loot his house of valuables while he was on a hunting expedition. When he returned home to find them both gruesomely murdered and his house ransacked, he was devastated and valiantly made a vow to purge the universe of all evil, beginning with his home world. At that moment, he was visited the first time by the Greatest Spirit. It could see the purity of this man and his intentions by his choice to not seek revenge upon the one that hurt him or to attempt to retrieve what was forever lost from this world. Instead, the man strove to make the worlds a better place for all the good creatures who inhabited them and protect them from the pain he had been forced to experience. Thus, the ability to tell good from evil was granted to him.

Once he had proven himself by ridding his home world of evil, he was visited by the Greatest Spirit a second time who bestowed upon him three gifts. A travelling cloak that allowed one to survive the perils of travelling the universe, a shield that could protect him from anything living, dead, or spiritual, and a sword that possessed the power to destroy anything that happened upon its blade. Ghaleon received these items humbly and with great thanks before using them to eliminate all evil from the universe at that time.

Once he had accomplished this, he had grown elderly and tired. He no longer had any goal to pursue or family to take care of and love, so he felt like he no longer had a purpose for which to live. The Greatest Spirit visited him one final time at this point. The Spirit tried to convince Ghaleon to remain of the worlds in flesh and blood to act as the protector against all that is evil in the times to come. Ghaleon refused, as he believed that he had already purged all evil so it could never return!

After much arguing, the Greatest Spirit decided to allow Ghaleon to pass into the afterlife and be reunited with his lost wife and daughter, but only after he destroyed the three gifts that he was given and hid the pieces properly amongst the worlds to be found again if the future ever needed them. Ghaleon of course insisted that the future generations would not have need of them, but he did as the Greatest Spirit requested. As he destroyed each piece, he sang an alluring tune that would allow them to only be forged together once again with one of his talents. He did this knowing that the type of magic bestowed upon him at birth was rare enough that in his travels he never once met anyone with the same talents, though he had heard of its presence in multiple legends and stories he had come across in various worlds. And so, duties believed completed, Ghaleon retired to the afterlife, ending his 1000-year life, and left the worlds to weave their own futures.

Evil was not so easily vanquished though, for it lived in the hearts of many creatures un-manifested and laying-in-wait for the precise circumstances to emerge. It was often unknown to the creature itself until the very moment came upon them. The Greatest Spirit realized this, and continues to search the worlds for others to replace the great Ghaleon before the balance between good and evil tips back to the latter.

Kylie lowered the book and closed it to look at the cover again. The warrior had a cloak flowing behind him as he was facing down the demon with his sword, and a shield was in the background behind the combatants. The warrior depicted must be Ghaleon and the demon some sort of evil that he was vanquishing. Was she supposed to be this warrior reincarnated? Was this 'Greatest Spirit' somehow inhabiting her? Why had Scilla wanted her to read this? She stared off into the darkness of her tent while she pondered all the questions that she had.

When her mind came back to reality, she noticed a faint green glow coming from the other side of the tent where she was staring. Her curiosity got the better of her, and she got out of bed holding a blanket draped over her shoulders to go investigate. As she walked toward the glow, it got brighter and brighter until she realized that the glow was coming from a mirror. She gasped. Her eyes were the source of that eerie green glow. After she had regained her bearings, she hurried over to her tent's entrance and poked her head outside the flap. She had heard voices and wanted to see if the passerby's eyes had the same glow to them.

Her hair was blown back by a crisp breeze, and she heard the crickets and frogs singing their nighttime songs. Fireflies seemed to flicker in and out of existence as they spontaneously lit up the darkness. There were multiple people still out and traversing the paths that wound between the neutral-colored sleeping tents aligned in an easily navigable grid system. The hour wasn't too late yet, and at a camp like this there would be some sort of bustle at any hour of the night. What she saw was mesmerizing, yet somewhat frightening. Many of the Saliek had the hoods of their black cloaks up over their heads to guard against the chilly night wind, and from beneath those hoods she could see a myriad of colored glowing eyes bouncing in synch with their owners walking gait. She saw a familiar orange glowing pair duck into a tent on the opposite side of the walkway. They had put her tent across from Anik's.

An idea struck her at that moment. She was supposed to be this great Spirit Master, right? So why should she be left behind from their mission tomorrow? Also, she wanted to see this brother of hers. Since she knew there would be no convincing her father, she would concentrate her efforts on Anik. Having made the decision to act instead of sitting around and moping had given a noticeable boost to her mood. She knew the details of the plans for tomorrow morning's mission per Anik and her father's dinner discussions, and it would just be a matter of inserting herself at the right time. She just had to come up with some way to convince Anik to take her along too...

She closed the tent flap and returned to the relative warmth of her room. Her ears and nose had gone numb from sticking her head outside for that short amount of time. She scurried across the rugs on the floor and wrapped herself into the blankets still warm from her body heat. She let her mind race as she lay there thinking of the most likely way to convince Anik to take her along.

Chapter 8

A transparent man traversed the halls of the place he had once called home. Dust powdered the shelves, and the volumes of knowledge he had collected were slowly decaying away. If he had committed one selfish act in his life, it had been to love his home and family too much. He knew it was time now, time to let it go. Somberly, he laid his hand on the great doorway and unlocked it to the world of the living. He prayed that the one to find this place would put it to the use of good. He would do his best to lead someone there.

Mory could barely contain his excitement as he closed the door to leave Scilla's working chamber. It was located in the cluster of rooms that Mory and Scilla lived their day to day lives in on the second floor of the library. There were more rooms on this floor than they could put to good use, so Scilla had spread herself out, often only using a room for a single purpose. Mory had decided that he really didn't need any more than the one larger room that he used as a combined bedroom and study.

Zhannah had talked to Scilla earlier this morning, and Scilla had agreed to allow him access to another part of the library. Scilla had just finished giving him instructions on how to reach this area as well as a key. She told him that finding it himself with her instructions would be better than her simply showing him how to get there. He had not felt this sense of adventure in a long time as he carefully read through his notes on Scilla's verbal instructions.

Yesterday's fireling fun was much too frightful to have been an adventurous feeling, and Zhannah's offer to teach him swordplay had honored him, but he was quite nervous. He feared that his talents would be sub-par to her expectations. At least he would be more useful as a skilled swordsman, he thought. As a skilled swordsman, he could protect those he cared for. The additional stories and information that he would find in this secret part of the library may sate his curiosity, but he wasn't sure as to how his knowledge would benefit many more people than himself. He was giddy nonetheless, for he really did love his books and exploring secret passages.

He wondered how he had not already stumbled upon this place in his earlier explorations. He had already unearthed a countless number of secret chambers and passageways hidden between the walls of the library. Many passages were dark and narrow, leading to secret exits from the library. Some were wide and spacious, as if they were supposed to be used often, and led to interesting rooms. His favorite of these rooms included a warm, bubbling hot spring deep enough for him to sit and cover his shoulders. He figured that the key Scilla had given him must make all the difference to locating the secret area.

This key was not shaped like any normal door key that Mory had seen before. It was a dense hunk of metal shaped into a miniature sword replica. Its length was close to that of his extended hand, and the blade was dull enough that he could grasp it and not be harmed. Its weight felt much heavier than it looked like it ought to be, and upon closer inspection one could see that the hilt was decorated with some sort of designs. He would have never guessed this to be a key if he had just seen it lying around. He would have assumed it to be some sort of decorative trinket. That was probably the intention of whoever made it.

Mory climbed down the spiral staircase leading to the entrance hall and walked through the corridor leading into the main area of the first floor where books were kept. He followed the outside stone wall until he arrived in a spot that he knew well. A decorated archway resided there that had been filled with stone and mortar for as long as he remembered. His best guess, until now, had been that someone from years past had been buried in a crypt back there, and then it had been blocked off from the rest of the library.

He examined the carvings in the red marbled archway having only a vague idea for what he was looking. Scilla had told him that once he got here, he should "place the sword in the stone." Along the arch, there were images of armies of women and men rushing into battle, some riding winged horses, all with capes flying backwards in the haste of their charge. Their opponents looked also to be women and men, but interspersed among them were firelings and other creatures that he could not identify. Other sections of the archway depicted scenery such as a dense forest of trees with immensely thick trunks that towered over the tiny humans within it, mountains surrounding a city, a speckling of stars overlooking a vast sea... Or maybe it was desert? In the age worn carving it was difficult to identify if the swells in the landscape were waves or dunes. He wondered at the stories beyond the images as he searched. There were so many carvings around the arch that he was beginning to worry if he would ever find the right place for the sword.

Then he saw it; he knew it had to be it. At the very top and center of the archway he saw the very same carvings that graced the front doors of the library: the courageous warrior wielding a great sword overtaking a tremendous demon. Mory had spent years trying to find the specific story behind the images on those doors within the library, but he had not found it yet. Seeing it again here confirmed his suspicion that it must have been significant at one point in time. Scilla had never specifically answered his inquiries on the carvings either. She only would say that they must be intertwined with the history of this place. It had occurred to him that she possibly didn't even know the answer herself.

He wandered off to find one of many stepstools scattered throughout the library used to reach books sitting high on the shelves and placed it in front of the archway so he could reach the carving. Now that he was tall enough, he could see that the miniature sword did indeed look like it would fit inside the carving of the warrior's sword. He leaned against the stone wall in front of him and placed it inside the carving very carefully. He held his breath for a moment... nothing happened. He felt a wave of disappointment coming over him, when suddenly the sword was sucked into the carving with the raspy sound of metal on rock. The next instant, he was tumbling and hit the stone floor the only way one can, hard.

Mory pushed himself up from the ground. Only slightly more than his pride had been bruised. Luckily, he hadn't been too far above the ground. He was nearly six feet tall, and had only needed to go up the first couple steps on the stool. He looked at where the wall used to be. The once rock-filled archway now looked semi-transparent. He experimentally placed his hand into the hologram looking wall, and to his amazement it went straight through. He then tried to walk through it back into the library on the other side but was met with a repelling force that pushed back. Mory felt a moment of panic then, not knowing how he would get out of here, but quickly suppressed it. He figured that he had yet to find the secret part of the library, and maybe there was a way out located there that Scilla had 'forgotten' to mention in her instructions. That would be very like her to leave Mory up to his own devices. She was either extremely forgetful, seemed to think he would learn more that way, or something else beyond his comprehension. Sometimes Mory found it rather irritating, but it was hard to stay frustrated long at someone who had taken you in when you had no family.

The dark staircase that the archway had opened into was lined with softly glowing orbs mounted in long intervals along the wall. They provided just enough light for Mory to see that it was a long way down. As he took his first step towards the staircase, he felt a quick stab of pain as he stubbed his toe on something metal that scraped across the stone floor with the slight momentum his foot had given it. After bouncing around for moment on one foot awaiting the pain in his toe to subside, he knelt down for a closer look to find a great sword lying on the floor in perfect condition. It couldn't have been lying there for very long considering the pristine condition that it was in. He picked it up and held it vertically with both his hands. A thought struck him, and he turned to face the archway again. There was a larger sword shaped indentation on this side of the wall, located at about hip height. So, that must be how he was to get out of this passage. The miniature sword key had somehow turned into a real sword after being absorbed into the wall, and he would have to return the sword to the wall to exit this place. At least, that was his theory. The testing of his theory would have to wait though, as he was still anxious to find the books that he had been promised access to.

Sword clumsily in hand, Mory began descending the long dark staircase to what he hoped would be the most magnificent part of the library. It was damp and cool, and he caught a waft of mold every so often. The sword had become his official cobweb slayer as he used it to beat down the sticky silk threads that otherwise clung mercilessly to his exposed skin. He hoped that he would not meet any of the creatures that undoubtedly resided within those webs. After descending what he guessed to be a half mile down, the staircase ended, and a short corridor led to a dusky room. He picked up the pace into the corridor, eager to be done with this staircase, when suddenly something monstrous in size dropped to the floor in front of him blocking his way into the room.

The creature had six legs and two muscled arms surrounded in dark red carapace. Each arm held a mace at the ready. What looked akin to a man's red tinted torso and spiral horned head extended out from an insect-looking body. It was poised for attack. It lifted his head back and let loose a blood curdling screech while Mory stood paralyzed in fear. The feeling ran through him like he had just swallowed molten metal. Realizing that he needed to do something instead of gawk, he fumbled with his cobweb covered sword and lifted it in defense. A malicious smile crept across the creature's face as it began to swing a mace towards Mory. He avoided the first attack but knew that he wouldn't stand a chance much longer against this beast. He dove to the ground and tried to roll under its belly hoping to find a weak point but failed when his move was countered by the beast lowering its midsection to the ground. Mory found himself chest to chest with his assailant. Faster than Mory could think, the beast lifted him up with his legs, and began to twist Mory into a tightly knit cobweb prison.

A very dizzy Mory heard a woman's battle cry. He was now dangling from the ceiling in a sticky, white cocoon with just his head poking out. He could feel the fine threads clinging to his entire body and couldn't do much more than wiggle his fingers and toes. Battling a claustrophobic feeling, he tried to look at where the sound came from, but each time he tried to get the cocoon to turn slightly, it instead spun him around more, adding to the dizziness in his throbbing head. He could finally discern through his spinning vantage point that the warrior woman was Zhannah. She had come to his rescue once again. That woman was a gem, and he was a buffoon who regularly needed saving. She made quick work of the spider creature, slicing off each of its appendages with the rhythm of an experienced warrior. When it had only the two back legs left, it squealed hopelessly as it toppled onto the floor until it could do nothing more than wriggle like a worm before Zhannah kindly put it out of its misery.

"Mory, keep your head low," Zhannah shouted up to him in warning before throwing one of her swords to slice the threads attaching him to the ceiling. Mory was worried for a moment as he saw the blade whirling towards him, hearing its blade slice the air as it passed nearby. Her sword flew true and sliced down the cocoon while keeping Mory's head fully intact. Following his relief at still having a head on his shoulders, Mory felt the butterflies of weightlessness infiltrate his stomach as he commenced his long fall to the floor. His landing was cushioned by the sticky threads that encased his body. Zhannah strode over and began to surgically cut him free of his cocoon with a knife that she pulled from her boot. She looked particularly angry.

"How could Scilla let you come down here all by yourself after yesterday? You didn't know any better, but she should have!" Zhannah was venting as she sliced off chunks of webbing with her knife and pulled them away with her free hand. "If the firelings were able to come to Thaer, who knows what other creatures could have been let loose here. This single grafter could have killed you before we had even begun! Did you know grafters can squeeze into crevices half their size to get inside places like this? Of course not, but Scilla should have!"

"Once Scilla let me know that she had given you a key, I came down here as fast as I could in case there was any danger lurking in the shadows. Thank the Spirits I did!" She was now slowly rotating him on the floor to repeat the slicing and pulling process. Mory wished she would stop yelling. His head was throbbing something horrible. Thankfully she did lower her voice as she continued, "I will speak to her later. Are you okay Mory? Any other damage done?"

He shook his head then stopped himself, "Well, I do have one killer headache."

Zhannah didn't seem too concerned about his headache, "Good. We will begin your sword training tomorrow. You will be able to defend yourself in no time. Let today be your first lesson in weapon care. You never want to impede the use of your weapon." She had freed him from the last of the sticky cocoon, cleaned the mess off her knife onto her pant leg, and stuck it back into her boot before handing Mory the mostly useless, cobweb covered sword that looked more like a fluffy cotton candy stick than a fearsome weapon. No wonder the grafter, as Zhannah called it, had smirked at him when he held it up in defense. "You will be happy to know that you have found the area of the library that contains the books about Krael and the various magics that it possesses," Zhannah gestured toward the dusky room that he had seen earlier as she began freeing his sword from the sticky mess that entombed it. "Please feel free to visit whenever you would like and study up. Knowledge is power on Krael."

Mory wasn't too sure that he could concentrate on reading right now with his headache, but he was determined to at least look at this place he worked so hard to find. He looked up at the brave swordswoman, "Thank you Zhannah. I will begin browsing as soon as my head clears." He sheepishly added, "I am sorry that you had to save me like that."

Zhannah chuckled, "No apologies needed. I've not had this much fun two days straight in years! Now up with you. I'll give you the grand tour."

Zhannah helped Mory up and retrieved her second sword before they walked into the room together. To Mory's surprise, it was not just a small room like one of the alcoves he often read in but another area just as large as the main library. It was a paradise. Mory's excitement from earlier today returned as he gazed upon the aisles of bookshelves. He couldn't fathom all the information that he would learn here. That was the fun of it! He needed to be able to expand his mind to expand his imagination, for if he couldn't even imagine something, how would it ever come to be?

Chapter 9

The ground turned crimson as the dragon lay motionless, chest inflating and deflating irregularly as it gasped for breath. Her midsection had been sliced open and her time left limited. A kind, wandering magician found the ailing creature, and his heart went out to her. He rummaged through his hooded, brown cloak and found a sample of a salve made from a plant with antibiotic properties. Using his magic, he increased the amount of the salve so there was enough to cover the wound on the dragon's belly. After applying the salve and saying some spells over her body, the magician propped himself against the dragon's head, teeth and all. Before falling asleep from exhaustion, he whispered into her ear, "You'll be well soon, Sister."

The next morning the dragon, with her stomach freshly healed, snuck away from the snoring magician. When he finally awoke, the winds whispered back to him, "Thank you, Brother," before giving way to the quiet day.

Kylie got up early the next morning and made her way to the pegasus field. She huddled in her emerald green cloak since the early morning air still had last night's chill in it. She saw colorful birds twirling with each other mid-air against a reddening sky as they darted from a deep green tree shadowing the camp tents to a purple flowering tree near the pegasus field. They had just begun to coax the first sun above the horizon with their twittering songs and others were joining in the chorus. She did not see much stirring within the camp yet, which was just as she had hoped.

Starshine trotted over to her as she neared the field, and Kylie gave her a good rub down. Her golden coat was soft as she ran her hand across it, and the little filly seemed to like being scratched where her wings met her shoulders, as she closed her eyes and heaved a contented sigh. Starshine was too small to carry a rider yet. It would be another six months before Kylie could probably give it a try is what her father had said at dinner last night. She was slightly disappointed that she could not just follow the ambushing party's mission upon Starshine's back. That would have made her plans so much easier. It was just as well though since she had no idea what kind of trouble she would be riding into. After all, not only had Starshine not had a rider before, but Kylie had never been steering while flying on the back of one of these magnificent creatures.

Kylie saw Bandit grazing peacefully not too far away and began to make her way over to the mare. Starshine was none too happy that attention had been turned from her and after a frustrated stomp, snort, and shake of her cream mane, followed Kylie over. Bandit all but ignored Kylie as she chomped on the dewy grass. That was fine though, Kylie had just wanted to be close when Anik came out to get Bandit. He did not disappoint. She saw his broad-shouldered form walking toward the field now. She was glad that he was an early riser because it would be harder to convince him with more people around. She felt her insides tangle up with nervousness as he approached.

"Good morning, Kylie! How are you on this fine morning?" Anik welcomed her and reached out to pat Bandit's shoulder, who in response raised her midnight head up to nuzzle Anik's pockets for treats. She was not disappointed when she grabbed a blapple out with her teeth and began munching away. "True to her name, she is," Anik chuckled as he lovingly stroked her coat. "She takes whatever she wants."

Kylie steeled her nerves and hoped that he didn't see that she was beginning to sweat with nervousness on this cold morning. Why was she so bad at this! "Hey Anik," she began nervously, "it is a beautiful morning, isn't it? Just came out to see Starshine here." She kicked herself, that wasn't her reason, "That and to inform you that my father had suggested that I ride out with you today to meet up with Sonu's search party. He decided that it would be a good idea if I came along... as a learning experience... you know?" Her confidence had failed her at the end, and she was looking up from the ground to Anik's eyes with what she knew were flaming red cheeks. Hopefully he thought it was from the cool weather.

Anik was giving her a funny look when she first met his eyes, and then he broke into a big smile. "Why absolutely! I would love to have you join me. At the request of my princess, and the suggestion of my commander, you shall ride with me safely," he declared earnestly with a deep bow.

Kylie was dumbstruck. She had thought that she had known for certain that he would deny her, and she would end up having to ambush him at the lookout area that her father had told him to man yesterday. "Oh! Um. Th.. Thank you," she stammered and then with more conviction, "and don't call me princess or do that bowing thing."

Anik rose from his bow and nodded, "As you wish, my lady." A half smile curled on his lips mischievously as he met her eyes, and Kylie felt her tension ease a bit. He obviously knew that would bother her too.

"Please, call me Kylie."

"Well met, Kylie! Please allow me to introduce you to Bandit. She stole my heart when I became a member of the Saliek and hasn't told me where she's put it yet. If I were to guess, it must be where she puts most of the other things she takes," he patted her stomach with a look that told Kylie he wasn't going to say it out loud for fear of Bandit hearing. She couldn't help but giggle.

"Nice to meet you, Bandit," Kylie said as she approached the pegasus and began to scratch her behind her ears. Bandit lifted her head from grazing again and nosed at her pockets. Finding nothing, she huffed and scooted away.

Anik handed her a blapple from his pack, "Try this; the way to this one's heart is through her stomach." Kylie slowly approached Bandit again. This time she held the blapple in her outstretched hand as a peace offering. Bandit gave her a quick sideways glance, appraising the situation, then raised her head and gently took the blapple from Kylie's hand. She now allowed Kylie to pat her while she happily munched. Anik had come prepared and had brought another blapple for Starshine as well, giving her the attention that she wanted while Kylie had been courting Bandit with her treat.

"We had better get a move on," he said turning away from Starshine. "My assignment is to act as a lookout for the approach of Sonu's party, and you will relay what we see back to Saliek'an Regithal through your link. We would not want to miss them by dallying here too long."

Kylie turned astonished to look at an amused Anik. Anik replied teasingly, "Apparently, you need to work on your shields while you sleep. Saliek'an Regithal found me at quite the absurd hour last night to warn me about your plans. At first, I was skeptical, as creating a mind link is quite a difficult task to achieve, but then there you were, standing with Starshine next to Bandit." Anik paused as he shook his head slightly in disbelief, "He thought it was better that I just allow you tag a long immediately, rather than having you attempt phase two of your plans. That would have just caused more trouble for all of us."

Kylie was really embarrassed now. She had gotten what she wanted, but it didn't feel quite as satisfying as she had thought it would in this specific turn of events. Maybe she should have just skipped talking to Anik and gone straight to the ambushing part of her plan. At least that would have had a sense of adventure to it. She replied ashamedly, "You must think me a fool or a spoiled child at the least."

"Not at all!” Anik exclaimed reassuringly. “Had I been in your situation, I would have wanted to come along as well. I was the one being selfish in agreeing with Saliek'an Regithal that you shouldn't be a part of the mission yesterday, when I knew very well that there would be no leaving me behind either," Anik explained as he cupped his hands together and lowered them to create a stepstool for Kylie to mount Bandit. She stepped onto his hands, and he gave her a boost to reach the pegasus' back, "Up you go!" He leaned on Bandit's shoulder looking up at her with crossed arms as she situated herself. The red in the morning sunbeams amplified the orange sheen in his auburn hair making the orange glow in his eyes more prominent. "You see, I have been the 'new guy' here for five years now, always being left behind or being given the most menial of tasks. That may have had to do with me living here for some time before becoming an initiated Saliek and people becoming stuck in a routine, but regardless, my pride felt the sting. I guess for a moment I saw you as the person to replace me in that aspect and felt relieved, but after Saliek'an Regithal talked to me last night, I had some time to think, and I've decided to help you not suffer the same fate as I had these last many years. I promise I will not allow you to be left behind, and I will help you find your place here," his expression was all seriousness when he spoke those words, and his gaze was determined.

Kylie had to break eye contact with him because of the intensity she saw in his eyes. He truly wanted to help her out. Her mind raced for the appropriate response to his generous offer, "Well, I do suppose I could use a friend here." She turned back to see him smile. Was that relief that she saw in his face? Before she could think too much on it, he whispered into Bandit's ear, and she knelt on one foreleg to allow Anik to ascend to her back. To her surprise, Kylie was not even jarred by the fluid motion of the pegasus.

He sat in between her and Bandit's neck, and she balanced herself by grabbing onto Bandit's wings. He noticed and said, "Now's not the time to be shy, please hold onto my waist tightly. I don't want my new friend to be falling off!" When Kylie wrapped her arms around his waist as he bid her to do, she felt his muscles tighten in his warm body for a moment before relaxing. "Spirits, girl! Not that tight, I still need to be able to breathe!"

She loosened her grip and looked down at Starshine who had acquired a pouty looking face, that is if a pegasus' face could indeed have expressions. "I'm sorry, Girl!" Kylie apologized, "Soon it will be just you and me going on magnificent adventures together. In the meantime, you stay here and have fun. I'll be back soon!" Starshine must have felt the same way that Kylie had last night when she thought she was being left behind. Kylie felt terrible, but she didn't know how Starshine could come along too.

Anik urged Bandit up as Kylie waved bye to Starshine. The steed's powerful wings beat with even strokes, and the tents of the camp shrunk as they ascended towards the pink and orange swirled sky. They flew through a low cloud, and Kylie was glad for Anik's added warmth as the cool droplets splashed on her skin. The views below were breathtaking in the morning sun. A nearby lake sparkled with glints of sunlight as the warm colors tinted its clear waters. The mountains loomed, pale grey soldiers with wisps of clouds hinting at colors weaving throughout their heights. Even the deep greens of the forest seemed to glow with morning light. The flight was not nearly as long as she wished it would have been. She would have to convince someone to take her on a flight just for the sake of flying some time.

Bandit began her descent, circling around a lighter spot in the forest. Upon closer approach, Kylie could see that it was a clearing covered in a field of golden grass, or at least it looked golden in the rays of sunshine. The grass crunched beneath Bandit's feet as she landed, and it came up to the pegasus' knees. Anik slid off Bandit's back and offered Kylie his hand. Remembering her last botched dismount off Valor in the camp, Kylie accepted his hand graciously and jumped into the golden grass. She smiled at the beauty of it all. She didn't think she could ever tire of the wonderful colors of this world. She realized that she still held Anik's hand, and let it go hoping he didn't think too much of her prolonged grasp. He was watching her with a smile.

"Seeing your wonder makes me realize how much we all take this world for granted here. I would be curious to see what Thaer is like in comparison. I wonder if I would stare as you do at all the unknown I would see," Anik explained.

"Thaer is similar to Krael," Kylie began, "but not as bright. It is not so obvious when that is the only place you have seen, but now that I have seen Krael, I am unsure if I could go back to living on Thaer without noticing that it was missing something. Some sort of vibrancy that this place possesses surpasses even the most beautiful parts of Thaer," she hesitated for a moment, "I would like to say that I would take you to Thaer one day to show you what I mean, but I truly don't know what my future holds since I have come to this place. There is a part of me that is excited, and another that is terribly scared."

"Well, let us hope that the adventures you have here will only bring you more happiness, and with any luck, the freedom of Krael from the clutches of Elasche as well," Anik announced confidently before he turned away and began walking towards a drop off at the edge of the field. Kylie waded after him in the tall grass. She turned back for a moment to see Bandit daintily nibbling the tips of the golden grass. Kylie broke off a stem so that she could inspect it more closely. Tiny bristles grew off tips of the grass and tickled her as she ran her fingers over them. They must be the seeds, she concluded as she held the stem to her lips and blew the seeds away into the morning air with a smile.

She eventually reached Anik and saw that the drop off they stood over was really a valley. Jagged red rocks lined the edge of the steep cliff, which ended into a grassy path and then rose once again up to their elevation on the other side of the path. She felt herself get slightly lightheaded as she overlooked the valley. From their vantage point, Anik and Kylie could see for miles in both directions. It looked as though this was the only passage through the mountains to reach Arbore.

Anik began scanning the valley with his eyes and said, "When we see their party coming down the path, you will let Saliek'an Regithal know, and he will prepare the ambush. Though we cannot see them, the Saliek are hidden among the rocks on the cliff. The Saliek'an has Spirit strong enough to keep them hidden for the whole day if needed. They hope to be able to quickly nab Prince Sonu and hide him in the rocks without having to fight the rest of the party. Obviously, we have prepared for a fight as well, but the Saliek'an tries to avoid costly battles when at all possible."

Kylie followed Anik's lead, and they lay down on their stomachs in the tall grass peering over the rocky red cliff to hide themselves from any prying eyes. Anik enlarged a dew drop for himself and another for Kylie. It turned out these large dew drops magnified objects in the distance and made it easier for them to spy on the valley. They hunkered in the grass in silence for hours watching, with a soft breeze causing the wavering grass to tickle her cheeks.

***

"Kylie, do you see that?" Anik unnecessarily whispered excitedly.

She must have been drifting off into a daydream or a nap because Anik's voice startled her back to awareness. Kylie repositioned her dew drop magnifying lens to look far down the valley. She saw it too. A group of people were slowly riding their horses through the passage. There were not as many of them as Kylie had thought. She had imagined an army alert at attention would be marching down the valley. Instead about twenty riders were nearing them in a seemingly disorganized fashion.

"Send word to Saliek'an Regithal," Anik insisted as he propped himself up for a better view.

Kylie focused her attention inward to attempt to contact her father like they had practiced in the cave. To her surprise, he answered her call right away. "Don't be too surprised," his voice entered her consciousness, "I had been awaiting you for hours now. There's not much to do down here hidden in the rocks."

She informed him of the party approaching their location and answered all his questions to the best of her abilities about the size of the group, what they were armed with, and other questions that would help the Saliek prepare for the upcoming encounter. Her concentration was suddenly broken when she heard yelling coming from where Anik had been lying. She looked to see him now wrestling with another man in the tall grass. Anik's black cloak was entangling him, while the other man was attempting to tie his arms behind his back. Anik seemed to be struggling to regain control of the situation. The air around the large man that he was wrestling with seemed to intermittently shimmer and blur. Kylie realized she needed to do something quickly to help her new found friend.

She scooted back and away quickly, heart pounding recklessly in her chest, and slid her knife into her hand. She hesitated a moment too long, intending to ensure her aim, when excruciating pain hit her head, and the world went dark.

Chapter 10

A pair of swords lay crossed at the chocolate brown base of a pink blossomed tree, discarded for the moment by their wielders in the depths of the green, feathery grass. The sun fell beneath the horizon, setting the skies on fire in rich, vibrant colors that mimicked the passion in the kiss being shared by the couple beneath the tree. A slight breeze picked up the woman's hair, and the man brushed his fingers through it lovingly while staring into the depths of her eyes, deeply entranced by the beauty he sees within her. The avaricious breeze also purloins some pretty pink petals from the tree, freeing them into the crimson and orange sky.

The second sun had set, and the shadows of the surrounding forest had begun lurking outside the light of their captors' fire. Anik had seen Bandit's figure among the trees earlier, awaiting his signal. She knew the drill, as they had been in similar situations before. Bandit, true to her name, could take pretty much anything she wanted. In these rescue type situations that often ended up being keys. She might be a large animal, but she could lurk about the darkness as stealthily as a shadow when the situation called for it. She had already nabbed the keys required to release Anik and Kylie's shackles from a negligent captor's discarded pack and was growing impatient in the woods.

Anik would have been out of this mess already if it

wasn't for Kylie's presence and the man who seemed to be protected from his physical and Spiritual attacks. As for Kylie, he wasn't sure how to transport an unconscious person, especially when he didn't know what other damage may have been inflicted upon her. His talents were not in healing. As for the large man, he had never met someone without a Spirit glow that could best his attacks when he truly desired to fight. He was admittedly irritated, but truth be told, he was mostly worried about Kylie's well-being.

Their captors had knocked her out when she had pulled a knife from her sleeve in an attempt to help him, and she had been out for a few hours now. They were currently shackled hand and foot to trees. Anik's shoulders ached from being pulled back for such a length of time, and he could feel abrasions forming on his wrists from their constant rubbing on metal. Kylie was slumped on the ground like a rag doll, head and golden tresses lolling about in front of her with her arms shackled behind the tree. The mere sight of her limp body lit an anger deep inside his chest. Those brutes couldn't think of a better way to subdue the girl than bludgeoning her on the head? He suppressed the flow of anger knowing that keeping a cool head would be better in this situation.

He should have known better than to have had both himself and Kylie looking over the ridge. One of them should have been watching their backs. Rookie mistake. It only made sense that Sonu's party would have had scouts of their own. No wonder why Saliek'an Regithal hadn't let him come with the main ambushing party. He surely would have found a way to mess that up too. He hoped that Kylie had been able to get enough information over her link to Saliek'an Regithal before she had been distracted.

Anik looked over towards the fire at their captors. Royal thugs the lot of them. The one who wrestled him was sitting on a rock cracking his knuckles habitually while staring into the fire. He didn't speak much, only when necessary. His facial expression was completely unreadable. Anik could not detect any sort of emotion from the man, even when considering his dark un-Spirited eyes. His completely shaven head shone in the firelight. Tattoos began at the base of his neck and were patterned down his leather brown skin over muscled arms and toned torso adding obscurity and mystery to his already menacing figure. One stood out to him. In red ink, there was a sword wrapped in thorns with two roses crossed along its hilt: the sigil of the Mahashta house. That meant this man was one of the personal guards to Elasche's family. He was a member of the Ignet, which explained his uncanny abilities. The personal guards of Mahashta were notorious and rightly feared by anyone who wasn't being protected by them. Anik hadn't stood a chance in his wrestling match.

From what Anik had learned in his studies at the Saliek camp, the Ignet were chosen at a young age to train with the eldest and wisest of the clan. They had to pass certain trials and tribulations to earn the right to wear each of their tattoos. The more intricate the tattoo, the better that individual had completed the test rewarding that tattoo. No one truly knew if their powers resided in the tattoos or if those only represented the powers within the person who they were painted on. If only he knew what each of those symbols meant, he might be able to craft a way to defeat the man.

Something else nagged at the edges of Anik's mind. He couldn't help but wonder why this man was here. He must have been Elasche's protector. Anik supposed she could have loaned him to Sonu for his current mission, but something seemed amiss. His unlikely presence had just secured the capture of the Spirit Master, no matter how temporarily Anik would allow their success to be.

This was no small coincidence.

The man who had knocked Kylie out stood off to the side watching the woods closely. He was tall and spindly and kept his hand on his sword that was sheathed through his belt. His greasy hair was tied back in a thinning ponytail. He had the bearings of a careful man who took as little risk as possible and was slightly jumpy. Spirit glowed faintly from his eyes, but Anik doubted he was strong in it. He seemed to be leading this scouting party, as he had been the one directing the camp set up and taking point in the discussions on their plans. There was one other member, an ill-tempered woman who kept pointing out whatever she thought the others were doing wrong. Anik found her quite annoying, and he'd only been around her for a few hours. How her colleagues put up with her the whole way here he couldn't understand. She was curled in her bed roll, shoulder length brown hair sprawled out, with her back to the fire. She had just finished engaging in an argument with the spindly man on how watches should be done for the night.

"What are you looking at, demon boy?" the spindly man sneered. Anik moved his gaze off the woman to the nervous man. He knew the reference he had made was to his eyes. Their orange glow had unsettled many a person in his day. The jeers used to bother him but not anymore. His eyes were a part of who he was, and he was proud to be a member of the Saliek. As a matter of fact, at a time like this, unsettling a person could come in handy. Anik glared as menacingly as possible into the other man's eyes. The spindly man turned away quickly, speaking in a threatening tone, "Don't you try any of your magic on me! I see you are strong in Spirit through your eyes, but you use none of it now. You must be an uneducated piece of trash. You're an embarrassment to the Saliek name!" Anik's black cloak must have given away his allegiances. Until then, he had had a small hope that Kylie's emerald cloak may have thrown them off. Anik had already decided to not reply to anything. He was clearly being goaded into either speaking or using his Spirit. Anik did not wish to oblige him either way for the time being.

"Awww, come off it now, Fauler. He's just the scouting boy for the Saliek. I doubt he even had a chance to warn his troops of the prince's arrival. No one wants to hear your bossy voice at this hour! Can't you see we're trying to sleep here?" the woman whined as she turned over in her bedroll to look at him before continuing condescendingly and chuckling to herself, "We got what we came here for, that girl that you decided to nearly kill. Prince Sonu will reward us lavishly, no doubt! Ha ha ha! You were so scared of a girl's knife that you had to knock her out? That amuses me so! Sonu told us that she most likely wouldn't know how to use her Spirit yet!"

Anik hoped they would say more. The more information he left with, the better. He was particularly intrigued by how they knew of Kylie's presence in the Saliek camp and how she had been targeted so quickly. His mind had leapt immediately to suspicions of a traitor in the camp, though no suspects came to mind.

"The girl is nowhere near dead, just unconscious. I've seen plenty of women skilled in weaponry. They are not to be underestimated. Unlike yourself, Itha..." Fauler defended his actions and threw the last words like knives at Itha who huffed and turned back into a more comfortable sleeping position.

The quiet man continued to stare into the flames unperturbed by the others' argument. Anik estimated that he was the real danger here. He would have to keep a careful eye on that one.

Fauler had turned his attention back to the woods surrounding the camp when Anik heard rustling coming from Kylie's position. He heard a slight moan as she peered up at him through her currently tangled long, golden hair. He felt his heart leap for joy. With another person to help, they could hopefully get out of this mess! He made a mental note to teach himself some basics on healing when he returned to camp. "Good morning, sleepyhead. Welcome back to the world of the living! Do you feel any pain coming from anywhere besides your head?" he whispered anxiously. Kylie peered back at him with a look completely void of comprehension. Her mind must still be fuzzy from the hit on her head. He thought he saw her shake her head slightly, denying that she felt any other pain. That was a good sign!

Before he could explain anything more, there was a quick movement in the woods coming in their direction. Branches cracked and leaves crunched as it hastily descended upon them from the forest depths. The trio of captors readied themselves for a fight. The quiet man stood, Fauler and Itha grabbed for their swords, and then Starshine came crashing out of the trees and appeared by Kylie's side. She took a stance that challenged anyone to oppose her. The quiet man returned to his seat, obviously thinking this was not worth his efforts. A young pegasus was not what he desired to fight today. Fauler was angry at being frightened and began marching toward Starshine, sword raised. Itha began yelling at him to come back at once, but he ignored her. A wall of ice suddenly appeared in Fauler's path and his forward momentum slammed him into it. His sword made a ringing sound through the darkened woods as it reverberated from the hit.

Kylie had pulled her shackles taught, getting as near to Starshine as possible, and was staring intently at the ice wall. Not too bad, Anik thought. She must have bid the condensation in the air to form into an ice wall. Very nice! And now was his chance. He whistled high and sharp, and Bandit came crashing out of the trees like a dark winged angel. Key locked firmly in her teeth, Bandit inserted the key into the shackle's lock and turned her head, unlocking Anik's hands. Anik took the keys from there and finished releasing himself and Kylie. Her wall had given him the time and protection he needed to get them out of there. Fauler must have still been recovering from his collision because the first person he saw was the quiet man running around the chunk of ice. Bidden by Anik, a nearby tree root pulled taught a few inches above the ground to trip the running Ignet. He crashed to the ground with an irritated grunt. Anik felt a burst of pride in his small successful workaround to the Ignet's magic. He had not actively used the root to attack the man, rather his own momentum had been his demise when he hit the root.

Not wanting to waste time with words, he took Kylie's waist and hoisted her onto Bandit's back then followed her up with a leap. Starshine had thankfully taken off towards the sky. There was not enough room for Bandit's full-grown figure to take off in the tightly clumped woods, so she folded her cumbersome wings down and bolted into the forest. Anik looked back momentarily to see that they were being pursued by Itha. Her brown hair whipped against her face, which brandished a look of anger and irritation. Bandit slalomed around tree after tree trying to shake her off, but Itha's smaller, more nimble horse was catching up easily to Bandit's hulking form. Anik attempted to knock Itha off her horse with a burst of wind, but the air shimmered around her when the wind touched her, just as it had done around the Ignet when he had been wrestling him. In his mind, Anik cursed the Ignet. He must have extended his protection to Itha for the time being. How far could his magic reach?

Anik felt one of Kylie's arms around his waist while the other was beating on his shoulder. What in the

Spirit's hell was she doing! They were running for their lives. "Slow down! I have to go back!" she yelled at him.

"Starshine is fine; she took off into the sky. She'll be able to find us later!" Anik yelled back trying to console her. He understood her worry but really wished she'd hold on tighter and stop banging his shoulder so he could better think of a way to shake their pursuer. Branches were whipping him in the face and tree trunks were scratching his legs where his tall boots ended into his leggings. Kylie couldn't be thinking this was much of a joy ride either. He was trusting Bandit to take them back to the open field where she could take off again and get away for good. She had followed them from there to their captor's camp, so she should be able to make it back again.

"Saliek'an Regithal orders you to slow down so I can return! You can leave if you want, but I need to go back. Not for Starshine. To spy! Don't you see? I can report to my father through our link. They never have to know!" Kylie was pounding harder on his shoulder now as her plea became more insistent. It was beginning to hurt. This was insanity! He just escaped those morons, why should he go back? There was no way he was letting Kylie go back by herself. Who knew what those ruffians would do to her? His mind wavered for a few more seconds before he made his decision. Ever so slightly he let Bandit know that she should ease her pace. It would do no good to let Itha think that they wanted to be captured again.

Anik hoped he didn't regret his decision later, but there was not enough time to think it through now. He spoke softly into Bandit's ear, "You keep safe and close if you can, girl. We have to go back. Watch after Starshine. No more surprises like that last one." He gave Bandit's neck a hearty pat and then pushed off her back in what he hoped looked like an action mimicking a hit by a low branch from Itha's point of view. He twisted mid-air to wrap himself around Kylie to protect her from the impending fall. He took the brunt of it on the shoulder that she had been punching earlier. Perfect. They landed in a pile of dead leaves and mud that slightly broke their fall. He didn't think they'd been hurt too bad.

In the moments they had before being recaptured, Kylie pushed herself off him onto the adjacent ground, breathing hard from their wild ride. Her green eyes, amplified in the darkness, met his briefly as she thanked him in between breaths. He wasn't sure if that was for softening her fall or for not leaving her alone on her mission. All he knew was he'd gotten himself into a much more complicated situation than he'd ever been in during his 21 years of existence. Had Saliek'an Regithal expected him to stay behind with Kylie? Ugh. He only hoped he was ready to be a mouse in the lion's den.

Itha swung herself off her horse with a smug grin stretched across her dirtied face. She drew her sword and pointed it alternately at Anik's neck and then at Kylie's who both scrambled on their backsides and hands into the base of a large trunked tree. "Clumsy fools, can't even stay on the back of a horse!" she hissed at them. "Now you both are coming back with me. It's a pity Prince Sonu wants you alive." She roughly tied their hands behind their backs and forced them to their feet at sword point. She must not have dealt with many talented Spirited people or had the utmost faith in the protection of her Ignet companion. Ropes would not have usually held Anik back, but their goal was now to be captured, infiltrate, and report so he settled his mind. He would have to fall into his role of despondent hostage. Well then... Let the game begin.

Chapter 11

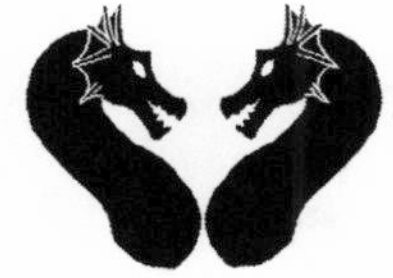

Wooden blocks scattered everywhere as a dark-haired boy ran through the construction of a small toy town on a grassy hill in the peaceful sunshine. He had somewhere to be and wasn't paying attention to the destruction he was leaving in his wake. Seeing the incident, a blonde boy meandered away from his parents' picnic. He picked up the pieces of the broken town, slowly and meticulously rebuilding it to its former grace. The blonde boy's shadow, unbeknownst to him, extended out for miles behind the hill, touching many cities. The pinnacle of the shadow's head ended in one surrounded by rocky guardians.

The evening air held the scent of rain as it blew through Liri. The skies were grey but not ominous. The town was slowing down as people headed home to eat and rest with their families for the night. Zhannah still had Mory in the training yard behind her cabin where the peaceful air was broken by the sound of swords clashing and Zhannah's firm voice shouting instructions. Mory's arms burned, and the palms of his hands were raw from being unaccustomed to holding and shifting the weight of a sword. The last part of the day was always the most difficult when all his muscles ached and his stomach growled for dinner. Zhannah had told him that he had been catching on quickly, but he still felt horrible. Zhannah could foresee every move he made, and he knew that she was taking it easy on him when she attacked.

Zhannah had given Mory a light sword, which she explained would most likely complement his fighting style. She thought that he would be more of an agile swordsman who utilized speed and finesse to take down his opponent rather than one who forcefully used strength to obtain his goal. She envisioned that he would be using his talents in stealth to gain close proximity before striking and not charging in like a bull. By the way his body ached with only using the light sword, he figured Zhannah had made a good assumption. The last few mornings had started off with a series of positions that challenged the flexibility and balance of his body. They would then move onto specific sword techniques and end with a duel. The dueling session was what they were engaged in now.

Mory had not been able to spend as much time in the newly found section of the library as he would have liked. Sword training took up the better part of his day, and his poor aching body demanded rest in the evenings. Tonight, he was determined to at least crack open the books that he had brought up to his room. Reading them was his passion. What he had found in the midst of the secret library so far had amazed him. Not only was there a wealth of information in the form of books, but there was an entire section devoted to the geography of Krael including many maps, spinning globes, and artistic renderings of its landscapes. He would be able to learn how to navigate the planet without ever having set foot there! Amazing!

Dust had covered the majority of the library, but that did not detract from Mory's wonder and admiration. In his eyes, it added to the atmosphere of timelessness when the dust particles hung weightlessly in the glowing light emitted from the wall sconces. Though it had been underground, the secret library had been well lit by a collection of stones imbued with light. Zhannah had explained that they were small relics, which had been brought from Krael. This had been necessary since the Spirit of humans was severely dampened on Thaer. Objects, however, seemed unaffected. This topic had sparked Mory's interest, and he had scoured the library after his tour for books that might help him understand the human Spirit barrier phenomenon on Thaer.

Mory's thoughts aimlessly drifted to Kylie as they so often did since she had been gone. He missed having a close friend around town to talk to and share his life with, even though he had been kept busy lately with all his training. Talking with Scilla, Zhannah, or the others around town just wasn't as fulfilling as teasing or plotting with Kylie. His life just wasn't the same without her everlasting energy, witty retorts, and headstrong nature. Mory hadn't realized just how much he had cared for her until she left, or rather had been taken away, so abruptly. He hoped that he'd be able to see her light-bringing smile again soon or that this hole inside would heal with time.

Zhannah mercilessly knocked Mory off his feet with one fell swoop of a sword. She began scolding him, “You'll have to stop your daydreaming if you ever want to survive a real fight, Mory! One second you are deftly deflecting an attack, the next your eyes get this far away look in them and your body enters autopilot mode. You say you're tired, or some other excuse, but it's obvious that your mind is elsewhere. What are you actually thinking about?" Mory was looking up at her from the ground, sword flung a couple feet or so away, and had a nice scrape on his leg with crimson drips oozing from it.

He started picking himself up, reached for his sword, and then responded, "Oh nothing, just thinking about doing some more reading tonight." He brushed the dirt off his legs and noticed that it was starting to turn into smears of mud with the light drizzle that had begun.

Zhannah sighed, "Yes, I suppose that would be a good use of the evening. I've been so preoccupied with your sword practice that I had nearly forgotten that you should also be spending some of your time studying." With a twirl of her swords, they were replaced in their sheaths. She had insisted that he learn to fight her as she wielded two swords. Her rationale being that once you had slain the dragon, the fireling was not so daunting. "You have just been such a great student, Mory. Catching on so very quickly to most everything I show you. I think we will be able to return to Krael sooner than I had anticipated." Zhannah nodded definitively to herself the way she did when she was making plans internally. Mory's heart leapt at that very prospect. How he would love to see that fascinating planet he had been learning so much about... and Kylie too, he silently admitted to himself.

"You are dismissed for the night, Mory. I will see you again tomorrow morning after breakfast," Zhannah concluded their training session. Mory nodded his acceptance, gathered his belongings, and placed his borrowed sword back into its slot in Zhannah's weapon rack. He began his walk back to the library across the muddying streets of Liri. He could feel the cool raindrops creeping down his scalp to run down his cheeks and neck, yet he didn't hurry. His muscles ached too much, and he didn't really mind the rain, especially if it was just this light drizzle. The droplets' cooling effect was pleasant on his overheated body. When he arrived at the entryway to the library, he turned his face up towards the sky and let the rain wash away the sweat from the day. As he turned his face back down and was about to enter, he saw a patch of flowers, yellow petals quivering as the light rain rolled off them, and a thought struck him. Instead of seeking refuge in the library, he turned to continue down the emptied streets of Liri, into the soft soil of the crop fields, towards the Zula River on the other side of town.

By the time he arrived at the riverside, he was soaked through and muddied. The intensity of the rain had increased, but he felt drawn to the river nonetheless. The weather had reminded him of the day that he had found the stone for Kylie by the river. He had been out walking the banks, enjoying the overcast day and brilliant blooms of the early spring flowers, when suddenly the clouds had opened into a downpour. He had seen something far too colorful wedged within a clump of drab looking rocks in the shallow water near the bank. Rain had pelted down his back as he had knelt down, retrieved the odd-looking stone, and pocketed it. He hadn't examined it too closely or decided to give it Kylie until he had gotten home that day.

He drew his attention back to the present since the terrain was becoming densely littered with slippery rocks as he neared the bank. He carefully placed his muddy, booted feet going rock to rock until the river rushed inches from his toes. He squatted down and let the warm water flow through his fingertips. The river always felt warm, particularly now in the cool spring rains. Mory had supposed this was due to some sort of hydrothermal vents beneath the water. After all, off in the distance he could see the outline of Mount Liriken through the rain haze. The dormant volcano had slept peacefully for as long as anyone Mory talked to could remember.

Mory looked back down into the swirling current of the river and thought that he saw something oddly colorful once more. Could he really be that lucky? He carefully walked out onto the stones beyond the edge of the river where the waters began to get deeper to get a closer look. He braced his footing, then reached out into the depths of the river knowing that the treasure would soon be within his grasp. Just a little further he stretched his arm out, his fingers could touch it now, and then something in his pack shifted. He had to quickly rebalance himself on the slippery rocks, miss-stepping in the process, and sent himself tumbling into the racing river.

Mory knew a moment of terror as he was tossed about in the eddies of the rain-enraged river. The water swallowed him up and stung as it rushed up his nostrils. He curled into a ball to facilitate ricocheting off the scattered submerged boulders. In the darkness behind his closed eyelids, he calmed his thoughts and stopped struggling for a moment. His body oriented itself in the correct position, and his head popped up above the raging surface of the water. He was still being strewn about like a rag doll, but it was easier to navigate his frail body away from the hard rocks that rushed up on him with his head above water.

He shook his soaked hair out of his eyes with just enough time to see that he was heading towards a funneling mass of water. He gasped in a gulp of air before the current pulled him under again. This time he couldn't find up. The current was dragging him at will to whatever destination it had predetermined. Mory fervently hoped this destination wasn't the afterlife, but he didn't know how he could regain control of the situation. After a few minutes of being submerged and tumbling, his lungs began to burn with suffocation. He longed to take a breath but knew that would be certain death. His chest felt as though it would cave in. A sensation of falling came over him, and when he knew he could no longer hold his breath, he surfaced.

The initial gasp of air he took upon resurfacing hurt nearly as much as not being able to breathe, but the pain was short-lived and welcomed, as he knew it was his life's breath that he inhaled. A tumultuous roar deafened his hearing. At first, he wasn't completely sure that it wasn't the sound of his thrashing heartbeat, but after determining that his life was his own again, he noticed the crashing waterfall behind him. The plummeting water splashed a warm spray onto his back and neck. That waterfall must have been connected to a whirlpool in the river above.

He was now floating in a pool of hot water under the ground, similar to one of his favorite secret places in the library. He could feel the bubbling vents tickling his feet beneath the water and laughed heartily with the giddy exuberance of being alive. He wondered if this pool was connected to the room in the library. Before chasing that trail of a thought, he remembered the original reason that got him into this mess. He kicked himself over to the edge of the hot spring and pulled himself onto the rim with his legs dangling in the pool. He raised his clenched fist up and opened it to reveal the stone he had been reaching for initially. It was nearly the same as the one he had given Kylie, but the swirled color patterns were unique to itself. He would have to investigate the river another day to see if there were more like it when there was less rain and slippery rocks to trip him up.

Mory looked around and saw that he was surrounded by a room full of grey stone rocks. The surfaces of those near the pool were smoothed to almost a glasslike texture. He found that his sopping wet pack had followed him along for the ride and was bobbing in the pool. He slid back into the water to rescue it, figuring that his clothes were already drenched anyway and the warm water felt good on his aching muscles. After nabbing his pack, Mory swam over to the waterfall and let the falling waters massage his back and shoulders for a time. Reluctantly, he decided that he would have to go find a way out of this place and get back home before somebody missed him. To Mory's great disappointment, he doubted that he would have as much time to read those books as he had desired before falling into a well needed and, he believed, well-deserved, rest.

Chapter 12

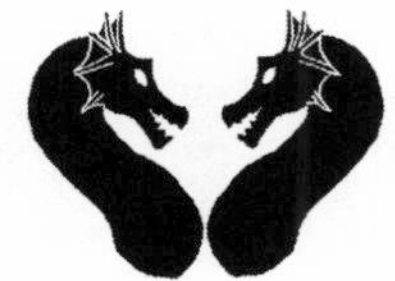

He could see deep into the souls of his victims. He could see their greed, their lust, their ambitions for power, and their insecurities. From each of their desires, he planted his seed. He let it grow year after year blossoming into a dark network of trees. Time was on his side. Their minds were putty in his hands waiting to be molded into a great masterpiece amidst his plan.

The walk back to the camp was seemingly never ending. This was due to a combination of having to walk back as far as they had ridden on a horse, the darkness concealing the best areas for footing on the trail, and Itha's endless chatter... Or should it be called whining? Kylie had never heard a person complain so much in her life and with so many colorful curses! Itha had decided to walk with her prisoners, her horse plodding alongside. She had connected Kylie and Anik's bound hands with a long piece of rope and had wound that around the saddle horn. Kylie believed escape would not have been so difficult if they had truly wished it.

Fauler must have done something in the past that rubbed Itha the wrong way because there wasn't a single kind word about the man that she had to say. This ranged from topics on how ugly and gross she thought he looked to her anger that Sonu had selected him to oversee of the scouting party. The only upside to her tirade was that Kylie had been able to learn a great deal about their soon to be travelling companions and their circumstances.

Fauler and Itha were both members of Arbore's ground forces and had served in the same unit since they had joined. Itha had aspired to lead her own unit and had dreamed of climbing higher in the ranks to obtain the status of general or an advisor to the royal family, but something had happened to curb her dreams. She chose not to elaborate on that topic, but in her eyes a storm had raged as she spoke around it. The units rotated through the duties of escorting Sonu's search parties, though they had no idea what it was in particular that he searched for. There were many rumors of treasures, ancient relics, lost libraries, dragons, and other such ideas but none were confirmed, and Sonu became very aggravated when asked. Sonu had randomly selected Fauler and Itha to scout out the cliffs before the rest of their group entered the narrow passageway between the Sentinels and had instructed his personal bodyguard, Dainn, to accompany them since a source had told him they may find his sister there.

For whatever reason, Sonu was keen on keeping Dainn away from his side, which seemed contrary to the point of having such a highly skilled bodyguard. Sonu's strange behavior towards Dainn had made the entire unit edgy around him, even though Dainn followed Sonu's orders flawlessly, and none could best his strength. Itha and Fauler had barely heard any words out of his mouth since they had begun their scouting mission, though he watched everything intently. Dainn's reticent behavior made Itha nervous and even more suspicious of him. Itha postulated about the tattoos that covered his back and arms, supposing that they indicated worship of the dark spirits and used that as her tangible excuse for staying clear of him.

By the time they had made it back to the camp, Kylie seriously doubted her decision to get re-captured. Itha had given up a lot of information freely, but it was torturous. Kylie had relayed the information back to her father and had fallen asleep to the seemingly endless bickering of Itha and Fauler. She thought that maybe the reason Dainn didn't speak was because if he did the first thing that would come out would be a loud, resounding, "Shut up!"

***

It was mid-afternoon of the following day, and Kylie kept playing back the events of yesterday evening wondering if there was anything key that she had missed. The weather was pleasant, but the trail down the edge of the cliff was physically demanding with rocky terrain. Kylie was beginning to tire. The day so far had not been very interesting. Their bonds had been secured more thoroughly, and therefore uncomfortably, for today's trek at the insistence of Fauler. Kylie had found out that the message that she had relayed about Sonu's forces had gotten through, but also the signal that Fauler had sent back to Sonu was received, and so Sonu's party waited outside the pass through the Sentinels and never made it to the Saliek ambushing party.

It would take them all day to get to Sonu's camp since Anik and Kylie were walking. They were secured to Dainn's horse's saddle, and she was unsure if either of them would have even attempted to escape from his watch even if they had the desire to. She had already seen him thwart Anik's Spirit powers, and Dainn's physical stature would easily overpower their own. Itha and Fauler rode up ahead discussing the details of the report to give Sonu. Kylie nudged Anik with her shoulder thinking that she could at least start a conversation to pass the time, "Why do you think those two hate each other so much?" She shot Itha and Fauler a sideways glance.

Anik studied the ground for a moment before answering, “Isn’t it obvious?” Kylie shook her head not being able to decipher what was so obvious about it before he continued. “They must have once been lovers, and something came between them. It’s not possible to truly hate someone without having loved them.”

Kylie let that thought soak in for a moment before she inquired, “How do you know this?” She had obviously entered uncomfortable territory for Anik whose face turned to stone and stuttered in his walking gait.

After what must have been an internal debate, Anik responded, “It is not of any significance, but my parents split up when I was a young child, forever arguing, trying to pit me against the other, and in general going out of their way to make the other’s life more difficult. Not unlike our friends here." Anik gestured his head towards the couple. "Unexpectedly, my mother contracted a deadly disease, and my father tried furiously to be by her side, but my mother’s friends denied him, saying that if she saw him, she would surely leave this world prematurely in her anger at him being there. For all the hatred he had for this woman and all the evil he had wished upon her, he was the one most deeply saddened by her death. He was so distraught that he took his own life in the regret that he had wasted so much of his time pushing her away and causing her pain,” his face remained emotionally stoic as he rendered the tale to Kylie and eventually finished, “That was after he had dropped me off at the Saliek camp, for he believed that I would learn to be a better person from them than from him.”

Kylie didn’t know what to say. She regretted asking the question and felt very uncomfortable, but how was she supposed to know the answer would be so personal? “I’m sorry, Anik," she begged remorsefully. He said nothing in response and just kept walking with his eyes averted from her. No wonder Anik was admitted as a Saliek so young. She considered how many years ago his story may have taken place. Her father had said he had been initiated about five years prior, but how long had he been raised at the Saliek camp before he had been initiated? She cleared her mind of questions before she prodded him anymore. A part of her felt sorry for him, but he didn't seem to be the kind of person who wanted others' sympathy for his situation. She decided to let the topic drop.

Kylie noticed Dainn peering at them from the corner of his eyes with the most interest she had seen yet. The moment was awkward enough already, so she decided to turn her attention to him, "So Dainn, what's your story?" His face showed a moment of surprise before critically inspecting her. Kylie held his gaze, as difficult as it was. His dark brown eyes nearly shadowed out the pupils within giving them an inhuman quality. She could see why no one dared speak directly to Dainn. It was frightening. Trembling as she was, it took all her willpower to stay on her feet. Her bravery was rewarded, ever so slightly.

"I am Dainn from the house of Mahashta, elite member of the Ignet. It is my duty to keep the members of the Mahashta house safe. That duty is my life. My 'story' so you call it," he replied in a very deep voice, and the foreign accent almost veiled the meaning of his words to Kylie.

As well as she could manage tied up and trembling legged, Kylie made a slight bow to Dainn, "It is my honor to meet you, Dainn." Dainn's eyes were now back on the road ahead.

Anik stared at her shaking his head, "You are one crazy person directly addressing a member of the Ignet like that! You could have been killed!"

"Itha said that Sonu wanted us alive," Kylie replied disarmingly. "Anyway, I never knew anything like that. I just figured he was a tough looking regular person." She heard some coughing coming from Dainn. Was he covering up a laugh? Men. She would never understand their need to look tough. Although Dainn accomplished the look well, others just looked ridiculous, she thought as her eyes drifted to Fauler.

Up ahead Kylie thought she saw movement. It must be Sonu's camp! She thanked the Spirits because she wasn't sure how much farther she could have walked. It was not nearly as orderly as the Saliek camp, but there were many tents and people bustling about the area. As they approached, she saw one tent that was larger and more ornate than the others. She assumed that must be Sonu's tent. As they neared the camp, an armed guard intercepted their small company. Many questions were asked of Fauler, being the group's leader, and Itha grudgingly kept her mouth shut during the interrogation.

After a pointed question on containing the magic of the Spirited ones, Fauler signaled to Dainn who nodded. Kylie felt nothing, but Anik's face lit with a moment of fear. "I'm shielded," he said after his shape shimmered momentarily. "I'm not sure to what extent though," he added for show looking around at the others. Kylie considered trying to access some of her Spirit but thought better of it for the time being. If she was shielded as well, so be it. Finally, they were allowed into the camp after an intensive search of their belongings as well as Kylie and Anik themselves. Two additional people joined their group, both whose eyes gleamed with a rich color of Spirit. When the welcoming guard had dispersed, their captors lead them towards the large tent.

Someone must have informed Sonu of their arrival. When they approached the front of the tent, the guards there remained standing straight and tall in their metallic armor and did not flinch from their positions on either side of the entrance. Their helms covered their faces completely with small slanted slits where their eyes would be and longer vertical slits stitched along their mouth. Horns curled out of the sides of the helmets, and whether for decoration or use in battle they proved to be an intimidating show. A strong voice darkened by a deeply-seeded hatred welcomed them, "Dainn, bring the prisoners into me. Leave your companions outside." The voice spat out the word ‘companions’ as though it was a painful word to say. Dainn dismounted promptly from his horse and ushered Kylie and Anik into the tent. As soon as the three of them had crossed the threshold, they heard a sudden clanging of swords from the outside guardsmen as they crossed their broad swords across the tent's entrance. Whether to keep people out or to keep the prisoners in, it was unclear.

The tent had not been intended to be erected for long and not much time had been devoted to its interior. There was only a single large cot, a fire pit, a mirror, and a pile of weapons thrown haphazardly into a corner on the dusty ground. A flap in the roof of the tent had been opened to allow the smoke to escape from the fire currently burning in the pit.

The man they met with was without a doubt Kylie's brother. His hair was blonde and eyes green, although his eyes did not glow as Kylie's did. His face bore the same structure as Kylie's but in a manlier fashion. He wore a light armor that had a golden sheen with a red cape swooping across his chest held in place by two intricate medallions. Even as he sat cross-legged on the floor, sword across his lap, and red cape splayed across the floor behind him, he maintained the bearing of a man who was used to being listened to. The crowned Prince of Arbore sat before them. "You will have a seat," he commanded gesturing in a circle around the fire.

Dainn untied Kylie and Anik from each other while still leaving their hands bound before helping them down to sit with the prince on the floor. Dainn took his own spot directly opposite the prince and began watching the dance of the flames. Kylie did not much like the feel of this place. Not even the warmth of the fire held its usual comfort. Instead, it flickered nefariously in front of her, almost as though it would lunge out of the pit and engulf her at any moment.

"So, my sister has decided to find me... how interesting," Sonu began as he considered the girl he had last seen as barely a toddler, "I had always planned to find you one day to succeed in my mission, but not this soon. You throw a wrench into my meticulous plans being here now, but I may need you eventually… if I ever locate those blasted artifacts!" Sonu's teeth were gritted as he spat out the last of those words. He threw his golden hair out of his face to look her up and down before beginning again, "So what shall I do with you? You always were our parent's favorite, you know, with your Spirit glow and what not. Always so concerned about protecting their special daughter they were. Well look at them now, cowering somewhere on Krael waiting for a day that will never come when they will reclaim Arbore." Prince Sonu's anger had grown, but he regained control of it before continuing, "Hmmm.... Well, at least it looks as though you have brought along a friend to ensure your good behavior. How kind of you!" A smile slinked across his face, but it held no kindness in it. "Oh, and he is a member of the Saliek that I so love playing cat and mouse with. This is indeed a treat!"

Anik remained perfectly still, staring off beyond Kylie's shoulder across the fire and making a show of not letting the conversation bother him. Only the sweat rolling down his face in the cool evening gave away his nervousness. "I know exactly what I'll do with you two!"

the prince suddenly proclaimed, "I'll send you back to the whor… cough… cough… horribly beautiful fiancée of mine in Arbore while I continue my searching." The prince glanced quickly at Dainn across the fire who still looked entranced by the flames before continuing, "Tomorrow, we will walk through Sentinel's Gate with your necks at the front of the line to ensure our safe and timely passage through the Saliek entourage that awaits us. Your escorts from today will be sure to keep you… safe." The prince chuckled to himself seemingly pleased with his plan.

Kylie was terrified but determined not to show it as she watched the crazed man that was supposed to be her brother chuckle maniacally to himself. She decided that just because they shared the same bloodlines that did not make him part of her family. She would make sure that she did her best to thwart whatever mission it was that he was undertaking. Suddenly, a large, hot spark leapt from the fire and landed on the corner of Prince Sonu's cape. It took him a moment to realize that he was on fire through his laughing, but he did notice it before it got too large to stamp out with his golden armored boots. Anik's eyes betrayed a glimpse of humor before he quickly cleared it away.

"Get out of my tent now you Spirit wielding freaks! I know this was one of your faults," the prince screamed at no one in particular. "Dainn, get them out of here now before I do something that I will regret," he spat out angrily while gripping his sword as if about to unsheathe it momentarily. Dainn methodically stood up from the fire and collected Kylie and Anik to lead them back out into the darkening evening. For a moment, Kylie thought she may have seen one of Dainn's tattoos along his arm faintly glowing red, but that was probably just a trick of the fire light.

Chapter 13

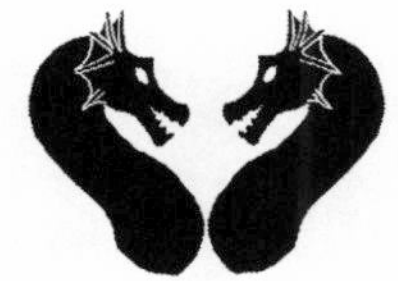

Rocky ledges whip by as a black dove careens through a cave-like maze. Its heart is rapidly beating, as it knows time is running short. Already knowing the way, the dove flies true around each corner and quickly chooses its way at each fork in the maze. The dove is nearly at the end of the maze when it hears the harsh scraping of rock on rock. The maze walls ahead of the dove begin shifting themselves. Barely squeezing through one last alleyway, the dove descends exhausted to the ground. It is still trapped in the maze but no longer knows the way forward.

The feel of cold steel chilled not only Kylie's neck but her heart as well. Never before had she felt so powerless. Itha held her knife against the tender skin of Kylie's throat with one hand and firmly grasped her arm with the other. Every so often, she would whisper demoralizing tidbits into Kylie's ear and give her calves a kick for good measure. Anik was not in any better of a position. Fauler held him tightly, and his knife hovered deathly close to Anik's throat. He was purposefully positioned in Kylie's view to, as Sonu had claimed before, ensure her good behavior. He had assumed that she was the dangerous one of the two. Kylie knew now to take everything Sonu said seriously. She originally had not thought that she would literally be leading the parade of the prince's troops through the Sentinel's Gate with a knife at her throat, yet here she was.

The Saliek had already retreated to their camp after Kylie had relayed her message to her father last night, so none of this was necessary. They had decided not to risk an assault to free the prince since the information that Kylie had provided them with had suggested that he was not under Elasche's control but working on a task of his own devising. She had not passed on the Saliek's absence to the prince's troops in order to keep her contact with her father a secret. As a result, she could feel Itha's weight shifting from one side to the other keeping watch for the Saliek that she still anticipated to jump out of the rocks at any moment. Kylie hoped dearly that Itha's hands remained steady.

In her mind, Kylie kept seeing images of the prince with his tangled blonde hair falling into his crazed eyes while laughing at them last night. It sent fearful shivers down her spine. She wondered what kind of trouble a man like that was capable of plotting. She would have to eventually figure out his mission. It would take them a couple of days of travelling to reach Arbore after they were done spending a day hiking through the pass. Anik and herself would be given a mount to speed up their transportation from that point forward. She had gleaned this from conversations that she had overheard from the troops earlier. Maybe those couple of days would give her the time that she needed to uncover his plans. She planned on talking to Anik if she could ever get a moment alone with him. He might be able to provide another point of view on the situation.

Contrasting the coolness of the steel on her neck, the heat of the midday suns beat down on Kylie's head disrupting her thoughts. She could feel the skin revealed by the parting of her hair on the top of her head beginning to burn and the rivulets of sweat dripping from her face. Itha complained profusely each time a drip would fall onto the hand restraining Kylie. Periodically, Itha would try to provoke a mean-spirited conversation with Kylie on the topic, but Kylie was not in the mood for the aggressive banter that Itha was prodding with, much to the dismay of Itha.

Kylie realized a moment of inspiration in the monotonous day. She was Spirited, so she could probably block the sun from her exposed skin if she tried! Kylie spent some time thinking back on all the information that she had read as Scilla's apprentice. She needed something that was simple so as not to drain her energy if she were to maintain it for an extended period of time, but effective. Ahhh, yes! She was covered in a layer of sweat anyway at this point, so why not put it to good use? She focused her concentrations on increasing the reflectivity of her sweat so that the heat would be reflected away from her as opposed to absorbed by her sensitive skin. She felt relief from the heat mixed with excitement at what she had accomplished. This would surely make the remaining trek more bearable, if she could maintain it. She may not be able to turn her talents against her captors yet, but she could at least use them to improve her own comfort level. She wondered if Anik was doing the same.

***

Anik's head was drooped over Fauler's knife while he silently brooded. Fauler was not being as careful as he had been instructed to be, so Anik had created a small shield in between his neck and Fauler's knife. This had turned out to be a good idea since multiple times now Anik had felt more pressure than he thought his unshielded skin could endure without puncture. The Spirit shield that Dainn was maintaining around him was essentially not letting Anik project his Spirit beyond himself, so he was still able to create this small protective shield around his neck without being impeded. He had learned the bounds of the shield with a few quick experiments and was content in his understanding of his limitations. He surmised that the shield must be difficult for Dainn to maintain. During the previous night, while he was sleeping, the shield had been removed, and today, he could sense it waver every so often. Since Anik had no intention of escaping yet, he was more than happy to know that their precautions were tiring the strongest member of their captor's army.

As for Kylie, he was unsure if Dainn had her shielded at all. His ability for this must be strained if he were picking and choosing between them. This was not too surprising after Anik thought about it. All energy had to be pulled from somewhere, and someone else's internal energy is not something that can be easily contained. He wondered if that meant Dainn's power of will was stronger than his own. Anik discarded that thought immediately. He did not want to ever get into a situation where that point would be contested.

Anik was not happy with the situation. He was fairly sure that he knew what Prince Sonu's ambitions were after last night's show he had put on for them. Anik had studied many books in his lifetime, and of those that were required reading for any Saliek member were the many books of Krael's legends and lore. One of these books contained the Legend of Ghaleon. If Prince Sonu had known growing up that his sister was allegedly the Spirit Master reborn, that would have been reason enough for him to want to keep her safe for the moment or rather as safe as they could possibly be at the hands of this Elasche creature he had heard so many horror stories about. According to the legend, without the Spirit Master he could never reconstruct the fabled cape, sword, and shield, which he assumed were the artifacts he was having trouble locating.

Anik wondered if Prince Sonu believed that he had found any of the required parts for their re-creation or if he had just been searching the places of deep magic that were the suspected hiding places for them. Books had told of a forest with trees that were not only taller than the eye could see but with trunks as wide as the base of a mountain. If one could find his way through the forest's twisted paths and perils to its center, the torn and tattered cape would await them. The shattered sword was supposed to be beneath the crashing waves of a vast and treacherous sea or perhaps beneath the ever changing, sand blown dunes of a scalding desert depending on which source was to be trusted. As for the shield, many believed that the legends pointed to its whereabouts being in Arbore. They indicated a great city surrounded by a mountain range. This was a point of contention, as many did not think it feasible for a city in existence today to have also been in existence at the time of Ghaleon. Still the resemblance of the descriptions was striking.

No one, of course, actually knew where these places of deep magic were, and those places that were suspected had been extensively searched by Krael's adventurers throughout time. None had been successful. The excuses of the failures always being that someone possessing a greater magic, possibly even the Spirit Master themselves, needed to be present for the truths to be revealed.

Anik had never been completely trusting of the books containing legends and myths, so he had not stopped to consider if these items of power actually existed. He was much more interested in the books of sciences that could help him further his talents in the Spirit. It was now clear to him that it didn't really matter if the cape, sword, and shield existed, but whether others believed that they existed and to what extent the believers were willing to go to achieve their ambitions. Prince Sonu scared him. He didn't think that he was a man willing to let morals get in the way of his potential power.

***

The evening breeze rolled into the room and shuffled the papers on her desk around. Scilla nabbed one piece out of the air before it fell to the floor and smoothed it back onto her lacquered wooden desk. The natural light from the window was getting too dim for her to continue to study, she noted as she readjusted her glasses. Not that she needed the glasses, but they were a good accessory for the part she played on Thaer. She pulled her dark cloak shut around her breast to fend off the slight chill of the breeze. Leaning back in her padded, ornately carved wooden chair, she stared out the window into the swirling hues of the reddening sky. She took a deep breath of the fresh evening air in an attempt to settle her twisting insides. She had known the days were numbered before her seeings came to fruition, but now that the players were in motion, it was getting harder for her to stay in her seclusion here on Thaer. It was true that she had done all that she could to prepare, but she was still uncertain if it was enough.

From this point forward in time, her visions had always swirled, like the colors of the sunset before her eyes. No sure path to take. Living this reality that she herself had foreseen unsettled her more than she could have ever imagined. Always before, she could prepare for what she saw, now she would be a spectator in the game. At a time like this, Scilla would usually reach out to a friend, maybe Zhannah, but no, not this time. There was nothing she could do. Zhannah would never be able to understand anyway. She was a swordswoman through and through. No, she would never be able to understand the problems of a seer. Scilla clasped her hands together with her elbows on the desk in front of her. An array of oversized bracelets clinked as they fell to her forearms. She bowed her head forward to touch her folded hands, and her hair closed upon her face in jet-black curtains. Then she began to pray to her Spirits for any help or guidance that they would be willing to give.

Chapter 14

A man appears onto this world from darkness with a great splash, blinded by a haven of colorful specks of light. One light in particular grasps his attention, and he follows it ceaselessly wherever he goes. He is enraptured by its light and cannot go on without it. He knows that he would be become lost and unable to find his way in this new world if the light ever escaped his sight. On he goes, endlessly following his guiding light. It will lead him where he needs to be.

Mory searched around the rock heaps in the damp, grey stone cavern and found a narrow passageway leading out of the room. For lack of any other choices, he decided to follow it. At one point, he even had to shimmy sideways to fit, dragging his pack along the floor beside him. Thankfully, he wasn't a very large person. The narrow passageway opened into a wider corridor. Dim lights, like those in the secret area of the library, lined the walls. He decided it must be a corridor as opposed to a natural cave since there were defined corners where the walls met the ceiling, and the stones mortared into the wall were linearly spaced.

Tiny streams of water were trickling through the ceiling and down the walls creating dark, jagged stripes. Greenish grey moss congregated in patches, soaking up the water as it descended. That combined with the amount of dust and spider webs clinging to the surfaces surrounding him indicated that this was not a well traversed path. He felt a spike of fear at the thought of the spider webs. Last time he had been in a long corridor with spider webs it had not ended well for him, and this time he had no sword. Mory's best guess was that he was under the library in another secret area that had been unknown to him.

His stomach growled irritatingly at him. He slid his pack off one of his shoulders so that it would swing in front of him and he could rummage inside to see if any of his snacks had survived the whirlpool. To his excitement and dismay, he found that all his snacks had survived his adventure earlier but were extremely soggy. He found a clump of once dried fruit. It had plumped back into a mushy wrinkled version of its former self after being submerged in the water. He also crammed a piece of spongy bread and cheese into his mouth and hoped that it would sustain him for whatever lay ahead.

Stomach somewhat satisfied, Mory made his way down the musty smelling corridor. The end of the corridor lead to an empty room. On the opposite side of the room, he noticed something familiar. A large stone archway filled with rock faced him. As he neared, he noticed that there were carvings similar to those in the library on the stone archway. The story they told was still unclear to him, as he had not found it in any of the books he had read yet. To the left of the archway was a rack of swords, each one slightly different from each other. This piqued his interest. There were three swords there, and Mory figured there would be no harm in trying them out. After all, he had been training to wield swords, so he may as well experiment with a few different kinds.

He grabbed the sword at the bottom first. It was the largest of the swords on the rack, and he could barely hold it aloft. He took a slow agonizing swing with it, grasping it in both hands, and then decided that he would move on before he dropped it on his foot or otherwise hurt himself. The second sword was a fat short sword. He could handle the weight in one hand but felt as though he would be too close for comfort in a sword fight against an enemy. The third sword was long and thin. It was the lightest of the three swords. The hilt fit comfortably in Mory's hand, and he rather liked the swooshing noise it made as he battled his invisible foe. He side-stepped briskly to the left and right as Zhannah had taught him across the old stone floor, combining thrusts and lunges with parries and retreats as it pleased him. Mory liked this sword. It seemed perfectly fit for him.

As he tried a large swooping stroke, he misjudged his reach and with a reverberating clang the sword slammed into the stone wall. Mory felt the hit through the sword hilt, cried out in surprise and pain, and dropped the sword. He shook the ringing out of his hand and then looked to the ground at the sword. It had broken. Mory felt his heart sink into his stomach. In the time that he had held the sword, he had subconsciously decided that he was going to keep it as his own. It was doing nobody any good just hanging on a wall down here. So much for that idea. He sighed to himself rationalizing the situation. It was old and had probably been rotting down here for millennia any way.

Not knowing what to do about it for now, he finished looking around the room. On the right side of the archway was a faded carving of the huge warrior Mory had gotten used to seeing in the library holding his sword and shield in the ready position and a cape flowing out behind his shoulders. This version of the carving was impressive in that it was life size. Mory walked up to the wall and brushed the layers of dust from it. Yes, it was the same carving. Only there was something missing… the sword. Not missing in the sense that it wasn't carved, but missing in the sense that it was a big hole shaped generically like a sword. Specifically, like the sword that was lying in pieces scattered on the floor on the other side of the archway.

Just his luck. He'd broken what was clearly the key out of this place. Not knowing what else to do, Mory knelt on the cold floor and gathered up the sword pieces. Not wanting to touch the sharp blade with his hands directly, he removed his shirt and used it to carry the pieces over to the carving. He carefully put each piece in its place. Once he got to the final piece, the very tip of the sword, he backed away quickly from the wall. He waited anxiously for something to happen.

A faint rumbling began vibrating the stone encompassed by the archway. The rumble grew exponentially in magnitude over the next few minutes until it was a deafening thunder, and Mory found himself crouched on the floor, cringing, and attempting to cover his ears with his shirt, completely unable to process a lucid thought. The noise eventually died down, and Mory gathered the courage to stand again. Through the fine cloud of debris that had accumulated in the air, he saw that there was a pile of rubble in front of the archway with dust swirling above it.

Freedom! For the second time today, he found himself laughing at something that wasn't particularly funny. If he had lost his mind, he wouldn't blame himself. Stepping carefully over the shattered stone strewn across the floor, Mory made his way back to the carving where he had placed the pieces of the sword. The sword... it was whole again! It looked even more magnificent than it had on its rack. The blade was shining as though it had been recently polished, and there were amethyst stones embedded in rings around the hilt. Mory gingerly reached out and picked up the sword. He was blinded.

Purple light flooded the room for an instant after

Mory touched the blade. He couldn't remove his hands from it while the light was in the room. The light subsided after a few seconds, and Mory's eyes readjusted to the dim light. A bright white sheath had appeared around the blade in the crevice. Warily, Mory reached out again to grab the blasted sword with a mind of its own. This time it let him take it without further complications. Any reservations Mory may have had about taking the sword had vanished. At this point he felt that he had clearly earned it. He fastened the sheathed sword to his belt, and it stood out against his now ragged clothes like a single white rose in an otherwise dead field. Feeling a bit self-conscious, he replaced his shirt in hopes that he looked a bit less like a ruffian.

Sword acquired, Mory began his ascent of the rock rubble pile through the archway. What a mess he had made. He hoped Scilla wouldn't be too angry with him. The archway led to a darkened spiral staircase. Mory paused for a moment and groaned. His muscles still ached from sword practice and his river swim earlier today, but he knew he needed to get out of this place soon. He had lost track of time at this point. After a long grueling climb, Mory heard the sound of running water. When he reached the top of the stairs, he looked out through a sheet of falling water into a distorted world of colors. A thin mist of water stung as it sprayed into his eyes. Closing his eyes, and bowing his head slightly, Mory slowly stepped through the thin sheet of water into a shallow pool that came up to his ankles. When he re-opened his eyes, he was taken aback at the world he saw.

The ground and trees were mixed shades of green and yellow that he never knew existed. The many colors of the flowers that dotted the bushes were rich and deep. Even the rainbow in the mist of the waterfall seemed more vibrant than anything he had seen before. Birds flitted merrily across the sky with their shimmering wings spread out wide. But upon a closer look, the birds were not birds. Their wings had been split into two sections each, beating at a high frequency. Each pair held aloft a different colored body containing tiny arms and legs. Fairies? “No, could it be?” Mory wondered aloud. Was he in Krael?

Books had not done the beauty of Krael justice. Mory was transfixed for minutes just admiring the scenery and soaking in the moment until he looked down into the pool of water at his feet. Glowing amethyst eyes overshadowed his blue ones. He was disconcerted for a moment but then remembered what he had read in the books about Krael. He was Spirited. Glee washed over him. Never in his wildest dreams did he believe that he held magic in his soul. The possibilities of the universe now seemed endless. There was nothing he couldn't take on with his new powers. How could Kylie not love him now! Mory paused for a moment… That thought had caught him off guard. Did he love her? Yes, Mory decided after a short thinking spell, he supposed that he did. Now that he had admitted that to himself, a goofy-feeling smile engulfed his face, and he felt warm and tingling all over, even while standing soaked in a pool of cold water, in a completely foreign world, with no way of knowing how to return home.

His next steps seemed obvious to him. He knew Kylie was on Krael somewhere. He would find her, help her in her quest, and let her know how he felt. Easy as that, right? He had spent time looking over the maps of Krael in the library; with any luck, he'd be able to discern where he was. But how to know where Kylie was, he wasn't so certain. While pondering, he noticed a smooth purple glowing sphere lying amidst the rocks at the edge of the pool. Mory waded over and picked the dense orb up with both hands. It was about six inches in diameter, and at his touch, it activated. Scilla's somewhat distorted face appeared and began speaking to him, "Mory, if you are listening to this, you are on Krael. You are a smart boy, so you have probably already figured that out. This object you hold is a memory sphere. I have imbued it with information that I am sure you will find useful in your impending travels..."

Scilla's recording continued for hours relaying information about Krael. Some pieces Mory had read in the books that he had found, but most of it he had not. He just hadn't had the time needed to scour the library as he had wished. He was currently located in an oasis in the desert that surrounded Mahashta, a city that Scilla portrayed as dangerous. The Saliek camp was located in the mountains surrounding Arbore, and he figured that was the most likely place that he would be able to get information about Kylie's whereabouts. Scilla had not mentioned how he was supposed to get from the middle of the desert to Arbore, so Mory would have to figure that much out himself. Scilla had provided him with maps of the various areas on Krael, which he could view distorted images of through the sphere. The last bit of her message had indicated that there was more to be said to him, and in time he would be informed.

Mory was sitting cross-legged on the bright moss-covered ground surrounding the pool holding the memory sphere. It no longer glowed purple. He shook it and nothing more happened. Scilla had said that to re-access any of the data that she had stored in the sphere, all he would have to do is think about a specific piece of information and be holding the sphere. He experimented with the map of the area surrounding Mahashta, and lo and behold it appeared. He made a mental note to study how these memory spheres worked next time he had access to books.

Krael was dark now, and Mory was so exhausted at this point that he didn't mind the thought of sleeping on the ground outside tonight. The moss even felt rather soft and inviting. Mory put the memory sphere into his pack and clutched it close to his chest. He yawned heartily and stretched before lying down on the sweet-smelling moss carpeting the oasis floor.

***

The fairies of the oasis shimmered in the moonlight as they zipped overhead investigating their new visitor who now lay fast asleep snuggled on top of a blanket of moss. Chattering amongst themselves, they decided that this Spirited human was not harmful to them. Only one of the fairies, whose light was slowly fading with age, had been alive long enough to remember the last time a human had visited their domain. She had been the Lady of Shadows, the one who had left the memory sphere by the pool. They could feel the boy was the rightful owner of the sphere through their own magic. They would protect him until he left the oasis, and then their pact with the Lady of Shadows would be fulfilled.

Chapter 15

Unbidden, she came with her cloak billowing in the wind and hidden within the darkness of the shadows. Without a word of explanation, she took matters into her own hands and saved those who were only capable of hiding and could not fight for themselves. With one fell swoop of her trained arm, their adversary had fallen. Before she melted back into the shadows from which she came, a sky dotted with stars the color of a rainbow appealed to her. Their debt would be repaid.

Mory woke up to a buzzing noise near his ear. He sleepily turned over and covered that ear. The buzzing returned in his other ear. He reached for a pillow, out of habit, to compress over his head. Not finding one after blindly patting the ground around him, he finally sat up, waving his arms irritably around his head.

"Hey! Watch where you are flailing those things!" a tiny voice chastised him. Mory rubbed the sleep out of his eyes and opened them. Within moments he was wide awake. The flood of color reminded him of yesterday's events, and he began looking for the memory sphere. "Don't worry, we watched over your person and belongings. Nothing is missing," the tiny voice chirped again. Mory turned to look towards the sound and saw a purple fairy hovering near him. She was a perfectly proportioned miniature human, no larger than the size of his hand, with light purple skin and darker purple hair.

Her transparent wings flitted so quickly as she hovered that he could barely see them move. She reminded him of a hummingbird. "Up, up, get up! You need to eat so you can begin your journey!" her voice rang once more at him. She flew to a nearby area where an oversized leaf had been laid on the ground and an array of food spread out for him.

Mory was beginning to pull himself up when the fairy zipped over to another nearby place where a pile of nice new clothes was folded for him. "These are for you too. From the looks of it, you definitely are in need of them," the fairy judged him as she looked him up and down in his present state. Mory looked down at himself and figured she wasn't wrong. His shirt and pants had been tattered through his day of adventuring yesterday and had acquired an unpleasant smell, probably from the river on Thaer. He picked up the white sheath and pulled the sword from it, just to look at it. The purple glow was gone, and it was now just a shiny steel blade. It still seemed beautiful to him.

"Pay attention!" the energetic fairy scolded him to regain his focus. "My name is Telovi, and I will be your guide here in the oasis. It is nearly midday now. You slept soundly through the night and should be well-rested, but now you have to prepare for your journey," Telovi said, pulling Mory's sleeve towards his breakfast, or maybe it was lunch now, and he began to mosey on over. The food was gatherings from the oasis, and its contents reflected that the fairies living here must be herbivores. There was an array of exotic looking fruits and nuts that he could not identify, and he was pretty sure that he ate a stick of wood. Telovi was watching though, and he did not want to offend the fairy folk, so he ate without complaint and expressed his gratitude.

Occasionally, he would see a glimpse of color appear in some nearby foliage only to disappear seconds later.

Mory's curiosity eventually got the better of him and he inquired, "Telovi, why are you the only fairy who talks to me? I saw many of you yesterday."

"Not many humans have entered this oasis in the last few hundred years. It is about one day's hard ride from Mahashta, but the magic of my people has hidden its existence in a mirage. We prefer to have the area to ourselves. Unless a person was to actually walk into the oasis, it will just blend in with the endless miles of sand. Because of this, only one of the fairies still living has ever seen a human before you came along. You are an oddity to us, and many are fearful of you," Telovi paused as a proud smile lit up her tiny face. "I, on the other hand, have volunteered to be your guide. You see, I am different from the rest, I am more curious about you. My grandmother is the one remaining fairy that has seen a human, and you do not fit the description of the last one very well." Telovi squinted her little eyes examining him again before continuing, "She told me many stories while I was younger, and they have fed my curiosity. Now that one of your kind has entered the oasis, I saw no reason why I shouldn't interact with you."

Mory chuckled a little, "I hope I've managed to make your learning experience interesting."

Telovi sighed, "No, not really. So far, I have deduced that humans are quite lazy. You slept nearly through the day! I was becoming impatient."

Mory had finished his food by this point and continued to ready himself. His new clothes fit perfectly. They were lightly colored and made of a soft breathable cotton so that he could be as comfortable as possible in the desert. There was also a hat that had a piece of cloth that fell behind his neck, as well as a wrap to keep the sand out of his face. He left those off for the moment, not seeing an immediate need for them in the oasis. The brown boots were made of a quality leather and came just below his knees. They would protect his legs well.

After he was ready, Telovi beckoned him to follow her. They made their way through the jungle-like oasis vegetation slowly, as there were no well-defined paths for humans to take. Telovi zoomed up on ahead and taunted him with various jeers hinting at how slow Mory's progress was. A cloud of tiny bugs had congregated around Mory's head, and no matter how often he waved them away, they would return in a denser cloud. There were multiple instances where he ate some, or they flew into his eyes. When he was sure that he could no longer bear the annoyance, at last they came upon an opening. Here the greenery was cropped short from the grazing of a herd of horses. The horses looked strong and beautiful as the sunlight coming through the canopy of trees dappled their shining, sand-colored coats.

Telovi began to explain, "These horses have bred in the desert for generations and have solid, quick footing, even in the sand. They can also go without water much longer than horses bred in other areas of Krael. The fairies will let you borrow one for your travel to Mahashta, for that is the only human city within reachable distance from here. Once you arrive in Mahashta, you can let the horse loose, and it will make its way back here. The way is not hidden from their eyes. You will ride across the desert tonight when the suns have set and should arrive in the city by morning. If you would find the horse a drink before letting it loose, I am sure it would be grateful to you."

Another fairy flew close and joined Telovi. This one was blue and not nearly as bright as Telovi with a slow voice that cracked with age, "Mory, I am under the impression that your survival is key to resolve an issue of major import to Krael. The fairies here generally do not meddle in the workings of the outside world, but for you an exception was made. Take care of yourself. Do not let the exception go to waste."

Telovi bowed with reverence to her grandmother, "Thank you for your wise words, grandmother," then shot Mory a meaningful look.

"I will do my best, honored one," Mory bowed too and hoped his response was adequate.

The afternoon passed uneventfully in the oasis. The fairies made sure that Mory had a pack full of food and water that would hold him through the night and then some. Mory explored the hidden wonders of the oasis with Telovi at the lead, and both learned a great deal. One memorable learning moment had been with a plant consisting of plump green bulges and bright yellow flowers with long, thin petals that waved in the wind like streamers. The green parts of the plant looked be covered with a soft fuzz that Mory could not help but want to touch. When Telovi wasn't watching him closely, he gingerly reached out to touch the intriguing plant. The fuzz had actually been fine rows of sharp thorns, and Mory had recoiled with a startled scream. Telovi had laughed so hard that she couldn't fly for a short time while she tried to catch her breath, and Mory pitifully extracted the thorns from his bristled hand.

Once the suns had set, Telovi and Mory returned to the clearing. A horse had been selected for him and awaited his arrival. He would be riding bareback through the desert, as the fairies did not have any tack for his use. As Mory mounted his horse, a multitude of fairies emerged from their hiding spots to bid him farewell. A rainbow of flecks dotted the dark night sky, as if the stars had gained vibrant color for the night. Telovi showed him the way out of the oasis, and once his horse had stepped beyond the boundary that she indicated, the oasis disappeared. Mory felt suddenly alone, and a breeze blew sand into his face, stinging his eyes. He pulled the hat and scarf out of his pack and put them on. The desert was cool during the night so he didn't mind the extra coverage on his head, and keeping the sand out of his face while riding would be important.

The sand dunes continued in stagnant waves as far as his eyes could see. The sky was black as pitch, and he could clearly see millions of stars untainted by any nearby lights. He could easily pick out the constellations on this night, and the stories surrounding them played back in his mind, keeping the sudden feeling of loneliness at bay. The moon had a slight orange haze covering it as it shed its light onto the white sand. He hoped that the horse truly knew where they were going and applied a slight pressure with his legs to urge him on. The horse took off immediately, nearly jarring Mory from his back. He grabbed a fistful of mane to keep from flying off and then hunkered down for the ride. Sand swirled in a vortex behind them as the horse galloped off into the night.

Just as the first sun was rising over the horizon, Mory saw a glow of light ahead that must be from Mahashta. A pale wall surrounded the city, and a castle rose from inside. Mory had never seen a castle before and stared in awe as the horse galloped towards the city. There were three cylindrical towers connected by a smooth white stone building. Tall, arched, gold-rimmed windows were evenly spaced in rows across the white castle. The center tower was tallest and was crowned with a giant golden bulb that looked like an upside-down onion. The two towers on either end of the building were also crowned with golden bulbs but much smaller than the one in the center. As he got closer, Mory could see that in each of the cardinal directions of the towers a downward pointed sword had been painted. The sword was wrapped in thorny vines, and a pair of red roses lay crossed at the hilt.

The horse stopped suddenly near the side of the white

outer wall, nearly jarring Mory from his back. Mory had expected to go in through the front gate. Suddenly, Mory startled as he heard a buzz and saw a flash of purple light before realizing Telovi had just zipped out of his pack. "Telovi! What are you doing here!" Mory exclaimed.

Telovi giggled, "You didn't expect me to leave you utterly on your own in this world you know nothing about, did you? I wasn't lying before when I said I was a curious fairy. I've always wanted to see the world outside the oasis. This seemed like an opportune time to do just that! This way, if you ever need to return to the oasis, I can show you the way. Also, I think that you will find my powers could aid you on your journey." Her hands were on her tiny hips and her head was cocked to one side.

"And what powers are those, if I may ask?" Mory questioned her.

Telovi replied matter-of-factly, "The same as the other oasis fairies. I can make it so others will not see you. You will be a mirage invisible to human eyes, as long as they do not walk into you or hear your approach. I can also sense strong magic, just like we sensed in you when you came to our oasis initially."

Mory considered this and thanked her for coming along. "Won't you get in any trouble for sneaking away from the oasis?" he inquired. Telovi shrugged, "I hinted to my grandmother that I might be accompanying you. She seemed to approve of the idea. Regardless, I am full-grown fairy, not a child! I've seen enough to make my own decisions and deal with the consequences." Telovi flew towards the gate around the corner of the wall, ending the conversation, and motioned for him to follow her, "I will make you and the horse a mirage so that you will be able to sneak in." Mory decided to trust her and followed her lead, urging the horse towards the open gates to Mahashta. They were manned on either side by a lightly armored archer. Slowly the horse walked into their eyesight, and Mory passed through the gates of Mahashta unnoticed.

Once inside the city, it seemed larger than he had expected. Other than the castle at the center, there were houses and shops built along roads extending from the castle walls to the outer city limits resembling spokes on a wagon wheel. The buildings were all small and boxy in comparison to the ornate castle. Sand blew across the empty street in front of him and a tumbleweed got itself stuck in a water trough outside of an inn. Mory dismounted and led the horse over to the trough for it to drink its fill before returning to the oasis.

Fully rehydrated, the horse turned to Mory one last time. The wind picked up its mane and twirled it haphazardly, causing the horse to shake its graceful head to realign it. Mory placed his hand on its forehead and thanked the horse for bringing him here. The horse looked at him with a wild look in his eyes. For a brief moment, his gaze cleared as he gave Mory a head butt in the shoulder. Without another glance, the horse galloped back through the city gates.

Telovi's mirage must have had a distance constraint, as the archers gasped in surprise at a ghost horse that appeared and began running across the desert. Mory chuckled to himself and wondered how long those ghost stories would last. He wished the horse safe travels and hoped that the stamina the fairies bragged so much about held true, or else how would he make it back to the oasis after bringing Mory all the way here through the night?

***

The grandmother fairy flew slowly, her body aching with age, to an old trunk shoved into a dark, rarely-visited corner study of her home, an ancient tree located centrally in the oasis. It had been locked and forgotten for centuries. Her faint glow lit the darkness of the trunk as she delicately opened it with a key she had worn as a necklace since that terrifyingly fateful day. Metal dust glittered blue in the fairy's soul light as it stuck to the spectacularly woven patterns of spider webs allowed to be spun undisturbed for generations. Beneath the stunning art was a silver brooch shaped like a snowflake, twinkling with the flutter of the grandmother's wings. She had never seen snow before in her many years of existence, so the image alone was magic to her. An endearing smile laced with hints of wonder danced across her lips as she gazed upon her treasure.

She took a deep breath, coughing slightly at the dust she inhaled, and reached through the cobwebs to retrieve the brooch. Gently, she brushed off the dust, removed the sticky webs, and rubbed it on her tunic until it was clean. She was nervous, but she had delayed the inevitable long enough. It was time to reconnect with the Lady of Shadows who had saved her race so long ago from certain destruction. The grandmother, out of gratitude, had done as the Lady had requested by fostering a love and curiosity for humans in her children, as well as the need for something more than the life offered to them within the oasis. The person the Lady had foretold had now entered the oasis, and the fairies had taken care of him. Her very own granddaughter had seen to it and was now adventuring at his side.

Unbeknownst to the innocent, darling child, her loving grandmother had cast a spell upon her. It was a tracking spell that she could use to follow the location of someone of her own flesh and blood. In the back of her mind, she could feel her presence now if she concentrated on her. Once her concentration stopped, her image would dissipate until recalled again.

The grandmother brought the now shining snowflake

to her lips and whispered the words she was taught long ago, "Awaken, My Lady, the Stars are calling." The snowflake began to glow with a bright, white light that extinguished momentarily, and she could clearly hear the kindred, welcoming voice of the Lady of Shadows within her heart. After a small polite conversation of times gone by, the grandmother relayed back the promised information of the whereabouts of the boy and the young fairy.

Gingerly, the grandmother placed the brooch back into the trunk and noted that the nervousness she had felt before was gone, and she was now smiling warmly. Maybe she would enjoy these conversations with the Lady of Shadows for her heart echoed with the joy of connecting with a long-lost friend.

Chapter 16

A tired old man with a crook in his back and a white beard so long that it swept the floor, slowly hobbled along on his cane up the spiraled stairs to the uppermost towers of a castle. The night was dark and the skies clear so his crackled voice would travel as far as it needed. On the balcony of the tallest tower, he looked down onto the city that was saved, knowing that the peace they had won for now was not completely stable. His secret would stay locked away, for now. He raised his head up to the skies and with a Spirit-enhanced voice called to his creations, "Sleep now, dear creatures. Rest well. A time will come again when you will be able to finish your task. Until then, you must remain vigilant and listen for the call."

The midday sun warmed Kylie's back as she sat astride the horse that she shared with Anik. Her arms were wrapped around Anik's waist to maintain her balance as Anik held onto the saddle horn. The horse was being led by one of Sonu's soldiers. Ever since they had completed their trek through the Sentinel's gate, she had been watching the city grow from a faraway bulge on the horizon to the great masterpiece before her. A grey stone castle rose above the landscape as a backdrop to the city. Tall spires punctured lazy, low-lying clouds as they drifted across the bright blue sky. Soft white, feathery swirls coiled around the tall and slender red rooftops, which glinted in the blinding sunlight. Green vines snaked their way aimlessly across stone patterns, racing each other in the endless maze of rock around the castle. Kylie stared, transfixed by its magnificence. Her hair flared out behind her in a golden flag as a breeze swept by, kicking up clouds of dust around the bay horse's ankles and blowing it up into her face. Eyes stinging, she pulled her face into the back of Anik's shoulder for protection. Anik jostled and quickly looked from side to side, startled awake by Kylie's sudden movement. "Were you sleeping?" Kylie asked him astonished, pulling her face back.

"Well, yea. It's been a long couple days, and with the warm sun blanketing us, it was hard to stay awake," Anik responded while stifling a yawn.

"But the view of the castle..." Kylie began to say before Anik interrupted her with a kindhearted laugh.

"Country girl from Thaer, eh? Never seen a castle before? Yea, this one here is a doozy. Largest castle I've ever seen to be honest. I've seen it so often though that its grandeur has worn off," Anik paused for a moment, recalling something to himself, "You should see it from the back of a pegasus!" He turned back to give Kylie a flash of a grin over his shoulder, and she returned his smile before refocusing her attention on the castle. Anik took that as his queue to give her a rundown of the various sights he could think of within the city that they would see on their way to the castle. He described the bustling bazaar with people shuffling every which way, competing to see and haggle for the best wares of the merchants. The merchants pushed around squeaky little carts piled high with goods or holed themselves up in wooden stalls capped with a slanted, taut white canvas to protect them from the elements. He promised to point out the best sweet shop, armory, and inns, in his opinion, that lined the main road leading to the castle entrance. In case they were ever freed, they could visit them. His general

excitement about Arbore radiated into his words and gestures.
Anik pointed up high to a carving on top of one of the rectangular stone pillars that hinged to the pointed, black metal gate leading into the city, and Kylie's gaze followed. The pillar, which looked grey from a distance, was actually comprised of a multitude of colors of rough-faced stone stacked tightly together. Kylie assumed the castle must be made similarly. The carving was a gargoyle shaped into a creature with a serpent-like head and wings extending out as if to take flight. Its mouth was open, revealing pointed teeth with a forked tongue sliding between split incisors. The forepaws of the creature gripped the precipice of the pillar with curved razor-edged claws, and a tail swooped from behind the creature plated in heavy armor. Anik’s voice continued to narrate the scene, "Gargoyles, like this one, are hidden away in many stone crevices around Arbore and also decorate the outside of the castle. Each one is unique to itself, or rather I've never seen any two that look the same. There is a story of how they came to be here, if you'd like to hear it."
Kylie's attention was pulled from her observations for a moment at Anik's remark. It was a remark very similar to what Mory had made to her several times before. He knew the stories behind everything, it seemed, and enjoyed relaying them to people with inflections and elaborations in all the right places. She reached to grab the small stone secured around her neck that he had given her and hoped that he was doing all right back on Thaer. She felt a sharp pang in her heart before releasing it and responded to Anik, "Yes, I'd like to hear it." Anik then began his story:
"Thousands of years ago, Arbore was under attack by an evil race of demonic creatures determined to steal the souls of the city's denizens in order to satisfy their

undying hunger. An architect, who also happened to be strong in Spirit, realized that sending soldiers against this soul-eating army would lead to worse than certain death for the attacking soldiers. They would forfeit their souls, condemned to live out the rest of their lives without direction, purpose, or meaning. Only an army of soulless creatures could be worthy combatants against the soul-sucking demons."

"In this realization, he created formidable stone-hearted gargoyles, and with his Spirit, he imbued the stone monsters with life...soulless life. He commanded them through a small, winged creature made of stone, for which he had attempted to craft a soul. Well, with what likeness to a soul a paltry human as himself could envision. The miniature winged gargoyle provided the battlefield information necessary for the architect to orchestrate the battle against the demons and relayed his commands to the stone army. Through the architect's efforts, the demons were demolished and the city of Arbore spared. Not knowing what else to do with his creations, the architect put them into deep slumber ready be awoken if they were ever needed again."

Kylie looked once again at the dragon-like gargoyle and critically assessed it, “It doesn't look like it's sleeping to me.” The eyes of the gargoyle stared blankly out into nothingness, but they were open.

Anik chuckled and shrugged his shoulders, “It is just a story. Who knows how much truth is behind it?”

They stopped underneath the dragon's intimidating gaze as the leaders of their convoy were conversing with the gate guards. Kylie wanted to reach out and touch the rough stone pillar, but she feared it was slightly too far and that she would fall off the horse. After a short wait, the screech of metal on metal pierced the air, and the black gates slowly creaked their way open. The gate guards had let the returning search party enter Arbore.

As their horse rounded the pillar and was led through the gate, Kylie did not see the grand city that she was expecting. She was looking down the main road that led to the castle and could see the gates in the distance, but the bustling streets that Anik had described were close to empty. Dust clouds in miniature whirlwinds carried small pieces of garbage to their final resting places, plastered to the bottom corners of abandoned buildings. The wooden stalls he had described were there, but mostly abandoned, and their white cloth covers sagged with mistreatment. There were no vendors calling out their wares or customers haggling. She just caught a few glimpses of people hurriedly crossing the street, heads down, as if passing through a war zone. As the party made their way down the road, Kylie looked from side to side into the alleyways and streets annexed to the main road. Most were empty and cluttered with debris and garbage. In others she saw piles of clothes, which she could only imagine were people huddled on the dusty ground. Arbore was akin to a ghost town.

"What happened here?" Anik was looking around in disbelief. "That was the best sweet shop in town! And... and Blauden could make the dullest edge of a sword as sharp as new again in a jiffy, where has his shop gone? And..." he hung his head low in defeat, cutting short his blabbering. His auburn tresses fell forward into his face. "I never knew Arbore was this far gone," he spoke again in a more rational tone, shaking his head. "It's been around nine maybe ten years since I'd last been within the city walls. It's incredible what has changed in that amount of time." Kylie did not remember seeing Arbore before, but it didn't look anything like Anik had described earlier. The person leading their horse turned at Anik's reaction, and shook his head mumbling something about an idiot.

No matter what she had thought of the surrounding city,

the castle ahead was still impressive. Another wall, made of the same stone as the castle, separated the town from the castle grounds. Every so often a pillar adorned with a gargoyle segmented the length of wall. Deep green trees hung their leaves over the castle walls, and the grounds beneath were sprinkled with dainty teal, yellow, and pink flowers shed from the trees. She could hear the trickle of water beyond the gates, indicating the presence of a fountain beyond her eyesight. An emerald banner with a golden dragon emblazoned on it, similar to the gargoyle near the entrance, was centered on the gate they were approaching. It was guarded by sentries wearing the same metal horned masks they had seen at Sonu's camp whose presence took away from the splendor of the castle itself. They added an element of fear to an otherwise inviting scene.

Upon reaching the gate, Sonu and Dainn made their way to the front of the party. Sonu made a grand gesture that must have signified the release of his troops, as they dispersed quickly into the town. Dainn took the reins of Kylie and Anik's mount and followed Sonu as he approached the sentries. The sentries respectfully saluted the prince and began opening the gate to the castle grounds. This gate didn't squeak as horridly when opened as the previous one. It must have been better cared for. Upon entry, Kylie was not disappointed. The castle gardens were beautiful!

The fountain she had heard from outside the walls was a white marble fountain with twists of pale green and peach throughout. Two dragons were the centerpiece. Their necks were intimately intertwined and arched elegantly positioning their noses inches apart as they stared into each other's eyes. The tails of the dragons constructed the bowl of the fountain carrying the water that spilled out of the dragons' mouths. The dragons stood ankles deep in the pool, which reflected their magnificence in the bright daylight. The fountain was encircled by perfectly manicured bushes that alternated in color from green to gold expanding outwards from the fountain creating walking paths lined with white stone.

Kylie was mesmerized by the fountain, but she was conflicted in how beautiful the castle was maintained compared to the city, which lay in ruins mere feet away. She forced her eyes away and saw that Sonu had approached the main door to the castle and was using the dragon head knocker to gain entrance. The doors were a deep red, matching the roofs of the towers, and the knockers that lined the front were jet-black. Dainn helped Kylie and Anik off their mount and handed the reins to a servant who had appeared when they had entered the castle grounds. The servant accepted the reins with an expressionless face and made a small bow. Dainn lead Kylie and Anik up the couple stairs to the door's front. As he did, one of them cracked open and Kylie could feel a small breath of air from the pressure difference between the castle and outside. The smell of a smoky incense tinged the air that escaped from the open door.

"Dainn, show our guests upstairs, and introduce them to Elasche," Sonu said with a flip of his hand and a smile that oozed malice. He continued walking down a long, central corridor, his metal shoes grating on the stone floor with each stride he took. There was a staircase on either side of the corridor that led up a second floor. The staircases were crescent shaped and a crimson carpet lined the steps. A chandelier glittering in the sunlight entering from a large overhead window was the centerpiece of the foyer. Tiny specks of light twirled in a ballroom dance beneath their feet as they ascended the steps. Dainn led them down a hallway lined with paintings of people Kylie did not recognize and many decorative doors presumably leading to guest rooms.

Dainn pulled a key from his pocket and bounced it in the palm of his hand a few times as they approached the final door in the hallway. Dainn knocked briskly twice before attempting to open the door.

"Come in!" rang a feminine voice with an accent matching Dainn's. Dainn opened the door with his key. A sweet perfumed smell overrode the smoky incense of the foyer as they entered.

"Sonu has presented you with a couple guests to share your time with, my lady. I hope you find them to your liking. This one is Sonu's sister. The other is a Saliek member," Dainn explained to a caramel skinned woman about Kylie's height with hair darker than night falling to her hips. Her deep red lips pursed as she nodded her ascent, and her near black eyes slowly swept across first Kylie and then Anik. Her gaze seemed to penetrate into Kylie's heart as she held it. Dainn nodded and with what Kylie thought may have been an apologetic look directed at Elasche, slid back out the door and secured it. They were now imprisoned with the woman that they had been taught to fear. Anxiety gripped at her chest before she realized that the door was locked before they had entered the room.

Chapter 17

Flowering trees in an abundance of colors dot a pristinely manicured garden inside of a floating glass sphere. A beautiful song bird perches in one tree, weeping. The sweet scent of spring surrounding her and the soothing trickling of a fountain are not enough to cheer her up. Many pegasi fly around freely outside of the glass sphere garden. One decides to change its course and slams into the glass sphere, shattering a hole more than large enough for the bird to escape. The bird sees that the pegasus is severely wounded lying in the center of the gardens. She flies over to the pegasus and begins to sing a song of healing. Once the pegasus has healed enough, they both escape through the hole in the glass together.

The room they had entered was decorated in shades of orange, gold, red and yellow. A large bed with a crimson comforter decorated with embroidery and a golden sheer curtain surrounding it was against the center of a stone wall. The ground had plush decorative mats strewn across it to keep the feet that trod across the floors warm from the cold-hearted stone. Elasche stared across the room at them from in front of a large window twice her height. Her shadow was elongated in front of her, and the tip of its head touched Kylie's toes.

Anik was frozen in position, eyes wide open, and mouth slightly agape. Kylie decided that he needed some help returning to his senses, so she gave his shoulder a good punch. "Owww! Hey, that kind of hurt!" Anik whined and cast a pitiful glance in Kylie's direction while rubbing his targeted shoulder. Kylie nodded her head in Elasche's direction indicating to Anik that she was going to approach her. Anik stayed back near the door rubbing his shoulder as Kylie walked purposefully towards Elasche.

Kylie extended a hand in friendly greeting, "Hello Elasche. My name is Kylie. It is a pleasure to meet you." Elasche looked skeptically at Kylie's outstretched hand and cautiously extended her own to daintily take hold of it. She nodded her head and then turned to look out the window once more. The view was an aerial of the gardens that they had passed through upon entering the castle. Kylie could see the dragon fountain was the centerpiece with colorful foliage spreading out around it. Smaller marble statues were scattered throughout the garden, and a maze of pastel hedges formed the perimeter before the outer stone walls barricaded the beauty inside the garden. Beyond the walls, Kylie could see the pitiful condition of Arbore in comparison.

Elasche must have noticed Kylie's expression darken because she chose to break the silence. Her voice was solemn and sorrowful, as if speaking of a recently deceased loved one, "It is horrible isn't it, the way he hoards all of the beauty to himself. He wastes all the resources on maintaining his missions, his gardens, and his castle while ignoring the strife in the city that he is supposed to protect. He is unfit to rule."

"You speak of Prince Sonu," Kylie declared. She needn't ask.

"Of course, I do!" Elasche's temper flared as her eyes briefly met Kylie's. There was a fire of resentment and hate burning in her gaze for a moment before she regained her composure and turned back out the window, placing one hand on the glass and staring at her bare feet. "I'm sorry," she apologized. "It's just that he has held me here as prisoner for two years now, ever since my parents relocated back to Mahashta. Well-fed and entertained in these elaborate quarters, never have I needed anything that was not provided to me, but he has stolen my freedom. I am trapped. No amount of riches can account for that loss." Elasche took a deep breath that slightly wavered as she inhaled, "He has told the world that we are betrothed, but I never truly accepted. He stole me through bartering with my parents. Apparently, all I was ever worth to them were some trade goods and lands."

Anik had made his way towards the girls and softly began to speak behind them so as not to startle them, "He must not be sure which one of you is the real Spirit Master. So, he is going to keep you both here until he finds the fabled sword, shield, and cape of Ghaleon."

Kylie recalled the story from the book she still carried in her satchel. What Anik said did make some sort of twisted sense. It was loathsome to admit that she was related to such a power-craving monster. She turned back to Elasche whose gaze had risen from the floor and back out the window. Both of her hands were now grasping a slender decorative wooden partition that crisscrossed the window. Kylie interrupted her musings, "What of your powers Elasche? Can't you just take hold of his mind and convince him to stop?"

"Phaw!" Elasche exclaimed irritated, shaking her midnight hair over one shoulder as she looked to Kylie again. "Those powers are rumors attributed to my looks. You saw how your friend here reacted when he entered the door. Completely frozen, jaw dropped, I could almost see the drool coming off his chin from all the way over here. Men don't like being considered weak, so they blame their reactions on my 'magic' rather than their lust." Her voice took on a hint of pride as she continued,

"I am actually skilled in the healing arts." Anik's face turned a hue slightly darker red than his orange glowing hair and began mumbling what sounded like incoherent apologies as he backed away slightly, rubbing the back of his head with his hand as he intensely examined the floor mat that he was standing on.

Elasche continued, "If I had trained more in combat, I may have been able to find a way out of this prison by now, but that never really appealed to me. I always had many guards of my own growing up, so I never felt the need to increase my proficiency in their same areas of expertise. As it stands, I am afraid that I am no match for the guards, Spirited or not, stationed around the premises."

Kylie curiously inquired, "All spirited people I have met on Krael have glowed with a color. You don't seem to have any color attributed to you. Why is that?"

This question brought a mischievous half grin to Elasche's visage, "Well of course I do. My color is black." That explained the intense shine of her dark hair and eyes. They were amplified by a dark glow. "It's actually not that rare of a Spirit color where I am from. The genetics are different here." Elasche sighed and backed away from the window, "Come with me now, I will show you the rest of my beautiful prison that we will be sharing. You might as well start getting used to it."

Kylie and Anik followed her across the room to another door. Elasche walked with a flowing grace that made Kylie feel like a foal just learning to walk. Elasche had been raised as a princess since birth, and it obviously suited her. Anik had entered a trance again as they followed her. Kylie could hardly blame him though, the sway of her shining smooth hair across her slender torso whisking along the tops of her curvy hips was hard not to watch.

Elasche opened the door, and it led to another large

room. This one was decorated in teals, purples, and other colors befitting of the sea. It was similar in size and proportion to the previous room and also included a large window spilling in light. Elasche gestured across the room to another door, “There is a third room like this room beyond that door. Its colors are more earth tones. The rooms were introduced to me as the sun room, the ocean room, and the forest room. I am unsure if there is any significance to their names other than the colors they portray."

Anik, awake enough from his trance now, shook his head with a frown, "We won't have need of these rooms… at least not all of us for long. I told Bandit to keep close, and she would have. She will take us away from here and back to the Saliek camp. We will take Elasche with us. With her, I see no need to gather more information here. She knows far more from being here two years than we will ever be able to glean in the time we'll be here."

Elasche's eyes widened in excitement, "You have a way out!" The smile that spread across her face would have made any person want to tell her yes, just to keep her wearing that smile, no matter the truth of the statement. When Anik nodded she began clapping and did a cute little twirl with a giggle. Kylie felt a slight stab of resentment knowing that she was nowhere near as beautiful as the woman that stood before her but then remembered that she knew how to survive. This princess had spent her whole life coddled and trained to be elegant. Kylie had been brought up to fight for her survival. She was quick of wit, intelligent, and could assess situations quickly to make a life-or-death decision. Her beauty was more than skin deep. Certainly, that had to count for something. She let her confidence in herself and her abilities swell just long enough to quell the uprising jealousy that she felt for this woman. They should be able to be friends.

"Anik!" Kylie took hold of his shoulder to turn him away from the look he was sharing with Elasche and explained what she saw softly, "You will only be able to take one of us with you on Bandit. There is not room for us both, and Starshine is not strong enough yet to carry a person on her back."

Anik turned to look at Kylie, "I know. I plan to leave one of you here while I take the other back to the Saliek camp. I would stay behind myself, but I am unsure of... well your flying abilities. You have not flown yourself before." Anik must have sensed that Kylie would not appreciate hearing about her shortcomings because he shied away slightly, grabbing the shoulder that she had punched him in earlier.

"I've got a better idea, smarty pants," Kylie retorted with more spite than she anticipated. Boys and their need to accomplish heroic deeds, Kylie thought to herself. It blinded their sight to how best to solve the problems at hand. "I'll contact Father, and he will bring Valor along. We will have to wait until night so he can arrive unseen, but then we will all leave together." Anik must not have seen a flaw with the idea because he cocked his head to one side thoughtfully without a response.

Elasche broke in worriedly, "What about Dainn?"

Kylie and Anik turned to her simultaneously and spoke, "What about him?"

The tones of their combined voices had a sobering effect on Elasche, "Dainn is my bodyguard. I was allowed to keep one servant of my choice with me when my parents bargained me off to Sonu and went home to Mahashta. It was assumed that I would take a handmaid to keep me company and to help take care of me, but I surprised them by selecting my most trusted bodyguard." Elasche's tone gained a nostalgic sadness to it, "I have never remembered a moment in my life that he has not been by my side, other than now when he parades around as Sonu's guard. He relays information back to me in my prison here. When he tells me of his expeditions, it's the closest I've come to seeing the outside world in two years."

Kylie's measure of Elasche increased. She must have some brains to have selected a bodyguard over a maid. She chose to forego her daily pampering for a sense of safety and freedom even though she may not truly have either. Kylie attempted to reassure the worried girl, "I am sure we can arrange for there to be three pegasi available tonight for our escape. Is there any way that you can coordinate with him to meet us here?"

Elasche nodded vigorously, "Yes, he brings all my meals. When he comes with the evening meal, I will let him know."

"Perfect," Kylie responded. Now they were getting somewhere.

Anik interrupted the planning momentarily, "Elasche, is there any way you could ask him to remove this Spirit shield that he has had around me since we've been captured?"

A knowing smile spread across Elasche's lips, "If you can get us out of here, I am sure Dainn will do just about anything you ask. You should feel flattered that he felt it necessary to shield you that way. Usually, he just trusts his own capabilities to take care of unwieldy Spirit users."

Anik prodded a little more with the confidence built by his small success, "What other 'capabilities' does he have? From what proximity can he use them? Also, why haven't you tried to escape with him, if he is as powerful as you insinuate?"

Elasche's smile melted away from her lips, and she turned her back to him once more before answering, "The first answers are not my secrets to tell. The answer to the last question is that we have tried… unsuccessfully. Even if we were to succeed, I am afraid we would have no place to go. My parents would only send me back here, and Prince Sonu would send his men out to find us. We would have to live the rest of our lives out in secrecy and on the run. We have been waiting for a better opportunity or a better plan to come along before attempting again. I think we may have found that in you. For that, I thank you whole-heartedly. Thank you for restoring my hope." Elasche became pensive for a moment before adding, "Maybe one day we can tell you the story of our thwarted escape, though here is neither the time nor the place. We should continue our own escape plans."

Anik bowed, "I respect your answers to each of my questions. I do hope one day to hear your tale, for I am sure it is a most riveting story."

Kylie thought she may have seen a hint of a blush creep up Elasche's caramel cheeks as Anik pulled up from his elegant bow, but she couldn't be too sure. She was right in that they should continue their own plans, though. Time was not on their side.

Kylie contacted her father as Anik signaled Bandit with a series of secret whistles into the wind indicating when she should meet them and trusting that she had kept as close as she usually did during their expeditions. When Dainn delivered a plate of steaming, delicious smelling food, Elasche gave him an unexplained request to visit later that night and with a brief gesture asked him to remove the shield from Anik. Dainn took it all in step, and the stoic expression engraved onto his face never changed as he abided by her words. In the time that elapsed before darkness, Elasche talked about her previous years of imprisonment. She must not have had very frequent conversations with people in that time. It showed in her growing exuberance as she told them story after story about exploring the castle and the gardens, witnessing the further decline of Arbore from its already sad state upon the leaving of her parents, and Sonu's excursions that had recently increased in frequency. She even delved back further into her past to when she was a happy carefree child growing up in a family that wanted her to care about extending the influence of Mahashta.

It sounded like she never really had a knack for politicking. She just wanted to have her pretty things and dance around the house. Her parents had tried to discourage this behavior without success, so they began to look for a suitable prince for her to marry so that she could spread their influence that way. They dragged her to meeting after meeting with the same result of the prince being overly interested and her not at all, until they had finally removed her choice from the matter and selected Prince Sonu. After all, she had grown up in his presence, and they could return to their home in Mahashta with Arbore cleanly within their grasp, as their daughter would be married to its Prince. Elasche now regretted not paying more attention to her other suitors. Surely none of them would have locked her away such as he did.

As night overtook the sky, a moonbeam crept into the room and fell upon the little triangle they had made on the floor. The ethereal lighting gave their bodies a ghostly hue in the darkened room. None of them had bothered to light the sconces since the moon was full and provided plenty of light for them see by. Dainn opened the door to their fancy prison and let himself in. He stood protectively over Elasche's shoulder as she continued to converse as if nothing had changed. Dainn was giving Kylie and Anik an appraising look that made it difficult to concentrate on what Elasche was saying. She must have noticed their discomfort because she gave his leg a nudge, and he looked away.

They had left the window cracked, and a slight breeze made the open curtains flutter chaotically. A darkness suddenly shadowed the moonbeam, followed closely by two more shadows. Anik jumped to his feet to fully open the window into the night, and Bandit hovered as close as she could to the open window. He stepped back, and with the window fully opened the pegasi and their riders filed their way in. Hooves clomping on the hard stone floor leaving a muddied mess to be found by the next person to enter the room. They would leave the sun room by the light of the moon.

Chapter 18

A great man walked the streets of a desert city during the busiest hours of the day. All gawked as he strode by mingling as though he were one of the common folk. He would cast smiles to his onlookers and stopped to say hello to a few of those watching him, patting the heads of small children as he went along. He made his way straight to the main avenue where the market stalls were set up and found a vendor of meat pies. He casually approached and waited his turn in line as people were whispering amongst themselves on either side, casting sideways glances in his direction. Once his turn came up, he requested a beef pie and told the vendor of how delicious he had found his wares to be the last time he was in the city. When the vendor handed him the pie, he vehemently refused payment wanting the man to have the meat pie free of charge. A purple velvet coin purse still found its way into the hands of the vendor containing far more coins than his entire baked stock was worth. "I always repay my debts," the man said before leaving the vendor totally dumbfounded.

Sand crunched in between Mory's teeth as he lay beneath the wooden deck of the Tumbleweed Inn. It was impossible to be free of the granules that hung in the dry air. His muscles ached from his long ride the night before as he stretched them out as best as he could in the cramped quarters. There was only enough room for him to lay horizontally on the ground and prop his head up on his elbows. There hadn't been much of a choice of where to sleep. He had no money, and even though Telovi could have kept him hidden throughout the day while he slept, people could have still physically run into him if he hadn't found a protected location. Under the deck hadn't been the most restful sleep he ever had, but it was well needed.

The boards above his head creaked as the inn's customers for the evening ascended the stairway to the entrance. Each step of theirs caused sand to tumble down onto Mory's back as he peered out from his hiding place into the crowded streets of Mahashta. It was difficult to distinguish any specific person, as all of their faces were partially covered with a cloth to keep out the airborne sand. He saw a vendor across the street with what looked like meat pies, their fragrance wafted over to him, and his stomach began to growl mercilessly. He reached into his pack and grabbed a bit of the food that the fairies had provided him with hoping that it would sustain him.

Telovi buzzed into his field of view and began chattering quickly in a high-pitched voice, "This is very different from the oasis. I never dreamed that I would see so many people in my entire life! What an adventure this is starting out to be! What are your plans for today?" A tiny smile beamed across her face.

"No real plans," Mory responded shaking his head, "Just playing this by ear. I've never been on an adventure such as this before." He scooched his pack forward along the dusty ground and rolled out the memory sphere willing it to show him the map of Krael. The orb shimmered purple for a moment, and then the map appeared. "Here," he said pointing to the mountainous area surrounding Arbore, "is where I think we should head next, but I'm not sure how we get there from," he spun the orb slowly to reveal more of the map, "here."

Mory pointed to the desert surrounding Mahashta.

"Ooo Ooo! I've an idea!" Telovi was bouncing excitedly in a "V" shape in front of Mory's face clapping her tiny hands, "The people of Mahashta need to trade in order to prosper. The best way to do that would be through a portal. Arbore is a city so great of import that even we fairies know of it. There must be a portal to Arbore somewhere in the city!" Telovi punctuated her idea with a small twirl that flared out her purple skirt in a wave about her hips.

Mory nodded. Her idea had a ring of sense to it. "That's a good thought, Telovi," he praised her. "I bet if there was a portal in town, it would be near the castle grounds." Mory cocked his head to one side pushing one of his elbows deeper into the sand-dusted ground. It would be difficult to infiltrate the castle, but with Telovi's mirage magic, he may just be able to pull it off. In the meantime, those meat pies sure looked delicious in comparison to the fairy food he had in his satchel. "Telovi, I think I need a snack before we continue on tonight. Do you think that you could cover me if I walked across the street to that vendor and uhhh... sampled one of his wares?"

"Yes, but..." she looked caught off guard by the sudden change in subject.

Mory cut her off before she could continue, "Great! I'll be right back!" He shimmied out from the cover of the deck and lithely danced between the pedestrians to make his way toward the coveted meat pie mountain that was spewing an intoxicating aroma from its peak. Mory could think of nothing else at the moment other than sinking his teeth into one of those pastry beauties. He made it across the pedestrian river without a hitch and was now along one of the sides of the vendor's stall. He tried to flatten himself up against it the best he could since the customers would walk right up and select their meat pie from the mountain before paying. If he could just contort his hand around the slight overhang of the counter, then he could reach the bottom meat pies on the mountain and bring one down to his position.

Mory carefully reached his hand upwards, and as he could feel the heat emanating off the pastry crust onto his skin, his wrist was pinched by a customer's large belly as they leaned close to the mountain. The pain was instant and severe. He tried to snatch his hand back, but it was stuck in between the counter and the man's belly. He must have yelped because the man jumped back in surprise, freeing his wrist, but causing a localized earthquake that set the meat pie mountain to swaying. The vendor gasped in horror as his wares began their inevitable topple to the dusty ground. Unsure of what to do, Mory reached out his arms to catch the falling meat pies. As they touched his hands, they disappeared into Telovi's mirage magic. After realizing his mistake, Mory made a break for it back to the Tumbleweed's deck and dived beneath it, still clutching a few meat pies.

He peered out from the deck to inspect the mess that he had made. The vendor was in a fit of anger over the meat pies scattered all over the ground, and the nearby customers were talking in hushed tones of a ghost. Mory would have the people of Mahashta convinced their city was haunted if he wasn't more careful. First a ghost horse, now a meat pie loving ghoul! What would be next? He felt horrible about what he had done to the poor vendor. He would no doubt take a loss for the day because of Mory's selfishness. Mory wanted to apologize or make up for the trouble that he had caused somehow, but he could not think of a way without blowing his cover. He took a bite of one of the stolen meat pies and let the warm, salty gravy run down his throat as the soft flaky pastry stuck to the roof of his mouth. Delicious. His stomach gurgled in contentment.

Telovi was staring at him incredulously. Mory shrugged as he stuffed the rest of the meat pie into his mouth. He didn't want to think about it anymore. He knew that he had messed up, but wasting the food he had just obtained wouldn't make amends to the vendor. He hoped that one day he could though. Licking the final drips of gravy from his fingers, Mory looked down the road. The castle was not too far away. "Let's go Vi," he said decisively. "The sooner we get out of here, the less I can screw up!" He pulled himself out onto the street where the crowds were beginning to thin as evening approached. He dusted off his knees and elbows the best he could before walking down the side of the street. Vi followed him wordlessly and didn't seem to react adversely to the nickname he'd given her. He figured he'd stick with it.

Being unseen made traversing the road slightly more challenging. Dodging pedestrians as well as animals walking the street in various directions became a constant chore. As he approached the castle, he saw two lightly armed guards protecting a large wooden, barred gate. Being invisible didn't mean he could melt through walls, so he'd have to find another way inside. There were thick vines covering the wall surrounding the castle that looked climbable to Mory. He adjusted his trajectory so he would end up where the vine grew thickest and greenest up the wall and gave the plant a tug. It seemed healthy and strong and not something that he expected to see here in the desert. There must be an inner garden where the vine originated from.

Mory swung his weight up onto the vine, shifting it so the vast majority of it was taken by the solid white stone wall. He clambered quickly up the vine feeling his fingers rub against the abrasive stone surface. Once he reached the top, there were small trickles of blood running down onto his hands. It stung madly as he used his spit to clean the shallow wounds. They would have to go untended for now. Mory sat down on top of the wall and took reconnaissance of the area.

In the fading light, he could still see the bright white wall that surrounded the castle's inner gardens clearly. It shone nearly as bright as the last glimmer of sunlight that was illuminating an immaculate fountain in the courtyard. A towering sword entwined with thorns and roses was embedded into a white stone. A shield lay against the stone, catching the runoff water and guiding it to the fountain's basin. He couldn't quite see the emblem emblazoned on the shield, but from this distance it resembled a serpent. Just beyond the fountain was a tree that was growing conveniently close to a castle window. If he could get to that tree, he would surely be able to leap into the open window, which was flung wide to capture the cool evening breeze.

It was good that Mory was not afraid of heights as he looked down the edge of the wall that he had just ascended. Nothing soft lay below, so he shuffled a few yards along the edge of the wall to a large bush that looked to be a soft, or at least a tolerable, landing point. He turned around and positioned himself buttocks outwards towards the bush and then pushed off the wall. There was a moment of weightlessness before he felt the shrubbery scrape against his legs. He heard a few branches snap as the bush engulfed him. Once he was sure that he wasn't going to fall anymore, he fought his way out of the greenery. There was a nice person-shaped indentation in the bush where he had initially hit it. Mory sighed in resignation. This was not his day. Scrapes now lined his legs and arms making his shorn knuckles seem like nothing.

Mory trudged on through the gardens towards the tree behind the fountain. The foliage was lush and colorful, even in the moonlight. This must be part of the oasis on which the city was built. Palm trees shaded the pebbled paths swaying slightly in the breeze, their shadows leaving only shifting slivers of the path visible in the moonlight. There was a sweet perfume smell emerging from some of the flowers overhanging the walkway, and Mory felt his mood lift as he strolled. The path opened up into the courtyard with the fountain. Mory paused to take in the view. From the viewpoint on the ground, the fountain was more magnificent. Its size seemed greater, and Mory could feel the slight splatters of water hit his face as he neared it.

Mory cupped one hand and drizzled the cool liquid onto his scrapes. The feeling was soothing, and he repeated it across his arms and hands. Unfortunately, he had nothing to spare to cover his wounds and prevent them from oozing blood, so he plucked a leaf off a nearby plant and dabbed off as much residue as he could. After tending his wounds, Mory dunked his head into the fountain, and it felt unbelievably refreshing. Inspired, he swung his legs over the side of the fountain, and stepped into the water pooling beneath the marble shield. Mory heard a click, and the next thing he knew he was propelled down a swerving waterslide into the darkness.

Chapter 19

An unnatural entity appeared out of the darkness. It should not have been alive. Maybe it wasn't. It came and left the world as simply as a door could be opened and closed, yet it was trapped. It was missing arguably the most important aspect of life and sought after it. What it hungered for most would be its demise, for only one with great life strength could withstand its gravity.

Mory yelled, clutching his pack close to his chest with both hands so as not to lose the valuables inside of it. Vi, who was clinging to Mory's satchel, hair and face drawn back due to the velocity of their descent, began short repetitive high-pitched screeching while they slid. The slide was two connected semi-circles made of marble with twists and turns that curved upwards bringing Mory frighteningly close to the edge, but not quite over. His return to the center of the slide would cause water to splash up into Mory's face making it difficult to see where he was heading. Mory felt his skin becoming slightly raw on his backside as he slid further down. The descent ended up plopping the two into a soft pile of squishy plants, much more comfortable than the bush he had found previously. He rolled over onto his now burning back and exclaimed aloud, "Ugh! The crazy things I am going through for this girl!"

Vi tentatively poked her head out of Mory's bag. "Hey, I've not caused any of this!" she disgruntledly crossed her tiny arms and stared up at Mory. He banged the back of his head on the soft mass a couple times before responding. He guessed that it wouldn't matter if he confessed his feelings to Vi.

"Not you, Vi," Mory said hopelessly, "A girl I knew growing up in the world that I came from. She was my best friend for years. Smart as a whip and beautiful as well. She has long wavy blonde hair and big beautiful green eyes that display whatever emotion she is feeling openly. She can take care of herself too. I bet she could beat me in a fight with her knife skills." A big goofy smile spread across his face as he continued, "I can't get her out of my head! Everywhere I look something reminds me of her. And each time I think about her, this warm intoxicating feeling takes over my mind and body, and I am unable to focus on anything else. Time stops for those few moments as I drift away from reality, and when I return, I hardly know where I am! When I close my eyes to dream, I see her smiling face. I awake each morning to the sound of her laughter. My heart has ached since the moment she was taken from my world of Thaer to this world of Krael. I hadn't known just how much she had meant to me until she was gone. She has stolen my heart without knowing it, and I intend to at least let her know!" Mory clenched his fist in conviction as he finished his soliloquy.

Vi had uncrossed her arms, and a warm smile had spread across her face instead. She sighed, "Oh, I adore a good love story! Have you decided how to let her know once you've found her?"

"Ummm... no not really," Mory stuttered with a bright crimson face. He could feel the heat spreading from his cheeks to his chest. "I figured I should find her first, then I assumed the words would come to me."

Vi chuckled in amusement, "Silly boy, you must be new to this kind of thing. Take my word for it, think about what you want to say to her before you find her, or else you'll just look like a babbling dumbstruck fool." Vi winked to show her jest and flitted out of the pack, illuminating a small area around her with a faint purple glow.

Mory rolled off the planted area onto a cold floor. He involuntarily shivered upon touching it. Vi had flown off into the darkness and wherever she went, a dim light sparked on. She encircled the entire room before returning to Mory and said, "I had heard about these devices in the stories I was told as a child, but this is the first time I have seen them in real life! You see, there is a light source beneath each of the orbs lining the walls, and if you shift the orb so that the opening in the orb overlays the opening in the wall, light floods into the orb illuminating the room!" Vi proudly surveyed her work around the room, and Mory assimilated himself as well.

Three of the four walls were bare stone. Along the entire fourth wall a mural had been painted. It depicted several items hanging on a wall and a large archway in the center. The archway was the same one he had seen in the library on Krael and in the room where he had found the sword. On either side of the archway various pieces of battle apparel adorned the wall. There were gauntlets, pauldrons, body armor, shields, swords, maces, and a myriad of other items. Mory walked closer to examine the mural. As he walked closer, the strangest thing happened. An image of his likeness appeared in the mural. It was as if he were watching a reflection of himself approach the mural. It wasn't possible. The mural couldn't have been a mirror. There were no other items in the room to have their images reflected. Mory hesitantly reached out to touch the mural mirror and watched his reflected image touch fingers with himself. It felt like a regular wall.

Mory noticed something then as he looked his

reflection over. In real life, his sword lay inert at his side. In his reflection, his sword was alight with a purple fire. He removed it from his scabbard watching his reflection. The sword grazed the wall as he was twisting the sword around in his hand, and the wall before him shattered to the ground. He took a startled jump back and smacked his palm to his head, groaning. Behind the shattered mural mirror was stark blackness. Mory lacked the courage to reach into the void and instead replaced his sword into its scabbard and knelt on the floor picking up pieces of the mural mirror. Telovi joined him, alternating looking into the blackness and at the shattered mirror on the floor, before stating the obvious, "That didn't seem very good."

"I know, I know," Mory replied. "These kinds of events have a way of happening to me every so often. Actually, more often than not of late. Vi, stay away from the darkness, I don't like the feeling radiating from it."

"You don't have to tell me that twice!" Vi shuddered in dislike and hovered over to the side of Mory furthest from the wall.

Mory had picked up a slightly larger piece of the mural mirror and was examining it as Vi shifted her position. Their reflections had flickered in the eyes of the mural mirror. "Vi, what was it you just did?"

"I suppose when I shuddered, I let down the mirage magic I had been subconsciously maintaining. I guess we don't need it down here really." They blinked out of existence in the mirror.

"Vi, I think this mirror can be used to see what our eyes can't!" Mory exclaimed excitedly. He snatched up the largest piece of the mirror he could find and slowly spun himself around while standing in the center of the room. "This room, its walls are decorated with the items we saw in the mirror! They are hanging on the walls!"

Mory avoided viewing the wall of darkness in the

mirror piece. Something about it rattled him more than he was willing to admit. Using the mirror as a guide, he walked over to one of the walls where he had seen gauntlets on a shelf. Carefully, he placed his hand where the mirror showed something would be. Sure enough, where his eyes showed him nothing, his hand touched a shelf jutting out from the wall. As his senses battled with the confusion, he grabbed the gauntlet off the shelf and pulled it towards himself. Once off the shelf and within his grasp, the gauntlet appeared in Mory's eyesight.

It was hefty and sturdy. A tornado of dust swirled around signaling that an insurmountable amount of time had passed since this gauntlet had last been disturbed. He coughed a couple times waving his hand to clear the dust before placing it back onto the shelf. The moment it touched the shelf, it blinked out of existence in the world and returned to the mirror. Mory tried touching the shelf himself. The world shimmered and swayed for a moment and he could see everything in the mirror as well as with his eyes, including himself. He slid his hand onto the wall and the world remained the same. The wall itself must be the source of the mirage magic. Mory removed his hand from the wall, and the objects evanesced into nothingness again.

Mory walked over to the archway to examine it. He placed his hand on the wall to see it clearly with his own eyes. He ran his fingers over the familiar carvings collecting a thin film of dust on his hand as he did so. He was unable to tell where the archway lead since it was filled with stone and mortar as had been the one that he had seen when he found the sword beneath the oasis. Mory waited for the disappointment to wash over him in his trapped state, but for once it didn't. He had figured this out before so he would no doubt be able to do again, right? That was strange, Mory thought to himself. His confidence must have increased significantly in light of recent events. A smile stretched across his face with this realization. He removed his hand from the wall, and with his newly discovered confidence looked at the reflection of the wall enshrouded in darkness.

Mory froze in terror. A pair of red eyes glowed back at him from the void. All feelings of confidence were quelled, and a paralyzing dread crept through his veins. The red eyes locked with his own through the reflection, and the demonic creature began to materialize. Above the eyes, two horns curved forward like those on a bull, and a bony shield extended partially down the neck ending in pointed tips. Long yellow teeth were bared in a menacing grimace, saliva dripping from their tips and a forked tongue snaking in and out between the bottom front teeth. The long serpent-like neck connected to a black and yellow body larger even than the grafter that he had encountered beneath the Ancient Archives. Its sharp claws curved fiercely, promising a swift death to anything they sliced, and a formidable tail swayed precariously in the air culminating in two spherical bone clubs on either side of the tail's tip.

As quickly as the nightmarish creature had appeared, it vanished from view in the mirror that Mory still gripped in his now clammy hands. He knew what that meant and bolted to the wall as a screeching roar pierced the air in the enclosed chamber. Mory hoped that he would be invisible to the creature when touching the wall if he could not see it in the mirror. If anything, he might be able to find and use some of the armor for protection. Vi was vigorously bouncing up and down and pointing him towards a shield. That would indeed be helpful in this situation. He broke into a run along the wall, careful to ensure that his hand was touching it at all times until he reached the shield. He slid it onto his forearm opposite his sword hand. It was the wrist he had hurt earlier that day, but it could still bear the weight of the shield. He could tell he would not be able to dodge as fast with it equipped, but with any luck, it would block incoming attacks that he would not have been able to dodge with his agility alone.

"Vi! I'll need your help! Would you mind using your mirage magic to blink me in and out of sight as I command? I am not sure how I'll get myself out of this mess otherwise," Mory yelled, anxiety threaded into his voice.

"Yes sir!" Vi replied giving a salute. "I am at your command!"

Summoning all the bravery that he could, Mory stepped away from the wall and ran screaming at the dragon creature. It had been surveying the room, so he must have been invisible to it originally. The dragon flung its clubbed tail in his direction forcing Mory to dodge before he could strike. An idea sprung into Mory's head, and he signaled Vi to cloak him. He next appeared in front of the stone filled archway and thankfully the dragon repeated its move. Mory dodged the club again and this time it hit the wall and the stone structure was visibly weakened. It would take a few more well aimed shots if Mory was going to get the dragon to free him from this living grave.

The dragon shrieked in irritation and in what Mory hoped was pain. Instead of whipping its tail around again, its next move was to lunge at Mory with its long neck. Mory hid behind his shield and felt the impact of the dragon's head reverberate into his arm. A puff of rancid rotting breath blew over him as Vi cloaked him once more to run. Mory ran towards the beast's belly and swung his sword valiantly. His swing tore mercilessly into the dragon's flesh. Mory hardly felt any resistance. He had always thought the hides of these creatures would have been tough and impenetrable from the stories he had heard growing up, but this one's skin sliced like butter.

Black ooze dripped from his blade, and the creature wailed. It retreated slowly back into the darkness. Mory was not too keen on following it in there. He hesitated to see what the dragon's next move was. He suddenly felt something ripping from within. It was the worst pain he had ever felt as it burned and clawed simultaneously at his chest. It was as if his very soul were trying to escape from his body. Mory imagined his body as an unbreakable container in the hope of preventing himself from shattering from this demonic magic. He cried out in agony and found himself wishing for help. In his mind he was crying out as loud as possible since he could no longer find his voice. He couldn't let anything escape lest it lead to his soul's severance from his body. Nothing else could have caused such torture.

Time halted, as it does when its passing no longer has meaning. As it does in the moments we wish to cherish forever. Whether it is because they are our last moments on this world or the moments when we are sharing thoughts and feelings with the ones who matter most to us. When the intensity of the flow of feelings and emotions in those moments overpowers the relentless forward movement of time, it has no choice but to slow down and eventually freeze for that individual. Mory had no idea how much time had passed as he held himself in a stalemate of wills against the soul-sucking dragon. The only thing he knew was excruciating pain as he maintained a tenacious hold onto all he was, is, and could be. There were moments when he was sure he could go on no longer. It would be easy to give in to this awesome power, but he would always find a reserve of resolve and push on. He found it took all of his strength to keep himself together and found himself hoping that the dragon would tire first. It couldn't maintain this grip on him forever... could it?

The world had long since faded and his consciousness was debatable when Mory thought he saw a bright light converging on him. So, this was death. There really was a bright light at the end of the tunnel. Could heaven actually have found him when he was standing at the gates of hell holding back a monster who could have been the devil himself for all Mory knew? This horrible power assaulting him surely could not have been wielded by anything less! He wondered what death would hold for him. Sweet release from this torturous agony that was upon him now certainly, but then he would never be able to tell Kylie how he felt. He would never have the chance to have her as his, as slim as his hope was that she might actually reciprocate his feelings. He wondered if he would at least be able to watch over her as a guardian angel. She would never know he was there, but he would shadow her every move and protect and help guide her until her light ceased to shine anymore. Then after she had lived a full, happy life, maybe she would remember him in the afterlife, and they could be re-united forever in endless bliss and happiness.

Mory's daydream lifted when he could no longer feel the pain anymore. He gasped in the air as his eyes shot open. He was still buried alive at hell's gate within the chamber he had slid into. Alive. His head was spinning and the immense weight of exhaustion held him down against the floor. He hadn't realized that he had been holding Vi protectively against his chest cupped in both of his hands until he felt a slight tickle from her wings on his palms. He released her. She seemed dazed but overall, okay. That gave Mory a feeling of reassurance. He pulled himself to a sitting position with agonizing slowness. His body ached terribly all over. He slowly rotated his head to survey the area and at first couldn't comprehend what he saw.

An army of stone creatures encircled him, standing at

attention, apparently awaiting his orders. Every sort of creature, mythical and realistic, stared intently at him, expectantly. He looked behind him and saw the stones within the arch had been smashed through. The exit was now open. "What happened?" Mory was hardly able to whisper to his army.

A tiny stone fairy, no larger than Vi, defied physics and flew to Mory's side to respond, "You called and we came. We've slain the soulless one who preys upon that which he cannot have. We had sealed him away all those years ago because he was the one that we were not strong enough to defeat. You wearied him enough for us to finish the job we started. Thank you, Master." She bowed deeply and sincerely.

Mory saw only part of a motionless black and yellow tail emerging from the void wall. Black liquid was splattered everywhere across the room. "Where does that go?" Mory rasped, nodding in the direction of the darkness since he needed both of his arms to remain propped in his sitting position.

"That is a hole in time and space ripped by the Spirit Master of our age to contain the demon. He closed the wall with a seal that could only be broken by the one who had a chance to defeat it. That one would apparently be you, Master," the stone fairy replied gravely.

"Call me, Mory. I am no Master," Mory's voice was coming back, but he still croaked his reply.

"May we return to our slumber Master Mory? There are no more soul stealers to slay," the stone fairy inquired.

"Of course, you may! I think a good deep slumber sounds pretty good myself actually," Mory responded, as he was finding it increasingly difficult to keep his own eyes open.

"Rest well, Master Mory. May the world ever bend to your kind-hearted wills," the stone fairy bid him farewell, and the gargoyles followed her back through the broken passageway. The last one that entered the archway was different from the rest and somehow familiar to Mory. It was a miniature wooden kitten with wings. It looked back at him and waved a wooden paw before following the other creatures through the archway. That was the last thing Mory could remember before torpor engulfed him, and he let his eyelids sink over his weary eyes.

Chapter 20

A chocolate brown cat weaved its way through the strands of space and time creating a beautiful tapestry. It spoke of comfort, good times, laughter, and love. The colors were generally bright and happy, but even the few undertones of sadness and solitude brought out a poignant beauty in the connection that was being woven. Either end of the tapestry was wrapped around a person. Their faces could not be distinguished in the realm of space-time, but the connection being woven between them was solid and strong. When the cat finished its work, it admired it with its shining, yellow eyes before stretching its paws and curling up in the soft center for a long well-deserved nap.

Kylie looked over her shoulder as she clung to her father's waist. They were bringing up the rear of the escape party, so she could see the curtains fluttering in the window they had left open to Elasche's prison. They had left swiftly and silently hoping to have at least until morning before their absence was noticed. Anik and Bandit were leading the way with a frightened looking Dainn averting his eyes away from the plunge to the ground below. It was amusing to see the tough warrior in such a state. Elasche had hitched a ride with Kylie's mother, Zhannah. Her presence had caused an emotional rush for Kylie, but there had not been time for explanations: a flurry of anger at being pushed away so abruptly, excitement to relay her recent adventures to her, and relief to see her again so soon. After the intensity of the farewell that they had shared when she had left for Krael, she had assumed it would be years before she'd see her again. Her relief had been palpable after the shock dispersed, and if it weren't for the urgency of their situation, she would have run into her mother's open arms to greet her. Kylie would beg her for the story once they had returned safely to the Saliek camp.

The night was clear, and the moon shone brightly, center stage, in the pinpricked night sky. Moonbeams danced across the slick metal surfaces on the pegasi tack as well as across the weapons that the group carried, creating haphazard glints flashing into the night. It was not the ideal night for an escape, as visibility was nearly endless due to the lack of clouds. Any pursuers would have an easy time following them. Gazing ahead and around, Kylie could see the stars continuing forever. It was beautifully boundless. She could almost feel her soul being pulled away from her body to chase the endless possibilities extending before her. It was the most enticing feeling ever. Her head began to spin, and her body felt lightened as she nearly gave into the release of her soul to the handsome night sky.

Suddenly, chaos was unleashed beneath the rhythmic beating of the pegasi wings, bringing Kylie back to reality. The castle seemed to be tearing itself apart. The rough sound of rock scraping on rock echoed through the night, and the coalescing dust clouds ascending to the sky were stinging her nose and eyes as they enveloped her. Pieces of the castle were breaking off and taking flight or galloping away across the ground leaving stone rubble in their wake. The same was happening throughout Arbore to buildings and stone walls everywhere. The gargoyles, Kylie realized, were coming to life. That was impossible! The soul-stealing demons from Anik's story had been vanquished eons ago. There was no way anyone with the capability to summon them was still alive.

A swarm of flyers was impeding their forward path as they forced their way upstream. The gargoyles were congregating around the dragon fountain, which was exactly in the opposite direction from which they had come. Upon closer inspection, they were disappearing into the basin of the fountain itself. Thankfully, the escapees weren't the target of the wrath of the stone creatures. Kylie jerked backward and nearly lost her grip when something thumped into her father. She heard a groan before he called back to her, "Keep your head flush to my back Ky! These stone monsters are not paying heed to anything that gets into their path." She hoped he was all right from whatever had hit him, but his back remained straight and muscles tensed as they flew on, so she assumed all was well enough.

She followed his command until something started stirring in her satchel. It was moving this way and that, attempting to escape its confines. Kylie carefully removed one hand from her steady grip to open the top flap of the satchel strapped across her body. As soon as she did, the carving that she had been working on back in the Ancient Archives emerged. It poked its wooden kitten head and front paws out to test the night air, and then, with a mighty push, lifted itself into the air and flocked with the rest of the creatures. Kylie was glad that she had had the foresight to give the little creature a pair of wings. She hoped that wherever its journey concluded that it would find a good home.

The skies ahead cleared of the gargoyles with only a straggler winging by now and then. The dust had clouded the sky and marred the view of their aerial escape from the ground. The city was steadily shrinking into a dot on the horizon as they approached the surrounding mountains. Her father's weight began shifting, and he was leaning noticeably to his left. Valor began descending unbidden by Regithal. Kylie felt panic beginning to rise in her stomach and pulled back her hand, frightened to see what she had begun to feel dripping warmly onto her hand. Blood, not her own, slid in between the lines of her fingers as she briefly held her hand out for inspection. Quickly she replaced her arm around her father's waist to help maintain both his and her own balance and to hopefully quell the queasiness simultaneously battling and enhancing the panic felt in her stomach. "Father, are you okay?" Kylie's voice quivered slightly in asking the question. He didn't respond.

She prodded with him with the mental connection and was astonished at the sudden assault that engulfed her. His unguarded, unguided mind was a capricious thing bouncing between images of battles won and lost, various Saliek missions from the mundane to the most important, and her mother and herself in various stages of their lives. She could feel the emotion behind each of the images. The fear and sorrow that he overcame during battles in order to lead his troops, the joy and thrill he felt while thinking through the design and execution of the Saliek missions, and yet overpowering all of the other emotions entangled within his memory strands was the driving love that he felt for Zhannah, Kylie, and more recently, Anik. It seemed as though he had taken the young boy under his wing early on and had seen personally to his training. Her father viewed him as a son. Kylie pulled herself away before she might accidentally see something too personal. That last bit had knocked the wind out of her. Anik was a brother to her when viewed from the mind of her father.

Valor landed smoothly, as always, and knelt down gently on the ground, shaking his head nervously. Kylie swung herself off the large pegasus' back, and her father slid slowly into her arms. He was heavy, but all she needed to do was ease him onto the ground, and gravity was on her side. He was unconscious for the moment. Kylie swallowed her fear and laid him out as well as she could on the grassy ground. Once situated, kneeling beside her father, she unwrapped his black cape and saw dark liquid matted onto the black cloth of his shirt. Knowing a little about medicine, she thought that finding something to clean and bind the wound would probably be a good decision. She got up and rummaged through the saddle bags as quickly as she could for the water canteen. Finding it mostly full, she thanked her lucky stars.

Returning to her father's side, she unbuttoned his shirt as nimbly as she could with her trembling fingers. She had to keep a cool head now. This was not the time to let her fear get the best of her. The shirt stuck stubbornly to the wound as she pulled back the fabric slowly to reveal the damage. Rocks were stuck intermittently in the blood-soaked, scraped, and punctured skin. With the shirt no longer there to hold back the flow, blood began oozing onto her hands as she held the dampened cloth to the skin's surface. Her head had begun to thump in rhythm with the heartbeats that were pulsing the crimson liquid out of the wound. Her hearing rang and then faded as cotton balls filled her head. She could hardly see now as the images of the wound swum before her, and she fought to keep her eyes open. Her eyelids, hands, and body were suddenly more weight than she could support. The pulsating of her father's life blood through the wet cloth onto her hand was her last feeling before the world blackened.

***

Warmth from the morning sun kissed Kylie's cheek softly to awaken her from the nightmare she was having. She heard bustling going on in the background and slowly propped herself up on her grassy bed to see what was going on. Her head spun slightly at the movement, but she recovered swiftly. What she saw reminded her that the nightmare was reality, and her heart sank. Her father was propped up against a large rock, blood drenching the white bandages wrapped snuggly around his waist and pooling red in the green grass beneath him. Elasche and Kylie's mother were sitting cross-legged beside him speaking in hushed tones. Dainn held Elasche as she sat, supporting most of her weight, as she looked near unable to on her own. Her father looked as though he was sleeping, if not unconscious. The steady rise and fall of his chest indicated that he was at least alive.

"Good morning, Sunshine," Anik's voice welcomed her. Kylie tore her eyes away from her father to see Anik smiling with empathy at her. "Rough night, eh? We all turned around and followed Valor when we noticed him descending. Upon landing, we saw you both were lights out, sprawled in a bloody mess on the ground. You had us in a good panic for a moment before we realized that you were both just passed out." Anik looked towards the ground, "Thank you for trying, by the way. That was mighty brave of you to try and stomach a wound like that with no medical training." Kylie felt a surge of annoyance bubble up at her inadequacy but said nothing and returned her eyes to her father.

Anik followed her gaze and replied, "Don't worry. He will be all right. Elasche was not lying when she said that she was a talented healer." A look of admiration crossed Anik's face as he spoke, and it filled the tone of his voice, "The moment she landed, she assessed the situation and went straight to work. She hardly knows Saliek-an Regithal but never hesitated once she knew his life was in danger." Kylie tensed at hearing that. She didn't like to think of her father's life being in danger. Anik continued, "Elasche worked tirelessly through the night, her Spirit guiding and speeding up the healing actions of his body. She is tired and weakened now but sounded confident that Saliek-an Regithal would heal up the rest of the way without her help." Anik ended his recalling with a self-assuring nod.

"It looks like one of the stone gargoyles hit him mid-flight. It must have had some serious spikes on its body to have punctured his stomach so deeply. The slicing and scrapes around the puncture indicate that the gargoyle must have shaken its head vigorously to get its spike out after it had impaled him." Anik's voice lowered before continuing, "Without Elasche's Spirit healing, he wouldn't have made it through the night." Kylie noticed Anik glancing at her out of the corner of her eyes before she began to needlessly examine one of her hands that were planted on the ground holding herself up.

Kylie owed the life of her father to this foreign princess. That was a debt that she was sure she could not repay anytime soon. Maybe Elasche could teach her how to treat wounds with her Spirit so that she wouldn't be helpless if this ever happened again? That thought faded quickly, as Kylie realized that it wasn't her inability to heal wounds that caused her failure, it was her inability to remain conscious while looking at a grievous injury. She wasn't sure if she wanted to get used to seeing wounds like that. Plus, how could she ask any more from this woman?

"Thank you, Anik, for relaying last night's events to me. I am really embarrassed that I couldn't stomach his wounds and at least help a little bit. I feel so useless. If you guys hadn't followed us, he... ugh... I don't know how I could have lived with myself," Kylie hadn't meant to be so honest with Anik, but he didn't seem to mind.

Anik sat down next to Kylie in the grass and wrapped his arms around his knees bringing them close to his chest. He talked quietly so only she could hear, "You know, as Zhannah and Elasche rushed to tend to Saliek-an Regithal last night, I took one look at his wound and felt terrified and queasy. I used you as an excuse to get away from the sight. I dragged you over here and watched over you as you slept. I've not gone back over since. All the information I've told you is because Zhannah has come back here to fill me in." He paused to let that sink in, "How about we both go over there now... together. It looks like they've cleaned and covered the wound well enough. It's possible that us weak-stomached creatures could tolerate being near him now." He needn't speak the part about the fear having abated now that imminent death wasn't in the air. Kylie understood. He got to his feet, offered her his hand, and gave her the same smile he had when he had first helped her mount Bandit.

Kylie felt better knowing that she wasn't the only one suffering from fear and inadequacy in this situation. Anik was right; they should go see how her father was doing now that he was bandaged up. She accepted his hand, and he pulled her up to her feet. In the brief moments that their hands were touching, she felt that his was trembling just as much as hers.

Chapter 21

The sky battled itself. Light tried to poke through the oppressive darkness, but darkness pushed back harshly believing only it could properly take care of the world that they encircled. The light persistently pushed on, until it finally occupied half of the sky around the world. Upon this day, the world underwent a wonderful transformation and thrived in the existence of both the light and darkness. As long as the balance was kept, the world continued to thrive.

Mory had not shown up for his sword practice that morning, but the bright sun shining through the sparsely clouded blue sky seemed to have lightened Zhannah's initial mood as she was making her way between her cabin and the Archives. The irritation that Zhannah had felt at the prospect of him sleeping in faded when she realized how hard she had been pushing the boy lately. It was just so important that he be ready as soon as possible to go to Krael so they could join the fight. Zhannah had been waiting almost twenty years now to return. The muted colors that painted the landscapes of Thaer, covered with a constant overlay of dusty browns could really dampen one's mood. Krael's brightly-colored landscape was fading into a dream world in Zhannah's mind. It might already have if it hadn't been for Zhannah's extended lifespan. Twenty years is a blink in time for one who's lived near 300. She also missed

Regithal and her pegasus, Storm. Zhannah pushed away those dismal thoughts and forced herself to not take her absence from Krael out on Mory. It may be that Mory deserved a respite. Whether or not that was true, she could not go completely easy on him for just not showing up at all this morning. Some sort of notification would have been appreciated. She replaced her thoughtful visage with a sterner one, preparing to scold him, as she opened the door to the Ancient Archives. Scilla was at the main desk area flipping through a book.

"Mory was not at practice this morning," Zhannah got straight to the point. "Has he come down from his room yet?" Scilla looked up from the book she was flipping through and met Zhannah's eyes. What Zhannah saw there alerted her that something was amiss. The paleness of Scilla's face amplified the red veins webbing through her eyes, and the purple bags wallowing beneath them indicated that she had not gotten much sleep the previous night. "What's wrong Scilla, did you see something important?"

Scilla put the book down on the desk and looked away from Zhannah, down into the halls of the Archives before speaking, "It's what I didn't see that was cause for last night's unrest." Zhannah felt that there was additional weight behind those words from Scilla's tone. Before she could ask, Scilla continued flatly, "Mory did not return here last night for supper, and he won't be returning here for a while." Scilla paused, returning her gaze to meet Zhannah's, "He's on Krael."

Zhannah felt fury build up within her for the second time this morning, "You knew he was leaving, didn't you? You never let me know! I could have prepared him better..."

Scilla raised her hand to stop the words cascading from Zhannah's mouth, "Yes, I knew he would go to Krael, but I hadn't known the precise timing. When he didn't return last night, I knew that was when. Zhannah, there is something I should let you know. Could you spare some time to listen?" Scilla had already begun walking away from her down the halls of the Archives, her tall boots clicking with her steps and long black dress rippling with her strides. Zhannah had no choice but to follow her friend in silence because she knew that if she started speaking again, her words would bite like the swords crossing her back in a battle. She would hear Scilla out. Her part in this was invaluable, and she deserved to relay her side of the story.

Scilla lead them to a comfortable alcove with two grey chairs adorned with red buttoned cushions. A pot of tea was set on the table in between them to share in conversation. Scilla motioned towards the chair and the pot. Zhannah took a seat pouring herself some of the aromatic tea. Cinnamon it would seem. Zhannah took a deep sip of the hot beverage and felt her inner rage calm slightly. She still didn't trust herself to speak kindly though. Scilla did the same, but following her deep sip, she began her confession.

Scilla had stationed herself in the Ancient Archives on Thaer a few years before Zhannah and Regithal had come with Kylie. She was a member of the Saliek but worked alone as many of the eldest Saliek did. As a seer, she let her visions guide her next steps across the universe, often planning decades or centuries ahead of the flow of time. She weighed in with the Saliek-an on occasion when her visions were of great importance and when she needed their help in shepherding the worlds down a path that didn't end in destruction. Scilla was one of the eldest members of the Saliek, pushing nearly 1000 years old in her immortal lifetime. She had known Andolin, the former Spirit Master, as a young man and was a trusted advisor. She had seen various worlds flirt with the brink of destruction only to return to a precarious balance between good and evil. She had orchestrated elaborate schemes, spinning complex webs of information that she had gathered from her network into coherent plans that gently guided the flow of time in the favor of good. She was a heroine in her own right, though songs of her great deeds would never be sung since she spent her life thwarting evil before it came, instead of defeating it on a battlefield.

All of this Zhannah had known, and she had always respected Scilla deeply for her contributions and knowledge. Over the past nineteen years though, Zhannah had become closer to Scilla as a friend and confidant rather than a mentor, and as such, sometimes forgot the reverence that was due to this accomplished woman. This was indeed one of those times. Zhannah couldn't help but feel betrayed by Scilla as she explained her most recent smoke and mirrors. Kylie was a decoy. Mory was who Scilla believed was the true Spirit Master of this age. Scilla had used her influence in the Arborian court to solidify the king and queen's surety of Kylie's powers and had arranged for her escape with the Saliek. Kylie was indeed strong in Spirit, but not in the same way as Mory. Scilla had lied about Mory's age to remove any thought that it was possible for him to be the Spirit Master and had actually rescued the boy herself from a burning building on Krael amidst the riots on the same night that Kylie had been flown away from her true mother's arms. Scilla did not go into the specifics about the boy's parents, but it seemed their fate had been a gruesome one that she could not thwart.

Scilla had foreseen Kylie's brother's dabbling with a greater evil to gain power for himself and had needed to draw his attention away from searching for the true Spirit Master with a decoy he could not resist: his sister. Instead of searching for the true Spirit Master, he wasted valuable time searching for ancient relics that even if he did stumble across, he wouldn't have had the means to repair or activate. Had he the true Spirit Master within his clutches, he would have been drawn to the relics, as Mory was now, or rather as Scilla hoped Mory was now. Scilla had explained to Zhannah that her foresight had ended last night. Everything that happened now was as unknown to her as an average person.

As Scilla returned to her sorrows at the loss of her lifelong gift, staring into her cup of tea, Zhannah felt as though she had wasted the last two decades of her life for naught. She understood the importance of it, but the sense of betrayal coursed like an acid through her veins. At least she had some time training Mory, but he would have been far more skilled in the sword had she enough time to train him properly. Scilla had apparently decided that his time was better spent in the library gaining knowledge than gaining physical strength. Zhannah looked upon the woman now, and her feelings softened. Before her was a morose woman who was mourning the loss of the tool that she had used all of her life to bring about her will. It was not only a tool to Scilla. It was her strength, her guiding light, and her treasure. The best Zhannah could liken it to, would be if she had lost one of her dual swords. She had depended on those tools her entire life. They were an extension of her being. Something tangible that she fully understood and took pride in that she could grasp for in her times of need as a base to keep her solidly grounded. Scilla had lost her version of Zhannah's dual swords, and now, in her time of need, had nothing to turn to. Her soul was wandering aimlessly.

Zhannah sighed in resignation and reached her hand out across the table as a peace offering. Scilla eyed it suspiciously. "Let's go together. Let's go to Krael and finish the path you've been cutting for years. We'll finish this the old-fashioned way," Zhannah offered as she winked and a mischievous glint crossed her eyes. Scilla continued to stare intently at her tea. Swirling it into a little whirlpool inside her cup. Zhannah tried again, "You know how your power has always been dampened on Thaer... maybe on Krael some of it will return." She thought she saw something spark in Scilla's eyes. Was that hope? Anger? Fear? It was too fleeting to tell. Regardless, Scilla removed one hand from her tea, and placed it on top of Zhannah's outstretched one and looked at her. Zhannah felt the frigid coolness of the tiny hand with black painted fingernails transferring into the wild heat of her own larger hand.

"To Krael we'll go. For better or worse," Scilla paused to look around the library, "There are too many memories here for me at the moment. It may do me some good returning to Krael for the time being. Let's spend the day making preparations and leave tomorrow morning."

Zhannah felt the giddiness of a child overcome her momentarily before responding, "As you wish, Scilla. I will meet you at my cabin first thing tomorrow morning. Let me know if you need anything before then." Zhannah got up to leave but felt Scilla's gaze penetrating her back. She turned to look at her friend once more.

In a quieter voice than Zhannah had ever heard Scilla use, she spoke, "Thank you Zhannah, for trying to understand... and for trying to help even if you couldn't fully."

Zhannah smiled in response, feeling proud of her results, "Anything for my friend." She pulled one of her swords from her back and saluted the small pale woman sipping tea before continuing her leave of the Ancient Archives.

***

Scilla looked back down at her cinnamon tea. She could see the remnants of the powder falling towards the bottom of the cup forming patterns at its base. Yesterday, those patterns would have meant something to her. Something would have clicked in her mind, and the future would have laid itself before her or at least one of the many paths it could take. She would have taken that future and noted it to be examined later along with other possible futures she had seen. Scilla would decipher the path of least resistance for all that was good in the world and do whatever was in her power to guide the river of time down the correct fork. Now that the future was no longer hers to see, the powder patterns were just random clumps and swirls at the bottom of a dish.

Maybe on Krael... no. She dared not hope. Loneliness and isolation had already engulfed her heart years prior, dark curtains drawn in on herself. She had foreseen her loss of the future as a young seer. Living her entire life knowing that her gift would one day be gone, she had cherished it, and searched endlessly for any path that would save her. Since she had seen no alternate path where the future was hers again, there must not be one. Yet still, she felt a slight flicker in her heart. A beam of light peeking through the drawn curtain. That fiery-tempered swordswoman always could light a fire when there seemed nothing flammable left. What a magnificent creature.

Scilla gathered the dishes from the table, placing them on the nearby flowered platter. The silence of the Archives was softened by the clinking they made as she bore them away. A warmth touched her back as the sun rose above the high window sill, infiltrating her dark realm. Scilla shivered slightly. It was during times like this that she thought he was here with her again embracing her warmly, telling her everything would be all right. Before she lost herself, she willed the curtains closed, and the warmth left her.

Chapter 22

He was trapped, bound in a cocoon of unknown origin upon entering his room. His own bed stood in the room's center beckoning to him to lie down. He shivered as something in the back of his mind reached out to him in warning. He would not be leaving this room. To the right of the bed was a window through which he could not see clearly, nor open. Succumbing to his fate, he laid himself down on the bed, as he was clearly expected to do… as he had known he had done countless times before. As soon as his head hit the pillow, a figure appeared outside the window, cloaked entirely in black, face hidden beneath the shadows of a sagging hood. "It is your time," an unknown, but strangely familiar, voice rasped from beneath the hood. Then it disappeared into the darkness outside the window once more clutching its staff.

Thick thorny vines began growing out of the bed, wrapping themselves around him as they lengthened. The more he struggled, the quicker they grew, thorns biting into his skin. Even when he stopped struggling, the vines continued to steadily entangle him. Eventually their grasp on him was so tight that he struggled to breathe. In one last gasping scream of pain, it was over. He floated over the bed staring at his own dead, bloody, mangled body, wondering how he had let himself become so irretrievably lost.

The castle was quiet as the evening passed into night. Prince Sonu could hear the chorus of crickets and frogs serenading the clear night sky as he paced his ornately-ornamented and orderly bed chambers. The noise grated on his conscience. The beauty of it made him jealous of all he was not, and his nearly overwhelming urge to control everything made it difficult for him not to imagine destroying every last singing creature so that he could have total peace and quiet. If he had the power he desired, he may have done just that at that moment. Instead, he strode over to the window and slammed the wooden shutters closed, drawing his red curtains shut across them to muffle the sound. He could still hear the songs if he strained himself, but he would just have to not do that for the sake of his sanity. His knuckles were clenched and pale from the blood being constricted from them for the last few minutes. He took a deep breath and unclenched them slowly, rubbing the feeling back into them as he sank into the large comfy chair at his desk.

The last few months had not been going well for Prince Sonu, and he found himself raging more often than normal to the detriment of the castle servants and his armies. He could hear the maid that he had punished earlier for not arranging his shoes properly still sniffling outside his door. Unfortunately, he had struck one her legs hard, so she would be there for a while until one of the other servants dared come near his door to retrieve her. The thought made him smile. He enjoyed the fact that the castle servants feared him. It gave him power over them. The way they looked down when he passed, not daring to meet his gaze, the way they hurriedly and meticulously met every demand he made of them, no matter how ridiculous, it gave him goose bumps just thinking about it. He actually didn't mind that he could hear the girl crying so near his door. It made him feel warm inside. Maybe he would make sure to peek outside soon so he could scare the others away from rescuing her, and so he could look at her red, tear-stained face. The thoughts that overwhelmed him at that moment made it difficult for him not to do that immediately, but he had work to do tonight.

Prince Sonu despised not being in control of every situation and not succeeding. He blamed all those surrounding him for his failures. He didn't understand why people would not just listen to his orders. If the maid had just followed his instructions, she would not be in the predicament she was in now. The decisions that he made were sound in every way. He needed no feedback from the other idiots in this world or any other worlds. His mind was far superior to all of theirs, and it wasn't his fault that they could not see the genius of his insight. After all, it was his master plan that forced his parents to run away from the castle, tails between their legs. It was his devising that led to the Saliek being misinformed at every move they made. They had even believed that Elasche was the one behind his devious plans! It was him who would soon be the ruler of as much of Krael as he could conquer, if only he could locate those cursed ancient relics!

Elasche, that irksome girl, tried his patience more than once trying to leave the castle. She had come close to the same fate as the young servant girl a few times, and only his impeccable restraint had saved her. He did not want to give her any additional incentive to leave, and if her family came to visit, he'd need to have her in prime showing condition. He had even locked her away in the nicest quarters of the castle with a view of his beautifully maintained fountain and gardens hoping that she would be less inclined to escape his clutches. With the amount of time that he was away from the castle, forcing him to leave her in the possession of the less skilled armed guards, he was always worried of a breakout attempt. He kept her bodyguard, Dainn, with him on his missions as insurance that she'd have to return for him. The girl seemed attached to the man, and admittedly, he had his uses in the field.

Prince Sonu doubled over as a nauseous feeling gripped his stomach, as it did when he was being called. It was a small price to pay for what he had been promised though, and it would go away as soon as he met his current Master's demands. The thought of having to call it "Master" amplified his sick feeling, but it was part of the arrangement. He looked up from the expensive baubles that were scattered across his desk to the mirror hanging on the wall. The mirror reflected more than merely his reflection. It reflected back his character as the evil he had bonded himself with stared back at him with his own eyes.

He felt its deep raspy voice reverberate through his body. It was almost as if he was being spoken to underwater, "You forget the part *I* played in your recalled successes." The voice reminded him, "Without me, none of this would be yours! Don't you ever forget that. You mustn't back down on our deal." The skin on his face in the reflection seemed to obtain a blackened purple hue.

"Never, Master," Prince Sonu responded, staring straight into the darkened, shadowed eyes in the mirror that overlaid his own. As much as it pained Prince Sonu to admit, it was right. The other servants of his Master across Krael had been organized to help his efforts, and his Master had bolstered his confidence so that he believed in his ability to do what was necessary. It was very important to his Master that the ancient relics of Ghaleon be found expediently. Prince Sonu had no real idea what exactly his Master was or why it needed those specific relics. He only knew that it wielded power so great that his un-Spirited body could feel it and that it had promised him the possession of one of Ghaleon's relics after all three had been mended by the Spirit Master and delivered. With a sword, shield, or cape of such powers, he would be sure to conquer Krael, and possibly other worlds if his hunger for power and order was not satisfied. He would only have to be rid of the Spirit Master of this age who Prince Sonu was quite sure he was in possession of at this time, whether it be his sister or his fiancé.

"You had best be planning your next expedition; I tire of watching your failures. I have been searching Krael for others such as you who are willing to do my bidding in exchange for the same rewards that I have offered you. I might actually select another one soon if you fail again," the voice threatened him, as it often did. Prince Sonu knew that he should be afraid of this force, but fear was a feeling that he had learned to suppress long ago, so instead he felt irritation at this creature and a rising anger at the fact that it dared to threaten him.

"Your dark thoughts give me hope, Sonu. Continue on," and with that the shadows across his eyes dispersed, and again he looked into his own green eyes, golden hair sweeping across his cheek, rose-colored from anger. Prince Sonu picked up a small golden globe bauble with a chain from his desk, intending to throw it at the mirror and watch it shatter in satisfaction, but he thought better of it at the last moment. He instead let the bauble fly towards the door, chain streaming behind it. It collided with a wooden thunk and a clink, leaving a small indentation before it fell to the floor. He grabbed a hunk of his hair in each hand and pulled until he could feel the pain of its tension. He hated that thing in the mirror and desperately wanted to destroy it. Letting go of his hair, he walked to the door to retrieve the globe, as it needed to be back in its place on the desk. Everything had its rightful place. Before kneeling to the ground, he ran his fingers across the newly marred door, feeling splinters of wood pricking his calloused fingers. Sometimes he forgot his own strength. He would send for someone to fix the door tomorrow.

Returning to his seat, Prince Sonu placed the globe back into its spot and unfurled a map of the area that he next planned to explore. He had brought it here from his library earlier. The ancient tales of Ghaleon's artifacts were all very consistent, but none went into the amount of detail that was needed to pinpoint the location of any of the relics. A forest, a desert, a mountain city... Yes, yes, he had been to many places that had matched those descriptions, yet none of them yielded the treasures that he sought. He was starting to think that maybe they were not located on Krael, but then he would have to find a way to travel to other worlds safely, and that seemed too ambitious at the moment. He wouldn't resort to that until he had exhausted all his options on Krael. Prince Sonu didn't want to work too hard without necessity.

His latest expedition, he thought, was quite clever. Within a cave far to the north, where the snow never ceased to blanket the ground and cold winds chilled the barren landscape, there was rumored to be a forest matching the descriptions in his books. He had only ever read of this forest in children's tales, but he had tried all of his rational options already. The creatures rumored to live there were unlike any that he had seen on Krael, if the children's tales were to be believed, and the magic there was unlike that seen anywhere else on Krael. This would be his furthest and most costly expedition yet, as he would have to make sure his armies were supplied for the cold and the possibility of not being able to find food in the snow-covered lands. He would also need to bring equipment for digging if the cave itself was buried…

Prince Sonu's mind entered the most peaceful state that he knew while he was focusing on the planning and logistics for his next mission. It was one of the clearest states his mind ever reached as the proper plans laid themselves out orderly before his demanding mind, and he took notes and drew routes and figures onto his maps. This was a time when the insanity abated into genius for a while. For as sure as his feelings were unlike the majority of those on Krael, his strategic mind when posed with a mission, exploratory or battle-oriented, could be surpassed by none. Anyone watching would never realize this, as when a particularly ingenious thought would cross his mind, he would giggle to himself, and the wild, passionate look overtaking his eyes would no doubt be construed as the raging look of a madman.

Prince Sonu continued his work long into the night, completely engrossed and unaware of the events happening just outside his closed window. Not even when the gargoyle above his room took off, throwing a trail of rubble against the shutters, did he flinch from his planning. The frogs and crickets continued their night song, and the young maid outside his door was eventually rescued by a fellow servant, unnoticed by Prince Sonu.

Chapter 23

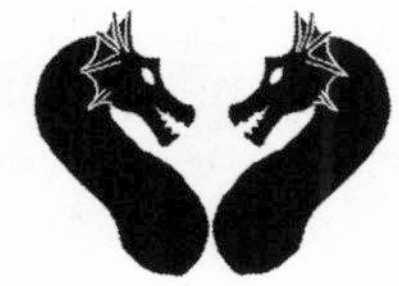

A golden lock of hair fell across the closed eyes of a sleeping boy. His head indented a plush, purple, silken pillow, and his hands were clutching an old stuffed bear. Sweat beaded on his furrowed brows as he tossed and turned through the night. His mind was filled with dreams of dragons and heroics, as most boys' dreams are, but his dreams were somehow different, more realistic, and they refused to release him. The night was a rough one for the dear boy, but the sun peeked through the curtains in the morning and warmed his flushed cheeks to awaken him from his nightmares. When the boy awoke, he looked the same as he had when he had fallen asleep, only slightly more disheveled, but in actuality, he grown into something much more powerful. An aura of strength, pureness, and light now surrounded the boy and his shadow stretched even further across the lands when he finally stood up out of bed.

Drips resounded hollowly and methodically in time to Mory's heartbeats, gently easing him away from the world of dreams and back to reality. He took a deep breath full of cool, damp air before opening his eyes. He sat up in the center of the floor, feeling the coolness of the ground on his legs and hands, and took in the situation. He had fervently hoped that his dreams had been reality, and this had been a nightmare, but everything here seemed too real. His sword was within arm's reach on the floor to one side of him, and the shield that he had acquired out of whim was on the other. In front of him, the abyss still stood as dark and ominous as ever, dragon tail lifelessly protruding from it.

Over his shoulder, the archway now lay open, rubble strewn around the entrance. The whole underground chamber was still splattered with black ooze that was starting to emanate a rotting odor. Much to Mory's dismay, it was splattered on his clothing and person as well. He brought the blackened ooze pasted onto his hand up to his nose and took a whiff. Fortunately, there was nothing in his stomach as he went through the motions of retching, abdominal muscles clamping down on his back-flipping stomach. After regaining his composure, Mory began to wonder just how long that he had been sleeping.

Vi was on his shoulder yawning and rubbing the sleep from her eyes. "So that all actually happened," she spoke in the most serious tone Mory had ever heard her use. So contrary to her usual upbeat self.

"Yea, I suppose it did," Mory said somewhat dejectedly, surveying the wreckage left in the room.

"I had hoped it was a nightmare," Vi shook her head, purple hair bouncing into her tiny face.

Mory nodded, sharing a glance with the fairy. The morose look on her face sliced into him as she stared at the ground, no doubt reliving the terror. He wanted to make her smile again, "Me too. But you know something, we made a pretty awesome team against the dragon. I mean, if it hadn't used its magic against us, we'd have totally gotten him without the help of the gargoyles!" Mory winked at Vi, whose spirits instantly inflated as she started zipping around Mory's head with a smile stretched across her face. Mory felt his own spirits lift off with the fairy. "I don't suppose you know how long we've been down here, do you Vi?"

Vi shook her head and responded shrugging her shoulders, "I fell asleep out of exhaustion about the same time you did."

"Well, I suppose we should get out of this grave now that we are both rested and awake," Mory sighed as he stood up and dusted himself off as best as he could. He collected his sword, put it back into its scabbard, and then looked over at the black-stained shield lying on the stone floor. Under the splotches of dragon blood, he saw the metal gleam in the dim light of the sconces. Something inside him was drawn to it. Mory couldn't explain it to himself, but he didn't think that he could leave without the shield. Maybe he was subconsciously grateful for its part in his survival. Whatever the reason, he retrieved the shield. He loosened the strap that had secured it to his forearm during the fight and slung it across his body to carry the shield on his back. It was surprisingly light. He looked around the room one last time before walking towards the archway and a set of stairs he could see beyond it. He knew that the events that happened in this room would haunt his memories forever and felt a tingle run down his spine.

Vi zipped over to the open staircase, and her glow illuminated the darkened corridor in a purple haze. Mory started ascending the first few steps when something caught his eye. In the center of the next step a small wooden kitten was curled into a peaceful resting position. Its wooden tail wrapped around its tiny paws, eyes closed, and wings nestled into its shoulders resting above its back. Mory reached out to touch the carving, but nothing happened. It was as if it had never been alive. He picked it up and immediately knew why it had seemed familiar before. It was the carving that Kylie had been working on in the library before she was taken to Krael with Regithal. Unbidden tears welled up in the corners of Mory's eyes, and the air stung as it flowed past them. A piece of Kylie had been there to help him earlier, and it had chosen to stay with him, for now. Mory refused to release the tears and brushed them aside, placing the kitten into his pack. A determined look crossed his face. He would make sure that he returned the carving to her safely, and in the meantime, it would keep him company. Just knowing that a piece of Kylie was close to him strengthened his resolve, and Mory continued to climb the ancient stairway.

Calves and glutes aching, breathing heavily, Mory finally reached the top. Vi had teased him endlessly during the climb insisting that she was the far more evolved creature of the two of them. After all, her legs didn't ache at all since her wings did all the work for her. In her opinion, they would have reached the top 'days' beforehand if Mory had a pair for himself as well. Mory had lost any idea of the passage of time other than pulling food from his pack to satisfy his stomach's rumbling hunger every so often, but he was quite sure it had not taken more than a day to ascend the staircase, contrary to Vi's jibes. Mory was beginning to think of what a nice purple lamp she would make if only he had a thick bottle to trap her in. One that sealed sound inside.

"Hey, why are you looking at me like that?!" Vi exclaimed. "That look in your eyes is downright devious."

Mory stifled a giggle at his internal joke. "Oh, it's nothing. Just thinking of how nice a lamp would be right now," he said with what he hoped was a straight face.

"We should have scavenged that area a little more before we left. I bet we would have found a lamp down there," Vi replied.

"We needed to leave that place, Vi. I had an eerie feeling that we were no longer welcome. We were lucky that nothing happened to us while we slept," Mory responded, unwilling to admit how terrified he actually was down there and that he hadn't really begun to think clearly until he had been about halfway up the staircase.

Mory turned his attention back to the staircase. It seemed to go straight into the ceiling. A dead end. There had to be some sort of trigger or something though. How else would all of those gargoyles been able to come fight on his behalf? Mory began searching the area by running his hand along the rough stone surrounding the staircase while Vi did a visual search, her purple glow lighting the way. Mory felt a cut in the rock that he thought was too straight to have been a natural formation and called Vi over to take a look at it. She flew along the cut and they found that it formed a rectangle above their heads. At the short edge of the rectangle there was an indentation in the stone that was large enough for a hand to grab and pull on. Mory and Vi backed away from under the rectangle, and Mory pulled down on the handle. He heard a click and a torrent of water came splashing down onto his face. Mory was beginning to be very sick of water incidents as he rubbed the water from his eyes. The stone door flipped down to reveal a ladder that was being drenched by the waterfall Mory had created.

Over the span of few seconds, the rush of water down the hole subsided into smooth fall of water around the edges of the hole with a rectangle of air in the middle. Vi burst through the thin wall of water and flew up and out of the staircase without prior warning. Determined to be out of this place and not be left behind, Mory stepped into the waterfall, grasped the slippery rungs, and climbed the short distance up into a pool of water. Without his weight on it, the door began to slowly close itself, sealing off the flow of water and allowing the pool to fill up again.

The crimsons and pinks of evening were beginning to fill the sky and reflected playfully off the blue waters of the fountain basin in which he was sitting. Brightly-colored petals from the late blooming trees of spring floated about him in the water and showered onto him in the evening breeze. Streams of black began to swirl out from himself as the dragon's blood was cleansed from him and his equipment in the fountain waters.

A reptilian foot carved of marble caught his eye beneath the black swirls, and he followed it up to the enormous fountain centerpiece of two dragons staring longing into each other's eyes, necks intertwined. It was beautiful. Mory was enthralled as he admired the curves of their backs, the breadth of their wings, and the swirls of peach and green intrinsic to the marble. Something this magnificent must have a story. Mory collected his items from the fountain basin after he thought most of the dragon blood was gone and sloshed over the side.

After a quick wring-out of his clothes, he searched the perimeter for a plaque of some sort that would tell him the story of these passionate dragons. He found one, but all it said was 'Arbore Castle'. Such a shame. The story must have been lost in time. A moment later something clicked in Mory's head. Arbore Castle! He was where he needed to be! Mory was able to put a bit of bounce in his step now.

Vi splashed around playfully in the water as Mory concluded his search. "Oh! The wondrous feeling of being clean!" she exclaimed in her high-pitched fairy voice while tossing a spritz of water into the air around her, no doubt from the happiness of being rid of the vile dragon blood. Mory whole-heartedly agreed with her. He pulled out the memory sphere from his pack and sat on the edge of the fountain basin as Vi floated peacefully on her back in the water with pink aromatic petals surrounding her purple body. The Saliek camp was in the mountains surrounding Arbore, somewhere. Somewhere looked quite large as he scanned the map for any promising areas. Mory took out the cat and absentmindedly stroked it while he pondered his next path.

***

The jolting of the cart was less than comfortable as Mory spit out some straw from his mouth, blowing it away from his face as best he could. Even though Vi's magic kept him invisible, he had decided it was prudent to remain hidden regardless. He was currently huddled within a pile of straw on the back of a trader's horse cart, contemplating the real risk of leaving his hiding place because wherever the straw touched his skin, it would tickle and itch horrifically. It was as if tiny bugs were crawling over his skin and were ceaselessly biting him. He shivered at the thought. It then occurred to him, that truly might be the case in this pile of straw, and he slowly inched his way out of the pile to join the rest of the goods on the trader's cart. Mory frantically brushed his hands all over his body to hopefully brush away any unwanted insects. A large cylinder of cheese was conveniently located between where he sat and the back entrance to the covered cart. He would rather rely on the mirage magic, which had not failed him yet, than sit in that pile of straw for another minute.

After re-provisioning and resting through the night in Arbore, Vi had helped him hitch a ride with one of the traders outbound from Arbore in the morning. The maps in the memory sphere indicated that Mory would first have to leave the Arbore area through Sentinel's Gate, the only pass in the Sentinel Mountains he could see on the map. The paths into the mountains outside the pass were much more gradual than the steep slopes that fell into the Arbore area, making it easier for him to explore.

So far, his trip had gone well, and the covered cart provided him with suitable comfort and protection from the elements. He had only had one hiccup in his plans thus far when a dog caught a whiff of his scent and almost gave away his hiding spot before the trip had begun. Mory had been lucky enough to have been out of sight from the owner of the dog, who just told his dog to calm down. Soon he would be through the pass, and he hoped his nervousness would dissipate as he started off on his own again.

In the late afternoon, Mory overheard the traders speaking of the pass ending soon. After a couple days of bumping around in the back of a cart, Mory was thrilled to hear it! He opened the flap of cloth that created a little window in the covered cart and peeked outside. Through the dirt being kicked up into his face by the cart, he could see that they were nearing the end of a long corridor of rock. Mory gathered his belongings swiftly and quietly, making his way towards the back of the cart. The horses were being held at a steady walk for the safety of the traders' goods on board while traversing the rocky ground of the pass, and so Mory hopped out of the back of the cart with minimal trouble, Vi following beside him. They hid behind a large boulder until their ride had moved sufficiently far away from them.

The canyon carved into the rock behind him was incredibly deep. Mory wondered if an ancient river had flowed through here long before the city of Arbore had been erected, its lifetime etched in the various colored layers of sediment stacking up to the top of the canyon. He walked over to the beginning of the cliff, where he examined the reddish layer that was just about his height. If he looked close enough, he thought he could see imprints of the bones and shells of creatures long dead. He ran his fingers along the creatures, dead in life, but frozen forever in time within a piece of nature's artwork and smiled at the wonder of it all. A bird screeched in the blue skies above, bringing him back to his current time.

Mory began his trek out of the last bit of the canyon and searched for any path or trail that might lead him closer to the Saliek camp or at least somewhere he could make a safe camp for the night.

Chapter 24

He bid his Ghost back into the land of living. A partner must be found for the young Master adventuring on his own, and the conventional means were not in play. He touched his two forefingers to Ghost's forehead and wished him luck. Ghost spirited through the forests, fields, mountains, and deserts of Krael searching for the one. He found him, alone and headstrong, in the mountains near Arbore. Ghost inhabited his body for a brief moment, and the stallion understood and began his journey. Ghost returned once more to the land beyond the living and was highly praised.

A cool breeze rustled through the canopy of trees Mory had begun hiking in, allowing the light of the moon to flicker in through the wavering leaves and dapple the moss-covered forest floor on this peaceful night. He had found a relatively level area on the slight incline he had been climbing and constructed a crackling fire, unrolling the bedroll that he had acquired in Arbore near it. After his re-provisioning in Arbore, he now needed to find ways to pay back people both there and in Mahashta. Mory sighed in resignation. A small rodent he had captured was roasting over the fire for his evening meal, and the smell and sizzle were making his mouth water. He couldn't wait a moment longer and removed it from the flames and sunk his teeth greedily into the meat. He offered some to Vi, but she politely declined preferring to forage the forest for food closer to her liking.

Licking the juices from his fingers, Mory heard the bushes whisper and saw a flash of purple through the brush. Eyes. He felt fear compress in his chest and then drop to his stomach. He was being hunted. Mory shook the thought from his head. No, that was just his mind playing games with him while he was alone in the dark. Vi had promised not to go further than the mirage magic would reach. Mory began scanning the perimeter of his camp for any trace of her purple glow to comfort himself in her presence. At worst, some animal had smelled his cooking. Failing to locate Vi, Mory held very still for the moment, trying not to shift or make any movement that could cause a sound. After what seemed an eternity, a massive horse-like creature emerged slowly from the brush. Its ears were slightly larger than expected and its fur coat white, smooth, and shining. Not very conducive to hiding in the green forest at night. Its nose and feathered feet were a shade too dark to be distinguished in the minimal light. Once it had fully revealed itself from the bushes, Mory saw that it had magnificent, powerful, feathered wings tipped in the same darkness of its feet and nose. Even though Mory had thought that he was invisible, the creature seemed to stare right into his eyes.

Fear began to overcome Mory, and he slowly began to reach for his sword to defend himself or scare the creature away. Partway through the motion, the creature cocked its head ever so slightly, blinked, and bowed its head as if in greeting. Mory halted his reach for his sword and instead felt drawn to the creature. Something inside of him wanted to give the creature a chance. Not only a chance, but he felt compelled to trust the creature, as incredulous as that sounded in these circumstances. Deciding to be wary in case there was some sort of magic happening of which he wasn't aware, Mory stood up slowly and took a step towards the white pegasus. It perked its ears up at the movement and began trotting off down a path. Mory, unable to let the beauty of the creature leave his sight, followed it. The creature created the illusion of floating away from him since the dark feet blended so well into the night.

Moments later, the pegasus disappeared. Not into the brush, but into thin air. Mory caught up to the place where he had last seen the tail of the creature flicking in the moonlight. All that was there was a large boulder. Mory looked over his shoulder, and noted that his campfire was still within sight, so he didn't feel as vulnerable as he could have otherwise. He sat down on the soft, green grass in front of the boulder, twisted a piece of it up from the ground, and began to nibble on it. He could taste the sweetness of spring while he let his mind wander off in his thoughts of the mysterious winged horse.

Suddenly, something grabbed his belt, and he felt warm slobber dribble down his backside as wet lips pressed against his back before he was suddenly yanked backwards. Bracing himself for the clunk of the boulder against his skull that never came, Mory fell backwards into a cold, wet pile of snow. The shocking change of temperature was almost as painful as a clunk in the head would have been. The snow on his unprotected ears stung as if he were being burned.

Mory got himself up quickly, shaking the snow out of his pant legs and hair, and stood in the shin deep blanket that extended as far as he could see. Behind him sat a boulder identical to the one in the forest he was just in. It must have been another warp gate. Someone should really label those blasted things. The pegasus was nowhere to be seen, but Mory had no doubt that it was its slobber on the small of his back drying in the chilly wind. He pulled his shirt over the top of his pants to block the chill. It was a silent night, wherever he was, and winter had a steady hold on the season. The blanket of snow surrounding him was growing deeper each passing second as the big flakes floated lazily from the sky to the ground.

Mory turned his face upwards, flakes swirling around him as the moonlight softly illuminated his body, and was awestruck. He had never seen such a breathtaking sight in his life. There were stars… Millions, no billions, of them… More than he had ever seen in his life. Some of them were large and bright, others just a dusting across a never-ending, impossibly dark blue palette. The only light dimming their brilliance was that of a moon over-shadowing those that were too near its yellow halo's glow. Each star, a sun with possibly its own solar system. A sun with its own life force, allowing others like him to create their own stories in life.

There was a fracture across the center of the sky. Deep black starbursts stark against a pale pink haze faded into light oranges and then a pale green sparkle around the edges of the fracture. Mory was gazing into the history of the galaxy, for the light that was being shed from those stars had taken near an eternity to reach his eyes here on Krael. He wondered if another being was staring at the same scene from a place far far away, and if they had a strong enough telescope, could they see the past of Krael? Would they be able to watch the story of the passionate dragon fountain transpire and anything else since the beginning of time here? Could Mory himself gaze into the moment of creation if he let enough light from the furthest reaching stars gather in his pupils?

He had read much about what was known of his solar system and the galaxy that held it. He had even read about how there were other galaxies, yet unexplored, beyond it, but nothing he had read could compare to what he was experiencing right now. It was a feeling of insignificance and awe when facing all that there was, mixed with hope and joy that there was indeed something more than his plain, ordinary life, topped off with the wonder at how it all came to be.

A flash of light traced across the sky releasing Mory from his ponderings as his eyes followed its trail. A tear of the sky... a shooting star... a meteor burning up in Krael's atmosphere was coming closer than Mory had ever seen. Its light streak disappeared into a darkened forest on the horizon briefly illuminating the barren trees prior to its impact. The night sky was weeping, and he wanted to go find its tear, the meteorite, left behind. He needed to. Maybe he could make the sky smile again. But his body yearned for warmth as he shivered in the solitude of the snowy night, and Mory was only able to stop himself from running into the white-filled darkness towards where he believed the star had landed, by promising himself that he would come back prepared for a journey across the frozen plain.

Reluctantly, Mory turned his face away from the ever-clear sky and back to the rock portal from which he had come. In less than three steps, he was back into a spring forest night. What had felt like a chilly night before seemed like a warm blanket enveloping him. He ambled back over to the campfire, hoping to find warmth and a place to dry off from the melted snow that had found its way into his boots. Instead, he found an infuriated Vi circling the fire.

"What do you think you were doing wandering off like that? I was worried sick about you! You could have been eaten, or gotten lost, or who knows what out there in this unknown forest," her tiny tirade continued in earnest for a few minutes straight before she realized that Mory was not listening or even paying attention to her. He had sat on an overturned tree trunk and was staring into nothingness, clutching the wooden cat in both his hands, a helpless, lost look in his eyes.

How could he give up his hunt for the Saliek camp and finding Kylie? It had taken the return to the forest where a canopy protected him from the allure of the night sky before he started to consider what his impulse for chasing a fallen star in an unknown location would mean. The pull had been so strong in the moment. It had seemed so unbelievably right and necessary to find the sky's tear. It was the powerful feeling that only he could console its sadness. His emotions tore this way and that at the confused longings of his heart until his mind was feebly able to inject something remotely intellectual. He had to adjust his perspective and not view this as a choice that needed to be made but as a sign showing him the way in the darkness. He didn't really know that Kylie was at the Saliek camp. He had just assumed that it was the most likely place for her to be. It was possible that the stars were weeping for his separation from the other half of his soul and guiding him to the correct place! Who was he to ignore the signs given to him from the stars? A warm feeling of happiness washed over him as he knew what he would do…what he had to do.

"Are you okay, Mory?" Vi inquired hesitantly.

Mory refocused his eyes to see Vi hovering in front of his face and put on a smile, "Yes, I am, now that I know the way."

Vi gave him a slightly confused look, and he filled her in on what had just transpired. She wanted desperately to see the beautiful sky that Mory had painstakingly tried to describe in words as he assured her it was far more fantastic in real life. Mory promised her that he would show her, but he wasn't sure if he could make it through the portal and back again without some rest. Knowing that it could take many days to prepare, they would start early the next morning to gather and create what they could from the forest to make a journey through the cold, snowy lands bearable.

Vi had forgotten her previous tirade and was bouncing in contagious anticipation for the upcoming day. The sunrise could not come quickly enough for her. Mory felt the same way as he laid down in his cozy bedroll. Dreams of a white pegasus with purple eyes danced through his consciousness as he entered the world of dreams, showing him the way through drifts of snow and a barren forest. It took sudden turns in a flourish of snow, weaving in and out of dark, sleeping trees, stopping in some locations, and swiftly passing through others. There were places where it would stare deeply into his dream-self's eyes, imparting a sense of warning. Mory realized then that the journey ahead of him may not be as simple as deciding to take it, but the possible rewards at the end outweighed the consequences in his mind. He would have to stay strong and remember the reason he was doing this, even if everything seemed to have abandoned him. If he could manage that, all his longings, fantasies, hopes, and dreams would be at his fingertips, and he could find eternal happiness. If only he could remain strong in his resolve. The dream pegasus seemed to approve of his mindset and continued bounding along the snow-covered paths of Mory's dreamland, giving him a glimpse into what his future contained.

Chapter 25

A cauldron of liquids hangs over a smoldering flame. They are each separated, like oils in water, either refusing to or unable to intermingle with one another. Stagnant void bubbles hover within each liquid. A spoon begins to stir the liquids together, and a poker wakes the fire. The stirring steadily increases in speed as the fire heats the cauldron. After some time, the originally stubborn liquids have blended into a solution. The stirring slows, and the heat dies down, but the once separated liquids have now congealed together to create one shining silver mixture, refusing to separate.

Regithal had been sleeping soundly for a few hours, wounds steadily healing, and everyone had congregated around him participating in idle conversation awaiting Elasche to deem him ready to be on the back of a pegasus again. Elasche was looking more rested as well, as she no longer required Dainn to support her weight when sitting. Kylie's mother had filled her in on how she had arrived in Krael, and Kylie was excited to hear about how Mory had fared in her absence. Her mother glowed about his talent in sword training, and Kylie hoped that he wouldn't get himself into any situations on Krael that would require his newfound skill. It hardly surprised her that Mory had somehow stumbled his way onto Krael. He always had a knack for being drawn towards trouble. She hoped that they could find him soon.

Anik and her mother froze at the same time, ending the conversation abruptly. Both scanned the edges of their vision without moving their heads, then looked to each other. “Something’s in the forest... watching us,” Anik stated.

Kylie’s mother nodded, “Not something… some things. Everyone act as natural as possible for the moment. If they attack, we’ll defend, but otherwise we stay here. Elasche, can Regithal be moved safely yet?”

Elasche thought about it for a moment tilting her head slightly and touching her finger to the corner of her mouth, “It’s still possible for the healing on the inside of his body to come unstitched. I could put more effort into the healing now, but I worry that then we would just be switching him for me.” Elasche folded her hands into her lap with a serious look on her face.

Kylie’s mother understood what Elasche was saying and made a decision, “We’ll stay then. You and Dainn will sit near Regithal’s side while Anik, Kylie, and myself will protect you.”

Dainn interjected with his deep seldom used voice, “I will help fight too. Elasche is well enough to sit next to Regithal. Fighting is what I am trained for. I will not stand by and be protected when I can contribute.”

“Then the four of us will defend as best we can. If my senses are correct, there are firelings in the forest as well as a few other types of demonic creatures. They will most likely attack us.” Her mother subtly shifted herself into a position from which she could readily stand.

Kylie had never fought a fireling before, although she remembered seeing them on the day that she had left Thaer, burning Liri to the ground. They were not very large creatures, but she would be in close combat with her knife, so their horns could be deadly if she miss-stepped. Before she could think any more on her strategy, a fireball roared through the air towards their little camp. A gust of wind precisely swirled about the projectile, extinguishing the fire, and then veered it off its course. Anik was staring at it in deep concentration until it safely crashed into a clear section of grass. A sudden assault of firelings came charging out of the woods towards them screeching a horrible battle cry, claws and weapons raised and ready. Within seconds, the charge was slowed and then halted as the ground beneath their feet turned soft. Sucking sounds could be heard as disgruntled firelings tried in vain to remove their feet from the muddy ground. Before their attention was brought back to the battle at hand, her mother had rushed in, beheading the lot of sunken firelings.

Outside the reach of the newly created quicksand pit, a few stragglers had reached Kylie who was putting her years of practice to good use. Her mind had entered a state of calm concentration as she skillfully sliced the tender necks of her attackers as they approached. They did not seem to focus much on defense of their vitals and instead put all of their effort into violent attacks. They rarely coordinated an assault, instead coming at her one at a time, resulting in an easy dispatch. When her assailants stopped appearing, Kylie looked back towards her comrades. Anik was taking care of crowd control of the groups of firelings that would emerge from the forest with his Spirit training in the elements. A large monster Kylie had not seen before was engaged in battle with her mother and Dainn. It had spider-like legs with a demon-like torso and head. They seemed to have it under control. Even the pegasi were doing their part; they had grouped together and with hooves flying would rear up and trample any of the tiny firelings that got too close. Even the larger creatures seemed loathe to mess with three war-trained pegasi.

A shadow briefly hovered over Kylie before she dodged quickly, rolling to one side. A giant creature with six muscled arms, furry clawed feet, and a bird-like head had swung a war hammer in her direction. It thumped the ground, sinking into the soft grass. Kylie took her opportunity and sliced at the creature as swiftly and precisely as she could, aiming for what she intuitively hoped were its vitals. Its skin was as tough as scaled armor though, and her knife refused to cut through its neck or torso. It was almost as if it were made of a similar material as the breastplate that it wore. If her mind had not been locked into its battle mode, she might have felt annoyance at this, but in her current mental state, her mind fluidly moved onto finding another solution. The creature had now recovered the hammer from the ground, and Kylie had to back away quickly to not take a hit. Dainn leapt in over her head landing on the back of the creature who even made Dainn's imposing figure seem small. He wrapped his own arms around the feathered neck of the creature and began compressing, forearms and biceps bulging with a single tattoo glowing red as he did so.

The creature violently shook, trying to fling Dainn from its back, but his vise-like grip held strong. Eventually, it was forced to relinquish its hammer as it tried to break Dainn's grasp with more of its hands. Kylie took advantage of the moment to harry the monster with her knife attacks but was still unable to find any place where she could break its rough skin. Eventually, the screeches that had been coming from its beak slowed and then stopped. Slowly, the creature began to topple over its own weight. Dainn's arms were still wrapped about its neck when it fell to the ground with a great thud. His forearms were bloodied where the claw like fingernails had sliced his skin, but other than that, he was not too much worse for wear. The beak of the creature had not been able to reach him where he had secured himself on its back. "Spirits burn this scurgel!" he swore as Kylie helped to pull him out from under the creature that she now knew was a scurgel.

The battlefield looked devoid of movement when she next scanned it. Anik was surveying the area with scrutiny, glowing orange hair plastered to his forehead, black cloak billowing in the wind. Her mother was inspecting the corpses lying about, nudging them with one of her swords. Kylie assumed this was to make sure they were all as dead as they appeared. Dainn went back to Elasche's side who was intently looking at the ground as she knelt near Kylie's father. He put his finger under her chin and raised it up so she would be looking into his eyes and spoke some words softly before embracing her and running his large hand through her wind-tangled jet-black hair comfortingly. Kylie thought she may have seen a tear fall from Elasche's face, but it could have just been some battle debris flying through the air. Her father was still fast asleep, sitting against his rock.

Her mind was slowing emerging from her battle mode, and she began to feel exhaustion creep over her from the recent battle. She walked over to Anik, carefully avoiding the pools and streams of blood that stained the bright green landscape. She kept a clear watch on his back while he continued searching for any latecomers. They stood silently for a moment, until he spoke, "I think they are gone for now. I saw a human-shaped figure holding a staff draw back into the depths of the woods after the last fireling wave. Its face was shadowed by a hooded cloak, but since it disappeared, no more monsters have emerged. It couldn't have been Sonu. There was no way for him to have gotten out here so quickly." Kylie hummed her agreement and began attempting to connect any dots in her head as to who the masked culprit could be.

"Zhannah is searching for any remnant of who could have been controlling the firelings. They are creatures that usually need to be bribed, tortured, or enticed in some way to fight for someone and usually carry their prizes on their person," Anik continued. "I've never seen them in this large of numbers in my entire life. They usually wander around in small bands, causing minor disturbances wherever they go, but coordinated assaults with multiple bands I've not heard of happening naturally before." There was a troubled thoughtfulness in Anik's voice.

Her mother made her way back through the carnage and stopped a few feet from them. She looked particularly frightening with a battle glow still raging in her eyes and a smattering of blood covering her clothing and yellow braid. The braid's normally golden color was enhanced by her pulsing Spirit energy, which Kylie noted, was a sun-colored yellow here on Krael. Frustration was plainly evident in her voice, "Nothing. Nothing at all! I don't get it! In all my years, firelings have always been the most predictable of all the irritating creatures in this world, and now I can't find a single item or marking to trace back." She turned away from them and began pacing back and forth, blonde braid whipping around with each turn of her heel. After her frustration had visibly fizzled down and she had ceased her pacing, Anik told her about the cloaked figure he'd seen. After pausing to think, her mother responded, "I'll plan to stop at the library when we return to the Saliek camp to do some research, or at least I'll ask Scilla to do some research since she is no doubt already ensconced with the books there looking for a way to find the artifacts mentioned in the tale of Ghaleon. Maybe there is some historical account of similar events happening in the past."

Kylie and Anik agreed with her assessment, and they made their way back over towards the rest of the group, each of them still alert to any changes to the current calm of the battlefield. Once they had all sunk down around the smoldering fire, Kylie noted that if Elasche had been at all upset earlier, she had pulled herself together and looked completely normal now.

"Kylie, I noticed that when you fought, you never once used your Spirit to aid you," her mother observed. "When we get back to camp, I'll try to take some time to teach you how I use it to amplify my ability with my swords by increasing my speed, precision, and concentration."

Her father's voice interjected hoarsely, "And I will, as well!" Everyone turned to look at him now that his eyes were partially open, and he tried to put a small smile on his face. "What did I miss?"

Kylie couldn't help herself, and a loving giggle bubbled out of her. She wasn't quite sure what made the situation amusing to her, but it seemed to merit a giggle. The crew filled him in on the battle that had just ended, and he claimed that he could not remember hearing a single bit of it. He thanked them all for looking out for him and especially Elasche for fixing him up so well. She blushed slightly at his compliments and asked him how he was feeling. He responded weakly, "I feel better than I did last time I was awake, that's for sure, but my abdomen hurts each time I move." He winced as he shifted his position slightly.

"That's not surprising," Elasche said. "You took a pretty big gouge from a gargoyle."

"Mmmmmm, yes, I remember that," her father recalled. "I thought I'd be fine if I could at least make it to the Saliek camp, but it looks like I misjudged the seriousness of the wound. I'll try not to do that again!"

Kylie's mother snorted and turned her back towards him, "Yea, that's what you always say, until the next time that it happens!"

"Awwww, you were just worried about me, that's

all," he gave her a slight playful nudge with his hand and as big of a smile as he could muster. "Elasche, when do you think I'll be able to leave this place. It's obviously not safe. The sooner we can get back to a known safe area, the better for us all."

Elasche nodded, "I understand. I think that after a full night's rest we should be able to prop you up on Valor with someone riding double and get you back to the Saliek camp to finish recuperating."

"Well, I think I'll start that process now then…" and with that Kylie's father dozed back off into the dream world, leaving the wearied group with more hope now that he seemed to be well enough to converse.

Chapter 26

Fireflies flit about a field during a peaceful night as a pale woman in a dark cloak strolls through the knee-high grass. Their lights are slowly pulsing on and then off, illuminating small patches of the darkened field. She is drawn to the firefly whose lighting rhythm matches that of her own heartbeat. She holds out her hand, and it flies willingly onto her palm. It closes its wings around the lighting bud on its back, but she can still see its glow. Gently, she cups her hands around the tiny bug, trapping it within her palms. The moment she can no longer see the light of the firefly, despair overtakes her being, and she collapses to the ground, releasing the firefly from her grasp. The woman scrambles to find the firefly once more, but when she looks around, she is surrounded by darkness. She kneels down on the ground and weeps. Under the breast of her cloak, a beating light awaits her to find it once again.

Scilla had found the library at the Saliek camp and tried to make herself at home knowing that the majority of her time would be spent there. It was easily the largest structure in the camp and the only one intended to be permanent. Its walls were made of large interlocking grey stone blocks standing like a castle in the center of the Saliek camp. The exterior was sparsely decorated, as it was built with the intention to survive an assault rather than impress a crowd. The basement floor, where she was now, was Scilla's favorite place to be. It lacked the large clear windows that flooded the upper floors with light. Her pale, delicate skin could not withstand the intense light for long. It was a remnant of where she had grown up as a child.

Royal purple banners edged with a gold trim featuring a rearing white pegasus, the Saliek emblem, were draped in even intervals across the interior walls of library. In between every other set of banners were portraits of the Saliek'ans of the past. The bookcases were in orderly lines with every other row exchanging the end bookcases for a wooden table and chairs, allowing the rows of bookcases to give those studying at a specific table some semblance of privacy.

Scilla sighed deeply, gazing at the stack of books on the table relating to Ghaleon that she had already read through and began thumbing the pages of the one she was currently studying. This library did not feel the same as the Ancient Archives, and a slight homesickness had crept over her since leaving. In the years that she had lived there, she had become attached to it. The ancient lore that was intrinsic to the Archives had rung through her veins, easing the tension that the years of her life had put on her mind. Scilla was not of Krael or Thaer. Her home planet was all but forgotten in her mind, and she could no longer even recall the name. Whether that was because her mind had subconsciously blocked it or because it had been so many years since that piece of information had last mattered, she didn't know.

That planet was where her foresight had come from. It was a magic different from those practiced widely on Krael but was a common blessing around her first home. Living in a world where everyone could see the possible trails of the future to some extent was very different from living on either Thaer or Krael. The possible trails were infinite and ever changing. Each person could try to alter events so that the future they wished for would come to pass, but inevitably other people would alter something else ever so slightly, ensuring that nothing could ever be guaranteed. The most relaxed and arguably wisest of the residents of her home planet were those who completely ignored their talents and lived life as it happened to them. The downside being they swiftly became the tools of others. The chaos had been unbearable for Scilla, and after a series of unfortunate events, she had found herself on Krael, unable to return home.

Initially, she had been scared and lonely, but the predictability and controllability of this world had boosted her spirit. She found her way into Arbore where her talent was easily appreciated, and she advanced rapidly from there. That was where she had met Andolin. They had been fast friends and worked together often to thwart demons and dangers from various parts of Krael to maintain peace. They hadn't meant to fall in love, but can anyone really plan genuine life-lasting love? When they had realized it themselves, they decided to keep it quiet, sneaking off into quiet corners to embrace for fleeting moments and stare affectionately into each other's eyes. They were both people of high importance in the Arborian court and neither knew if it was socially acceptable. Eventually, they ceased caring what others thought, as they knew Andolin's time on this world was limited, and this was the only life that they could remember living.

Andolin was the reason that Scilla had carried on until now, and it was because of his loss that she simultaneously wanted to give everything up. A constant battle of wills raged in her mind and heart. This quest that she was on to ensure Mory ascended to his rightful title of Spirit Master was all for Andolin. She had promised him that she would lead the world to peace as best as she could, even after he was gone. It had proven more difficult now than when she had made the promise with him at her side, but she knew it was necessary. No one else was in a better position to do so. Deep down she also knew that he wanted to make sure she had a purpose to live, a reason to not voluntarily follow him into the afterlife. He had valiantly tried to protect her, even in death. Her life was eternal unless she were to be killed, thanks to the Saliek initiation ritual. Andolin had been fated to live 1000 years to the day.

As it did each time that she thought too much of Andolin, a void opened in her heart, darker than the world she was doomed to live in now that the light he had shone on her was extinguished. It slowly expanded until she could feel a physical pain in her chest threatening to make her collapse in agony. She clutched frivolously at her chest, looked to the ceiling, and waited for it to pass. The grasp that it held her with refused to release until she could drag her mind away from his memory. How pathetically cursed she was. Her happiest memories in life were with him, but each time she recalled them, a pain so deep would overtake her existence that she could not focus on anything else until it had dissipated. The pain was worth it though. The years of happiness and joy that they had shared were feelings worth any amount of torture that she needed to endure now. They would be reunited eventually. She knew it had to be true, or she risked losing her mind.

A loud thudding of boots on stairs announced Zhannah stampeding into the basement. After the thudding stopped, the large wooden doors at the bottom of the stairs slammed into the stone walls as Zhannah pushed them slightly too hard. She winced abashedly at her mistake and then carried on down the aisles of books to find Scilla sitting silently at one of the tables. Scilla was glad for the interruption, hoping that the void would release her heart soon.

"That incorrigible man!" Zhannah exclaimed plopping herself across the table from Scilla. "I swear he thinks that he is invincible just because he has eternal life. What kind of fool doesn't let others know when he is mortally wounded? I'm married to a fool, Scilla, a complete utter fool! The worst thing is, this isn't the only time he's done it!" Zhannah was holding her shaking head between her hands, elbows on the table.

Scilla knew she was referring to Regithal and felt the edges of her mouth twitch slightly upward. She spoke soothingly to Zhannah, "Hush, child. Is he all right now? You should be with him. There may come a day that you wish you had spent more time at his side."

Zhannah calmed slightly, "Yes, he is doing well now. Elasche fixed him up, and with the help of the healers here, he should be as good as normal tomorrow. He is actually the one who suggested that I come find you and ask how your studies have been going. Have you found anything of use to us in locating the ancient relics of Ghaleon?"

Scilla put down the book that she had been studying and started leafing through her notes that she had taken, pushing her glasses snugly onto her face. Thoughtfully she said, "I did actually find something noteworthy and obscure enough that it may have been overlooked for years by treasure hunters." Scilla found what she was looking for in her notes and put them down as she pulled a thin book out of the stack at the table. She opened up the children's book to the page she had indicated in her notes and slid the open book across the table for Zhannah to read. She seemed mildly surprised at first to be reading a children's book, but the confused look in her eyes swiftly changed into a mischievous smirk.

"You are brilliant, Scilla!" Zhannah stated matter-of-factly with a big smile on her face.

"Of course, I am," Scilla said with a flick of her wrist

as she sat up a little straighter and winked at Zhannah who chuckled.

The book told the tale of a young boy who lived in a frozen northern world where the suns stayed up all night or hid all day depending on the season. He would go out to play in the snowy land and come back with wild stories of a beautiful, warm, fruitful forest with magical creatures unlike those he had ever seen and the greenest of trees with wide, circular trunks that towered nearly to the sky. All the children enjoyed his stories, but their parents thought he was just inventing them to bring attention to himself. They scolded him often, chasing him away from the other children until he was a known outcast. He would try to convince others to come along with him so he could show them around his secret forest, but the parents of the other children never let them go, even if he could convince one of them. One day the boy disappeared and never returned to his frozen home. His parents mourned him for dead, while the others secretly were relieved that they no longer had to protect their children from the crazy boy.

Many years down the road, a difficult year came around where food was scarce, and many of the villagers died of starvation. A strange young man came to visit the village and only said the words, "Follow me; you'll be safe." The people were in such dire need that many followed the stranger willingly, including the parents of the lost boy. The young man took them on a journey through a dark cave, and when they exited the other side, warmth and beauty was laid out for all to see. An abundance of creatures frolicked through the trees and fields of the colorful forest. When all had thanked the young man for saving their lives, he approached a woman who had tears streaming down her cheeks. Through choking sobs, she managed to say, "I am sorry, son. I should have believed in you." The young man embraced her as her tears flowed freely, forgiving his mother for her mistake that she had made so many years ago.

"So, you think there is a hidden forest in the Frostlands?" Zhannah inquired.

Scilla nodded, "It's the best lead I have so far, so it is probably worth investigating. I will stay here and continue my research if you and Regithal can gather and supply a party to go investigate. I will attempt to narrow down the area for you to search, if I can."

The next few hours Scilla spent planning with Zhannah. They determined that Regithal should stay behind at the camp to perform his Saliek'an duties and also to act as a messenger to the search party through his connection with Kylie. Zhannah, Anik, Elasche, and Dainn would accompany Kylie. There would be no additional Saliek joining them to limit the number of people who knew about their mission because the suspicions that Anik had relayed about a possible informer of Sonu's in the Saliek camp had made everyone slightly uncomfortable. Elasche and Dainn would be joining them. Not only because they had proven to be helpful companions previously, but because Prince Sonu would have a much more difficult time finding moving targets than stagnant ones, if he decided to send a group to find the missing princess and her bodyguard. After they had a general idea of their plan, Scilla and Zhannah went to find the rest of the crew to help fill in the details of the logistics and to fine tune them. Scilla secretly hoped that their plans would intersect with Mory's path because he should innately be drawn to the ancient relics and show them the way there.

The grandmother fairy had contacted Scilla with updates on Mory's whereabouts until he had dropped off their radar in Mahashta, or maybe Arbore. The grandmother's link with Telovi had diminished towards the end and had eventually broken off entirely, so her reports may not have been completely accurate. They both came to the conclusion that Telovi, and most likely Mory as well, had entered an area of intense magic that must have wiped the tracking spell from Telovi. From what the grandmother fairy had told Scilla, it sounded like Mory had already retrieved the sword of Ghaleon before entering the oasis or if not that, a sword that emanated an extreme amount of power.

This news had given Scilla some additional confidence in her ability to locate the relics of Ghaleon, as she had always suspected that somewhere near the secret oasis was where one of his artifacts was hidden. It had also brought her a bit of frustration that she could no longer track the boy's whereabouts as he galivanted about Krael retrieving them.

After the majority of the camp had retired to bed, Scilla pulled off her cloak and went for a walk outside in the comfortable night air to clear her mind. The only time she was able to safely leave her skin exposed was in the soft essence of the moon that approximated the intensity of the lighting of her home planet. Zhannah had filled her in earlier on what had transpired at the battle site where they had fought to protect Regithal. She was relieved to hear that Zhannah had not told Kylie that she was not the Spirit Master. Eventually, she would have to learn, but Scilla felt that information should be saved until Mory knew what he was.

Something tugged at her irritatingly about the cloaked person that they had reported sighting in the forest. The way he seemed to command the firelings and other demonic creatures without having offered them any tribute. She halted suddenly, a swirl of fallen pink petals mixed with dust floated around her calves beneath her floor length skirt before they settled back to the ground. Had she not been reminiscing of the past earlier, she may not have had this thought... Was it possible? She followed the trail of the thought into the depths of her mind, and it acted as a key to unlock the memories of her past flowing back to her now that she required them. Every detail of her exile, every painstaking moment of her youth bombarded her. Each second was as vibrant as if she had just lived those moments. They were just as vibrant as the future had once been to her… and he was there.

He was only a boy at the time, equivalent in age to her but with guile enough for someone who had lived twice their lives. He was the reason she was here, and if he was the man in the cloak, she needed to proceed cautiously. He must have traded the firelings knowledge of their future for their help. That's why Zhannah could not find trinkets or treasures on their bodies. The worst part was, if his talent for seeing the future had not been squelched out as well as hers, he could change the future that he had shown those firelings to suit his own purposes… his purposes that Scilla had never known to be good as the selfish, power hungry, divergent that he was.

The night suddenly seemed colder, and she turned around posthaste, black riding boots thumping in the dirt until she reached the library once more and pulled on her cloak hugging it close. This was going to be a late night.

Chapter 27

Lightning crackles across the sky, crashing into the clouds in waves of thunder. The silhouette of a dark bird appears out of the ebony night, growing steadily as it nears the ground. It is plummeting out of control, swirling helplessly in the torrential, frigid winds and rain of a foreign place. Barely clinging to a thread of its life, the bird makes one final attempt to spread its wings. As it does, another nearly identical dark bird emerges from the first, and each takes flight mere feet before they would have crashed to their death on the solid ground. Without glancing back at each other, hearts beating frantically, one flies towards the mountains, the other towards the snow.

Scilla poured over her own prophecies one by one, day after day, reliving each as she read their accounts. She had been diligent in keeping written record of anything that she had foreseen, knowing that they could one day be of use. Paper and pen were essentials on her person at all times, and she still carried them, even now that the visions were gone, out of habit. Oftentimes she had been able to control the images and feelings that overtook her when the paths of the future had lain before her, but other times, the visions would take her unsuspectingly and leave her in the throes of a violent stream of imagery… occasionally, at the most inconvenient times.

Scilla had been focused primarily on studying events that furthered her purpose of peace on Krael throughout her lifetime and had overlooked anything that seemed trivial to her at the time of her sightings to avoid oversaturating herself with information. Even though she had considered some events trivial, she still kept record of them. These were the prophecies that she was studying now. Not only did she hope to find something that might shed light on a more specific location in the Frostlands to search for the hidden artifact, but she yearned to find a piece of information that could lead her to Kaitzen or possibly hint at his purposes. Kaitzen was the name of the man she believed to be under the hooded cloak.

Studying through the nights and sleeping during the brightest part of the days, Scilla invoked fear, or at least uneasiness, within the Saliek camp in those who didn't know what she was. She was unperturbed though. Nothing could distract her when her mind was this focused on something. It had been years since she had felt this sort of thrill. In her brief breaks that she took, her mind would wander onto matters concerning herself… If she could meet Kaitzen again, what would she do? Would she enact revenge? How so? Had she forgiven him? Would she long to embrace him as an old friend from a world long forgotten, or would his goals be so in opposition to hers that she would be forced to fight him? One would think that she could determine her own reaction, or possibly plan it, but Scilla had lived long enough to know it was nearly impossible to predict her personal feelings about an incident until it happened. Even when she could foresee events, sometimes she would be overwhelmed in emotion when they came to pass, even though she knew they were coming.

***

Kylie looked down at Starshine from atop the back of a pegasus introduced to her as Galaxy. There was a mixture of hurt and anger in her small visage. Kylie cooed down at her, attempting to ease the filly's feelings. The group had needed to employ the help of the pegasi to reach the Frostlands that Scilla had suggested they search, and Starshine was still too small to carry a rider. Kylie wondered if Starshine would ever forgive her for leaving her so often in such a short time.

Dainn and Elasche were also introduced to their own pegasi which had agreed to help them on this mission and would return to the Saliek camp afterwards. Flying lessons had been a must for the three newbies, and after a few bouts of comical episodes and one possible near-death experience, everyone had seemed to get the hang of flying.

Kylie had spent the last many days training with her mother on how to enhance her fighting skills with her Spirit. At first it was awkward thinking about when to properly decrease the mass of her limbs to speed up her movement and when add it back to increase the intensity of her thrusts, but she was a quick learner and soon able to take down a person twice her size when she employed the techniques properly. Anik had spent the days showing Elasche around the camp and telling her stories of his prior accomplishments. It didn't go unnoticed by Kylie that they spent much of their free time together and would giggle and smile constantly in each other's presence, catching each other's eye when they thought no one was paying attention. She was happy for them and hoped that they didn't end up being separated after their mission together had been accomplished. Dainn did not seem particularly thrilled by the attention that Elasche was giving Anik and would frequently cast threatening glances at him when he was in her company.

It wasn't long before their respite at the camp concluded, and her mother declared that they could waste no more time at the camp and needed to start their journey.

Galaxy pawed the ground anxiously as Kylie waited on the rest of her party to ready themselves. Her mother slowly stroked her fingers through Storm's grey mane, twisting it on occasion as they watched Anik attempt to help Elasche onto her pegasus, Silk, who was proving to be as slippery as her namesake. Elasche nearly fell off the other side of her back because she was too busy staring deeply into Anik's eyes. Dainn was fuming silently on the back of Rock, and Kylie thought she saw one of Dainn's many tattoos glow momentarily. Anik lost his balance, released Elasche's hand, and fell onto his backside. Elasche laughed heartily as she clutched Silk's mane. Anik looked around, confused.

The pegasi would be heavily laden, as each not only carried a person, but also a large roll of provisions and supplies for them to use when they arrived in the Frostlands. This would most likely prolong their journey, but Kylie thought it provided a nice back rest behind her saddle for the time being and relaxed against it while Anik finally mounted Bandit. Kylie bid Starshine a final farewell, handing her a blapple to chew on, and they formed up the pegasi with her mother in the lead taking off into the soft pink of the morning sky.

Spring was bursting into summer, and the brightly-colored flowers that had adorned the trees now blanketed the ground, leaving behind a sea of many shades of green in a delightful patchwork as she gazed down from Galaxy. The warm air played with her hair as she ascended higher, and she couldn't help but grin noticing strands of Galaxy's black mane intertwine with her own golden locks as the breeze took hold of them. The temperature dropped as they entered a fluffy white cloud, blinding her to anything other than its pristine white presence, and she felt cool droplets of water begin to condense on her skin. As quickly as they had entered, they exited, and the world reappeared around her just as it was before. She was flying, in a world of magic, atop the back of a pegasus. She didn't think this feeling would ever get old.

And it didn't, at least not in the days of travel to the Frostlands. Each day the scenery changed beneath them, always a new surprise to behold, and each night they spent in good company with one another chatting about each person's past and their feelings on the various happenings of the world. Even Dainn felt comfortable enough to eventually open up to tell a few of his stories from younger days. He even admitted to the magic that his tattoos held, like all those of the famed Ignet. The bodyguards of the Mahashta house needed to have some advantage to safeguard those they were sworn to protect. He reverently told the histories behind a few of the more intricate tattoos and the trials he had survived to obtain them while the party listened entranced. He did not tell them everything about every tattoo, even if specifically asked, but he divulged just enough to clear away the total haze of mystery about them. Elasche only smiled knowingly. It was clear she knew all this and more about Dainn already.

Eventually, the air began getting chillier, and Kylie had to retrieve the warmer cloak that she had packed, tying its hood snuggly over her head. The scenery below began to get greyer and hunting for dinner at night became more difficult as game became scarce. When the wind had nipped at her reddening nose to the point that she could hardly feel it anymore and the tips of her hair that escaped from her hood were freezing solid instead of moving fluidly with the breeze, her mother finally motioned for them to land at their destination. Galaxy's feathered feet were covered nearly to the knee when his hooves crunched through the untouched snow.

The soft falling of tiny snowflakes surrounded them in an austere land. It seemed that no other creatures had walked within miles of their location, or if they had, the snow had already covered their tracks. Up ahead a forest loomed, completely unlike any forest Kylie had seen on Krael thus far. The trees were arthritic skeletal hands protruding from a stark white wasteland, grasping at a grey streaked midday sky. Brittle bark of white, black, and grey peeled away from the gaunt trunks, marring the white snow beneath them with dark flecks. No sign of life was in plain sight.

"It's hibernating," her mother explained referring to the forest. "We've crossed to the opposite hemisphere of Krael, and the seasons are switched. We are so far from the equator, that the suns will not be lighting this land for long or very brightly during the winter season. We should make the best of the small amounts of daylight that we will have." And with those words, she urged Storm forward, breaching the tree line. When Kylie and Galaxy crossed into the forest, she immediately felt uncomfortable and unwelcome. The others seemed to feel it too, as she noticed them eyeing the trees suspiciously and shifting their weight in their saddles. Only her mother seemed un-phased. Kylie supposed that could have been from years of experience, or maybe she had expected this, or had been here before. For whatever reason, it helped give her strength to see another person standing strong.

They had known that they would be unable to fly once they had reached the forest and had planned ahead for this. Scilla had not yet been able to discern the exact location of the cave they would need to enter. Although, she did continually send updates to Kylie on her research status through her father every evening. They would have to search for the cave the old-fashioned way for the time being.

Anik had admitted to studying how vibrations travelled through different types of sediment and hoped to put that to good use in finding the cave. He was quite proficient at creating mini-earthquakes. He would just have to control them at a non-destructive level and open his senses to the way the ground vibrated in response. He seemed confident that he would be able to tell if there was a cavity in the ground nearby. Kylie hoped he was being sincere about his confidence level, or they might be wandering through this cold barren forest longer than she had anticipated.

***

Scilla was taking one of her nightly walks, gazing up at the stars and letting her mind wander unfettered by any tasks when she had the epiphany. It stopped her in her tracks as she raced through all the data in her head that she had been researching. It all made sense, the pieces all fit, and it was inconvenient, which with her luck meant it was most likely true. Kaitzen had been hiding out in the Frostlands for all these years, waiting for the right moment to strike. He would have been well-hidden there, as no one in their right mind visited that area. He also seemed to have the eternal life granted to those who completed the Saliek initiation, which took place in the Frostlands. Whether he stumbled upon it accidentally or had been spying on one of the initiations, Scilla didn't know for sure.

He would most likely have strong and dangerous allies, as he could grant them the gift of knowledge of their futures, knowledge of how to alter their futures, or even the secret of the immortal Saliek for their cooperation. This meant that the crew they had sent into the Frostlands to find a magical hidden cave were in significantly more danger than expected. Scilla hoped that Kaitzen had befallen the same misfortune as herself and had lost his ability to see the strands of time. If not, he could be an adversary that was impossible to surmount. She needed to warn Kylie as soon as possible so that they could be prepared for the worst. Scilla began striding towards Regithal's tent as she continued thinking. Maybe even a backup contingent from the Saliek could be sent to support them, though that would take days. If only she could nail down the location of that cave, she would go join them herself. Kaitzen… What is your purpose? What is your goal on this world? Scilla was beginning to think that she may not have the time she needed to find out all of the answers before it was too late.

Chapter 28

White flakes floated past the entrance to the hollow of a hibernating tree. A raven perched inside the hollow, shackled to its horde of random shiny objects glinting in the daylight making its way into the tree. It peeked outside of the hole in the tree, face twitching quickly from left to right, watching the world as time passed by. Slowly the horde beneath the raven grew as the seasons changed rapidly, slowing only when the death of winter came around each year. At the base of the tree, a dark circle's diameter steadily increased, sickening all life that came within its perimeter.

The aged cabin creaked eerily as a cold wind whistled through the rafters announcing the arrival of winter. A fire crackled in one of the rooms, warming the single occupant of the cabin as he relaxed in a worn, bronze-colored armchair with his feet propped up on a matching ottoman. The room was a cluttered mess of objects, and one could barely see a large, brown floor rug along the paths weaving in between the carefully cared for objects. A gaudy chandelier shone down on the piles, enhancing the flickers of light frolicking over them from the frenzied fire. The chandelier swayed slightly as the cool air that penetrated through the tiny cracks of the cabin swirled with the fire's warm updraft.

It was Kaitzen's favorite time of year. The suns were hidden for the majority of the day, barely skimming the surface of the horizon when they were visible. This allowed him more freedoms outside his cabin without his cursed cloak hindering his movements. The brightness of the suns was the worst of Krael's attributes in his opinion. He could almost feel his skin yearning to ignite when it was touched directly by the suns' rays.

Zen, as he had taken to calling himself, watched out the window. He leaned back in his cushioned armchair as the snowflakes piled themselves higher and higher onto the ground around the ragged-looking shrubbery and trees surrounding his log cabin. He didn't mind the snow or the cold. He appreciated that its existence provided him with the solitude he needed to work. He turned his pale-skinned, pointed face away from the window and looked back onto his treasures with his long, thick, black ponytail hanging over his shoulder. His treasures were his pride and joy. He spent much of his free time sitting in his treasure room, admiring the beauty of his horde and basking in its magical essence. He had spent the past hundreds of years adding to his collection, researching ancient tales and following them to find the treasures they hid. Krael was a deeply magical planet, and he was fortunate that his ancestors had not known to what extent before they had exiled him here.

Each treasure in the room had a useful magical imbuement. Some had been unused for years, others he used frequently, but Zen did not discriminate when it came to his treasure horde. He loved each piece of it equally, as long as it was his and no one else's. His eyes gleamed with greed as he wrung his hand possessively around the staff that he had taken to carrying around with him. The staff allowed him to cast a multitude of spells that were stored within it, so long as it was in his grasp. Associated with each spell, however, was a recharge time before he could cast it again. The staff needed to sap strength away from nearby objects to regain its lost power. This proved to be a hindrance at times, but he had found ways to maximize its usefulness.

Although he adored each one of his treasures, none were the one he truly desired. The cloak told of in the Legend of Ghaleon was his personal holy grail. It would allow him to travel across the universe without fear of death. Enslaving minions across Krael to do his bidding in his attempt to rise into power here was an entertaining pastime that he hoped would sustain him indefinitely, but more than anything, Zen wanted to return to Tendyis. Not only did he crave to return to his home planet to wreak havoc among those who had wronged him, as his goal had been for years, but he also believed that if he returned there, he could reclaim his ability to foresee the future, which had recently left him so abruptly. His underlings on Krael had yet to know of his blindness, and he intended to keep it that way until he could see yet again. The anxiety and frustration he felt wrenching his soul at the loss reminded him of when he had been exiled. He believed that it was only his years of life experience that kept him from becoming mentally unhinged and physically sick at the moment.

When he had been exiled, his prosecutors as well as himself had known the possible ramifications of portal hopping across space without proper protection. The longer the distance that you travelled, the more likely you were to die in route. His exile was a probable death sentence. Those with higher degrees of magic in their blood tended to survive more often, but nothing was ever certain. He could still remember that night centuries ago as though it were yesterday. His heart had been beating in rhythm with the throbbing hums of energy on the Plain of Portals beneath the soft glow of the night sky as a council had decreed Zen and his twin sister's sentence.

Zen, as with most Tendyians, did not have the ability to foresee the paths of the future beyond the planet he was currently on, and the strength of this power was only as strong as the magic intrinsic to the planet. His unknown fate had unnerved him to the brink of insanity, fighting his escorts violently all the way to the golden base of the large circular portal, it's diameter of twice his height looming down on him. His sister, in contrast, had held her head high, accepting whatever fate had in store for her beyond the swirling colors of the portal illuminating their planet of eternal twilight. Her last words to him had been, "At least we are in this together," before her escorts pushed her through the portal destined for Krael, a planet in a nearby solar system. He never understood the compassion he heard in those words and knew he did not deserve them after what he had done. Yet, he still believed that what he had done had been necessary.

For that reason, he had left Scilla alone all these years. Her altruistic pursuits had not contended with his rise to power until recently when reports from his networks indicated that the true Spirit Master, as well as Scilla, were back on Krael. This would ordinarily not have upset him, but it coincidentally aligned with the vanishing of his ability to see the future so he could not properly track either of them down the streams of time. Zen had not foreseen this, but he knew it had to be her workings. It reeked of Scilla. Zen had thought the Spirit Master descendant lost when it and Scilla both disappeared from his vision years ago. He had even instructed Sonu to find the one who should have replaced it. Instead, contrary to his theory, Scilla and the Spirit Master had just hidden on Thaer until the time was right. He was quite irritated at himself for not having figured that out sooner.

Awhile back, the firelings under his control had stumbled across a portal leading to Thaer and had reported the suspicious behavior of the Saliek occurring there. After a few weeks of reconnaissance, he had sent the firelings and a smattering of other beasts to flush them out of Thaer and back onto Krael where he could keep a better eye on them since his foresight had not functioned beyond this planet. Soon after that, his foresight vanished, and the reports of the reappearance of the Spirit Master and Scilla were reported by his networks. Now Zen had an overwhelming desire to exterminate the true Spirit Master -after it mended the cloak of Ghaleon for him- as Zen believed that it was the only person strong enough to halt his conquest of Krael, and he despised the lack of control he had over it without his foresight.

Scilla was a proper member of the Saliek. An annoying army-like group of Spirit wielders that his underlings often had to deal with in their workings. He had heard that they had the ability to create cloaks that allowed a person to travel between worlds close by, or at least in the same solar system, but not beyond that. A mere pittance in comparison to the universe opened up to him should he find Ghaleon's cloak. He had obtained a specimen of a Saliek cloak from an unsuspecting victim during an outing where he had viewed the Saliek initiation ritual but had not attempted to use it yet. It shimmered slightly in the firelight on a peg in the wall of his treasure room. The initiation ritual was conveniently completed in his forest in the Frostlands, so he had been able to learn the secret of their immortality without having to become a member of the wretched group.

A curious stream that never froze bisected the Frostland forest. Along this stream grew small, sturdy plants that were resilient enough to survive beneath the heavy snows of winter. If a person was able to dig up one of these plants and crush the leaves into a tincture to be ingested, they would be sick for many days, but it would be the last sickness from which they ever ailed.

Something about the plant left the person immune to all disease and poisons. It allowed the organs to finish development, if the person was young, and preserved them in a healthy, ageless state as long as they were not mortally wounded physically. This gave the Saliek, and any others who knew the secret of the plant, a seeming immortality. Zen also enjoyed this privilege without having to serve the Saliek. The violent throes of the self-inflicted illness were well worth it in his opinion.

His mirror across the room began calling to him as a deep purple and black swirl slowly worked its way out from the center to the ostentatiously carved dark wood of its exterior. It was not dissimilar from some of the Tendyis' portals that he had been reminiscing about. This specific relic connected to any other mirror across Krael, and sometimes it could even establish a connection, though less clear, with other reflective surfaces. It also allowed him to see into the thoughts of the creature on the other side, making dealing with the demons he plotted with easier. Most often, he was the one doing the calling, but there were times his underlings were given permission to contact him. This particular calling was one he had been anticipating while waiting in the treasure room. Zen got up and unhurriedly snaked his way across the room through his treasures. His staff softly thudded the carpeted floor with each step he took during his approach.

When he stood a few feet away from the mirror, he waved his hand across its width, and an image of a blonde prince appeared. The gullible boy actually believed that Zen would give up one of the relics of Ghaleon. Zen smirked to himself at his deceit. Zen would of course allow him to rule as an underling on Krael but never to the extent that the boy imagined. He had a vivid imagination amplified by a vision that Zen had shown him of a future where Zen had given the boy a relic prior to the loss of his vision. What the prince didn't know was that fate was not carved in stone and that there were multiple trails that the future could flow down predicated on the choices made by the surrounding people.

***

Prince Sonu had brought a well-supplied, although small, army across Krael to the Frostlands, taking advantage of ancient travelling portals identified by his Master to travel more efficiently. Prior to his departure from Arbore, he had left a trail of ruin. While he had been planning this very mission, his castle guards had let his potential Spirit Master candidates escape. This had angered Prince Sonu beyond reason, and he had personally disgraced and executed at least five members of his castle guard who had been on duty that night. Without any more time and nor anyone who he felt was competent enough to lead a search party for his missing quarry, he left Arbore in a leaderless distressed mess that he intended to clean up himself when he returned. He would now have to re-locate one or both of the young girls that he suspected to be the new Spirit Master if he wished to mend any relic that he may find in the Frostlands.

The snow fell onto his small camp of wary and weary soldiers just inside the perimeter of the Frostland forest. Though the soldiers all maintained a healthy fear of their moody commander, there was a level of respect they felt for him as well. He had not only well-provisioned the troops for the cold climate with thick hide tents, plenty of fat and protein rich foods, and strong hardy horses, but had also promised each person accompanying him a monetary compensation equal to twenty-five percent more than their regular pay, if they completed their mission. Prince Sonu had accepted volunteers from across his entire army for this mission and then thinned them to reflect the best of the group.

The people drawn to this kind of mission were the desperate and greedy types, so the character of their leader was a minor obstacle in their minds. The camp was eerily quiet and tenuous as the soldiers pointedly avoided each other and talked amongst themselves sparingly. None of them knew how to trust. Each knew that that they themselves would stab any other member of this company in the back if it meant their advancement in some way, so they would expect nothing less from their fellow soldiers.

Prince Sonu was currently tucked away in his sparsely-furnished tent this evening. He had locked himself in as best as he could to make a call to his Master and inform him of his location. Prince Sonu felt a thread of nervousness, as he had never attempted a call to his Master before, but rage at his feelings quickly overpowered his nerves prior to the call. Feeling nervous was a sign of weakness. Prince Sonu did not see himself as a weak person.

The familiar black and purple hues distorted his appearance in the mirror as he felt his Master's voice begin to relay to him instructions on how to reach the place that it believed Prince Sonu would have the most luck in locating the lost cave he desired to search.

Chapter 29

A renowned warrior of the light took on a pupil as a favor to an old friend. The student was a daydreamer and learned the art of the sword much too slowly for the liking of the warrior. Still, day after day, the warrior taught on, showing nothing but patience towards the pupil even though a fire of frustration raged inside. One evening, years down the road, long after the pupil had left his teacher, a score of bandits ransacked the town that the old warrior was living in. The warrior was caught in her nightclothes and unprepared for battle when her house was infiltrated.

She battled bravely and ruthlessly until they had her cornered. When all hope was lost, a silent killer emerged from the shadows and took down the contingent of bandits in the old warrior's house. Before her savior left, he pulled down his dark hood and winked at her with a smile. Her eyes widened in recognition, and her jaw dropped before he hopped out the window and into the night.

Zhannah hadn't the slightest idea where to begin looking for the hidden cave, so in order to maintain a sense of purpose for the group, she steadily made her way towards the Saliek initiation grounds. Magic had a tendency to beget magic, so it was as good of a place to start as any. She had been there countless times while attending many of the younger Saliek's initiations at

Regithal's side. Even though she could still feel the strangeness of the forest in her blood as she walked through it, she had become accustomed enough to the feeling to not let its disturbance within her be perceived by the others. Anik, who had only been to the forest once for his own initiation, still had beads of nervous sweat dotting his forehead. The others were showing their discomfort in various tics that Zhannah took note of for future reference.

The air held a cold bite to it that clamped down when the winds blew causing the crew to huddle deep into their cloaks. Snowflakes twirled in a beautiful yet violent ballet as the howling music of those winds guided them across the sky. The pegasi were slow-moving as they trudged their way through the knee-deep snow, fanning the flurry of impatience that Zhannah had yet to master in her long lifetime. They had prepared for these conditions before leaving the camp, but that didn't make them any more enjoyable to bear.

She signaled Anik up to her lead position, and he urged Bandit forward to ride abreast Storm. Zhannah asked, "What kind of cadence can you maintain with your earthquake magic without tiring yourself out too quickly?"

Anik thought about the question for a moment before answering, "The tremors are not so difficult to create in the small magnitudes that are required, but I have not practiced the trick more than in isolated instances. I can start looking for the cave now, if you'd like. I will make it a priority to not tire myself out to the point of exhaustion or inability to continue on, unless you give the command."

Zhannah nodded her consent, but Anik did not back away immediately. Instead, he asked, "Are we headed towards the Saliek initiation grounds? This path seems familiar."

"Yes, we are," Zhannah replied. "It's the only location I really know in this forest, so I decided to make our journey simplest at first and then decide where to go from there."

Anik hummed in agreement, and she saw the corners of his eyes crinkle as he closed them in concentration. She could not feel the tremors that he manifested into the earth and decided that was a blessing with how jumpy her comrades were in this forest. She made it her job to watch Anik's back as he put his concentration and efforts into finding any hidden caves beneath the deep covering of snow. She thought that she saw something large and white shift in the snowy blur in front of them and pulled Storm to halt. A small bunny scurried between his legs in a hectic rush to be somewhere other than there. Kylie let out a small yelp, and Elasche veered Silk into Rock in an attempt to be closer to Dainn. Anik did not let his concentration break, trusting Zhannah to take control of the situation.

"It's okay guys. We just scared a bunny out of its hiding hole. No need to be so jumpy. We'll keep a sharp lookout for any real dangers," Zhannah reassured the group. She wished someone would reassure her though, as she could have sworn that she had seen something larger up ahead. It was gone now though, and she could not find a reason to cease their forward progress.

The rest of their trek to the Saliek initiation site was cold and uneventful. Anik did not look too spent from Spirit use, and the rest of the group seemed slightly more at ease. The dark tree trunks finally gave way to a clearing and a sparkling stream ran across their path. The skies darkened more as the last of the group entered the clearing. Zhannah looked up through the scraggly dark branches to the horizon where the suns grazed this time of year and saw Ontan beginning to overtake Tuon. This was the day of an eclipse.

Anik faced Zhannah with a serious look, “I think I found something.”

“The cave! You think you found a cave?” Zhannah felt excitement and relief bubble up inside of her momentarily, before Anik carried on.

“I found a cave, yes, but that wasn’t what I was referring to initially… I think I found an army,” Anik said gravely as he pointed east of their current location. “Over that direction, about one to two miles away. They seem to be headed towards this place as well. The cave is to the west, approximately the same distance.” The white haze surrounding them made it impossible to see more than a hundred feet at best. There was no way they could see the army approaching.

Zhannah’s brief moment of relief evaporated into concern. No one else knew of this place in the Frostlands because no one else knew of any reason to come here. The Saliek initiation grounds were a well-kept secret among the Saliek, and she had never known anyone else to have lived such long lives as they did. Her mind reeled through an endless number of other possibilities, but the only one that kept coming back to her was that this place was what was drawing them. She hoped that they were just an ordinary group of adventurers or treasure hunters, but her gut instinct told her otherwise.

Zhannah took control of the group immediately. They would take advantage of the low visibility and hide until they had a better look at the army headed their way. If the army looked benign, they could wait it out or come up with a plan to shoo them away. If it looked like trouble, they would pick them off one by one until they were noticed and then battle as necessary. She relayed her plans to the group and gave scouting duty to herself, as Storm’s grey coloring would mask him better in the snowy curtains. The others were to locate good hiding spots in the meantime.

Zhannah took Storm approximately one mile east, using her Spirit to give his legs additional strength and endurance to travel more nimbly in the snowy conditions. She peered cautiously through the trees and snowy haze the entire ride, and once she found her quarry, she knew that battle was imminent. The army was a group of treasure hunters, but of the worst kind. Prince Sonu's army stood before her huddled in fluffy, white winter gear braving the ice and cold. They stayed further apart from one another than what a solid army unit usually would have in an unknown environment. Zhannah supposed that was because they didn't expect anyone else to be in the vicinity. She knew that she definitely wouldn't have expected anyone. These treasure hunters must be after the relics of Ghaleon as well. Anger welled up inside of her as she contemplated taking one of them out now, but she thought better of it and rode back to her friends, hopefully unseen by their enemy.

Zhannah relayed her findings to them, and quickly, the close-knit group set into motion. Zhannah had located the end of the line of soldiers, so they bee-lined there as quickly as possible in the mounds of snow and whipping winds. By the time they had reached their position behind Sonu's army, they were only about a half mile away from the stream, and the pegasi were panting from trudging through the deep snow so quickly. Slowly and methodically, one by one, the back of the line of soldiers shortened. Some fell to knives, others to swords, magic, and even pure brute strength. Any way that it happened, the trail of death left behind in the forest was enough to merit the unsettling feeling that it had invoked in everyone.

Finally, they came upon a couple of soldiers travelling next to one another as opposed to the single file string that the others had been in. Zhannah had not been expecting this, and so as not to be too hasty, she signaled over the closest member of their group, Kylie, to talk it through, "These two will be more difficult to take down. They have clearly travelled with one another before and are each keeping close watch on the other's blind spots though it may not seem obvious."

Kylie nodded and looked closer so that she would be able to select her target. "Itha and Fauler," Kylie stated in disbelief as she pulled back slightly in surprise. Zhannah gave her a quick appraising look.

"You know those people?" Zhannah inquired.

"Yes." Kylie stated assuredly. "They are the ones that captured Anik and me; they were Dainn's companions initially. We could ask him what he thinks their weaknesses are when they are together."

Their brief hesitation and conversation were their demise. One of the two caught whiff of something amiss in the wind and relayed it forward. They called back to the person that had been following them, and after no response was received, they gathered a group to go investigate. Zhannah swore under her breath. They had taken down about half of the small army that Sonu had brought, and they still had the advantage of being the hunters, but many soldiers still remained as well as Sonu. They would now be alert, and fast action would be necessary before the army could group up and assess too much.

They moved as a team, Zhannah sending them the signals to wait for the opposing army to find the last body and then begin their attack. It was almost too easy. The soldiers were well-trained with their weapons, well fed, and in astounding physical shape, but they did not move as one. They did not think of helping their team, only of surviving themselves. It was just a matter of pulling one slightly away from the group, and their demise came about quickly.

Zhannah went up against a man twice her size with skills in the sword that rivaled her own Spirit-enhanced abilities. She had never felt this challenged in her years of life, and it was exhilarating. He could parry her dual-bladed blasts with his one great sword as efficiently and effectively as if he had trained against her in the practice field or maybe had the same instructor. Each swing of the sword bore the weight of her mortality. She fell into the rhythmic clinking of metal on metal as each one advanced on the other and retreated. Sometimes Zhannah thought she could see tiny sparks fly in the dim daylight from the contact of their swords. Battle rage built up in his eyes, and she knew it was mimicked in her own. She would not give up. Neither of them would. Fire burned inside her stomach creating an inexhaustible pool of energy fueled by adrenaline as she fought on.

The fight seemed endless; the muscles in her arms and torso now burned and her legs trembled. She backed up one step to absorb a powerful blow from her worthy adversary, and as her foot penetrated through the snow, it hit a rock. Her weakened muscles gave out on her, and she fell backwards into the snow. She tried to draw on her Spirit, but it wasn't quick enough, and she was too near exhaustion. The man was over her in an instant. Zhannah was too tired and too pumped with adrenaline to feel fear. As she watched the sword fall towards her face, she felt nothing, although her mind raced. She relived each of her valued moments and recalled all her regrets of the goals she had not accomplished in her life. She hoped that she had left enough of a light in those she left behind that she would be remembered and traces of her existence would be carried on. She hoped that her sacrifice would be enough for those left behind to prevail.

When Zhannah had accepted her death, swords still in hand, staring into the eyes of her killer, the skilled swordsman made an unexpected jerk in his movement, which hampered his swing. The battle rage evaporated from his eyes, as well as all other emotion. He dropped his sword and fell to the ground beside her, sinking into the snow to a depth where she could not see him from within her own snow imprint.

Another swordsman stood above her now. One who was sheathing his sword and extending a helping hand out to her as the eclipse formed a halo around his head. Snow sticking in his wind ruffled blonde hair and wearing the pelts of various animals to keep warm, Mory pulled Zhannah up and out of the snow.

***

Sonu peered beyond the wide trunk of a tree, bow drawn, looking down the shaft of his nocked arrow to sight his quarry. His sister knelt before one of his men pulling her bloodied dagger from his stilled chest. Sonu had been watching her fight. She was good, very good. He realized that his arm was beginning to ache from holding the string drawn for so long without firing. Something warm filled his heart for a moment, and out of hatred for himself for feeling any sort of compassion for her, he nearly let the arrow fly. The voice of reason in his head stayed his hand and reminded him that he needed a Spirit Master, whoever it actually was, to make the artifacts whole again. That was a rational reason for allowing her to live. He would get the artifact first, then collect his escaped potential Spirit Masters when he was better equipped.

Sonu tore his eyes away from the golden hair that matched his perfectly. He carefully released the tension from his bow string and placed the arrow back into his quiver. When he turned back, Itha and Fauler both stood staring at him, judging him with their eyes for the deed he had almost committed. "Let's get a move on before they realize where we are!" Sonu grumbled harshly to them. No other words were said as they remounted their horses and continued to trudge onward through the bitter cold of the snow-filled Frostlands.

Chapter 30

Ontan cringed and groaned as a crying Tuan was ripped from his embrace once more. Like she was every time he succeeded in stealing her away. Strong arms held him back as he struggled fruitlessly to return her to his embrace. He knew he would have bruises later and hoped fervently that Tuan would not be hurt as they threw her haphazardly back onto the carriage to be delivered to her betrothed, required by promises made too long ago. The guard tied him up roughly and left him in the corner.

Ontan had become deft at untying the knots that they always left him in, but he was never quick enough to rescue Tuan twice in one day. Rubbing the burn out of his newly-freed wrists, he peered out the window into the star-speckled night. The smell of the sweet summer grass filled his nostrils as he watched the wind toss the seeds of the cotton-like flowers into the sky to float effortlessly away. The carriage was nowhere to be seen. He turned sullenly away from the window, and there, sitting on the edge of his bed with a coy smile stretched across her face, was beautiful Tuan. His jaw dropped in surprise. Her hair cascaded down her shoulders, and her long legs were crossed before her. She lifted her chin slightly to meet his eyes, and her deep red lips moved to speak, "I realized my love for you had no boundaries. So, I changed the story. I came to you."

Ontan scanned Tuan's body over quickly, and there

was indeed blood and bruises marring her perfectly smooth skin. He hurried over to her side, and they nestled momentarily in each other's embrace. He pulled slightly away and softly brushed his fingers over a darkening bruise on her face, a look of concern and question entering his eyes. Tuan responded, "These matter not, as they will heal with time. Our love is worth the brief moments of pain and struggle. Now..." she stood up purposefully and held out her hand to him, a stare from her eyes holding his, "may I have this dance?"

The room filled instantly with a song written by Ontan, and they circled each other in a waltz happily into the night.

Kylie pulled her dagger from the last of the felled soldiers on the battleground, using the snow to cleanse the red stains from its blade. Near the end of their battle, Zhannah's attention had been completely occupied by the largest man that Kylie had ever seen, and so the rest of the group had banded together to take out the others. She had not fought Itha, Fauler, or Sonu and hoped that one of her comrades had seen to them. She scanned the snowy battlefield for any signs of movement hiding behind trees or otherwise.

She saw a swordsman wearing the pelts of multiple animals standing above Zhannah, sheathing his sword, and offering a hand to the fallen woman. Zhannah's former adversary was lying partially submerged in the snow, dark red liquid soaking through the back of his clothing. With Kylie's blood still boiling from the heat of the battle, she ran over to protect her mother from whatever danger this swordsman may pose. He was clearly not a member of Sonu's army from the way he was dressed, but the way he carried his sword and had taken down a man that had given Zhannah trouble, made

Kylie wary about him. Something inside of her was drawn towards him, whether his intentions were good or evil.

By the time she had reached him, her mother was already standing up, brushing the snow off her backside. Kylie jumped up onto a log protruding from the snow behind the man and placed her knife at his neck intending to demand for him to tell her his intent and purpose for being there. He chuckled. Kylie's insides froze nearly as much as her extremities had on the outside from the weather, eyes growing wide as they did. She knew that chuckle. She removed her knife from his neck, and Mory turned around to face her. He was disturbingly close to her but smiled one of his usual smiles. The ice that had seemingly encrusted her body, melted in that moment, starting from within and slowly working its way to her extremities. When she felt the flush flooding through her chest and cheeks, she turned away quickly apologizing in a mumble, finding that she could not convince her body to move any further away from him. This feeling… Fear? Wonder? Embarrassment? She couldn't place what it was, but it had her solidly rooted in place, even though every inch of her mind was screaming at her to run away from this feeling that she didn't comprehend.

He placed his hands on her waist, lifted her from the log, and placed her down beside him with a tremendously goofy grin still plastered on his face. The places where he touched her waist burned with intensity. She could feel them even through the thick clothing that she was wearing to ward off the cold. He stared down at her for moments that seemed like centuries with eyes filled with emotion, before pulling her in close and embracing her shamelessly, "Oh, how I've missed you, Kylie! Words cannot describe how much! I would have travelled to the ends of all of the worlds to find you! I beg of you, never leave me again!" He slowly stroked his hand through her long hair, and Kylie finally obtained a state of mind where she was able to command her arms to wrap themselves around him, rubbing and patting his back in comfort.

Kylie was at a loss for words and so just remained in his warm embrace for a while before answering him, "I… I missed you too."

He pulled her in just a bit tighter acknowledging her response, placing his forehead briefly on her shoulder. He hesitantly put her at arm's length away from him and looked down into her eyes once more. His gaze had intensified in emotion and took on a serious look, "Kylie, I love you, with every square inch of my being. You are the reason for every breath I take, why I wake up in the morning, why I have travelled aimlessly across a foreign planet, why I took up sword training, and so much more. You have enabled me to become who I am today because of my subconscious need to impress you and be near you. I cannot live without you by my side. Your intellect, your beauty, and your skills combine together to create the most enticing angel that I have ever had the good fortune to meet and are surpassed by none. Your silky hair glistens as it flows in the sunlight, your soft skin is so delicate and pale, your green eyes glow with light and happiness, and I now realize that I cannot willingly take my own eyes away from their stunning gaze. My very soul cries out when your presence is not near, and I cannot think of anything or anyone else day or night. Thoughts of you fill my mind constantly, and I would not have it any other way." He removed one of his hands from her waist and brushed a finger lightly across her cheek as he continued to stare at her admirably.

When Mory had finished, the fearful side of Kylie's emotions had taken over in her brain, and she tore herself away from Mory's embrace and ran headlong into the darkened forest just as the eclipse had reached its peak, and Tuan began to pull away from Ontan once more. The concept of Mory loving her was much too daunting for her to consider at the moment, and so she ran as fast as she could in no particular direction weaving through the trees and any other obstacles in her way. She had never been in love before truly, so the thought of it frightened her, and as unreasonable of a response that her flight had been, it was the only option that her mind had given to her in that moment. Not even the deep snow that had been a hindrance before seemed to slow her pace or tire her as she ran.

She found a sizable boulder that had been partially covered by the snow and hid behind it. It had veins of silver running through jet-black rock, and from her curled up position with her arms pulling her knees close into her chest, she was able to trace her fingers along the lines of silver, reminding her of her old habit in the Ancient Archives with her favorite geode table. This action comforted her somewhat, and she was almost able to think clearly again, using the tracing motions as her beacon back to reality.

Her mind returned to functionality slowly as the effects of being close to Mory had worn off. She contemplated what he had confessed to her, and what it could mean for her. Did she herself reciprocate his feelings for her? Should she really be involved in a relationship with her best friend? Was what she had felt for him after finally seeing him after being apart for so long proof of her love for him? Kylie had never really thought too much about love before now, since she had no real reason to examine the concept. Now that life had pushed it to the forefront of her mind, she had no other choice.

After tumbling the concept about in her mind for what seemed like an eternity, she decided that love was more than finding someone physically attractive and intellectually stimulating. It was more than sharing common interests, finding them fun to be around, and thinking you could put up with each other long enough to create a life together. Although each of those helped in creating love between two people, undying true love, in her opinion, was built on much more than that. True love being a love that would last beyond aging, sickness, disagreements, long distance, and even beyond life itself. It was feeling a base connection to someone on the soul level, admiring and connecting with the way that person perceives the worlds around them. It was feeling motivated to succeed through their support, and an unselfish want to support them and to see them succeed in their own life endeavors. There would be a mutual respect and admiration for each other that would transcend any hardships along the way. It was finding someone who could make you truly happy and bring color to your life when your entire personal universe was falling apart, and the last thing you wanted to do was smile. It was having your souls twisted together in a helix so tight that you could feel each other even when physical distance separated your bodies and you yearned to be together once more, no matter what the consequences.

Yes, Kylie decided, she did in fact love Mory, and she had run away from him as he was spilling his heart out to her. How awful of a person was she to do that to him! She was appalled at herself for being so selfish and heartless. He was probably an emotional mess right now, and it was all her fault. She had no idea of the pain and hardships that he must have gone through to reach her all alone on a planet he had never set foot on. She needed to go back and talk to him, to explain to him her reaction, and most of all to apologize.

***

Mory watched as Kylie's golden waves waved goodbye to him as she bolted across the snow at an inhuman speed in these conditions. He stood transfixed on her figure as it faded into the winter white haze of the forest leaving a trail of footprints behind her. He wanted to chase after her, but he knew he couldn’t. He had frightened her. He had seen it in her eyes, as he had been looking much further into them than the surface. He had imagined that she would be overwhelmed with joy and leap into his arms, maybe even kiss him. They would have both been astoundingly happy and giggling together as they embraced. Instead, he felt depression, inadequacy, loneliness, and anger at himself. What an idiot he was, dumping all of that on the poor girl. She would never love him now. She would never want to even be his friend again! He should probably run back into the forest where he came from and hide from the rest of the world forever, as he was clearly too stupid to be allowed to walk amongst the rest of the people here.

Tears freely streamed down Mory’s eyes as he plopped into the snow on the ground unable to convince his body to move. Telovi popped out of his pelt cloak to console him, “Shhhh now. Everything will be all right. She just needs a moment to let everything sink into her mind.” Her voice turned somewhat playful, “And I’d love to tell you that I told you so, but this seems to be an inappropriate time to do that… Oh wait, oops.” Vi winked at him mischievously.

Mory ignored Vi’s playful jibe, as he was not in the mood for levity at the moment. Zhannah rested her hand on his shoulder before sitting down beside him looking down the trail of Kylie’s footsteps as she gave him silent companionship. The others in the group followed suit behind them, watching the forest for any remaining soldiers. They all were in need of rest regardless, so the respite was welcomed heartily. After nearly an hour, Zhannah broke the silence, "Thank you, Mory, for saving my life."

She turned to look at him, and he nodded before responding solemnly, "Anytime Zhannah. It's the least that I could do for all that you have taught me."

Zhannah seized her moment of opportunity, "And the least I can do for you giving me back my life is to give you my consent to pursue the girl I have raised as a daughter. I would be honored if she chose to spend her life with you."

Mory's head lowered noticeably and replied dejectedly, "You saw her reaction. She hates me. She ran from me. She wants nothing to do with me."

Zhannah responded, increasing the forcefulness of her tone without losing the softness entirely, "Yes, I saw her reaction. She clearly feels the same way about you, or else she wouldn't have run like that. She was scared of the feelings that she felt inside of her, not of you." Zhannah pulled herself to her feet once more and offered her hand to Mory before continuing, "Now follow her footsteps and find her. She has had enough time to herself to think, and it could be dangerous out there alone. I think you may find her more receptive of your thoughts this time. I'll regroup here with the rest for the time being. We'll give you an hour before we come looking for you.

Mory grasped her outstretched hand and stood up once more. He was terrified of finding Kylie. He was scared that she would push him away again, but he had a spark of hope now that Zhannah could be right. After all, who would know her better? Also, she was right about another thing. Kylie might be in some sort of danger out in this forest all alone. He might be able to at least provide her with some protection. His ego patched for the time being, Mory signaled his departure to the group.

"Be careful out there, Mory," Zhannah warned. "Remember to keep yourself safe first. You won't be able to talk to her again, if you don't live to find her."

Mory nodded his consent and began to retrace Kylie's footsteps into the forest, his feelings of hope and excitement in a constant battle with his fear and anxiety. Not even the icy winds and snow could chill the heat of that battle inside of him as he felt the crunch of the snow beneath his boots with each step that he took closer to Kylie.

Chapter 31

In shades of black and white, two boys attacked one another with wooden practice swords, giggling and running before they crossed their weapons again. In between bouts, they would half drag, half carry their heavy wooden weapons, which were nearly as long as they were tall, across the drying autumn grass of the open field. They had "borrowed" the swords from the practice arena, as they were too small to actually take part in weapon drills. After a while, they became exhausted with their play, having to put their entire body's weight into each swing, and one tripped and tumbled down an unseen set of stairs at the far end of the field.

The strong, weathered arms of a ceremonially-garbed guard caught the tumbling boy before any harm came to him and brought him back up to his friend. The tired boys collapsed onto their backs in the grass, and the old guard chuckled to himself, recalling what it was like to be their age, "Do you boys know where you are?" They looked at each other shrugging before shaking their heads in unison.

"These are the catacombs of the lord of this land. Beneath the soil here lies the graves of the family members long since passed from this world. There are actually four entrances, each one located in one of the cardinal directions surrounding the estate," the elderly guard explained warmly as he pointed in the directions

of the other three entrances and the boys' eyes followed his finger. "Where the tunnels cross beneath the ground, something extraordinary is being built for the son of the lord. Though his time has not yet come, his father wants to ensure that when it does, he is honored appropriately. He expects that his son will visit from Thaer soon and wishes to have it ready for him to see in this life. Would you boys happen to be interested in seeing the tomb of Ghaleon?"

Mory felt tension build within his chest and a slight tingle spreading throughout his torso as he often did when sensing another's presence in the solitude. He looked up into the winds to see the great white pegasus that had been his guide in glimpses and his dreams standing magnificently across his path. The outline of its white figure was broken up by the flurry of snow, but the eyes shone purple and penetrating, ensuring him of its existence. As it had so many times before when he nearly reached its position, it turned and trotted away, disappearing into the storm. He continued placing his own boots into the smaller footprints Kylie had left behind, enlarging them with each step. If he had not been entirely sure of his actions before, the phantom pegasus had just confirmed them to him.

He had been searching for the sky tear before he had stumbled upon the group in the clearing and had remained hidden within the trees for some time, just staring at the way Kylie fought her enemies. She fought with grace, ability, and efficiency. He could tell that she did not relish the thought of killing but did not balk at it, as she clearly knew it was them or her friends. Nostalgia had enveloped him as the scene brought back memories of his childhood, hiding on the rooftop of the cabin watching Kylie practice her knife skills in the practice field. He could hardly believe the woman before him was the same girl he had watched so long ago. His reverie had been cut short by a sharp cry from Zhannah, and motivated by the inner strength he had seen in Kylie's fighting, he emerged from his hiding and thrust his sword cleanly through the man standing above his teacher and Kylie's mother. It was the first person he had ever killed.

He thought that he would feel some sort of regret, but none entered his mind. Only relief and pride in his ability to have been able to react in time to save the life of a person he held dear to him. Briefly, he wondered about the people who may have cared for the sword master he had slain, but his brooding time was limited. Moments after he had pulled Zhannah from the snow, Kylie had decided to grace him with her presence in her customary fashion. He smiled involuntarily at the freshly-made memory, as he did with any that involved Kylie's interaction with himself.

Up ahead he saw the footprints turn behind a boulder that glistened silver in the dimming light. Mory stood astounded for a moment. The sky tear stood before him, a pitch black, jagged rock laced with silver. He felt drawn to it as he ever was, but he needed to find Kylie, so he resisted his urge to inspect the meteorite and turned the corner around it. He saw her there, sitting in the snow in silence running her slender fingers across the silver lines of the sky tear. Her golden hair was sticking out of her drawn emerald hood, wet and matted with snowflakes. He couldn't think of a more beautiful sight at the moment, and his earlier reservations were forgotten. He reached out cautiously to place his trembling hand on her shoulder reassuringly. Nothing could have prepared him for what followed.

A feeling unlike any other came over him as he felt his entire self and existence dissolve and reshape itself. He was flowing through the veins of silver, his essence completely intermingled with that of Kylie's. He hadn't any idea of what was happening, but this closeness and oneness with her was intoxicating. He could feel the strength of her resolve, her thoughts, her fears, all of her emotions, and could even see her wildest dreams. He could understand all her thoughts and her rationale for believing them as though they were his own. For in this swirl of a moment, they were his own. His memories were her memories, and nothing could separate them. They were one and neither could exist without the other. He wondered briefly if she could feel him as he did her, but then quickly realized that he already knew that she did. They shared a brief moment of anxiety and fear before opening up and flooding each other with their emotion, passion, and love. Their Sprits completely intertwined with one another.

The moment that could have been an eternity, for all they knew, ended too soon. The sky tear spat them out onto the cool, damp floor of a cave, separated by their earthly bodies once more. Mory was gasping for air, soul yearning to escape and return to the existence he had just shared with Kylie. He heard Kylie's own gasps coming from beside him and knew she fought the same battle. He turned to meet her green glowing eyes, and before he could say the words, she replied to them, "I know; I love you too. Hush now. Let's figure out where we've travelled to. It seems like we have our own little world down here."

Mory was glad that she had told him to hush because he couldn't come up with any words to encompass his feelings at the moment. Instead, he smiled his most winning smile and got to his feet, offering Kylie his hand to bring her back up as well. Their eyes still locked in a deep trance that neither seemed willing to break, he pulled her in close and held her tight to his chest. It wasn't nearly close enough after what they had just experienced, but it would have to do. She began to explain as best as she could, "I was thinking about flowing through the silver veins, following them around the rock when you touched me. Your touch must have triggered… something." Kylie pulled away from his embrace far too quickly for Mory's liking, but he let her go, knowing she would be back. He knew how she felt about him now, after all.

They walked hand in hand, exploring the depths of their new cave, matching stride for stride and every so often holding each other close as they fumbled their way through the dimly lit area. Neither could see what the path held ahead for them or if there was even a destination to be reached, but there looked to be only way to go. They continued on, knowing that they could count on one another for support should any danger come to pass and knowing that the destination didn't truly matter as long as they both made the journey there together.

***

Mory's form disappeared into the ongoing snowstorm, and Zhannah returned her attention to the rest of her group. They were a sorry looking bunch huddled near each other for warmth and even after their recent respite, were near exhaustion from the recent trek and fight. She could empathize, as she felt her own aches and pains being amplified by the cold air. She decided they should build a small, quick fire to rest around while they awaited Mory and Kylie's return. They dug a circle out in the light, fluffy snow until they hit ground and began building a fire there. The slight entrenchment helped to block some of the wind as they huddled close to the fire, soaking in its warmth. The warmth seemed to work miracles on the group, relaxing their tired muscles and other ailments from the battle. Elasche worked her way around the fire, tending to their wounds as needed, as she had not engaged in the battle herself.

After they had a few moments of quiet to themselves, Zhannah had each of them report on their battle achievements. It seemed as though the majority of the enemy had wound up dead with the exception of three noteworthy individuals. Prince Sonu himself was not accounted for and neither were the two characters Kylie had referred to as Itha and Fauler. This news had earned a consternated look from Dainn who began to keep a closer eye on their surroundings. Anik was showing the most exhaustion of the group, as he had not held back his Spirit in the battle even after he had been using it to locate the hidden cave beforehand. His head lolled slightly on his left shoulder as he slept sitting up next to the fire. Zhannah let him be, for she did not know what the rest of their day had in store for them.

The hour that Zhannah had given Mory went by more quickly than she had imagined it would. While everyone rested, she occupied herself with thoughts of where Prince Sonu and his remaining cronies could have escaped to and was trying to assess their current danger level. Zhannah believed that Sonu would not want to re-engage them after this big of a loss and was most likely resting himself as her group was here. There was also the smaller chance that he would have continued on with his quest with his smaller group. If that were true, Zhannah's crew might be able to follow their tracks, after Kylie and Mory returned to their camp, and ambush them later. With any luck, Sonu's remaining men would do the difficult work of pinpointing the entrance to the cave.

Anik had slumped over onto Elasche's shoulder now, with a low rumble of snoring escaping him with each breath he took. She had a small smile of contentment on her face as she leaned her head on top of his. Dainn sat close to her other side, still steadily scanning their perimeter with his stoic eyes. Looking beyond her friends, at what could have been a beautiful landscape, Zhannah felt her spirit sink at the death and destruction that surrounded her. Bodies in positions that were not achievable by one that was living, red splotches -slowly turning black- stained the otherwise clean snow and writhing tree trunks, along with the putrid odor of decay all began to bombard her senses. If she cleared her mind enough, she could almost feel the souls of the dead mourning those left behind before leaving this mundane world for something else.

Had any of these people actually deserved death for their beliefs? Couldn't there have been another way to humanely come to a conclusion throughout all these years the Saliek had been battling, or had malevolence and evil already taken over these souls, and they were looking for the sweet release of death to allow them to realign? Was it possible that there were good people who legitimately believed in Prince Sonu or who were forced to fight for him because of desperate circumstances? These thoughts and many others circled around Zhannah’s mind as she recollected the images of each person’s face that she had killed during the battle. It was a sobering, selfish ritual that she had started many years ago to remember those she had sent to the afterlife. It was her small way of apologizing to them and accepting the responsibility for what she had done, though she knew it in no way absolved her from her actions.

She had been in many battles over the years, but every so often she was reminded of the price that had to be paid for the lives of those she considered her friends. She had trained herself to not think about it as much, but here, in the quiet, pristine white of winter, her depressing thoughts engulfed her once more. It must have been her own recent near-death experience that triggered her emotions this time.

Zhannah looked to the sky and realized that more than an hour had passed. She regretfully glanced at the tired group but knew they would all have to go together. If Mory and Kylie had not come back by now, something must have gone awry and everyone's help might be required. She got up and looked closer at their tracks leading into the woods. They would need to be quick before the snow filled in the last of their traces. Where there had once been well-defined footprints, there were now smooth indentations in the snow swept up to one side by the wind. It would have to do. Zhannah had tracked down prey on much less defined trails in the past.

She returned to the small camp and smothered their fire with an armful of snow. She let the rest of the crew mount their pegasi, but she herself would walk beside Storm so she could see the trail better through the swirling snowstorm. Galaxy followed riderless in their wake. The tracks ended at the most beautiful boulder that Zhannah had ever seen, but she spared no time to examine it for that purpose. She walked around the entire boulder, even tried pushing it herself before she enlisted Anik for his help.

The tired, yet devoted, Anik agreed to use his Spirit to see if there was anything beneath the boulder. After a moment's concentration, he confidently assured Zhannah that there was indeed a cavern beneath the boulder, but he regretfully admitted that he was too tired to move it without more rest. Zhannah could not blame the boy, she was exhausted too. It had been a very long day. So Zhannah made the decision to delay their search for Kylie and Mory until morning, hoping and praying that they found safety wherever they may be.

Chapter 32

A small, brown spiked ball wedged itself slowly into the ground. It was hideous, with tints of yellow and signs of rot on its woody exterior. The spikes would prick anything that got too near, and if something did manage to bite the shell, the acidic taste would deter any further attention being paid to it. Eventually, the ball buried itself completely into the ground. The pressure of the dirt surrounding it on all sides was too much. The sturdy shell cracked, and within was a seed as green as a new shoot of grass and as fragile as a newborn. It glowed with hope and promise. The seed shyly escaped its protective shell emerging into its new environment and began to sprout into something unique and wonderful.

Small globes dotted the earthen wall where it met the ceiling, shining a dim light upon the ruins buried for an eternity. Great cream stone columns rested broken against one another as a vibrant green moss crawled over their remnants in patches. It infiltrated the cracks and crevices that had patterned their smooth ribbed surfaces over years of erosion. Finials and plinths once separated by lengths of stone now lay scattered mere inches apart on the moss-blanketed ground. Building walls that had once towered on high were now diminished to rocky stubs short enough that a child could peek over them. Time, the greatest enemy of all, had taken its toll. Even the great workmanships meant to last forever could not withstand its constant beating. But even in its demolished state, there was beauty and a magical essence that a soul nearby could not help but sense about this place. A person visiting here would without a doubt stop a moment to look twice at this panorama hidden beneath the surface of Krael.

The vertical slits of the maw of a grey stone helmet as large as a building protruded from the ground, chin hidden beneath the dirt and rubble. Two humans walking abreast could easily fit in between the stone slits and then look up and out from the collapsed half of the top of the helm. Small rodents scampered quickly across the rubble inside causing tiny chips of rock to shift and fall from their precariously balanced positions, tippity-tapping across the stone surfaces on their way down to the soft ground. At the back of this helm stood a sarcophagus. The sharp edges were now worn and rounded, and the inscriptions in the stone were smoothed over, rendering them unreadable. The one recognizable aspect remaining was the statue of a man standing behind it. Contrary to the many other depictions of him across Krael, Ghaleon was not poised for combat. He stood tall, his sword held clasped within both hands pointed down in front of him, cape lying undisturbed and in perfect symmetry across his back, and eyes staring proudly ahead. His famous shield was carved onto the front face of the statue's rectangular base.

Leaning against the base, on opposite sides, were Itha and Fauler. Moisture from the ground swirled around their sleeping bodies in a deep fog that blanketed the dirt before drifting through the front of the helm as though its breath was condensing on a cool day. The helm's breath weaved its way across the ground, over the ruins, and beyond where the glow of the lighting reached. After it travelled a bit further, it found two more living bodies present in the usually desolate, dead, and forgotten catacombs beneath Krael.

The musty air filled Kylie's nostrils with dirt and her skin with grime as she awoke from her slumber. The air was chilly, but it held nowhere near the frigid bite of the snow-filled Frostlands above. She had snuggled close to Mory with the back of her head against his chest and legs intertwined with his, sharing his warmth for their rest. His steady breathing flowing across her neck sent shivers down her spine now that she was awake. His cape of animal pelts had made for an excellent blanket for them both beneath the surface of Krael. She was quite content to stay here forever.

Mory must have sensed her waking and pulled her in closer for a big bear hug, "Good morning, my love. Ready to explore what lies in the light ahead?"

Telovi emerged from Mory's bag excitedly, "I am! I am! I always love a good adventure!"

Kylie giggled at the fairy's antics. She had met Telovi while they had been walking through the tunnel earlier and had liked her immediately. She was so glad that someone had been able to keep Mory company while he had been adventuring around an unknown world. He had told her stories that she could hardly imagine to be true, and the sword and shield he now carried were beautiful and magnificent! His muscles had hardened and become more defined since she had last seen him, but the mischievous glint and laughter in his eyes were still there, softened now by their purple glow and with what she could only imagine to be love.

Kylie sighed and stretched before answering, "Yes, I suppose I am." The trio got up and ate a small breakfast from what Mory had in his pack, and then worked their way towards the lit part of the catacombs. On their way along the pathways the previous day, they had stumbled over old bones and found indentations in the walls that had likely been used to house the dead of centuries ago.

The deeper they wandered, the older the ruins seemed to be. Whatever lay ahead must be the oldest, most important part of the catacombs that they had seen yet. Why else would it be lit, while everything else slept eternally in darkness? They had specifically chosen to sleep in the darkness, outside the reach of the light, in order to hide from whatever dangers may have been lurking up ahead.

It did not take them long to reach the light, and once they did, all three of them stopped in their tracks and gasped astounded at the enchanting sight. It took them some time to take it all in. The helm was positioned immediately in front of them at the center of the cave, surrounded by the collapsed ruins.

"Well, what do we have here?" a masculine voice rang from the helm causing them to stop gawking and bring their weapons to ready. Fauler walked out of one of the great helm's slits, Itha appearing momentarily after through a different slit.

Itha cackled slightly as a devilish smile crept across her face, "Looks like a crew seeking out a beating. The prince said to kill anyone who came too close while he was gone." She raised her sword to inspect it nonchalantly. "This must be our first blood!"

Fauler held his hand up to signify a pause in their approach, "Hold off there, Itha! The girl, you see her? That's Kylie, isn't it? Prince Sonu will be thrilled if we can capture her again! And who's this boy with her? She must have dumped her old escort for a new one. I'll just delight in taking him down."

Itha purred at Kylie in a voice that sounded more threatening than soothing, "I guess we were meant to be travelling companions yet again, Kylie. Come over here now, and make this easier for us both. I would not like to mar that pretty face of yours without being forced into it." Itha used her sword to point to a location next to her where she wished Kylie to come.

Kylie gripped her dagger tighter in her hand. There was no way she would be coming peacefully. Those two must have passed them as they slept, or maybe there was another route down here. Kylie remembered the other cave entrance that Anik had found before their battle outside and deduced that they must have come from there. There was no way they could have gotten through the meteorite without being strong in Spirit. She responded to Itha with a tone of threat in her voice, "I would be more worried about your life than my face, Itha. If a fight is what you want, come and get it. If not, let us pass through and investigate the ruins ourselves."

Itha rolled her eyes and positioned her blade threateningly, "Well look at you, trying to talk reason. Sorry, but our orders precede any deals on the battlefield. I will take you hostage willingly or by force. Doesn't matter either way to me. Just trying to make your life easier. You would have thanked me later."

As if on cue, Itha and Fauler began approaching Kylie and Mory simultaneously. Kylie and Mory readied themselves for defense. Kylie thought she saw Sonu's lackeys hesitate momentarily once they saw Kylie and Mory had no intention of retreat, but they had already committed to the fight and so had no choice but to jump into the fray.

Neither was a pushover with the blade. Kylie was having trouble keeping pace with Itha since her sword gave her an advantage in reach. Kylie's daggers were more suited for throwing from great distances or sneaking behind one's enemy as opposed to one-on-one battle with a trained sword duelist, but she was not going to give up so easily. She knew Itha did not intend to kill her at least. She only intended to take her hostage once again. Unlike last time though, Kylie had no intention of letting that happen.

Hardly any time seemed to have passed when two rocks fell very precisely knocking Itha and Fauler in the head almost simultaneously. Kylie looked at Mory for a moment, not believing their luck when they heard Anik's shout from behind them, "You two okay? You looked like you might have needed a hand."

Kylie waved her hand in thanks as Anik, Zhannah, Dainn, and Elasche worked their way over towards Mory and herself. Itha was groaning on the ground, rolling back and forth, holding her head, and Kylie made sure to kick her sword far away for good measure. Fauler was not moving or making any sound at all.

Zhannah began to explain, "We were worried when you didn't return after an hour had passed, so we came after you. The boulder was blocking our path though, so we had to wait for Anik's strength to return to move it. I am glad we were able to find you in time to be of service. How were you able to get inside these catacombs without moving the boulder?"

Mory spoke up excitedly, "The boulder is actually a meteorite that I saw fall from the sky, not that it really matters at this point. Through some connection of our Spirits, Kylie and I were able to travel through the veins of silver within the meteorite and then pop out underneath it. I have been drawn to that meteorite for as long as I have been in the Frostlands, and only when it spat me out down here with Kylie did I feel its ever-present pull cease to hold me." Mory shrugged after finishing, "I guess it wanted me to find this place." Zhannah nodded, appeased by Mory's explanation.

Itha had pulled herself over to where Fauler lay on the ground and was avidly looking him up and down, panic growing in her features. The blood from her wounded head dripped from her matted hair onto his unresponsive body as she looked down on him. She suddenly began to appeal to the group, "Help him! Can one of you please help him? He isn't reacting to anything!" She moved an angry glare to meet Anik's eyes and demanded, "It was you who did this wasn't it!? You can fix this. Fix it now!"

Anik shook his head, raising his arms, not knowing what to do. Elasche, seeing his hesitation, slowly walked over to Fauler, knelt beside him on the ground, and spoke to Itha, "I am a trained healer and just want to get a quick assessment of his situation, if you will allow me to touch him to focus my concentration." Itha nodded her consent and warily looked at the young girl. Elasche placed both her hands on Fauler's torso and closed her eyes. Her long dark hair fell over her shoulder as she concentrated. Minutes later she re-opened her eyes and gave a report of Fauler's status, "He has a fractured skull, and his brain is bleeding out. He will likely not survive the next hour without treatment."

Itha let out a shoulder-racking sob, "No! That can't be right. You can fix him up, can't you? He'll be okay if you use your Spirit to mend him?"

Elasche looked backed to Zhannah. Zhannah used her cold emotionless voice to respond, "She will do no such thing at this moment, Itha. You both intended to kill our friends here, why should we go out of our way to save someone who wants one of our own dead?"

Itha begged, "Anything, I'll do anything! Just name it, what do you will of me?"

Zhannah waited a few long moments before speaking, "Very well. First, you and Fauler will not harm any person in this room or of the Saliek for the rest of your lives because it is at our decree that Fauler would have life beyond this point in time."

"That is yours; never will we harm anyone in this room or of the Saliek so long as we both shall live," Itha said hurriedly awaiting the other demands that would likely follow.

"You will tell us of your business with Prince Sonu and his intentions and answer any other questions about him and his plans that we may come up with, after Fauler is healed."

Itha gulped. She had to know that at this moment she was betraying her Prince and commander for Fauler's life. She had to know that neither of them would have a place in his army after today and would be labeled as traitors. Her dreams of advancement would be crushed to nothing more than past thoughts and hopes. Yet, still she answered softly, "Yes, I'll do it. Please, just help him before it's too late." Blood, sweat, and tears ran down Itha's cheeks as she spoke those words.

Zhannah gave Elasche a nod, and she went to work mending Fauler to bring him back from the brink of death. Itha watched eagerly across the other side of his motionless body awaiting his return.

Anik had found his way over to Kylie's side and nudged her shoulder gently, "See, I told you!"

"Told me what?" Kylie asked.

"That they loved each other once, and that there are still remnants of it deep down, regardless of how awful they treat each other, and regardless of how many times they deny it. Their allegiances will always come to each other first, especially in times of great need," Anik reminded her of the conversation they had when they had been captured by Itha and Fauler, seemingly so long ago.

Kylie smiled at him and replied, "I guess you were right about them, Anik. Love is a strange thing, isn't it? It must differ from couple to couple, from story to story, because it never looks the same to me. It's a shame they have squandered something so beautiful with hatred, anger, and manipulation all these years."

Chapter 33

Two pink blossom petals twisted happily around each other as they floated effortlessly in the breeze across a puffy-clouded, cerulean blue sky. The searing sun peeked out from behind one of the white clouds, and the petals began a playful race towards to the ground. As the friendly spirit of their race diminished, the petals slowly began drying up into crinkly brown debris. A mere moment before one of them became a disembodied powder of dust, the sky took pity on the couple and blessed them with another breeze. A friendly cloud hovered over the parching sun and began to spritz them with a healing drizzle revitalizing them from their withered state for one more chance at a life together in the skies.

Fauler awoke as ungrateful and grumpy as ever, and Itha abandoned her post at his side to join Zhannah, Kylie, Mory, and Anik who were sitting on various-sized pieces of rubble inside the great helmet. Elasche remained by Fauler's side to ensure that he did not do anything to worsen his condition, and Dainn sat close to Elasche to ensure that Fauler did nothing to harm her.

Kylie felt pity for Itha and disgust for Fauler as she watched Itha approach the group. She had bargained for his life, and he didn't seem to care one iota. It was as if he had just expected it of her. Kylie knew deep down that Itha would never see anything in return for her actions, and that made her heart cry for her. Itha sat across from Kylie. The tears that had streamed down her face earlier were gone, and her emotional shields were back up. Her face was expressionless except for if one looked deep into her eyes, they could see a hint of pain. Pain that she was so used to experiencing that she had become proficient at covering it up with her sarcasm and ill-treatment of others. No one could hurt her if she didn't let them get too close.

Kylie knew that there had to be other better ways of hiding the pain, or even healing it, but she did not know how to broach the topic with Itha. So, she sat quietly, examining the woman across from her, wishing she could reach her somehow.

Without any preamble or prodding, Itha began, "Prince Sonu was never very forthright with his troops, but I can tell you what I've seen and inferred from his actions. For the past many years, he has been searching for the Spirit Master and for something else. I've never known what that was, but I've been sent out on many search parties with him for it."

"There were many nights where he went to his tent early, and it sounded as though he was talking to himself for a period of time. This usually concluded in some sort of display of anger or frustration, so the troops would avoid the area around his tent at any cost during that part of the evening. Many rumors circled the camps about him, but the most plausible ones were that he was genuinely mad, possessed some sort of ancient relic, or maybe possessed a magic himself that allowed him to speak to another across many leagues."

"After retreating from the battle yesterday with Prince Sonu, we stumbled across a cave near a stream that led us here. The horses would not fit through the opening, so we tied them up loosely where they could reach the stream. We also left their feed bags out in case we did not return in a timely fashion and they could not find any vegetation for themselves. We each grabbed only the essentials that we needed to hike with, but Prince Sonu also brought along a handheld mirror. I only noted it because it seemed strange for him to want to burden himself with such a menial thing. I think it must be of significance to him, maybe it's even the relic that was rumored to allow him to communicate with someone else far away." Itha paused for a moment looking to her captive audience for a reaction. There was none in particular as they listened intently.

"When we arrived at the ruins, we searched the area for a while, and Fauler found a tunnel behind the statue of Ghaleon. We would have missed it, as it was covered by a slab of stone and years of moss growth, but the ancient, cracked stone shattered under the weight of Fauler's step, and he fell back onto the ground. After a bit of minor excavation, we were able to discern that a human could fit through the hole. Prince Sonu insisted on going in first and ordered us to stay behind and guard his flank. The look in the prince's eyes when he said that was a wild one, filled with fear, anger, and greed beyond which I had ever seen before. So, we asked no questions and let him go in alone. He has not since returned." Itha was bending forward with her hands folded together, elbows atop her knees, and was staring at the statue when she finished her report. She took a deep breath as though a large burden had been lifted from her shoulders.

There was only silence for a minute before Mory declared, "I'm going in after him. I have a feeling..."

Zhannah heard him trail off and consented, "Then go on ahead. I'll stay here with Dainn and Elasche. Would you take Kylie or Anik with you, also?"

Mory replied, "Kylie. I would take Kylie, if she would not mind." He turned to her with his winning smile and gazed into her eyes. She could not say no to him. She had every intention of following him into the tunnel regardless of whether he had asked her to or not!

She beamed back at him and replied, “Of course! I’d have it no other way!”

Anik coughed a little drawing attention to himself, “And myself?”

Mory cocked his head thinking about it for a moment before responding, “No, I don’t think so. If we don't come back in the same amount of time that Prince Sonu has been gone, you guys come in after us.”

Anik looked to Zhannah, who shrugged a little, “Whatever seems best according to your judgment, Mory. Before you go though, I think I should let both you and Kylie know something so you understand why I am giving you so much weight in this decision.” Kylie and Mory both stopped what they were doing and looked to Zhannah before she continued, “Scilla and I believe that Mory is the true Spirit Master, not Kylie. It’s a long story, but essentially Kylie was your cover, Mory, while Scilla raised you. Your age is the same as hers. Your powers exceed hers. You are the remaining hope for Krael and the Saliek, so please take care of yourself. Follow your intuition, but use your brain as well. This may not be the only world whose future is tied up in your success.”

Kylie was stunned. She hadn’t realized how much she had clung to her supposed title of Spirit Master. It had assured her that one day she would be more competent than she was now and maybe even be useful in this world. Along with the disappointment, though, was relief and pride. There was relief in that she would not be expected to save Krael and pride that the man she loved was destined for greatness beyond which she could even conceive. She watched Mory as he unsheathed his sword to inspect it closely, turning it over in his hand. He then gingerly placed his hand on the strap of the shield across his chest, taking it in between his thumb and forefinger. A faraway look entered his eyes as he stared at nothing in particular.

Zhannah had been watching him as well, "Yes, Mory. I see that you are putting the pieces together now. That sword you hold is Ghaleon's sword of legend, and that shield is his also. I suspect that through this tunnel you will find the cloak and become the most powerful Spirit Master that has walked the world of the living since Ghaleon himself. One day you will have to relay to me the trials that you had to withstand to obtain those, but today, all I ask is that you recall them, and remember that what lays beyond this tunnel is not to be taken lightly. It sounds as though your Spirit is leading you here, so it must be your destiny to find the relics, but that is no reason to walk into a battle unprepared."

Zhannah walked over to Kylie and placed her hand on her shoulder, "Before you go, can you please relay a message back to your father about what has transpired in the last couple days. I am sure he and Scilla are sitting on pins and needles in anticipation."

***

Crickets were chirping as the evening descended into night. Scilla sat anxiously at a desk within the library at the Saliek camp. It didn't feel as right as her desk in the Ancient Archives did. She had always felt like she could think more clearly there. There was only a small window above her here, letting the moonlight shine in onto the old, splinter-filled wooden desk. The chair she sat in was adorned with a worn, blue cushion that she could only sit on for short intervals before needing to stand and rub her rump and lower back until the aches subsided. The past many days had led to her increased discomfort. Scilla mentally scolded herself for being too posh and recalled times when she would sit on a vacant tree stump or fallen log in the forest to complete her studies when she had been younger and travelling the world laying the groundwork for her master plans.

The world had taken another step towards the peace that she strove to corral it in. Regithal had stopped by earlier to inform her that Mory had been recognized as the next Spirit Master and, miracle among miracles, had already located not only the sword, but the shield of Ghaleon as well. She yearned to ask Mory about the locations and trials of these ancient relics so that one day she could go back through notes of her previous prophecies and correlate them, but all that mattered right now was that he was in possession of them. A sense of pride hung in her mind as she realized that she had at least generally located two of the three ancient relic's locations: the oasis and the Frostlands. If Mory had been drawn to the place in the Frostlands as he had the previous resting places of the sword and shield, the cape would no doubt be hidden there.

Prince Sonu was beyond a doubt one of Kaitzen's minions in this world who was tasked with locating the fabled cloak of Ghaleon. If Prince Sonu ever returned it to Kaitzen, Kaitzen would have the ability to travel to whatever world that he desired without fear of death. Scilla was quite sure that he would use it to travel back to Tendyis, though for what purpose she wasn't sure. For now, she would nervously remain at the Saliek camp until they heard word from Kylie again on the success or failure of Mory's acquisition of Ghaleon's cloak.

***

When Kylie finished speaking with her father, the group ate a hearty meal before Mory and Kylie's departure into the tunnel. Fauler was still under strict orders from Elasche to remain lying down, so she fed him herself as he grumbled in discontent. The sight could have been construed as comical, as the fog that hovered slightly above the ground covered the majority of Fauler's body giving a translucent look to him, leaving his head as the only solid feature. Kylie felt nervous so she didn't eat as much as she usually would have, but her resolve was strengthened when she would catch a glimpse of Mory looking in her direction. When they were done eating, they packed their travelling satchels with what they thought they might need and headed over to the tunnel opening.

Mory waved his hand around the opening in an attempt to clear the fog away and get a better look inside, but he only succeeded in making it swirl about his hand causing Kylie to giggle. Mory sighed, and Kylie could see a flash of worry flit across his visage. "Normally, I would say ladies first, but I think in this case I will take the lead," Mory said with a taste of teasing in his voice and winked to Kylie before ducking into the tunnel.

Kylie, taken aback for a moment by his words, jumped in quickly after him. She would get him back for that eventually. She could have definitely led the way through this cramped, stinky, squishy tunnel. Her knees sank a good inch into the moist moss covering the ground, and she could feel a cool blast of stale air blowing at her face as she crawled forward. After a short distance of crawling, the tunnel opened up into a room wide enough for her to stand. Mory was waiting for her on the other side, staring ahead into the neon green glow that lit up the mists in front of them.

"Do you have any idea what is causing that glow?" Kylie inquired, mesmerized by the ethereal sight.

Mory shook his head and pulled out his memory sphere, "I'll check in here though. Vi, stay back for a moment, will you, just in case." The purple fairy had started to fly forward to get a closer look.

"Aww you're no fun, Mory! I was just gonna take a little peek!" Vi complained before flying back and hovering above his shoulder as he tried to extract useful memories from the purple glowing sphere to no avail.

"There's nothing in here about it," Mory said disappointedly before scanning the area quickly. "I don't see Prince Sonu's body near here though. So, if it's dangerous, it probably won't harm us immediately. You two wait here while I try to clear a path through with my Spirit." Mory took a few steps closer to the mist and closed his eyes to concentrate. A loud fizzling noise suddenly filled the silent room, and the green glowing mists started to expand their domain. Kylie felt panic rise in her chest, but instead of retreating back through the hole from which they came, she lunged forward to grab Mory. He was already limp when she got to him, and she could barely hold his weight. Before she could drag him back, she felt her head beginning to lighten and her legs beginning to weaken. The world became a muddled, fuzzy blur and then ceased to exist as her mind entered another realm.

Chapter 34

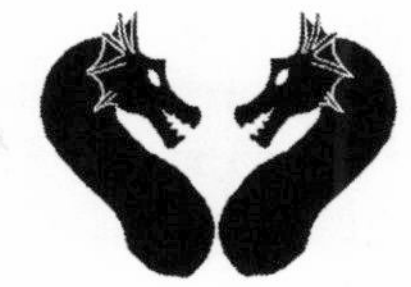

A proud, transparent man peered through a window into another world and cringed at what he saw. A large man with various blood-stained weapons secured around his person sported an avaricious glare in his eyes and stood poised above a rock pedestal presenting a priceless treasure. The avarice was tinged with hints of anger and insanity as the man briefly looked back upon the rest of his contingent. They were dead. He had single-handedly killed them all upon finding the treasure.

His hand released the long knife that had committed his dirty deeds, and it fell with a clink onto the buckle of a leather belt strapped across the bare, muscled chest of the last man he had killed. The last of his breath was pushed from his body, and his eyes stared blankly into the clear blue sky. That body had belonged to the man's best friend and brother.

Before the man turned back to his treasure, a ghost appeared and solidified in front of his eyes. The man froze. He was shocked for only a moment before a sword cleanly removed his head from his shoulders. "You have cost me," the solidified ghost spoke as he dimmed slowly back into nothingness, "but I fear there would have been a far greater cost had you gathered my treasure. I now see a test of conscious will need to be implemented. Thank you for showing me this necessity. I will not dally."

Coarse sand squished between his bare toes as a salty wind playfully messed with his golden hair, tossing it waywardly into his eyes. The sky was a clear, bright blue, and the sun shone down on him hot and brilliant. He was shirtless and could feel the sting and stick of the sand and salt in the air as it prickled his bare chest. There was a vast body of water to his left that spilled its navy countenance eternally in every direction, except towards the pale sanded beach he was standing on. The waves rose variably above the surface of the water capping in crashes of white before they rolled up the smooth wet sand of the shore. To his right, the beach faded into a thick forest of luscious palms and brightly flowered bushes that ended abruptly at the face of a jagged, black rock cliff. He didn't know where he was or why he was here. He only felt a great emptiness inside of him that steadily throbbed as his heart beat blood through his veins. His life currently was pointless and destitute, no matter how gorgeous the scenery was here. Who was he again? Oh yes, he was Mory. Too often he would find himself forgetting here.

Mory looked over his shoulder at a girl about his age who was following him. She had short, dirty blonde hair whisking her shoulders that was in constant disarray from the wind being channeled by the cliffside. The eyes that met his were blood red and contained a strange swirl of darkness within them. The constant sun that Mory and she were exposed to had bronzed her skin, amplifying the color of her hair and eyes. This made her a bewitching sight to be held.

She stepped along behind Mory, face set in its usual disapproving frown, whining at him to slow his pace so that he would be back at her level. He knew that she never smiled for real. Sure, her lips would curl into the shape of a smile, especially if she was manipulating him to do something, but the curve never touched her eyes, not even when Mory spent the time to joke with her. It felt as though she had been following him for years. They hardly spoke, but she took what she needed from him when he hunted or fished for food, and he couldn't deny her a share. He felt as though he had to take care of this being that weighed heavily on him day after day. He tried to teach her to be self-sufficient, but she refused to learn, preferring to take, and seemed too fearful to leave his side.

All she ever wanted to do was dance in the sand. Many men would have found her dancing alluring, and at first Mory was entranced and complemented her endlessly. The girl had taken advantage of this and soon forced him to watch her dance each and every day. It slowly blotted out any other activities that he had enjoyed, and she ferociously strove to remove all acquaintances that were not herself. She even went as far as forcing him to learn how to dance, criticizing his every move harshly with her sharp words even though she was the one who forced this upon him. Mory was her personal slave, and he could not seem to writhe himself away from her clutches since she would either guilt trip him into staying or threaten him with one of her violent tantrums. She had taken his tender heart that had shown her kindness in granting her his protection so many years ago and caged it away such that he could not show it to anyone else. He could not grow any of his interests or follow any of his goals with her claws lodged savagely into his skin.

Day after day they walked the endless beach. Mory could not figure out the point of this monotonous, restrictive life. Each day, time marched on slowly and repetitively, and his heart ached more with the emptiness growing inside. Each night, as they returned to their encampment built of palm wood, animal pelts, and weaved palm fronds, he would lie down next to her, and a foreboding darkness would seep into his mind. A depression penetrated his soul, needling it seemingly beyond repair. The ocean would beckon him into its depths during these times. All he had to do was walk out a little too far, and the currents would sweep him away from his worthless, unfruitful life to a more peaceful and possibly purposeful one. He believed that he could leave her that way. She would have the cache of supplies that he had stored up on hand to survive for years on her own. She also had her talents in dancing that she could no doubt make a living on, if she gave herself the chance. Mory leaving this way would force her to take that chance and give her the opportunity to become who she really wanted to be. The opportunity that she was too scared to take in her present, comfortable situation.

After tossing and turning through a night like that, Mory would try suggesting that they go inland and climb the palm trees with leafy emerald fronds to find the succulent coconuts that he loved, but she did not like the fresh white meat of the coconuts or the sweet, thick milk that they housed, so he was not allowed to partake in that unless it was a boon that she granted him. He tried taking her into the ocean and swimming with her through the rainbow of reefs, admiring the schools of fish whose scintillating scales flashed silver in the sunlight as they weaved their way through retracting anemones, but she never liked it when he spent too much time in the water and always made him get out as soon as possible. She would under no circumstances let him go into the water alone or let him do anything in general without her permission. So, he was stuck fantasizing about the ocean's beauty and alluring pull from dry land. He tried suggesting that she go inland and converse with locals that he had made friends with during his hunting expeditions to try and find others like herself, but that was always met with vehement refusal and tears that he was trying to get rid of her. Mory felt stuck with no way of escape. He knew full well that he was no more than a slave to her whims and did not actually provide her with any real happiness. He was just a safety blanket so that she could live her life dancing in the sand.

One night, after many years of endurance, Mory took out his old pack and began to rummage through it in hopes that it would keep the sinking depression that clutched for his mind at bay. He found a purple translucent orb that he could hold in one hand. The purpose of the orb had faded with time from his mind, but holding it did bring back a shadow of happiness as he rolled it carefully between his hands. He looked to the shield that sat in the sand and ran his fingers lovingly down the emblem on the front. It had been so long since he had last required its use that he could not remember exactly what it was for. It also tugged at his heart's strings. His sword, always nearby, held a faint purple glow that lit the small encampment with a dim light as he removed it slightly from its scabbard. The depression began to retract from his mind as the energy contained in these objects soothed his emotions. He reached into his bag one last time, intending to attempt to sleep again afterwards, and pulled out a carving of a wooden, winged cat and stared wide-eyed at it.

The world seemed to stop on its axis for a moment as an intense passion overtook him. Thoughts of a time past berated his consciousness begging to be let in but were denied through some constructed barrier. He only knew he needed to go to the ocean. The beautiful place that he was forbidden. The pull was so strong that by sitting still he nearly felt his insides being ripped out towards the direction of the water. He heard its waves crashing onto the shore over the pounding of his heart in his chest whispering in a sultry alto, "Come to me." He smelt and tasted its sweet salt floating in traces through the air,

"Come to me, Mory." He peeked out of the tattered cloth flap used as a doorway to their little hut and saw the now rippling blackness of the ocean sparkling calmly in the light of the full moon. It melted seamlessly into the sky where the sparkling ripples were replaced by the twinkle of the stars. "Come to me, Mory. You are meant for so much more than this." He flung his shield and old bag onto his back, strapped his sword about his waist, and bolted to the water's edge. The cool water touched his feet refreshingly and invited him in. "Come to me, Mory. Please," the voice of the ocean whispered soothingly into his mind.

With all his senses engaged, nothing would stop him now. Not even the screaming demon that ran behind him, for his companion had transformed into its true form once it knew it could no longer keep Mory hostage from his destiny. It rampaged, throwing rocks and shells at Mory as he stood on the shoreline with the water lapping at his ankles. The demon slammed its massive hands on the sandy ground, shaking its horned head in frustration, and then ripped the roof off their hut with a shriek before taking off after Mory.

Mory jumped into the depths of the ocean and followed his heart without looking back onto his old life. He swam with his sword slightly drawn to light the way through the depths of the water. On impulse, he willed the water to separate into gaseous oxygen and hydrogen in front of his face so that he could breathe and open his eyes beneath the ocean. Fish swam away from the glowing purple form that sliced through the ocean like butter, leaving a trail of fine bubbles in his wake. Mory bee-lined to where he felt the pulling in his soul and slowed when he saw a large bubble encasing the most beautiful woman he had ever seen. Her long golden locks twisted around her unconscious body, which emanated a green glow. Her head was tilted slightly upward towards the surface, lips slightly parted, as the rest of her body floated limply in an upright position ending in her toes pointed down towards the depths beneath her. The clothes that remained on her body were tattered and worn but still covered the necessary places.

A tug on Mory's foot awoke him from his trance, and he turned to face his demon companion. She had grabbed both his feet now and was taking him deeper into the ocean and further away from this girl he needed to save. He was descending too fast, and he could feel the pressure increasing in his head. He tried in vain to kick her away from him, but she held fast with her vicious grin spreading across her face. For the first time, he saw the smile reach her eyes. She was enjoying the thought of hurting him.

Any compassion that he had felt for her was lost in that moment as he realized the true nature of the one he had been protecting. Mory fluidly unsheathed his sword and sliced through her arms at the wrists, provoking a horrible soprano screech, "Mory, why did you do this to me? I loved you! You took care of me!" The demon's face morphed back into the creature that he had cared for as it looked back and forth at its handless arms spewing out gore into the pristine ocean waters. Tears filled its eyes as it tried to guilt trip its prey into staying within her clutches one last time.

Mory began kicking away from the creature and shouted over its cries, "You clearly don't know what love is if you thought that what we had was true. Shed your selfish, manipulative shell and maybe then you will find and understand love! Learn to give, and strive to improve yourself daily, then love will find you." Mory did not immediately understand what he meant by those words, but he felt it ring true within. He needed to save this bubble girl, and maybe his memories would come back to him. She had to be the key.

Mory swam unfettered for the first time in what seemed like an eternity. It was too dark to enjoy the colorful corals he knew to be surrounding him, but the ocean still felt beautiful to him. He didn't need to see its treasures to feel its wonder. He reached the bubble once more and this time did not hesitate. He reached his arm out towards the fit girl's body intending to carrying her out of the water, but the moment he touched her the world swirled once more, and he was no longer in an ocean saving the most enchanting woman he had ever seen. He was nowhere.

There was nothing but Mory's essence in the place the girl, Kylie, had taken him. He knew her now. His memories had returned, and he was ashamed that he had let his demon companion enslave him for so long while Kylie sat stagnant beneath the ocean depths awaiting his arrival.

"Do not fret, young Spirit Master. You have passed the trial that I deemed worthy of you," a booming male voice resonated through his essence. "I needed to know that you would not let others drag you down and take advantage of you when you have a far more important purpose to be serving. Even if that person acted like they required your protection, you needed to be able to see through the hoax. I needed to know that your core values penetrated deep enough into your subconscious that a small sign could point you in the right direction. Your own kindness and sense of duty are also your greatest weaknesses. Keep your eyes open in the coming trying times, and I will help you when I can."

"Mory, you are a person worthy of adorning my cloak. I wish you the best of luck in your future endeavors. May the pure goodness and love in your heart always lead you to the necessary course of action, no matter how difficult the choice," the voice faded away into the nothingness, and Mory felt a great sense of relief flood through him. He had chosen correctly. Now he must go find the real Kylie, his true love and his life.

Chapter 35

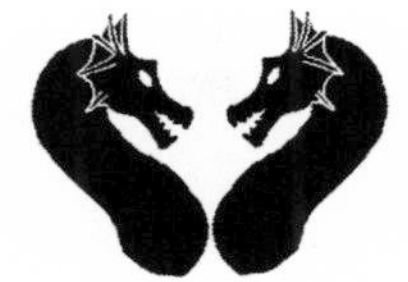

The young dragon had grown into a beast to be feared, although gentle she was. She searched fervently through the forest trying to find her treasure again. She refused to let it go, even when it drifted away from her. The trees peeled away layer after layer until she saw the golden-haired boy near the edge of a waterfall. He sat, eating a bunch of grapes, kicking his bare feet back and forth in the pool beneath him smiling back at her. He was no longer the child that she had grown with but a man who carried a sword and shield who could defend himself. She cared not, and curled up near the gentle splashes of the waterfall ready to defend him from whatever perils came his way. Once she had unwillingly been made his defense. Now she volunteered.

Dried and dead leaves crunched as Kylie ran through the red and gold forest. Her pursuers' horses crashed through the brush behind her as they closed in with each staccato of hoof beats. She'd have to find a place to hide quickly. Kylie ran between the closest-spaced trees she could find, hurdling logs and ducking under branches as required. Finding a thicket of thorny bushes, she hopped inside, thankful for her thick warm clothing keeping the thorns at bay. She pulled up her hood to protect her face from the briars and huddled down into a dug-out portion within them. An animal must have recently rested there. Tucking her knees beneath her body and crouching down, she could hide the majority of herself beneath ground level. The pounding of hooves increased in volume as they neared her hiding spot. She could hear the commander shouting out which directions to check, and she was glad that they did not have dogs to sniff out her trail.

She knew they would give up the search eventually; they had who they really wanted: Mory. She was just a nuisance and a cleanup mission for them. The acrid smell of smoke that the crisp breeze blew in her direction worried her more. After the riders passed, she would need to escape the forest hastily before the dried leaves and branches shed by the trees for the coming winter were engulfed by the fire raging down from the mountains. It saddened her that the beauty of this autumn forest would soon be destroyed due to an ill-placed lightning strike.

Four… Five… Six… That was all of them. Kylie finished counting them off as they sped past. The sixth rider rode double with an unconscious Mory in front of him in the saddle. She was alone now. Kylie could not remember the last time that she had been truly alone. Growing up on Thaer she had always been with one of her parents, Scilla, or Mory. Sure, she had gone on walks by herself or found secret places in the Ancient Archives to hide away and read, but she had always known for certain where to go looking for someone if she needed them. On Krael, her comrades had steadily increased over time, and she had become accustomed to travelling and fighting alongside them. She had thought that Mory and her trip to this planet, Blaet, together was going to be an extravagant adventure, and it was until a group of bandits had come upon them unexpectedly.

Blaet was a planet where Spirit magic did not function, so Mory was out of his element. He had become accustomed to using it over the many years he had now been the Spirit Master fostering peace and prosperity on Krael. Kylie did not use her powers as often as Mory, even though they were practically joined at the hip. She had not forgotten what she had learned in her childhood on Thaer, so when they were ambushed, Kylie smoothly dodged her would be captor and got in a good stab at his torso. They would need to bind the wound soon if he were to live. Mory, on the other hand, had instinctively reached for his Spirit and came up empty. His attacker gave him a good clunk on the head and successfully dragged him away and up onto his horse before Kylie could reach him. After dealing a possibly mortal wound to her attacker, Kylie scanned the area noticing the four other riders surrounding her. These were not ordinary bandits looking for loot. A sigil on the breast of the leather jerkin worn by her assailant sported the skull of a horse with smoke rising from its eye sockets on a red and black checkered background. It gave Kylie pause as shivers raced down her spine before she bolted off through the forest to hide and regroup. The Syn had come to capture Mory while he was vulnerable on Blaet.

The Syn were a group of Spiritless rebels that believed that the presence of magic within another person was evidence of evil. This made Mory the epitome of all evil in their minds. She and Mory had known of them on Krael and had tried to assuage them, but their beliefs were ingrained too deeply. Now they had Mory, and she was unsure what they would do with him. There had been rumors of their torturous rituals that were used to purify the evil from Spirited ones that they captured, but Kylie had never born witness to one nor had anyone that she had known. Those stories now flooded her mind as she cowered in her thorn bush causing her to tremble as the fear and anger washed over her. She could never let the Syn hurt the man that she loved more than life itself!

The weight of her loneliness began to crush her as she let the fear and anger at the Syn subside. She would have to formulate and execute a successful rescue plan herself for the first time in her life, and Mory's life was at stake. Zhannah would have known what to do right away, formulating a plan and executing it flawlessly. Anik would have been able to track them down and obliterate them with his incredible skills at everything. Regithal would have just killed all six of the miscreants with his long sword in the first place and had never been in this situation to begin with.

Hush hush! She told her brain before it derailed into a mess. Worrying did no good. She would just have to complete this mission on her own with only her talents for once. Kylie tried to boost the confidence in her mind but found it hard to concentrate with the fear she was battling. A flicker of flame in her peripheral vision finally jarred her away from her hiding spot. The fire was still far away but was getting too close for comfort so she carefully crawled out of the thorns, a few of them pulling at loose strands of her long braid as she extricated herself.

She straightened herself out, carefully picking out the thorns that had stuck to her clothing, and looked back towards the fire-streaked sky. The flames had claimed the mountain now. They licked the sky with their yellow and red tongues leaving a grey breath of smoke above them. She could see the charred stumps cluttered around her from another recent fire. Black on one side fading to a light grey on the other, they clawed their way out of the ground, giving her a taste of what was to become of the surrounding area. Fires must be common in this place, keeping the trees and vegetation relatively young. In their autumn garb, the trees were adorned with the same colors as the flames, almost as if trying to camouflage within them in an attempt to save themselves from their burning fate.

Camouflage. That was her key. The smoke was drifting down off the mountain and into an open valley. Conveniently, it was the same valley that the forest would be clearing into very soon. She could hide herself within the smoke and take down Mory's captor in stealth. She needn't worry about the other five if she were careful. She'd prefer not to kill them if it wasn't necessary. Once Mory was freed, they could make their way back to the portal and return to Krael to inform the others of the arrival of the Syn. Then they could discuss what actions needed to be taken. She would have to keep her travelling cloak safe if she wished to return in one piece, Kylie thought to herself as she ran the fingers of her left hand across the silky, dark fabric that she had tied into a roll attached to her belt loop.

Kylie set off at a brisk pace towards where she knew the edge of the forest lay. Unless the smoke had gotten too thick, she should be able to see where the Syn had scurried off to when she reached the clearing ahead. Upon reaching the last rows of trees, she carefully hid behind one, investigating the situation from afar. There was a grassy field of green and yellow swaying in the breeze before her. Beyond that, she located the small group of Syn on a flat of rock in the distance that surrounded a pool at the base of a waterfall. A small creek ran from the pool into the forest east of where she stood. They must have intended to wait out the impending flames there before moving on to wherever their final destination was. She wasn't sure if they wouldn't still suffocate from the flames in their location, so she would have to act quickly and rescue Mory with enough time to reach the portal or find safer ground before the fires came down.

She decided to make a short stop at the creek to wet a

cloth and swathe it across her face to lessen the effects of the thickening smoke cloud on her lungs before stalking her prey through the field. This also gave the smoke cloud time to better obscure the area. She could feel her eyes begin to sting slightly in the haze and knew now was the time to strike. She lowered herself into the waist high grass and quickly, but softly, stepped her way across the field. The blowing breeze combined with the smoky haze should have been enough to hide her advancement on the small camp of Syn.

Kylie's mind had entered her battle phase now. All other emotions, including fear, had been subdued by her overwhelming need to accomplish her desired purpose. Time did not seem to advance for Kylie in this state of mind. Its movement was only distinguished by events. It mattered not how long it took to complete a task, only that it was done and she could move onto the next one. So, the length of time it took her to traverse the grassy field was negligent in her mind, and once she started feeling the ground transition from soft dirt to solid rock, she slowed to a stop.

The smoke cloud had thickened even more, and she was glad that she had kept an eye out on the locations of each of the six Syn members as she had been approaching. The one with Mory should be to her right near a ledge overhanging the pool. Mory was awake now, sitting atop his captor's horse, but bound well so that he could not really be expected to escape on his own. Kylie saw the man dismount and walk to the side of the pool to dip his head into the water, most likely to wash the smoke sting from his eyes.

As he bent over the pool, Kylie let fly a throwing dagger straight into his kidney. The man sunk forward into the pool, only a brief gurgle escaping his lips before any further sound was muffled beneath the depths of the water. She let a second blade fly flat-first into Mory's chest. At first, he was surprised, but he quickly caught onto the situation and began sawing through his rope bonds. Kylie watched the other five in the group who were staring at the advancing fire. It seemed to be decreasing in intensity as it descended the mountain, but it would, without a doubt, burn straight through the dry, grassy field to their location. The fire was close enough now for them to hear the crackle of the flames and feel the sting of the debris in their eyes.

If only the horse Mory's captor had left him tied to would move a little closer, Kylie thought as Mory finished freeing himself. An idea popped in Kylie's head. She pulled a blapple from her pocket that she had been carrying for her pegasus on Krael and sliced it in half. Carefully, she stuck her hand out of the tall grass where she was hiding to allow for the horse to sense the delicious treat that she had in store for it. The horse gleefully tossed his head, eyed the bait, and cautiously inched its way forward. The other Syn in the group noted the movement of the horse, but when it stopped wandering away from the group, they turned their attention back to the encroaching fire. Either they assumed their now dead comrade had it under control, or the smoke was addling their brains.

Kylie scratched the soft fur of the horse's nose as it munched away on its treat, and Mory silently slid off its back into the brush. He looked to Kylie and grasped her firmly by the shoulders looking intensely into her eyes, "You are the most amazing girl that I've ever met, my love. I am now even more in your debt than I was previously just for you allowing me to be a part of your wonderful life." Mory, being a romantic as always, made Kylie beam and blush even though they had known each other forever. She kissed him softly and quickly on the lips as her pride in herself for completing the rescue mission swelled. She grabbed his hand, and they began to make their way back to the portal.

Kylie felt the world escaping her grasp as her essence floated into nothingness. She could no longer distinguish her separate five senses but could feel everything around her intensely. A powerful voice became present around her, "Congratulations on passing a test worthy of the Spirit Master himself. You would have made an excellent selection had he failed." She felt the presence hum to itself thoughtfully, "Before you passed through into the realm that holds my cape, as the deepest love of the Spirit Master whose duty it is to cleanse this universe of evil, I needed to know that you could believe in yourself enough to go it alone. There will be times when people will not be there to help you, and you will have to make decisions and act solely on your own discretion. I could see into your heart and tell that your own adequacy was your greatest fear. You had to know that you were capable of doing this, even when the stakes were high, so that you could continue as Mory's right hand and his guiding light eternally. Welcome, my dear. You will always be cared for in this life and the next."

The sensation of being omniscient faded, and life as she was familiar with regained control of her mind and body.

Chapter 36

A sullen ghost roamed the abandoned halls of his home. He had finally been released from his bedroom but not from the thorns that bound him to this place. The severed vines were draped about his body and dragged along the floor behind him as the chains they really were. He reflected back onto life, and with each poignant memory, he could feel the sting of another thorn gouging into his ghostly body. After wailing for an indeterminate amount of time in the hallways, without a doubt disturbing those of the living with his sorrow, he came to a realization. He could no longer bear the weight of his past, so he would forgive himself and try to shape his future for the better. With each burden he forgave, a thorn disappeared and vines disintegrated, one by one, until only a single thorn remained between his shoulder blades. He was freed.

An infinite number of mirrors lined the walls of Sonu's confines. He had wandered the hallways for an indeterminate, endless seeming, amount of time, yet he saw no end or hint of a way out. The pathways were lit just enough for him to see the reflections in the mirrors and the bluish grey stones that they were mounted on. The mirrors were not entirely ordinary. His reflection peered back at him from some of them with his tousled hair and fear-stricken eyes. He was quite the mess. His red cloak was torn and tattered, dirt was smeared haplessly across his face, and his clothing felt as disgusting and greasy as it looked in the mirrors. He was not at all the image of the princely figure that he was supposed to represent.

As much as those mirrors irked him, the other mirrors frustrated him more. They were the ones that opened the doorway into the fear hidden deep within his cold, hardened heart. Some of them showed him a series of images as though he were watching the events in them unfold as a spectator. The images were reflections of his memories, extending past when he had left the situation, showing him what had happened in the aftermath. Often the cruelty and pain that he had spread in those instances had laid the groundwork for troubles that found him later.

He saw the time where he lost his temper when the food that was brought to him was slightly overcooked. He had thrown the plate onto the floor in frustration, smashing the serving girl's foot in the process. He scolded her for attempting to serve him such tainted food as she cried on the floor unable to move with her broken foot. After he had gone back up to his rooms, leaving her alone on the floor for another servant to take care of, the servants had banded together in creating a shortage of Sonu's favorite food, which had irritated Sonu extensively for a month.

He saw another time where he had invited neighboring lords over to his castle to discuss matters of state that he wished to resolve with them. They spent hours listening to him as he made his points and arguments, letting him proceed as he wished. Many, he saw through the mirrors, were bored out of their minds and thought his ideas to be illogical, not well thought out, and utterly ridiculous, but they gave him their time and attention politely. Afterwards, one of the lords had offered a reasonable counter-proposal during which time

Sonu had stared into space and then started playing with his sword at the discussion table, making it very apparent that he did not care for the discussion at hand. The lords at the discussion decided that he was an incompetent leader at that point and never again invited him to their castles for diplomatic discussions nor returned to his. That small act of disrespect had cascaded into practically every problem that he now had with trade and commerce in neighboring lands.

Other mirrors showed him images that he did not remember from his life, and those were even more torturous. They all seemed happier, and the people surrounding him in them were content. He himself even looked jovial in those images. Seeing that joy more than anything cut into the shield he had constructed around his heart. That he was capable of experiencing happiness such as what the mirrors showed, terrified him more than anything. A cold sweat drenched his body as feelings he had believed himself long dead to flooded out. Some of which he couldn't even recognize.

He continued his way down the mirror-lined corridors, trying to only look at the floor or the myriad ornamented casings that housed the mirrors. He felt himself trembling as he often did before a fit of rage overtook him. The corridor eventually opened into a room where the lighting gave everything a bright sapphire hue. At least this was a slight change in scenery from the long, dark corridors that he had been traversing.

In the center, propped on a foot-high cylinder of stone, was the largest mirror that he had seen yet. The image inside of it contained a gleefully smiling version of himself standing regally in his red and gold robes with his ceremonial armor glinting beneath them in the sunlight. A compact crown consisting only of a plain golden ring adorned his head, symbolizing his station as Prince of Arbore. His eyes sparkled in delight an instant before a beautiful smiling girl in a long white dress leapt into his arms, and his image twirled her around as she giggled. The girl had long brown hair the rich color of a tree's bark in the summer. It waved down to her waist and had white flowers weaved into intricate braids around her head. The braids pulled the hair slightly out of her delicate face, accenting her large eyes, shapely lips, and high cheekbones that held a perfectly pink blush. Her hazel eyes beamed up into his as he held her up, and the rest of the world mattered not for those few moments.

The scene backed away so that he could see more in the mirror. His sister, Kylie, was there beaming and clapping in the background as she bounced in her chair. She sat next to his parents whose eyes glistened with tears as they watched their boy in his happiness. The castle garden had been set up with a beautiful white arch facing the dragon fountain. He was witnessing his wedding, an event that never actually happened since he was younger in the image before him. He recognized the girl now. She was the servant girl that he had beaten the night he had begun his plans to come to the Frostlands.

He felt tears sting his eyes for the first time in years as realization flooded him. The mirrors were showing him what he could have been. The choices that he had made in his life had turned him into who he was. He was not destined to have been a powerful and lonely man. He had shaped his world to be that way with each decision he made. Every time he let his temper out of control, every bribe he ever took, every person he treated with disrespect, even his dealings with the darkness that was his 'Master', those were all choices that he had made… choices that he could not undo now that they were in the past. A new feeling grasped at his heart: regret.

Sonu walked up to the mirror and gently placed his forefinger on the cheek of the smiling girl that might have been his love. As he did, she looked in his direction, feeling what she thought was a tickle in the breeze, for the past, present, and future were all connected in the place that Sonu was in now. Her big eyes met his unknowingly for an instant, and he collapsed to the cold, stone floor, curled into a ball, and cried uncontrollably at the pain and warm emotions that filled his previously frozen heart. His wedding to her was an opportunity lost, a door that was closed unknowingly by his own selfish decisions. In the current reality, he didn't even know her name.

A voice carried down the hallways to find Sonu in his pitiful state on the floor, "Prince Sonu of Arbore. I believe you understand now. I feel the change that has overcome you." Sonu choked in his sobs before righting himself into a cross-legged position on the floor, doing his best to contain himself now that he knew he wasn't alone. The voice pressed on, "You have no need to hide your true feelings from me, dear boy. I can sense them regardless." Prince Sonu took a deep breath and steadied himself as he looked from side to side unable to distinguish where the voice came from.

"Very well, I will show myself to you, as I think you understand what must happen now." The ghost of Ghaleon appeared in the sapphire glow of the room. Transparent as he was, he still carried himself as a warrior and wore a proud fatherly look on his face. The ghostly reminiscence of his renowned sword, shield, and cape all accompanied him on his body as they would have in the physical world. Sonu was taken aback at the brilliance and simplicity of the man he saw standing before him. He did not adorn any superfluous garments or baubles, only that which was needed for his duties.

"Oh, great and mighty Ghaleon, I hope you find it in your heart to forgive me for what I have done in this life," Sonu begged as he bowed his head in reverence before the spirit. "I see the mistakes I have made now, and if given the chance, would spend the rest of my life in recompense. I may not be able to change the past, but I could alter the future. I see this now. If only the chance were given me, I would help to lead this world and all the others to peace and goodness. I would strive to help others see what I did not before it was too late and protect those whose mission it is to save."

Tears dripped from Sonu's bowed head onto the stone floor, creating a small puddle as he sat in silence. He realized the great Ghaleon was judging him in those moments. Judging his words and his sincerity. Sonu knew not what would become of himself and almost wished that he could die and forget his past mistakes, but something inside of him ate at his conscience. He could do more if he tried. He could change and make the world a better place if given the chance. After seeing all the pain and agony he had been responsible for played back constantly in the mirrors for however long he had been in this stony prison and after seeing the happiness and joy he had given up, how could he just die? That would be too easy a punishment for him. As a matter of fact, it would be a reward compared to having to continue living with what he now knew.

"I have decided," Ghaleon's ghost stated, and before Sonu could look up to meet his eyes, he felt Ghaleon's ghostly sword penetrate his back. Sonu let out a blood-curdling scream. The sword cut through his body as though it were a solid sword. He saw its transparent blade pierce through his stomach and stared at it, momentarily lifting a quivering hand to the puncture wound before collapsing back onto the stone floor.

"Mercy!" he tried to wail but could not form the word with the liquids bubbling through his esophagus that should not be there. He passed out momentarily, before rising again. He stood and saw his mortal body lying in a bloody pool before him. The excruciating pain was gone, but a burning sensation remained in his back where Ghaleon's sword first struck his skin. Sonu lifted a hand in front of his face, turning it slightly to examine its now transparent nature. "So, you decided to relieve me of my mortal pain. I thank you Spirit Master Ghaleon for your kindness," Sonu spoke gravely as he looked into his eyes. "I guess this is what the afterlife feels like…"

Ghaleon chuckled before Sonu had a chance to continue, "No, boy, I have not done you a service. You are not dead but neither are you alive. You are doomed to travel between the worlds of the dead and the living until I decide you have atoned for your worldly transgressions. You will not know peace until then. Krael and many other planets across the universe are in peril of descending back into evil. You must be the messenger between myself and others passed on, to the living that can make changes in the worlds."

Sonu nodded, acknowledging his new duty, "Where do I begin, Master. Also, what of this burning in my back, will that cease with time?"

"The burning will remain as long as there is a spark of life in you. It is to remind you of how you got here. Please, do not call me Master. The Spirit Master title has been passed on to another now, and I do not own you. You are completing your task as messenger on your own free will. You yourself said that you would spend the rest of your life in recompense, and I have just given you the means to do that. When you failed my trial of worthiness to don my cloak, the penalty you were to pay was your life, but desperate times call for desperate measures. At least you are not wholly alive. Your help will be greatly appreciated in the times to come." Ghaleon clasped Sonu's hand within his own, and their pact was complete.

***

A dark-cloaked figure faded from a single mirror on the wall leaving the reflection of a dead man strewn on the floor and two ghosts shaking hands solemnly. Zen's grasp on Sonu had faded the moment the ghostly sword had torn through his body. The thoughts that Zen had felt coarse through Sonu prior to his death disturbed him greatly. He needed to act fast. It was pretty much assured that Ghaleon's cloak would be in the hands of the Spirit Master soon from the information Sonu had relayed to him previously and the discussion Zen had just witnessed. Zen was still without his prescient nature and now also his chief minion. He did not have any reliable means by which to take the cloak from the new Spirit Master, especially if they had the blade and shield of Ghaleon as well.

Zen pounded his staff on the floor once, forcefully, as he gritted his teeth and grunted angrily. Losing was not a condition he was accustomed to. He took one last look around his Kraelian treasure trove before turning to his back-up plan. The Saliek cloak hung motionless on the wall as it called to him. He had survived the jump to Tendyis with no protection once. At least this time his odds would be increased significantly.

Chapter 37

A black dove slept as fireflies spiraled around her delicately feathered body in the soft light of the moon. One had landed on her breast, over her heart, and never ceased its glow. She opened her eyes momentarily and looked up towards a tumultuous cloud moving steadily across the sky. A raven peered down at her with malicious eyes before he turned away. In her last glimpse of him, she saw there was a treasure clutched between his talons.

Ghaleon had warned Sonu that he could only interact with the living world for a limited amount of time before his life spark would need recharging. He would have to experiment with his limits before he knew what his true capabilities were. His hands could grasp objects if he willed them too, but that cost him life energy. In his current state, he could walk through a wall or climb it, depending on if he chose to use his life spark or not. Either way, the pain of it constantly burned between his shoulder blades where the sword had initially come into contact with his skin. Ghaleon suggested that Sonu contribute to the world first by carrying Mory and Kylie's bodies out of the dream mist and into the realm where his cloak had lain hidden for eons. There they could wake up and find their reward for their journey. This would be far faster than waiting for the mist to dissipate and having them awake on their own.

Sonu carried Mory's limp body slung over his shoulder through the green-glowing room and up a small flight of stone stairs into a vibrant forest realm, inaccessible through normal means on Krael. In his short life, Sonu had never seen anything as magnificent. Even the gardens that he had required his servants to keep meticulous in Arbore, he cringed at the thought now, were nothing in comparison to the beauty he saw here. The leaves on the trees were the brightest shade of green imaginable in nature. They seemed to glow against the bright, blue sky that shyly peeked through the dense canopy as the branches shifted in the breeze. Colorful birds sang the most enchanting songs as they spritzed like confetti through the leaves of the trees and tumbled around in the soft air currents.

Curious fuzzy creatures poked their noses out of the ground and from hollows in the reddish-brown tree trunks to watch the interesting happenings in the clearing and gain a scent of the new creatures in their domain. The thick grass that carpeted the ground was soft and short as it tickled his feet, until he realized that feeling in this world also sapped his strength. He immediately ceased the sensation allowing the green threads to pass through his eerily grey-blue, transparent feet, erasing his footprints from the ground. He placed Mory's body in the grass near a grey, granite rock with teal and green swirls throughout. The rock was in a clearing encircled by trees with wide, crooked trunks that were so tall that it was dizzying to look up at them for too long. The canopies of the trees were so widely spread that only in the center of the clearing was light allowed to enter unhindered. This light shone directly onto the rock that Sonu had lain Mory beside.

Sonu returned quickly to the cave to bring Kylie up before his waning strength disappeared completely. He felt great remorse as he carried his sister up to the wondrous grove cradled in his arms in front of him. He wished he could apologize to her for all he'd done. He wished he could attempt to explain all his foul actions and maybe be able to reconnect with her, but those conversations would have to wait, for now. She needed him to get her away from the mist that was keeping her unconscious. He laid her down next to Mory and gingerly brushed a strand of hair out of her face as he looked down at her sadly before fading once more into the world of the dead. He didn't want to push his luck… yet.

***

Sun shone brightly in Mory's face when he awoke. He blinked furiously as he was initially blinded by its brilliance then sat up quickly and began rubbing his eyes.

"Mory, why is it that whenever I go adventuring with you, I wake up and have no idea where I am or how I got there! On top of that, this time my head is full of memories of crazy dreams!" Telovi complained jokingly as she stifled a yawn. Mory couldn't help but laugh at his playful friend.

"If I remember correctly, you were the one that snuck away with me to begin with! You can't blame me for your bad judgment in companions!" Mory countered winking at her.

"I'll blame whoever I want for whatever I want!" Vi placed her hand on her hip and bounced up and down in the air while shaking a finger at Mory.

"What's all the commotion?" Kylie said, woken up by the clamor around her.

"Oh, Vi was just complaining as usual," Mory responded as she flew around him in a spiral to come to rest on his shoulder. Vi shrugged with a little smile and made herself comfortable.

"Where are we? It's so beautiful here!" Kylie wondered aloud, admiring the grove around her before looking to Mory "Did you have the same dream that I did?"

They spent the next few minutes sharing the challenges that Ghaleon had given them, listening carefully to each detail as the other related their story. "So, the cape must be here somewhere then," Mory said after they had finished swapping stories. Vi had flown off to look around the grove at some point during their conversation. A trial had not been offered to her by Ghaleon. Instead, she had just been plagued by hallucination-like dreams and preferred not to recall them.

Kylie was running her fingers across the swirls in the large rock next to them giggling to herself, "So many pretty rocks on this adventure!" Then she reached into the breast of her shirt and pulled out the rock necklace that Mory had given to her for her birthday, which seemed like ages ago, and smiled gazing into his eyes. Mory could think of no more beautiful sight than Kylie sitting in front of him in this bright and colorful grove with her legs bent within the soft, green grass brushing her thighs and calves. The slight breeze played with strands of her thick, golden hair as she leaned back slightly on one hand while the other fingered the rock necklace lovingly. "I never stopped wearing it, you know," she said.

A smile broke out across Mory's face, beaming brighter than the sun on the rock in front of them. He hurridly dove into his pack and rummaged around for a moment before pulling out the second rock that he had found in the river. "This is the rock that led me to Krael!" he exclaimed as he put it next to the one around Kylie's neck and smiled at the similarities before handing it to her. "Oh, and I have another gift for you!"

he spoke excitedly, wanting to prolong the perfect happiness of this moment that they were sharing. “Well less of a gift that I got for you and more of one that I am returning to you after safekeeping.” Kylie’s eyes scrunched together cutely, clearly not knowing what he was talking about.

He reached into his pack and slowly pulled out her winged cat carving, and Kylie’s eyes widened in surprise. “It came to me one night when I was fighting a dragon in the place where I found this shield, Ghaleon’s shield,” he explained excitedly as he raised the shield up slightly at the mention of it. “The cat and its friends gave me the strength I needed to defeat the dragon. Without them, I would not have survived the encounter. Since then, whenever I have needed strength, I’ve pulled it out of my pack and held it close to my heart. It seems to have worked so far.” Kylie's eyes glistened in the sunlight for moment before she scooted over next to Mory on the summer grass and lay her head on his chest while he wrapped his arm around her.

“Please, keep it,” Kylie responded, rubbing her forehead on his shoulder. “Knowing that it gives you strength in your times of need brings me far more happiness than my possession of it. It is my gift to you.” Mory grasped them both tighter within his arms, never wanting to ever let either of them go.

“Thank you, my love. You have my eternal gratitude.” Mory thanked her, setting the cat onto his lap so he could stroke Kylie’s long, soft hair as she lay comfortably on his shoulder for a few moments. He bent forward and kissed her gently on the forehead, which prompted Kylie to turn her head up to his. Her shining green eyes stared up lovingly into his, wrestling any form of thought away from his mind. He placed his hand on her blushing cheek and carefully pulled her in for a soft, passionate kiss sending pleasant shivers down his spine as they both sat in this magical realm, alone and undisturbed for the moment by the troubles of their everyday lives.

In Mory's mind it could have been a moment or an eternity, for time flowed differently in that segment of his life, just as it had when he was battling for his soul with the dragon. Although this was entirely different, being a time of bliss, pleasure, and delight unlike any he had experienced before. He wished it would never end, and so he let himself be completely enraptured in the moment, letting his mind stray no further than the illustrious magic before him.

Too soon it was over, and they were left just staring into the eyes of one another. Neither one was able to catch their breath or pull away from each other. Mory was thankful that Telovi had flown away to explore giving Mory and Kylie the moment to themselves, but she must have decided that the moment was over now and prodded them onward, "You silly lovebirds! Come have a look at what's on top of this rock!" Mory gave Kylie an apologetic smile and stood up from the ground, offering her a hand. She followed him quickly, not wanting to miss out on the new discovery.

On top of the swirled granite, laying perfectly centered in the sunlight streaming through the trees, was a mound of tattered fabric. At one point in its life, it may have been white, but now it was grass-stained and yellow with streaks of off-white visible through the dirt and grime. Mory made a face indicating that he thought it was pretty disgusting, then reached out to grab it, hoping for the best and expecting the worst.

When he touched the cloak, a strange sensation hummed through his body. The cloak began to lift itself off the rock on its own accord and wrested itself from Mory's delicate grasp. The air surrounding the cloak shimmered slightly as it straightened itself out. Slowly, but surely, the cloak began mending itself. The holes and shreds in the cloth were shrinking and the color was brightening. Mory was unable to take his eyes off the magical sight. When the mending was complete, the cloak was a pristine white color with a faint purple glow. It lowered itself back onto the granite slab folded crisply. Mory looked back at Kylie and Vi who enthusiastically motioned him towards the cloak.

Mory picked up the cloak, which now felt more substantial, and wrapped himself up in it. It fit him perfectly. He turned towards Kylie and Vi, and they both gasped with joy lighting up their eyes.

"I think you'll be an extraordinary Spirit Master, Mory," Kylie spoke after she regained her composure. Mory looked once more around the grove, and between the trees, he saw a flash of white. His guiding pegasus paused for a moment to look him in the eyes once more before trotting off into the trees. Mory sent well wishes off to his winged guide, hoping their paths would cross again.

"Let's head back to our friends, now," Mory suggested. "I'm sure they will all be eagerly awaiting our return. I've no way to tell how long we've been gone, and I don't want them sending anyone else into that dream mist!"

Kylie and Vi agreed. They began the short trek back to their comrades, taking just enough time to admire the beauty and whimsy of the forest as they strolled. A faint, seemingly familiar whisper in the trees guided them back to the room previously occupied by the dream mist. Upon their return, the green mist was gone, and instead they found themselves in a red, stone room with a massive, ornately carved coffin in the center. They paused for a few moments to honor and pay their respects to the Great Ghaleon before crawling back through the narrow tunnel to their friends.

***

Scilla was walking back in the darkness of night to the library from Regithal's tent in the Saliek camp. He had just relayed to her that the squad they had sent out to the Frostlands was on its way home. Mory had acquired the cloak and appeared to have all three ancient relics that had belonged to Ghaleon in his possession. The others said that they could feel the aura of his power as he neared them, although Mory himself did not seem to act any differently. This all boded well for Scilla. She had accomplished her task to see the next Spirit Master into power.

Scilla thought that she would have felt relieved at this point, but there was much more work ahead. Mory would have to use his powers to restore peace and prosperity to the lands that had been touched by evil in the past couple decades that Andolin had been gone. The thought of Andolin did not hurt as much as usual. It actually felt warm inside of her. Almost comforting. He was there with her, she could see now, and she should not work so hard to keep him out of her thoughts anymore. She no longer needed to close those curtains around her heart. She didn't have to be alone anymore. She had never needed to be. It was only because of her own mourning mindset that she had isolated herself in the first place.

The king and queen of Arbore had to be retrieved out of hiding, and Kylie would need to meet her true parents. She would also need to take up her duties as the princess and sole heir of Arbore now that Sonu was presumed dead. Kylie had reported over her link that they had not found a single trace of his person after he had tried to enter the realm of Ghaleon's cloak. They assumed he must have failed the trial he was tasked with and was no longer with this world.

Though all of these tasks seemed important, a connection deep inside Scilla nagged at her. She tried to think about what it was as the fireflies faded around her before she opened the door to go inside the library for the night. Suddenly, something akin to a vision overtook her, and she fell to her knees on the warm, early summer grass hoping to better control any vomit that may result from the tumultuous feeling in her stomach.

A vision came to her mind in fleeting spurts. “Goodbye for now, Krael. I will return soon with my powers restored. Maybe then I will find and confront you, Scilla,” a man in a Saliek cloak stated in a voice laced with anger and a trace of fear before he disappeared from her feelings. He was on barren, mountainous terrain, a storm brewing around him with wild winds whipping his hair and cloak in all directions as he stood resolutely amidst the chaos. He had to be Kaitzen. Somehow his mentioning of her name in the place where the portal to Tendyis was located, travelled along their internal connection as twins to her. He was going back home. His power was gone too. She needed to follow him somehow. Krael would be in more trouble than ever if he returned with his prescient powers restored and there was no one to counter him.

She knew what she had to do now. Spirits give her the strength and luck to help her succeed, or at least make it back alive.

Ready for the next and final book in the Legend of Ghaleon series?

Stars Calling

Available on Amazon in Ebook, Paperback, and Hardcover

About the Author

Aerospace Engineer by day, fantasy author by night, Theresa Biehle has never let increasing age or responsibility dampen the wilds of her imagination or prevent her from following her dreams. Spirits Entwined, her debut book, is the first book of a series she has been longing to write for years, and she is thrilled to see it become a reality. She grew up in the small town of Ida, Michigan playing backyard baseball, reading fantasy novels, taking juicy bites out of garden-fresh tomatoes after splashing through muddy creeks, and sneaking through cornfields to make wishes on magic trees before obtaining her Bachelor's Degree in Aerospace Engineering and a Master's Degree in Space Systems Engineering from the University of Michigan. Job availability herded her into Leesburg, Virginia where she resides now. Softball equipment now sits in her basement, fantasy novels cover her bookshelves, tomatoes grow in her garden, and she has never stopped believing in the power of wishes and dreams.

Social Media

Follow me here for information on future writing endeavors!

Facebook: biehletheresa
Instagram: theresabiehle
Goodreads Author: Theresa Biehle
Website: **www.theresabiehle.com**

Newsletter signup available on website.

Made in the USA
Middletown, DE
23 April 2023

28966687R00196